Arthur Moore Jr.
1968

The Devil in Harbour

THE
Devil in Harbour

by Catherine Gavin

William Morrow and Company, Inc.

New York 1968

To Robin Denniston

Author's Foreword

The research for this novel was carried out in Leningrad, Oslo, Amsterdam, London and the Orkney Islands. I am unable to make the usual claim that all the characters in it are fictitious, because Admiral Jellicoe, Admiral Scheer, Sir Alfred Ewing, Captain W. R. Hall, R.N., Captain Herbert Savill, R.N., Jack Cornwell, V.C., and others were actual personages, who played leading if various rôles in the drama of 1916. Most of the episodes are founded on fact. For example, the capture of the *Magdeburg's* naval signal book took place exactly as narrated here, while the passing of the fake code book into German hands at Amsterdam was suggested by a similar operation successfully planned by Captain Hall. In writing about him and other real people I have put words in their mouths which they never uttered, but which I believe to be consistent with their characters and actions, as revealed in the chapter of history which they adorned and helped to write.

Contents

✷

Wednesday, August 26, 1914

The Great War came to Odensholm two months after a double murder at Sarajevo set fire to Europe.

The seven families who lived on the small treeless island off the north-west coast of Russian Esthonia heard of it first through the newspapers, which reached them irregularly by boat from Spitshamn. Then a Russian detachment arrived from the mainland to guard the lighthouse. The fishermen of Odensholm, Swedish by descent and speech, took both the war in Europe and the Russians calmly.

Nevertheless their island lay in a stretch of water which was an old battleground. Here, during the Napoleonic Wars, Admiral Saumarez and a British squadron chased the Czar's fleet across the Gulf of Finland from Hangö to Baltisport, and captured the Russian warship *Sevodlod*. Here in the Baltic campaign of 1855 the British frigate *Arrogant* and her hunting mate H.M.S. *Hecla* had cruised endlessly between Hangö Head and Dager Ort, waiting for the Russian ships to leave the shelter of Kronstadt. Now, as the newspapers told the fishers of Odensholm, Russia and Britain were allies and the new enemy was Germany. But the Gulf was still the Gulf of Finland, dangerous to coastal shipping in its reefs and shoals, given up to fogs and frosts in spring and autumn, bound in ice from shore to shore in winter.

Two Russian cruisers, the *Pallada* and the *Bogatir*, were hovering off Odensholm on August 26 when one of the first of the autumn fogs came rolling down upon the island. Children helping their fathers to mend nets on the beach saw the smoke from the Russian vessels gradually merging with the mists and becoming invisible against the darkening sky. Ashore, the foghorn began to blare from the lighthouse. The little wooden houses took on new angles

1

in the fog and men loomed up like giants. At sea, such a gigantic shape appeared off Odensholm with terrifying suddenness. It was a German light cruiser, the *Magdeburg*.

Caught by the *Bogatir*, the *Pallada* and the fog, the *Magdeburg* went aground upon the rocks of Odensholm. The mighty crash when she struck was followed promptly by the reverberations of her guns. There was a German escort ship further down the Gulf which might arrive in time to tackle the Russians, and the *Magdeburg*'s captain was not disposed to give the enemy an easy victory. Through the fog the fire from the three cruisers stabbed in orange flashes.

Two Odensholm children, a boy and a girl, had run away from the beach across the rocks when all the others raced for home. The noise of the guns seemed to pursue them, the shaken earth to open at their feet. They found shelter at last in a cove they knew and fell down in the shingle with their faces buried in each other's necks. They were no more than ten years old.

Presently the boy plucked up courage and scrambled to his feet. He saw inside the curtain of fog a boat, lowered from the hard-pressed German cruiser, which two sailors were rowing frantically out to deep water. They were carrying a passenger, clutching a large dark object in his arms.

While the child watched, there came another flash, much nearer, and a reverberation, and then the boat was blasted from the water. Human limbs and spars and oars fell in a bloody fountain on the surface of the sea. Somewhere behind the fog there was the sound of cheering.

When the boy dared to look again, he saw that one of the German bodies, hideously maimed, had drifted inshore and was lolloping in the shallows at the entrance to the cove. The legs, in seaboots, were submerged in water; the hands were still clenched tenaciously across the breast. The bleeding head bumped on the stones, and the ripples broke redder on the shingle with every movement of the tide.

The terrified children fled sobbing to the village in a new and merciful silence. The *Magdeburg* had surrendered to the *Pallada* and the *Bogatir*. The fisherfolk slowly gathered to watch the Germans marched aboard the Russian cruisers. It was rumoured that there were several Russian dead and many wounded.

There was nobody to see the Russian patrol boat nosing round the island, exploring every tiny inlet, or hear the wild shout of triumph when the Russian sailors found the body on the shingle of the little cove. They floundered in the knee-deep water, hacking with their sheath-knives at the corpse's hands, and howled their joy as they stripped the lead from what had lain beneath them. Long after the sailors had carried their prize to their Russian captain the reddened ripples from the cove at Odensholm, returning to the waters of the Gulf of Finland, carried a fatal message round the world. For the dead man was the Yeoman of Signals of the cruiser *Magdeburg*, and the treasure he had guarded only too well was a copy of the signal book, complete with codes and cypher key, of the Imperial German Navy.

I

Monday, March 20, 1916

The curtains fell across the Maryinsky stage, blotting out the realm of the Snow Fairy and the swirling white tutus of the corps de ballet. From the house rose the hum of satisfaction which at that moment of the *Nutcracker* was the only permissible expression of applause. The dancer Tamirova, for once on the public side of the footlights, quickly arranged her lips in a public smile.

"I think the child was excellent!" she said to her elderly companion, in a clear voice meant to be heard by their neighbours.

"Claire or the Snow Fairy?"

"Snow Fairy, of course, the Luba child. She was quite charming."

"She's very promising. What did you think of Fyodor?"

"Oh, Fyodor." The dancer dropped her artificial manner. "Fyodor led Luba, all the way through. He wasn't supporting her, he was leading her. D'you think he'll try that on with Katia Kirillovna?"

"We shall soon find out, Elena!" said the old man.

The house lights came up slowly to half strength. The audience groped its way to the exit doors; the orchestra had already left the pit. Elena Tamirova took a pair of mother-of-pearl opera glasses from the red plush ledge in front of her and focussed them.

"They can't hang out the 'House Full' signs, can they, maestro?"

"Hardly, my dear."

The opera glasses travelled to the Imperial box. Before the war, Tamirova had never appeared on the Maryinsky stage without curtseying at the end of the performance to the Empress Dowager, or the Czarina, sitting with the young Grand Duchesses in the ornate box now dark and empty.

"None of the Family are here, I see."

4

In an undertone: "They haven't budged from Czarskoe Selo for months past."

The glasses swept back to a point opposite. "Our host doesn't seem to have arrived yet."

"Yefimov often comes late, but I've seldom known him miss a new ballet."

"The *Nutcracker* a new ballet?"

"Well, with Kirillovna dancing Sugar Plum for the first time," Maestro Borelli said. He looked nervously at the dancer. But Elena Tamirova was studying the two occupants of the absent Yefimov's box.

"Nelidov is there, I see, how charming. I wonder if he's been asked to supper too. Have you any idea who the fairhaired man could be?"

"He's a stranger to me. But then so many people are, these days," said the old Italian.

"He was staring at me for most of the first act."

"When both of you should have been looking at the stage. Not that I blame you; the party scene was deadly slow. Do you remember how fast I made you take it, when you first danced little Claire?"

"Oh heavens, how old that makes me feel!"

"Now you're being morbid, child; come and walk with me in the promenade."

"I haven't been there since poor Mikhail was killed."

"But I think you ought to let yourself be seen tonight, my dear."

He stood aside to let her pass, bowing as she swept her pink chiffon skirt into one hand and left the box. Borelli had known how to present Elena Tamirova since he took her himself to the Imperial School of Ballet, a thin long-legged child of ten; and now, of course, she was magnificent, with legendary jewels at her neck and wrists and her glossy dark head held high. He handed her into the promenade room, on the night intended for another woman's triumph, as proudly as if Elena Tamirova were Grisi or Taglioni, come back to shed her light on lesser mortals from a ballerina's heaven.

5

"How terribly this place has changed," Elena murmured as she smiled and bowed. Eighteen months of wartime neglect had taken some of the freshness out of the Maryinsky promenade's white paint and gold leaf, and faded the crimson curtains drawn across the double windows. But the change was less in the room than in the promenaders; they had lost the style and self-assurance which had made an interval at the Maryinsky almost a part of the ballet, a graceful chain of pas de deux in which men showed off their women and women their evening gowns and splendid jewels. The men moving round were elderly, or boys in students' dress escorting their mothers; the few who were young wore uniform. Not the gala uniforms of the Chevaliers Garde or the Preobrazhenski regiment, but grey service dress such as Russian officers had worn in the Pripet marshes or the retreat from Tannenberg; their faces were beaten and bitter. The noisy, voluble and often brilliant conversation of other days had died down to a few muffled comments on the *Nutcracker* and the corps de ballet: the only dancer Elena could hear mentioned was Fyodor Surov.

"Would you like a glass of champagne, Elena Petrovna?" asked Borelli.

"Yefimov will have a magnum on the supper table," she said indifferently. "Let's go back to our box now, maestro."

"You're anxious for the second act to start."

"Naturally."

The orchestra was tuning up as they took their places, and the fairhaired man opposite again levelled his opera glasses upon Tamirova. But her eyes were fixed on the stage as the house lights dimmed, and Tschaikovski's music welled up through the expectant hush. Then the curtain rose on the glowing interior of the Palace of Sweets, with the starry sky above the terrace walls, and to the plangent sound of violins the Nutcracker Prince and little Claire stepped out of the boat which had carried them safely down the rosewater stream. Softly, gracefully as a blown petal Katia Kirillovna, in the pale rose-mauve dress of the Sugar Plum Fairy, began to dance her welcome to the Kingdom of Candy. By Borelli's side Tamirova's breathing quickened, and he knew she was counting the beats of each movement, which she knew by heart.

6

She relaxed slightly during the Chocolate, Coffee and Tea diversions, and the Cossack dance which followed, but when the Waltz of the Flowers began she was tense again as Sugar Plum in her brief mauve-pink tutu and the Nutcracker Prince in silver embarked on their grand pas de deux. The young Kirillovna was nervous at the start, but Surov's authority held her up triumphantly, and her solo variation was as brilliant as a Maryinsky audience could desire. The applause, repressed all evening, broke out before the final pas de deux was over.

"You mustn't appear to be running away," said old Borelli, under cover of the noise. Tamirova was applauding with her hands held high, and her public smile at its most brilliant. The baskets of hothouse flowers being handed over the footlights to Katia Kirillovna might have been piling up at her own feet, but the old ballet-master felt her frantic impatience to be gone. "Don't let's be the first to move," he said.

Surov led out Kirillovna, not once but four times; then he led out Luba, who had danced Snow Fairy; then Kirillovna herself, curtseying to her partner, directed the applause of the house to the Nutcracker Prince. It was a Maryinsky ovation, stylised and time-less as the ballet itself, and as the occupants of the stalls rose and surged forward to the edge of the orchestra pit, with their clapping now resembling the beat of a metronome, the first movement out of the circles began. Borelli touched Elena's elbow and opened the door of the box. He had arranged with an attendant to be ready with their cloaks at the top of the grand staircase. Outside, in the Teatralnaia, a red carpet extended across the swept pavement to the kerb, where several limousines were already drawn up in line. By the side of the theatre, a number of sleighs and droschkis were allowed to wait for a favoured few. Borelli, as a former master of the Imperial Ballet, was among these, and an attendant who saw him emerge from the grand entrance ran ahead to warn his driver.

"A great success, barin, eh?" The man pulled open the door of the old-fashioned sleigh and took his fur hat off as Elena passed.

"Yes, splendid! splendid!" Borelli said mechanically. "Thank you, Ivan"—as the man tucked the fur rug round them both— "Tell him to drive to the Astoria, will you?"

"To the Astoria Hotel; yes, surely, sir. Good-night! Hark to them clapping!"

Wave on wave of applause came through the Maryinsky doors, now pulled wide open. The sound engulfed the square and reverberated from the walls of the Conservatory opposite, as the space of trampled snow began to fill with the noisy and delighted audience. Tamirova and Borelli could still hear the cheering as their sleigh drove off across the Moika.

On the other side of the canal, in a street of tall dark houses, Tamirova spoke for the first time.

"I'll never forgive Poliakovski—never!"

"My dearest girl, I've told you a dozen times already he'd no idea you would be available to dance tonight."

"He knew perfectly well I had to stop in Petrograd to get my new costumes fitted, didn't he? He knew I wasn't due to dance in Stockholm until Wednesday! The *Nutcracker* is *my* ballet! If Poliakovski wanted to put it on tonight, he could easily have sent for me to dance the Sugar Plum Fairy."

"Antonia dell' Era called it *her* ballet, when you were an infant in arms in Arkhangelsk. Come, Elena! You were bred in the Imperial School; you know better than to think any ballet is the property of any one girl or boy."

"Tell that to Katia Kirillovna! After tonight, she'll claim the Sugar Plum part as hers—"

"Ah, you thought she danced so well, then?"

Sulkily: "She was very good at the beginning and the end. But she stumbled once in the grand pas de deux, and Fyodor saved her from a fall . . . And did you ever see such a ridiculous tutu—like the paper frills the English put on their lamb cutlets!" Borelli heard her angry laugh.

"Elena, my child." He tried to take her hand. "You're over-tired after that wretched trip. Shall I make your excuses to Yefimov, and have them send some supper to your room?"

"And let that old gossip spread it all over Petrograd that I came back green with envy from Kirillovna's triumph, and went to bed to bite the pillows?"

8

"I only thought you might want to get a good night's rest," he said humbly.

"Why? To be fresh for a trip to Stockholm and a tour with Vassily Bronin?"

"Kamnov—" he began, but Elena interrupted with:

"Maestro, I've been a fool to stay away from Petrograd so long. All those performances for war charities—what have they done for me? Given the Katias and the Lubas a chance to step into my shoes, that's all. And now this Scandinavian tour, *your* wonderful idea! I wish I'd never agreed to it. I might as well have gone to America with Diaghilev, as bury myself in Christiania."

"It's only a short engagement," he said. "You'll be back here before the end of April."

"And the season ends in May. Well, the first person you and I are going to talk to when I do come back is the great Director, Poliakovski. We've got to take a firm stand, *now*, about the parts I'm going to dance next year—"

"Kamnov is the person you'll have to take a stand with, first."

"*Kamnov?* The *régisseur* on tour?"

"I know you think he's young and unimportant," said the old man wearily. "But he's a clever fellow, Elena, and the Director listens to what he says."

"More than he does to you?"

"Because my day is over; it's the day of men like Kamnov now." He hesitated. "Try to do your best for him on tour, and get on as well as you can with Bronin. He's a good dancer, though he'll never be in Surov's class. You did admire Surov tonight, didn't you?"

"Fyodor? Ah, yes," she said, softened. "He truly is a *danseur noble*. I'll be very glad to dance with him again."

Borelli patted her hand in satisfaction.

"But maestro, why are there so many people in the streets?" she said abruptly.

They were driving along the north bank of the Moika, through a residential district where only a few corner groceries and small restaurants broke the line of tall granite buildings with nineteenth-century façades, anonymous in the lightly falling snow. Although. it was nearly ten o'clock, eating-houses and shops were crowded.

Groups of men stood arguing beneath the bare trees or leaned to talk on the parapet of the canal. Elderly women had scraped the frozen snow from the park benches by the water and were sitting with shawls wrapped round their heads, watching the passers-by. The carriageway was crowded; the sleigh driver pulled his horses almost to a stop.

"The Petersburgers always liked to walk at night," Borelli said.

"But so many, and so late? And carrying those little children? Do you think there's been a fire somewhere?" Tamirova put her head out of the window. The moon, obscured by clouds and snow, shone faintly on the canal and the moving crowd. There was no red glare in the sky to indicate that fire had broken out in Petrograd.

"Get on, man," said Borelli to the driver. The people were walking faster now, hurrying into St. Isaac's Square, but here the sounds of argument were stilled. A detachment of mounted police was clearing the Voznessenski Prospekt.

"Are they rioting?" Tamirova whispered, and the old man shook his head. There had been riots in that aristocratic district at the outbreak of war, when the citizens of St. Petersburg attacked the newly built German Embassy, and gaps in the sculptures on the roof of the now empty building bore witness to that frenzy; but this crowd had not, apparently, come to riot. Men, women and children were merely walking, shepherded by the police, round and round the square, pausing only to stare as they came abreast of the War Ministry, where every window was ablaze with light. Tamirova and the old ballet-master looked at each other without speaking. They shared the same presentiment: there must be bad news from the front.

There were two policemen on duty at the door of the Hotel Astoria, a granite building as heavily Teutonic in style as the former German Embassy. They wore swords, black astrakhan hats, and black ankle-length greatcoats, of far better quality than the shabby garments worn by most of those who had chosen this snowy night to promenade around St. Isaac's Square. The policemen were alert, but not in a repressive mood; they even permitted a little crowd to gather when the hotel porter opened the door of Borelli's sleigh and helped the beautiful dancer to descend. She was recognised immediately. "Tamirova!" someone said, and there was some muffled applause from mittened hands.

Yefimov was waiting for them in the lobby. He was wearing his Civil Service frock coat, with pale-blue piping and gold on the collar above which his long withered neck was stretching like a fowl's as he watched for his guests in the crowd. He had an imposing title, which the dancer had difficulty in remembering: Principal Civilian Assistant to the Minister for War, or some such thing. She had known him, almost since her first appearance on the stage, as a connoisseur of the ballet, and also as a fussy, effeminate old bachelor, one of the earliest patrons and intimates of Diaghilev.

"My dear Elena Petrovna!" he said, and bent to kiss her hand.

"Maestro! Not too badly delayed, after all, by those foolish people roaming in the streets tonight?"

"But what in the world has happened?" the dancer cried, as old Borelli gently took the cloak from her shoulders and gave it to a white-gloved page. "Why is the Ministry of War lit up?"

"Because we've all been working there all evening," Yefimov said gaily. "Celebrating another Russian victory, my love!"

"Oh, where?"

"You shall hear, all in good time. But my other guests arrived before you, and are waiting—"

"What other guests?"

"Monsieur Nelidov, and a visitor from the United States, a Mr. Ericssen. Il faut parler français ce soir, ma chère—the American speaks no Russian."

"What's an American doing here in Petrograd?"

Yefimov shrugged. "Something in connection with a munitions contract, I believe. However, that's nothing to do with my Ministry; he's Nelidov's affair, not mine. A delightful young man—"

He led the way to the Palm Court. The mirrors with which the foyer of the Hotel Astoria was walled showed Tamirova the flattering reflection of a very slender woman with graceful bare arms and white shoulders just covered by folds of rosy chiffon. With assurance, she entered the palm-filled salon where on a corner table an empty carafe of vodka and a plate of canapés bore

11

witness to Yefimov's care for the earlier arrivals. Two men in evening dress got up at once.

"Madame Tamirova," said Yefimov formally, "You and Monsieur Nelidov are old acquaintances, I know."

"Of course we are." With a faint smile, Elena shook hands with the owner of the great Nelidov ironworks and shipyards.

"Delightful to see you again, Elena Petrovna."

"And this is Mr. Karl Ericssen, who has made a remarkable journey to Petrograd from Milwaukee."

The man who had studied her at the theatre bowed over Tamirova's head. He was very tall, and conspicuous in a room where every other man was either in uniform or sporting medal ribbons, by wearing plain evening dress. His fair hair was brushed back from his forehead, and his eyes were grey. He was clean-shaven, and there was a marked indentation in his chin. All this Elena Tamirova took in as she said laughingly:

"*Enchantée, monsieur.* You and Monsieur Nelidov made a remarkable journey from the theatre to the Astoria, since you got here so long before us."

"We came in Monsieur Nelidov's motor, madame."

"And we by sleigh." She took the arm Ericssen offered, and they crossed the hall to the restaurant. As they went down the few steps he said confidentially:

"You were right of course—that's how one pictures you: wrapped in furs, with horses in the troika, driving through the snow with sleigh-bells ringing—"

It was said with the intimacy of an old friend or a lover, and Elena looked up at him, surprised and intrigued, as the head waiter bowed them to their places. Yefimov had reserved the best table in the room, in an alcove to the left of the entrance, banked by a screen of potted palms and hothouse flowers. It afforded a clear view of the little dancing floor, crowded with officers in uniform and pretty women, some of them wearing the hobble skirts in fashion at the beginning of the war. The band, on a dais, was playing for the bunny hug and the turkey trot. The dinner tables were lighted by electric candles with pink silk shades. The table linen was pink, and vases made of crystal cut to match the great crystal chandeliers held pink carnations and delicate maidenhair fern. There was already a faded, pre-war charm about the Astoria restaurant, although it was the show-place of the capital, and only four years earlier the eldest Grand Duchess was said to have cried her eyes out when the Czar, for security reasons, had refused her permission to attend the gala opening. Every visiting foreigner was expected to express delight and amazement at the luxury of the Astoria; Elena Tamirova was faintly irritated that Mr. Ericssen from Milwaukee, calmly shaking out his pink table napkin, was showing no sign of being overwhelmed.

"How marvellous to be back!" she said across the table to her host. "If you knew what the hotels were like on tour!"

"You've been travelling, madame?" said Ericssen.

"I've just arrived from Kiev."

"She's been doing her best to kill herself," grumbled Borelli. "Dancing for war charities in every town between Petrograd and Vladivostock, it seems to me!"

"You exaggerate, dear maestro. What about you, Mr. Ericssen? Have you seen much of Russia, or are you like so many of our visitors—content to stay in Petrograd?"

"I'd like very much to see Moscow, but that'll have to wait till my next visit. I haven't even had time to see all the wonderful sights of Petrograd."

"Five days he's been here, showing us what Americans mean by hustle," said Nelidov. "He spent the last two of them going through my shops and yards at a pace the managers won't soon forget."

Elena turned to Ericssen. "Are you an ironmaster too, monsieur?"

"Nothing so grand, madame. The representative of a munitions firm, that's all—"

"One of the most important in the United States," said Nelidov. "We're working out a little purchase agreement, I hope to the profit of both sides—"

"Now, gentlemen, no shop talk before supper," said the host gaily. He waved forward the waiters and their huge bowl of caviar, served with chopped eggs, onion rings, and hot buttered toast.

13

"Vodka! Everybody fill their glasses! We'll drink to the incomparable Tamirova and her success in Scandinavia—"

"We'll drink to the victory," protested Elena. "Yakob Ivanovich, you promised to tell Borelli and me about the victory—"

"Ah yes." Yefimov's face fell. "Very well then, the victory first and Tamirova second. Here's to our troops, the conquerors of Ispahan!"

"*Ispahan?*" Elena set down the glass. "You mean you were working all evening, and hundreds of people turned out in the snow, just because we've occupied some dusty little dump in Persia?"

"Come now," said Yefimov, "it's not a triumph like the capture of Erzerum last month, but it's very important politically. It keeps the young Shah committed to our side—"

"I didn't know there were any Russian troops in Persia," said old Borelli innocently. "Who *did* take Ispahan?"

"Persian Cossacks, officered by Russians, of course. And now our way's clear to the Persian Gulf—"

"Very important," said Ericssen, "since the British let you down so badly at the Dardanelles."

"But surely the Germans aren't anywhere near the Persian Gulf?" persisted Elena Tamirova, and Nelidov signed to the waiter to refill his glass. "Beautiful ladies aren't expected to understand grand strategy," he said. "We drink to you and *your* victories, Elena Petrovna!"

"Thank you all so much." The dancer smiled, and Yefimov rubbed his hands. "That's more like the thing! Waiter, bring more caviar . . . I've ordered the simplest of wartime suppers. A dish of chicken à la Kiev, with a salad, and then a soufflé au Grand Marnier, which I trust you'll all enjoy. Have some more vodka, Mr. Ericssen . . . And now, will one of you take pity on a poor hardworking official, and tell me how the ballet went this evening?"

"Elena Petrovna is the best qualified," said Nelidov, with a touch of malice.

"Katia danced extremely well," she said at once, "and Surov was superb."

"The Tartar; it's good to have him back again. But he's doomed to be compared forever to poor Nijinski with those stunning elevations. What do you think, Mr. Ericssen?"

"I never saw Nijinski or Surov, sir. As far as the show tonight went, I enjoyed it very much, but the last time I saw the *Nutcracker* the same lady danced Sugar Plum *and* the Snow Fairy, and that I consider a real *tour de force!*"

"What lady was that?" said Elena with a laugh in her voice.

"It was yourself, madame."

Yefimov had seated them side by side on a sofa of purple velvet, while he and the two older men faced them on gilded and cushioned chairs. It was easy for Ericssen to turn to the girl with an effect of intimacy, laying his arm along the back of the sofa, behind which rose the screen of flowers and leaves.

"You were magnificent that night," he said, "I've never forgotten you."

"But—I thought you said this was your first visit to Russia?"

"I saw you in Berlin," he said, "when the English King and Queen were there in 1913, for Princess Victoria Louise's wedding to the Duke of Brunswick."

"You travel extensively, monsieur."

"My firm sends me abroad a good deal. And then my grandparents were Norwegian-born; I still have relatives in what they called the old country."

She had been wondering about his looks, for Karl Ericssen was more like the Englishmen she had known in London than her idea of an American, but Norwegian blood explained the extreme fairness and the cool grey eyes.

"She had a triumph in Germany," said the old ballet-master, "she danced there as a guest artiste all that summer. But I forget, my dear—was Surov or Bronin your partner in Berlin?"

"Neither, maestro, it was the German, Klaus Albrecht. Surov and I haven't worked together since London in the Coronation summer, when I danced Myrtha to Pavlova's *Giselle*."

"I have a wretched memory," said Borelli apologetically to Karl Ericssen. "Forty years, sir, I've been in St. Petersburg—in Petrograd as we must call it now; forty years of ballet, and I've seen many dancers come and go in that long time. But of them all the dearest to me, and I believe destined to be among the greatest, is this child here, my very own discovery . . . our lovely Tamirova!"

"Hear, hear!" Yefimov pounded on the table. "*Sommelier!* Where the devil is the wine-waiter? Open the champagne, you idiot. You know I detest it over-chilled!"

It was the magnum Elena had predicted, a Dom Pérignon *brut* of the great vintage year, 1907, and as the champagne frothed into the tulip glasses a new ease and sparkle seemed to be added to Monsieur Yefimov's supper party. Prompt service was not among the Astoria's luxuries, and as always there was a long wait between the caviar and the chicken à la Kiev; but four of the five persons round the table were accustomed to it, and the visitor from Milwaukee seemed happy to sip his champagne and look deeply into the eyes of Elena Tamirova. The problems of the war had been by silent agreement shelved. Nelidov and Borelli were engaged in giving their host the desired analysis of that night's dancing, step by step and pas seul by pas de deux. Ericssen was soothing Elena's earlier vexations by accomplished flattery.

"Aren't you exhausted after you've danced both the parts— Snow Fairy and Sugar Plum?"

"Not especially. After all, the Snow Fairy scene only lasts ten minutes, and then there's the interval."

"It may only last ten minutes, but what skill is needed to make the two parts different! That's what you achieved at Berlin, you know. You made the Snow Fairy quite a different personality from Sugar Plum. Both those girls tonight danced as if they were printed from the same stereotype."

Pleased: "I'm going to dance the double rôle again at Copenhagen."

"Is it your favourite rôle?"

"*Giselle* is my first favourite, then Odette-Odile. But what's the use? The romantic ballet isn't in fashion nowadays."

"Tell me about this tour of yours. Are you dancing in all the northern capitals?"

"It's started already. I mean, Vassily Bronin opened in *Petrouchka* at Helsingfors tonight, and Vera Polidova will be his

16

partner there tomorrow. Then I'll join them, and we'll go on to Stockholm for a four nights' engagement at the Royal Opera."

"And after Stockholm?"

"Copenhagen, Christiania, Amsterdam. Mostly *divertissements*, because that's what the foreigners like best—selections from our repertoire. Vassily and I will dance Puss in Boots and the White Cat, Bluebird and Florine, Prince Charming and Aurora—you know what I mean?"

"Yes, of course. But no complete ballet, anywhere?"

"The *Nutcracker*, once or twice. And when Vassily goes to London and Surov takes his place at Amsterdam, he and I will dance the whole of *Swan Lake* and *Giselle*."

"Fortunate Amsterdam! . . . How are you going to get there from Christiania?"

"Not by train through Germany, that's obvious! By a Norwegian steamer direct to Rotterdam."

"A dangerous route these days. The British cruisers are always hanging about off Horns Riff and the Jutland Bank, and there's a good deal of submarine activity as well."

"We'll be safe enough under a neutral flag."

"I hope so." The waiters had brought the chicken à la Kiev at last, and Yefimov, urging his guests to eat, browbeat the head waiter into seeing that the soufflé followed it immediately. At the high point of perfection, with little beards of gold running down the outside of the fluted china dish, the soufflé au Grand Marnier was put before them. It was just finished when the electric lights flickered and went out.

There was a sigh of dismay from the diners, and the orchestra stopped in the middle of "Alexander's Ragtime Band". By the light of electric torches flashed on by some of the waiters, the dancers groped their way back to their chairs.

"This is ridiculous; the Astoria should have its own generator," said Nelidov angrily.

"Does it happen often?" asked Ericssen.

"Only when the power load becomes too heavy at the war plants. We're working three eight-hour shifts a day now, as of course you know . . . At least they've made some preparation for

17

it," the ironmaster grumbled, as the head waiter hastily lit the four pink candles placed round the carnations on their table, in readiness for an emergency. The piano and one violin began to play an old Russian melody.

"They're playing 'The Red Sarafan'," Elena told Karl Ericssen.

"You know it?"

"Know it? I *dance* it—on the stage."

The candlelight, which changed the elaborate restaurant of 1916 into a place of shadows and mystery, and touched the marble statues round the walls to life, had subtly altered the values of Tamirova's face. Until then, Ericssen had seen her only as a very pretty woman, with something artificial in her smiling mask. By candlelight her mouth appeared more tender, her high Slav cheek-bones more pronounced, and her wide-set eyes, which he had supposed to be brown, were revealed as the true Russian hazel, sparked with light. The actress had changed into a young and vulnerable girl.

"Will you dance with me now?" he said.

"Dance here? I haven't danced in a restaurant since I was a coryphée."

"That was only yesterday. Dance with me!"

He had questioned her about her journey crisply, almost professionally; this was a return to the earlier tone of intimacy in which he had spoken of the troika travelling through the snow with the bells ringing. Over a gesture of protest from Borelli, Elena stood up and put her hand on the man's arm.

Ericssen swung the dancer on to the floor. For a shocking instant she thought "He will carry me off my feet!" and then her partner settled to a smooth, graceful step into which she slid immediately, following him as if the candles of the Astoria were the footlights of the Maryinsky theatre.

"Sew not, dearest mother mine, the scarlet sarafan,
Useless will thy labour be—"

She knew the air, she knew the words; she had never known this kind of dancing, where the man led and the girl followed,

18

held close in his embrace. On the stage, Elena was well accustomed to the hands of men, supporting her in her pirouettes and arabesques, clasping her waist in the lifts, or more intimately seizing the inside of her thigh to swing her low. Very often the men—she thought, perhaps all her partners except Fyodor Surov—had epicene hands which took no pleasure in a woman's body. Even when they mimed romance and the act of love they, like herself, were counting—the beat, the steps to the end of the bar; and if they spoke it was in little grunts, the "push!" and "*allez!*" which the audience never heard. But this man held her at waist and hand as if it was a joy to have her in his arms. They moved together in complete harmony. When the piano stopped as the electric light came on again and everybody clapped, Ericssen kissed her hand. "It was like dancing with a flower," he said.

"Bravo!" said the older men, rising as she returned to the table, and Borelli added, "Mr. Ericssen, you are a *danseur manqué!*"

"Pray sit down, dear lady; I've just ordered coffee," said Yefimov, seeing that Elena made no move to return to the sofa. Poised beside the table, she said "No thank you, Yakob Ivanovich; it would keep me awake for hours . . . And you must please excuse me now; it's after midnight, and high time I went up to bed. The train leaves so horribly early in the morning!"

"Are you staying in the hotel, madame?" said Ericssen.

"Yes, I spent the weekend here. Now I must say good-bye, Mr. Ericssen; I wish you a safe return to your own country."

"Good-night, madame, I hope we'll meet again."

She gave him a smiling nod, and turned to Borelli. "You mustn't dream of coming to see me off tomorrow, maestro. It's much too early and too cold for you. Yes"—in answer to his begging eyes—"I'll be very good. I'll do everything just as you told me."

"May I send my car to take you to the station?" asked Nelidov. "I don't like to think of you setting out alone in a droschki before daylight."

"That would be very kind."

"What time should my chauffeur call for you?"

"Would six o'clock be too early? I like to be at the station half an hour before the train leaves."

"Six o'clock it shall be."

Elena included them all in a graceful gesture that mimed "good-night", and turned to walk up the steps from the restaurant like a dancer leaving the stage. Yefimov trotted politely at her side.

"What a delightful party," she said as he escorted her through the hotel lobby, and he reproached her: "I think you might have stayed a little longer, Elena Petrovna. You made quite a conquest of the young man from Milwaukee."

"Gentlemen like to be left to their own devices after midnight. Don't drag my poor Borelli along with you to the gipsies! Put him in a droschki and send him home."

"Poor old fellow! While you were dancing, he told us he was thinking of going back to live in Italy—"

"After forty years in Russia? He'd hate it. He'd forgotten all about Italy until the war began. Now he keeps talking about Garibaldi, whoever Garibaldi was, and the Austrians, the eternal enemy, and so on . . . Please ring for the lift, Yakob Ivanovich."

He kept his finger on the plate beside the bell. "Borelli also gave us the impression that you weren't very happy about the Scandinavian tour?"

Elena saw the gleam in Yefimov's eyes. She knew that any ill-judged words of hers would be repeated, with embellishments, to Poliakovski, the all-powerful Director of the Imperial Ballet. She made herself smile, and said "Oh nonsense, I'm looking forward to it. And I'll be back in Petrograd in six weeks, you know. This is not good-bye for ever."

The lift, unsummoned, came creaking down through its grilles of iron lattice into the middle of the lobby, and the lift man opened the polished brass gates to let the passengers emerge. Inside the lift itself, lying across a stool, was a pile of newspapers, with "Victory at Ispahan!" splashed over the front page.

"Here's the first news of your victory, Yakob Ivanovich. They must have printed a special edition."

"So they must." But the Principal Civilian Assistant to the Minister for War did not look elated: his long neck, instead, seemed to withdraw itself inside his gold-laced collar like the neck of a moulting pigeon. He kissed Elena's hand with dry lips.

"Au revoir, dear lady. Blessings on your journey." He watched while the pink chiffon dress disappeared above his head, and thought how completely a creature of the theatre she was, able to turn a rattletrap hotel lift into a piece of stage machinery for lifting the star up to some tinsel heaven. Then he sighed heavily, and went back to join his guests.

The elegance of the Astoria Hotel ceased abruptly above the ground floor. On the second, where Tamirova had her suite, the halls and corridors were covered with drugget, already worn by four years of hard usage, and the few ornaments and paintings might have been bought in one of the cheaper booths at the Gostinni Dvor bazaar. The *dezhurnaya*, huddled in an armchair, lay sleeping with her mouth open, her white apron crumpled and a grey shawl twisted round her head. Elena roused her gently.

"Excuse me, *barinya*, I only closed my eyes for a moment—"

"Never mind, it's very late. Have you got my key?"

The woman hastily took the key to suite 23 from her keyboard and hurried to open the door for Elena.

"Will the lady require anything more tonight?"

"Nothing, thank you. But remember my orders for the morning; I have to catch the train for Helsingfors."

She bolted the outer door on the curtseying servant. Her evening cloak, she saw, had been placed on a hanger in the entrance hall, which like everything else on the Astoria's bedroom floors had been built to accommodate a giant. The huge cheerless diningroom held a mahogany table and twelve chairs. In the bedroom, where a light had been switched on and her nightdress and peignoir laid ready, were two brass double beds, a walnut dressingtable, and three mahogany wardrobes, one with a broken latch. All was heavy, cumbrous, depressing in the style of the country which was now Russia's enemy, but Elena, contrary to her own anticipation of the evening when Kirillovna danced at the Maryinsky, was not depressed. She felt extraordinarily elated. Her body was still tingling from the contact with Karl Ericssen's hands.

She reflected that she should have told the maid to open the bedroom window. Night air was not approved of at the Astoria, and on two previous nights she had had to struggle with stiff

21

fastenings. She pulled back the dark velvet curtains—these at least moved easily—and looked out. St. Isaac's Square lay in the pallid lamplight, with very few people now to be seen between the huge violet and bronze bulk of the cathedral and the equestrian statue of Czar Nicholas I. The lights in the Ministry of War had been extinguished, except in the duty officer's room on the ground floor. The crowds which had turned out to salute the victory of Ispahan with such glum faces had gone back to their dark tenements, and only twenty or thirty people, mostly men walking with women and here and there a stumbling child, still shuffled along the snow-encrusted pavements. The dancer, watching, was reminded of the compulsive movement of that other column, of officers in grey service uniform and women in evening finery, which had mechanically circled round the Maryinsky's faded promenade.

II

Tuesday, March 21, 1916

It was just after five o'clock when the *dezhurnaya*, who had slept all night in her armchair on the landing, entered Elena's suite with her pass-key and touched the sleeping dancer's shoulder.

Elena awoke immediately. "Tell the waiter to bring my breakfast in three-quarters of an hour," she said, in the act of getting out of bed. The woman, of course, made no attempt to hurry, but through the glass door which led to the diningroom Elena could see her spreading a white cloth over one end of the vast mahogany table. There was no time to lose. She hunted in the chest of drawers for the shabby garments she wore for practice on a travelling day. The heat in the bedroom radiator had been turned off after midnight, and she experienced a moment of freezing chill as she stood naked on the sheepskin rug. Then the darned silk tights and shapeless jersey were bundled on, and using the brass bed-rail as a barre the dancer began her daily exercises.

She performed the first set mechanically, while the hands of her travelling clock moved on from five to twenty past, and the sweat began to break out on her body. Arabesques, entrechats, pliés, grands jetés—holding the improvised barre or standing free, she went through the routine Borelli had worked out for her to follow on mornings when she had no access to a practice room. It was not as good as the hour-long "Cecchetti class"—the scheme Borelli's great predecessor at the Imperial Ballet School had expected his students to follow on every day of the year—but it worked, and it had come to be the basic discipline of Elena Tamirova's life. Without music or words of command, her body responded to her brain. The trained reflexes of sixteen years carried her through the routine until the moment when she hurled herself into the bathroom and turned on both taps to let the tub fill while she tore the soaking practice garments from her body.

The Petrograd water, very soft and slightly brackish in colour, lapped Elena comfortably for the five minutes she allowed herself to lie at full length in the bath. A brisk towelling, and she was quickly dressed, finishing her packing and putting her jewels, all but one diamond spray, into a soft chamois roll. The spray she pinned against the shoulder of her dark travelling dress. As she put on her sable cap she heard movements in the dining-room, and the floor waiter tapped on the door to say *"Madame est servie."*

Breakfast consisted of a pot of tea, a copper kettle of hot water on a spirit lamp, sliced lemon in a saucer not matching the other china, a pot of raspberry jam, some cold burned toast and a plate of pickled herring. There was no butter or sugar. Elena stirred a spoonful of jam into a cup of tea, took a piece of toast and ate standing. Wartime shortages, although not apparent at Yefimov's party, had reached the Astoria—the Petrograd bread was as coarse and tasteless, she noticed, as the bread in the provinces.

It was just after six when she put on her travelling cloak, lined and edged with sable, and took up her morocco bag. She was travelling light, for her heavy luggage had been registered through to Stockholm when she arrived from Kiev, but still there was one large valise to be strapped and left for the porter. Downstairs in the hall she identified Nelidov's chauffeur at once, in his correct blue livery and polished leggings. He was a tall, grey-haired Frenchman, who stood watching the lift for her to appear, holding a large bouquet of violets in one gloved hand. Elena was the only lady in the lobby at that hour of the morning, when the cleaners, shuffling along in felt *valenki*, mingled unceremoniously with the officers and businessmen crowding round the cashier's desk. The night reception clerks, still on duty, looked pallid and grimy beneath the electric lights, and there was a smell of stale food and tobacco in the hall.

"Madame Tamirova?" The chauffeur saluted.

"Yes, good-morning."

"Monsieur Nelidov's compliments, madame, and I'm to drive you to the station. He begs you to accept these flowers, with his respectful homage."

"How delightful. Will you keep them, please, until I pay my bill?"

"Has madame's baggage been brought down?"

"Not yet, but the porter has been told to fetch it."

The valise was in the lobby before the cashier was ready with her receipt. The dancer gave the porter tea-money, and let Nelidov's chauffeur do the rest. She was glad to get outside and breathe fresh air for a moment before she was installed in the Daimler, with a beaver rug solicitously spread across her knees.

"To the Nikolaievski Station, madame?"

"No, to the Finland Station, please."

The chauffeur smiled. "Madame is travelling west today?"

"Quite a long way west."

The car started with a purr and Elena, contemplating the Frenchman's grizzled neck, wanted to ask if he wished to be travelling west too, away from Petrograd and back to France, or if he was glad to be too old, too secure in the service of Nelidov, to be fighting in the trenches round Verdun. But the car's glass partition was raised between them, just as the footlights and the curtains cut a dancer off from her audience, and Elena sat silent in her cushioned corner, inhaling the scent of violets from the bouquet in her hand.

The car went up the east side of St. Isaac's Square towards the little Alexander Garden which lay beneath the windows of the Admiralty, where the statues of Russian poets, snow-covered, gleamed white under the street lamps. It was a place of sad memories for Elena Tamirova. She tried whenever possible to avoid the Alexander Garden, especially at the outset of a journey, and crossed herself instinctively as the car swept by. But already they were in the Palace Square, huge and almost deserted, although there were lighted windows in the General Staff Headquarters and drivers standing by a line of army vehicles drawn up beside the Arch. The statue of Czar Alexander I, on its tremendous column, dominated the centre of the Square. On the Neva side the egg-shell blue and white façade of the Winter Palace showed lights only in the guardrooms; the Czarina was in the country, the Czar with his soldiers on the western front. Elena's driver turned into

25

the Millionaya. It was the street of small palaces where his master lived, where princes of industry like Nelidov had established themselves among the princes of the Russian Empire; but Elena's eager look was given, as the car sped past, to the little bridge across the Moika and the humbler houses on the far side of the canal. There her life in old St. Petersburg had started; those back streets and alleys held kindly memories of her childhood, and in the very swiftness of the car's passing she had an intolerable impression of the illusion and the transience of her life. She wanted to knock on the glass partition, to make some human contact with the stranger at the wheel. He was driving her out of the Millionaya, down the French Quay along the Neva. Now they were in the heart of the splendid city, where the winter darkness was beginning to be pierced with streaks of lemon-coloured light, gilding the needle-slim spires of Petrograd from the golden cross above the fortress of Peter and Paul to the golden ship on the spire of the Admiralty. They crossed the Lityeny Bridge. A light wet snow had started to fall, but against the purplish granite walls of the Neva quays only a rim of broken black ice jostled; the river was running free from bank to bank. On Viborg Side there were lights in all the tenement windows, and workers muffled to the ears were hurrying off to the factories as the hooters blew for half past six. The chauffeur handed Elena out on Simberskaya Street at the entrance to the Finland Station.

A porter, almost as broad as he was long in a hooded sheepskin jacket and smelling of beetroot and *kvass*, came up at a slouching run to seize Elena's large valise.

"Is this all, *barinya*?"

"That's all. But has the train come in?"

"It's due in fifteen minutes."

"I *thought* madame had decided to leave the hotel a little early," said the chauffeur.

"I'm sorry," said Elena. "I'll go into the waitingroom."

"I'll make sure this fellow puts madame's valise in the van," the chauffeur volunteered.

"Thank you very much. And will you bring me a morning paper, if you can?"

The unroofed platform of the empty westbound track was already crowded with those who had bought tickets for the "hard" coaches, waiting patiently in the thickening snow to make sure of a seat. There was another crowd in the waitingroom, for the Finlandski Voksal was not large, and shawled women guarding children and shapeless bundles tied up with newspaper and string were huddled on the benches round the pot-bellied stove. Almost a whole ship's company of young sailors, with "Baltic Fleet" on their cap bands, monopolised the centre of the room. They looked wretchedly cold in their short peajackets, but were laughing and joking with the girls who had come to see them off. The floor was covered with tobacco juice and sunflower seeds. Elena Tamirova, standing as near the door as possible, was thankful to see the chauffeur brandishing a newspaper outside the window, and the porter waiting for his tea-money.

She tipped them both at the door of the railway coach and sent a message of thanks to Monsieur Nelidov. The Baltic sailors went charging past, for the coaches reserved for the Navy transport were behind the engine, and the sweethearts and wives ran screeching after them into the teeth of the rising wind. Then the conductor took Elena's ticket, and bowed her in to the "soft" coupé reserved in her name. She was alone in the warmth and privacy of the tiny house on wheels, with its two red plush settees which could be turned into beds for night travel, its red velvet window curtains now drawn over the inner curtains of white muslin, and the folding table on which a steward would serve sweet cakes and glasses of tea from the inexhaustible samovar in the corridor. Elena turned the knob in the sheet of mirror glass which covered the lavatory door. There were fresh towels and abundance of cold water, but no hot water and no soap. She hung her cloak and cap on the pegs provided, for the coupé was over-heated, and sat down. The train left on time. Over the sound of wheels she heard wailing from the platform and shouts from the sailors up ahead. The coupé wall, of solid inlaid mahogany, and the breadth of the corridor were between her and the grieving women left behind. Elena pulled impatiently at the red plush curtains. On the window side of the coupé there was nothing to be seen but coal sheds and a signal cabin, blurring as the train gathered speed. The sun had not yet risen, but the lemon-yellow light was growing stronger, and flooding over the belching factory chimneys and grimy roof-tops of Viborg Side. Once again, a solid plate glass window was interposed between the dancer and reality.

The newspaper Nelidov's chauffeur had brought Elena was the French-language daily, the *Journal de St. Pétersbourg*. It carried the same banner headline as the Russian paper she had seen in the lift at midnight: *"Victoire à Ispahan!"* The text beneath followed so exactly what Yefimov had said to his guests about the importance of the Persian front that she guessed he had been quoting to them from a communiqué he had drafted for the press himself.

She skipped the rest of the war news. For months past, with the sole exception of the Grand Duke Nikolai Nikolaievich's great victory at Erzerum, it had been nothing but a tale of disaster. Total defeat at Tannenberg and the Masurian Lakes. The loss of Poland, of Lithuania, and all of Courland except Riga. The failure of the British to open a supply route to Russia by way of the Dardanelles. And always, on every front, the tragic story of Russian heroism defeated by Russian inefficiency: no artillery, no shells, no transport, and Russian soldiers "offering their bare breasts to the foe". Elena Tamirova's heart had sickened at it long ago. All that interested her now was the press opinions of the *Nutcracker* ballet.

The editor of the *Journal* had given it two full columns. The review was as lyrical as Tschaikovski's score for the ballet: everyone from the child who danced Claire to young Luba, making her début in a leading rôle, received words of praise. As for the stars —"F. Surov," said the critic, "can justly be compared with V. Nijinski in his best days; and next time the title of ballerina is bestowed on any dancer of the Imperial Theatres, the choice should unhesitatingly fall on Kirillovna II."

Elena Tamirova read the review twice through, while angry tears came to her eyes. If old Borelli had been there to act as audience she would have sobbed and raged, accused the Director of favouritism and Katia Kirillovna of having bribed the ballet critic of the *Journal de St. Pétersbourg*; but in the solitude of her coupé she could only light one of the black-paper cigarettes she carried in a man's gold cigarette-case engraved with a double eagle, and make one of her very rare attempts to face the facts of her career.

She was twenty-six years old, graded in the rigid hierarchy of the Imperial Ballet as a *première danseuse*, while Katia Kirillovna, five years younger and of the same rank, was now publicly mentioned as a future ballerina. No one had said as much of Elena Tamirova at twenty-one, although in 1911 she had been regarded as the rising star, whose appearances in supporting rôles at Covent Garden had been one of the successes of the English Coronation summer. She thought now that 1913 had been the crucial year, when Nijinski was *maître de ballet* and Diaghilev presented *Rites of Spring* in Paris. She had never understood the music or the mood of *Rites of Spring*; it was a century removed from the ballets she had been taught to interpret and love; and after that had come her rupture with Diaghilev. Anna Pavlova had left him too, and had increased her fame thereby; but Pavlova was an established ballerina with an international following, which Elena Tamirova had not yet become. Back in St. Petersburg Elena learned that even Russian audiences clamoured for the new music, the new barbaric costumes and décor; no one wanted to see Tamirova dance *Giselle* who could watch Karsavina as the Fire Bird, or see *Petrouchka* and *Scheherazade*. Then had come her affair with Mikhail, and after that the war; and if she was to be honest with herself she must admit that the tours for war charities, undertaken "for poor Mikhail's sake", also served to hide the fact that the great rôles at the Maryinsky had ceased to come her way. She had no idea what the Director had in view for her in May, and in May all the Imperial Theatres (including the Zimin at Moscow, where she was a favourite) would close until September. Because of the war, she could no longer expect to make guest appearances in Berlin or Vienna, or earn a large salary anywhere in Europe unless she was prepared to do what Vassily Bronin meant to do after Amsterdam —appear in variety at the London Coliseum, on a bill including jugglers and acrobats.

She knew quite well that the old Italian ballet-master was right when he told her to do her best for Kamnov during the coming tour. On his report to the Director her whole future might depend: she might oust Kirillovna from her new precarious perch, or she might drop downwards from the star rôles to dance Myrtha again instead of Giselle, the Princess Mother instead of Odette-Odile. Then, to dance those parts away from Petrograd, in places like Simbirsk or Novgorod. Then, as long as she lasted, endlessly travelling, and not in "soft" coupés, but tired and hungry . . . as she was hungry now.

"You rang, *barinya*?" The steward opened the door immediately. "I was just coming to bring the lady this. From a gentleman in the next coach—a foreigner."

On the steward's little salver was a sealed envelope containing a plain white card. The message read: "Will you share my break-fast basket with me? Please!—K. R. Ericssen."

Elena looked up, sparkling. "Please tell the gentleman to come. And bring us tea." She passed her powder-puff quickly across her face. Karl Ericssen appeared almost before she snapped her hand-bag shut. He was smiling. He was as good-looking in travelling clothes, at nine o'clock in the morning, as he had seemed in the Astoria restaurant.

"I told you I hoped we'd meet again soon," he said.

"I didn't know it would be *so* soon!"

"But this was what I meant." He opened the door of the coupé a little wider, and another steward carried in a tea-basket and spread a white cloth on the table.

"You've taken very quickly to Russian travel, monsieur. Carrying your own provisions—"

"There's enough for two," he said calmly. "When I knew you were travelling on this train I had Nelidov telephone the Transport Ministry at one o'clock this morning and get me a reservation."

"Good *heavens*! Is that what he meant by American hustle?"

"Probably."

"And where are you going to—Helsingfors?"

"To Viborg first, and then to Reval via Helsingfors. The Gulf is open for passenger travel now."

"Not back to Petrograd?"

"No, my business in Petrograd is done."

Elena's steward brought the tea in tall glasses, with lemon slices and beet sugar cubes on saucers, and Ericssen opened the tea-basket. It contained plates, knives and napkins, hard-boiled eggs, thin black bread sandwiches filled with cucumber or smoked salmon, and apples.

"It isn't much, but it's the best the hotel could do at such short notice," said Karl Ericssen.

"I thought you were staying at Monsieur Nelidov's house."

"No, at the Hotel Europa on the Nevsky Prospekt. It's not bad."

"This is a feast."

"I was sure you really didn't know how to look after yourself," he said calmly. "I would have come to you at the station, but I knew the chauffeur was there, and no woman wants to be sociable at seven in the morning. I waited until all the fuss at the Finnish border was over before I sent my note."

"What fuss? A customs man opened the door and touched his hat to me at Terijoki, that was all."

"They're more particular about foreigners. And you're Elena Tamirova, the famous ballerina—"

"No, that I'm not," said Elena bitterly, "and according to the *Journal de St. Pétersbourg*, I never shall be!"

He understood her at once, with the quick sympathy she had felt at the Astoria. "I read that paper too," he said. "I can't read Russian. You haven't been worrying about that ridiculous review, have you? Because Mademoiselle Katia Kirillovna simply isn't to be compared with *you.*"

"You think not?"

"Of course not. Why do they call her Kirillovna II, like royalty?"

"It's the custom. She has an elder sister, now retired from the ballet, who was Kirillovna I."

"And was *she* a ballerina?"

"Of couse not. Oh, perhaps the day will come when any little coryphée will be styled a ballerina, but as yet the title goes to very,

very few. Pavlova, of course, and Karsavina; and the prima ballerina assoluta is Kchessinskaia II."

"I see," he said, "there's a chain of command in the ballet, as in any Service—"

"You aren't laughing at me, are you?"

"Of course not"—gravely. "I'm only wondering how carefully you read the rest of this morning's paper."

"I looked at it; why?"

He shook his head. "You missed it then; too bad. You put your finger on it, too, last night."

"What *are* you talking about?"

"You said, why should all those people turn out in the snow for the capture of some dusty little town in Persia."

"Well?"

"It had nothing to do with Persia. Nelidov was certain of it, and after you left us he insisted that Yefimov and I should go home with him for a nightcap. Signor Borelli was tired and went off to bed. And it didn't take us long to get the truth out of Monsieur Yefimov."

"That sounds—ominous, somehow."

Ericssen reached across the table and took the *Journal* from the settee where Elena sat. "There *is* a line about it in the paper," he said, and turned the pages. "Here it is in the financial column, tucked away beneath the market prices."

"Oh, I never read those!"

"It says: 'Forward patrols under the command of General Baluyev made contact on Saturday with the enemy in the area south of Lake Naroch.' That must be one of the shortest communiqués ever issued, and they wouldn't have issued it at all if some clerk hadn't leaked the news early yesterday evening. That's what brought the people into the streets! The fellow's been dismissed, of course."

"But where *is* Lake Naroch?"

"About sixty miles east of Vilna."

"On the Polish front!"

"Yes. Obviously that was where the Czar—or his Chief of Staff—had to order an attack to relieve the pressure on Verdun

32

and the Salient. The Russians are attacking von Hindenburg's right centre, and on the first day—that was March 18—they made good headway against General von Eichorn's troops."

"What do you mean by 'good headway'?"

"They pushed the Germans back several miles along the road to Vilna."

"So, if it all began so well why should the War Ministry want to keep it secret?"

"Because they want to be able to announce more than success in a preliminary skirmish. And they don't know if this operation can succeed."

"Why not?"

"Look out of the window," he said. "See the soft snow falling. The thaw has started, even in Finland. It'll be raining further south. The Czar has timed his new offensive badly. Soon the road to Vilna will be impassable, and the terrain round Lake Naroch will be one vast bog."

"Oh God," said Elena Tamirova, "it could be the tragedy of the Pripet marshes all over again."

Ericssen was silent.

"So that was why they were walking in the night," said Elena, and there were tears in her eyes. "The people are superstitious: they felt disaster on the way. Oh, how I hate this war! This vile, murderous war!"

"Forgive me," Ericssen said quietly, "I didn't mean to distress you. I know how much sorrow the war has already brought to you."

"What do you mean, Mr. Ericssen?"

"It was Monsieur Yefimov who remarked, when we were back at the Millionaya, that your fiancé was killed in the first month of the war."

"That old gossip! Did he tell you the name of my—fiancé?"

"He did."

"Then you know how unlikely it was that he would ever have become my husband."

Elena faltered. These were matters which, in her proud reserve, she had never discussed with her closest friends in the theatre, far less with a stranger, but already Karl Ericssen was no stranger to her. He had a quality of concentration, a quiet but absolute attention which invited confidence. She said,

"I don't mean the Family didn't behave most generously—they did. For one thing, I was allowed to keep the jewels Mikhail gave me, although some of them were heirlooms—"

"The diamonds you wore last night?"

"Those diamonds, and this brooch, are very clever copies. A person called Timmermann in Amsterdam, a theatrical jeweller, made them for me. The real ones have been in safe deposit almost since Mikhail's death. I never wear them when I go on tour."

"I'm sure you're very wise."

"He was so terribly young," she sighed. "So young, and so dedicated to the Navy! His father was in the terrible defeat at Tsushima, ten years before this war started. He brought Mikhail Mikhailovich up to believe in vengeance for what the Japanese did to Russia at Tsushima and at Port Arthur, until all he lived for was the time when the Russian Navy would win a great victory. He lived for—"

"*Der Tag!*" said Ericssen.

She paused, and looked at him intently. "That's what the Germans call it, so I've heard. But poor Mikhail's dream of victory never came true. He was in the *Bogatir* when his ship attacked the German cruiser *Magdeburg* in a silly skirmish at a place called Odensholm—nothing that mattered, nothing that could possibly affect the course of the war in any way—but Mikhail was hit by a shell splinter . . . killed in his first naval action . . . and buried at sea."

"How very sad," said Ericssen gently. She looked out of the window, tearless, as the train stopped slowly at a wayside station. Some of the Baltic Fleet sailors got out, and ran along the platform looking for a vendor of meat patties or *kvass*.

"Do you know where we are?"—still gently.

"Well inside the Grand Duchy of Finland. They have their dreams here too," Elena said.

"How long to Viborg?"

"About an hour." She knew the countryside well. It was here,

34

but in summer weather, that some of the happy hours with Mikhail had been spent.

"Let's get the man to clear all this away, shall we?"

The steward came and tidied up, folding down the table and at Elena's request, opening the window. The pure cold air of the Finnish forests drove the stuffy heat from the coupé.

"You mustn't catch cold, though," said Ericssen, rolling it up when the train started again. The coupé still smelt freshly of Nelidov's violets in a glass of water, and of Russian cigarettes. Outside, the spring snow was falling in huge flakes on evergreens bowed beneath their load of white.

"I don't want you to think," the man began carefully, "that Monsieur Yefimov said anything about you at the Millionaya last night that he couldn't have said in your own presence. He spoke of you—and Mikhail Mikhailovich—with great respect and admiration; so did Nelidov."

"Yefimov is a notorious gossip," she said indifferently. "But Monsieur Nelidov is always correct, and very kind. Think of this morning—his car to take me to the train, those lovely violets—"

"But you don't like him, is that it?"

"I don't *dislike* him. I just try to—avoid him when I can. He has no idea of the reason."

"Tell me."

"If I told you, then you would know a great deal about my life—"

"That's what I want to know."

"Well," she drew a long breath. Before her lay an excursion into the past which Elena Tamirova had not meant to take, but once again Ericssen's close attention encouraged her to give him her full confidence. She began:

"Did you ever hear the story of Bloody Sunday in St. Petersburg, eleven years ago?"

"When the Cossacks massacred the crowd who went to present some petition or other to the Czar? My God! Were you in that? You must have been a child then—"

"I was fifteen, quite old enough to understand what it was all about. Young enough to be safe inside the Imperial Ballet School with all the other boarders . . ." Elena paused to consider, and began again:

"I was born in the north, a long way away, by the sea. There were a lot of us at home, and when I was about nine my father's sister, Varvara Tamirova, took me to live with her in Petersburg. She had steady work there and a small rented apartment—a roof over our heads. She'd been an actress, but probably not a very good one, bless her heart, because when I went to live with her she'd left the stage, and was assistant to the wardrobe mistress at the Dramatic Theatre. I think she hoped that I'd become an actress too. She used to give me elocution lessons—reciting Pushkin and Lermontov, that sort of thing. She was the sweetest person, my little Aunt Varvara."

"You didn't plan, then, to become a dancer?"

"No. Tell me, last night when you left the Millionaya, did you drive over the bridge and down the Moika, on the way back to your hotel?"

"I remember crossing a bridge, and a canal—"

"Then you passed Dom Pushkina, the Pushkin house, and that's where I lived with my Aunt Varvara. Oh, not on the Moika side, nothing so grand, but behind it, where there are very old tenements built round a courtyard with a little ornamental pond and a fountain. Signor Borelli lived in one of the larger flats, across the way, with his back windows looking into the courtyard."

"So that's where Borelli discovered you. He saw you dancing."

"He saw me *skating,*" she corrected him with a smile. "I was a rough little girl from the north, and I loved skating with the boys after school. Borelli watched from his window and thought I moved well, and might make a dancer. I was rather too old to start—nearly ten, and the right time to begin is eight—but he was a very important teacher then, and he got me accepted as a pupil in the Imperial Ballet School."

"So you had to leave your aunt alone?"

"That was the sad part. Even in the summer vacations I had to live with the other girls from the School, at the government villa on Kamenny Island, but if I had good marks in class I was often allowed to spend Sundays with Aunt Varvara . . . But not *that*

36

Sunday in January 1905. The city was in a ferment, and the pupils were ordered to stay in. I imagine Aunt Varvara waited a little while for me, and then went out. Because she was certainly in the Alexander Garden when the massacre began in the Palace Square. It was her favourite Sunday walk."

Ericssen took her hands in his. He had been fascinated by her long fingers, fluttering as she unconsciously mimed the child skating on the frozen pond beneath the lamplight of St. Petersburg; he wanted to stop them from twisting in pain.

"Well, you know what happened," she went on. "Father Gapon led a procession of citizens, carrying ikons and portraits of the Czar, to the Winter Palace. They were to present a petition to the Czar, who wasn't even there. The Grand Duke Vladimir ordered the troops to fire on the crowd. They died by the hundred in Palace Square, and when some tried to run, the Cossacks pursued them into the Alexander Garden, and killed the women and children like my poor Aunt Varvara, who were just strolling, just happened to be there . . . She was shot down and trampled to death by the horses."

Ericssen bent over her hands, and kissed them. He felt her fingers tighten on his own. He looked up. The hazel eyes were staring and wide.

"And Nelidov?" he hazarded.

"Yes, I've told my story backward, haven't I? I should have explained that the unrest in the city began when the men at the Nelidov ironworks decided to go out on strike. It was that, much more than the quarrel about the Duma or the war with Japan, which started the trouble in St. Petersburg. Grigori Nelidov had just taken charge of the business, after his father's death, and no doubt he had his own reasons for opposing his workers, and refusing their demands for better pay and conditions in the works and shipyards. But I've often thought since then, when I pass his house in the Millionaya or see him in his box at the Maryinsky, that if he had been a better employer—had done more for his workers all those years ago—then we might have been spared Bloody Sunday, and a lot of humble people might still be alive."

"Are you a socialist, Madame Tamirova?"

37

"*I*? I'm nothing. Neither a socialist, nor an imperialist, nor a patriot, nor an intellectual—I'm just a dancer. The theatre is my whole life now. But if I could do anything—anything in my power to help the poor men at the front, or the sailors, or the people like my Aunt Varvara who're being trampled down by something far too big for them—then I'd do it, with my whole heart."

Karl Ericssen moved to the red settee beside Elena, and put his arm around her. "You do so much for them already," he said, "you bring them beauty."

He felt the girl relax against his shoulder. She was looking away from him, at the snow-laden pines now gleaming beneath a clear blue sky, for the snow had stopped, and with his sure and brilliant insight into the mind of another Ericssen knew that his words had carried her over the border of reality and back into her world of fantasy.

"You were born to dance the grand romantic parts," he said caressingly. "You *are* the Snow Fairy and you *are* Odette. But above all you're you, you're Yelena Petróvna—" he pronounced her name in the Russian way, and she looked round with an enchanting smile, "and you make us all believe in your own truth. When you were telling me about your childhood, with a movement of your hands you made me see that city courtyard, and the poor children skating underneath the lamp; and that's how you touch the hearts of all of us—with your compassion."

The train rolled on through the bright forests, and in the forward coaches the Baltic sailors sang. The coupé was a little house on wheels, cosy and intimate; the world beyond the plate-glass window was the dancer's familiar Realm of Snow. She sighed as Ericssen's arms enfolded her.

"But is that enough—to dance, and act compassion on the stage?"

"There's always more that one can do—"

"Tell me what—"

The touch of his hands was so compelling that she missed Ericssen's long shaking breath as he felt for the words which had to be finally and exactly right. "Well, for instance," he said, "there's a charity for neutral seamen that I'm interested in; you

38

could perhaps help with that while you're on tour. Poor devils, they're among the greatest sufferers of this war—"

"Oh, the poor sailors, yes, I would love to do something for them."

"You really are divinely kind!"

A voice in her own head warned Elena that here was something which rang false: that an American munitions salesman was an unlikely champion of European victims of the war. She silenced it. She whispered:

"Say my name again, the Russian way."

"Yelena Petróvna."

But already the identity of Elena Petrovna was merging with a new illusion of love as she turned in his embrace and felt his mouth come down hard upon her own.

III

Wednesday, March 22, to
Saturday, April 1, 1916

Wednesday was one of the rare mornings when Elena Tamirova
did not exercise at the barre, real or improvised. The whole Maryinsky Ballet Company, as this group from the Imperial Theatres
was called on tour, was ordered to go to bed and rest after the night
journey by steamer from Helsingfors to Stockholm. The Gulf of
Finland, although open to traffic, was rough and choppy, and those
of the company overstimulated by the evening performance who
sat up after the steamer sailed at midnight, drinking and smoking,
soon retired seasick to their cabins. Elena shared a cabin with Vera
Polidova. She had meant to find out when the steamer passed out
of the Gulf of Finland and think, although it lay far south of their
route, of the island of Odensholm where the futile battle between
the *Magdeburg* and the Russian cruisers had taken place, and say
prayers in Mikhail's memory. But Vera was exhausted and Elena
worn out by travel and emotion; when they woke up the steamer
was passing the Kopparsten, up channel to Stockholm. Odensholm,
deserted and forgotten, lay miles astern in the darkness.

There was a rehearsal call, of course, on the stage of the Royal
Opera House at four o'clock, and there for the first time Elena
encountered Lev Kamnov in his new position as manager and
maître de ballet of their company. She already knew him as one of
the youngest instructors at the Imperial School when she was the
star of the graduating class. In the world of ballet everybody knew
everyone else's business, and Elena was well aware that Kamnov
had aspired to become a choreographer, but had been defeated by
the superior talents of Fokine. He was a ballet-master of the new
style, who took his rehearsals in working tights and a thick sweater,
chain-smoking when he could and talking polyglot slang to the

stage hands—very unlike the classic deportment of Borelli, whose dancers bowed and curtsied to him as the embodiment of Imperial Theatre authority. Kamnov had worked with Diaghilev, and had made the great transition from romantic interpretation and the supremacy of the ballerina to eccentricity and the team-work of the entire company. Elena guessed that the programme he was rehearsing was not much to his own taste. That it pleased the serious, attentive Stockholm audience was beyond all doubt.

Their first performance at the Royal Opera House was a triumph. Tamirova, said the theatre critic of *Svenska Dagbladet* next day, had been a revelation. Her pas seul from Act II of *Giselle*, when she crossed the stage diagonally on points with a lily in her hand, added unearthly, immaterial beauty to technical virtuosity. "Tamirova in her first appearance in Stockholm," the reviewer continued, "has challenged Anna Pavlova as the supreme interpreter of love beyond the grave." Bronin, her partner in the pas de deux, reminded the critic of *Dagens Nyheter* of the late Serge Legat, especially in his pirouettes and tours en l'air. Bronin sulked at Thursday morning's practice. He was no more fond of being compared to Legat than his rival, Fyodor Surov, liked being contrasted with Nijinksi.

"At least," said Elena to the ballet-master, "they compare me to Pavlova, not to Kirillovna II!"

Kamnov smiled non-committally. "You're sending your press cuttings back to Maestro Borelli, I imagine?"

"Two sets. One for him and one for the Director."

"Very wise." Kamnov was pleased, she thought. He took her to luncheon at Operakällaren as a pale March sun was thawing the drift ice in the Norrström, and Stockholm began to emerge from the harsh sheath of winter like a great granite flower. Tamirova was recognised, and there was a pleasant hum of admiration in the restaurant.

Kamnov returned to the theatre, and Elena walked back alone to the Grand Hotel. She had a suite there, as her contract required whenever possible, and Kamnov was staying there too. Bronin had a new attachment in the corps de ballet, a sloe-eyed boy called Nikolai Levin, and nicknamed Kolia, whose lips were darkened on and off the stage to so purple a shade of red that Elena imagined his tongue like a chow dog's must be purple too. Bronin was treating his fancy to a few nights at the new Strand Hotel on Nybroviken, and the rest of the company were scattered through the theatrical pensions in Ostermalm. Nobody was likely to report on any visitor to Elena Tamirova's sittingroom, on a quiet winter afternoon.

Ericssen had told her exactly what to do. "Just pick up the telephone and call Herr Dr. Petersson at this number. Say you want to see the president of the Neutral Mariners' Fund. When he comes, give him this packet, and that's all."

"But what's in it, Karl?"

"Just some subscription lists. Take a look, and then I'll seal the envelope. You see—just a list of names and addresses of people in New York and Milwaukee. Some in Washington. More in Stockholm and Christiania."

"And Namsos. And Bergen, too. And Aarhus—where is that?"

"Denmark. Most of the men we're trying to help are shipwrecked Norwegian and Danish sailors, who've lost their livelihood through the war in the North Sea."

"You—why don't you want to send it by the regular post, Karl?"

"Darling, it would take ten days at least to get from Viborg or Reval to Stockholm under war conditions. Just think of the delays in all the Russian mail! In your hands it'll get to Petersson in forty-eight hours."

"And he's a shipowner?"

"He has large shipping interests, yes."

"I won't know what to say to him."

At which Ericssen laughed, and drew her to him, and when the train reached Viborg she was so drugged by his kisses that the sealed envelope was forgotten, stuffed deep into her handbag beside the fake jewels. Elena heard only his last words, spoken at the open window before the train carried her on to Helsingfors:

"I wouldn't leave you now, Yelena Petróvna, if I didn't know it was for so short a time . . . I'll be at Copenhagen on Saturday week to see you dance the *Nutcracker* . . . I'll come to your dressing-room before the show . . . goodbye . . . and don't forget—"

She hadn't forgotten. She telephoned to the number Karl had given her from the little glass booth in the lobby of the Grand Hotel, and went upstairs to wait for Herr Dr. Petersson. He was with her in half an hour—a grey-haired, grey-faced man with formal manners, who unfortunately spoke no French.

"You speak no German, madame?"

"Only a little, I'm afraid."

"Why is that? You have never been in Germany?"

"Oh yes. But I didn't care to learn the language."

Grunt. "And you speak no English?"

"Well, more than I do German."

"Why is that?"

"I danced two seasons at Covent Garden, before the war."

"*Ja-so!* And do you speak English, may I ask, with our friend Herr Ericssen?"

"We speak French together." To forestall another interrogation, and a complete survey of the European languages, Elena got up and fetched from her locked portmanteau the list of subscribers to the Neutral Mariners' Fund. Dr. Petersson, with a word of thanks, put it carefully away in an inside pocket, and after a few platitudes about the ballet season discreetly took his leave. It was an awkward little meeting, and left Elena regretting that the language barrier had prevented her from learning more about the work of the Neutral Mariners' Fund. Quite deliberately she dismissed it from her mind. There was too much to enjoy in Stockholm—the sense of freedom which all the Russians felt in their first visit to a neutral capital since the war began, and the enthusiasm of the Swedish audiences. That night they presented a Russian national programme, with Bronin as the Tartar Chieftain leading the corps de ballet in the Polovtsian Dances from *Prince Igor*, and partnering Elena in the polonaise and mazurka from Act II of *A Life for the Czar*. The evening ended with Elena's solo, the Russian Boyar Dance, in a choreography by Borelli which included "The Red Sarafan".

The next evening—Friday—she danced the famous adagio from

43

La Fille mal Gardée, and with the entire company in a cut version of *Chopiniana*. It was not until Bronin led her out for her first bow that she saw Herr Dr. Petersson in an upper box, grey-faced as ever, and accompanied by an obvious spouse in steel-grey satin, with an aigrette in her sternly plaited hair. Both were applauding enthusiastically, and the orchestra leader gave a significant look in their direction as he handed over the footlights an exquisite bouquet of gardenias and stephanotis. Elena curtsied to the box, to the audience, to Bronin, ran off to lead in Vera, went through the protocol of the curtain calls. All the time she was gripping the silver foil round the stems of the flowers. She could feel something hard and square there. As soon as she could dismiss her dresser she locked herself in the dressingroom and examined the bouquet. Inside the foil was a small box, padded with velvet but without a jeweller's name. It contained a brooch of sapphires and diamonds, obviously of considerable value.

It was not unusual for a dancing star to receive—in Russia, and from rich men—a gift of jewels. Foreign admirers of the ballet were not in the habit of throwing away their money on dancers in transit, although beautiful presents had been given to the principals when the Russian ballet made its first tremendous impact on London, and official gifts were sometimes made as well. Elena had even received a diamond clasp, designed by the Kaiser himself, after her appearance at the command performance for his daughter's wedding. It was a tasteless thing, composed of the happy couple's initials, V. L. and E. A., and Elena had sold it to Mr. Timmermann, the theatrical jeweller of Amsterdam, to be broken up into separate stones.

But this sapphire brooch was different. Elena Tamirova weighed it in her hand, pinned it to her dress, asking herself Herr Dr. Petersson's favourite question, *Why is that?* Back in her hotel room she placed it in the chamois roll in which she carried the fake diamonds. She was aware of it lying there all next day, as she went to practice, shopped with Vera Polidova for new ballet tights and shoes, and spent an hour preparing the shoes for use in the way Pavlova had taught her long ago. Soak the points and tread them down, sew plaited tape into the points. Insert the cork supports.

Put them on before the curtain rises and then float out into the warm semi-circle of bright light, prepared on those hard little platforms to dance the thirty-two fouettés of Odile. The fluent arms, the rippling fingers worked their seduction on Prince Siegfried. Down Bronin's painted cheeks, beneath the closely curled black hair, the sweat ran in streaks, as sweat was running between Tamirova's breasts. They smelt the harshness of each other's bodies as the corps de ballet closed in behind them and the curtain fell.

Much later, as the night train raced across Sweden on its way to Malmö, Elena watched the blue light in the ceiling of her sleeping compartment, and wondered why she had not wrapped the sapphire brooch and sent it back to Petersson. She was fond of jewels—all the ballet world knew that—yet in keeping the sapphires she knew that she had gained nothing but possibly lost some of her integrity.

At daylight the train ran on to the ferry steamer. The Russians, heavy-eyed and weary, clambered down from the coaches, crowding to the rails to exclaim and admire as the copper spires of Copenhagen, stained by sea air to the blue-green of verdigris, rose gracefully from the waters of the Sound. A free day stretched ahead, and the dancers went thankfully to their hotels. They were all lodged in the same delightful quarter near the theatre, the principals at the Hotel d'Angleterre, the others at the Cosmopolite. It was Sunday morning, and the church bells were ringing.

Thus tranquilly a week of growing unease began. The Maryinsky Ballet Company was not as enthusiastically received in Copenhagen as in Stockholm. The Danes had a famous ballet of their own, which had produced a prima ballerina of international stature in Adeline Genée, so that the newspapers were only too ready to play the dreary old game of comparisons. Tamirova (compared to Genée) was reproached for being too cold in *The Sleeping Beauty*. "Although technically assured," said the critic of *Berlingske Tidende*, "Tamirova is lacking in emotional depth." Vassily Bronin received a similar sentence of praise and blame, for the Copenhagen papers, unlike the *Journal de St. Pétersbourg*, had no columns to waste on a visiting ballet company. The war news filled the pages, for although Denmark, like Sweden, was strictly neutral, the country

45

was far nearer to the North Sea and the Western battlefronts. The London, Paris and Berlin newspapers were on sale in Copenhagen with only twenty-four hours' delay, and everybody in the company could read at least one of them: the war news went from mouth to mouth as it had hardly done since the days of Tannenberg. For the first time the Russians learned of the colossal sacrifices the French Army was making at Verdun, and how civilians in London were standing up to repeated bombing from the air.

Up to this time, the Maryinsky Ballet Company had shaken down together fairly well. Tamirova, the star, was too reserved to make scenes at rehearsal. She never gossiped with the other girls, although she was good friends with Vera Polidova—they had been coryphées together in the old "wagon" at the Maryinsky. Bronin made scenes on the slightest provocation, but for professional reasons only. His affair with the damson-lipped Kolia was still in the honeymoon stage, and the only tiff between them was when the boy asked Kamnov if he might understudy Bronin as the Tartar Chieftain in *Prince Igor*. Bronin screamed that Kolia was getting too big for his boots, and tears were shed.

But this was a commonplace in their backstage life. What was more uncommon was the new preoccupation with the war. In so large a company there were bound to be some who had friends and brothers on the Russian fronts, or who had been bereaved; but they had lived all their lives inside the fortress of the Imperial Ballet, and until now the war had come second, the theatre first. There were outbursts of despair and weeping when slowly and inexorably, just as Ericssen had predicted, the Russian advance towards Vilna began to bog down in the marshy land round Lake Naroch.

Bronin and the boys booked into the London Coliseum were chiefly interested in the Zeppelin raids. As that wild March ended, and the bomber's moon burned over England, the raids spread from the capital to the Midlands. The British retaliated by bombing the Zeppelin headquarters at Nordholzen near Cuxhaven. With a shock, the Russian dancers realised that Cuxhaven was less than one hundred miles from the Danish border.

Bronin in particular was obsessed by this. He had war maps in his dressingroom. He pinned up newspaper photographs of the German ace pilots: Peter Strasser, Linnarz, Heinrich Mathy and Breithaupt, four men who had had London at their mercy in the previous year. For the very handsome Breithaupt, with his straight blond hair brushed back, his clean-cut features and firm indented chin, the Russian developed a special interest, mixed with love and hate.

"Isn't he a gorgeous creature, darlings?" he giggled to Vera and Elena, as he showed them this Rogues' Gallery in the middle of the week. "Do you realise he bombed *three* theatres in London one night last October—simply *flying* down the Strand as if he were riding a bicycle, and nobody *dared* to stop him?"

"Aren't you scared, Vassily Ilyich?" fluttered Vera, and, "What if he bombs the Coliseum while you're dancing?" asked Elena.

"*Dusha moya*, I should die, I know I should! Oh, why did I ever sign that London contract?"

"Kolia would love to take your place," said Elena, and was rewarded by a glance of malice from Bronin's slanting eyes.

On Saturday Elena went to the theatre not long after the matinée, in which Vera had partnered a young dancer called Lensky who understudied Bronin as *Petrouchka*, in scenes from *Daphnis and Chloe* and *The Firebird*. She had left the room she shared with three other soloists when Elena looked in, and the whole backstage was very quiet. In the star dressingroom Louise, the elderly French dresser who knew Elena's habits, was waiting with the *Nutcracker* costumes hung up in readiness. These were the new dresses fitted in Petrograd, which had arrived in Copenhagen only three days ago and were now to be worn for the first time on the stage. Snow Fairy's glittering bodice and white gauze tutu were traditional and timeless, but remembering Kirillovna's sickly rose-mauve "pie-frill" Elena congratulated herself on her own innovation for Sugar Plum—a costume which really was the glowing red of a ripe plum, frosted over with sparkling strass. Both tutus were in the romantic style of Taglioni—modestly veiling the dancer's slender legs.

47

"They're beautiful, madame," enthused the dresser. "I like them even better than the new dresses for *Swan Lake*."

"So do I, especially the red. And my dinner dress, you have it ready too?"

Louise drew aside a sheet, and showed the sapphire blue chiffon dress on its padded hanger. "Madame is supping at a restaurant tonight?"

"I expect so. Now help me out of my street clothes."

"Shall I prepare a glass of tea while madame rests?"

It was Elena's custom, before a taxing performance, to rest on the dressingroom sofa for half an hour before starting her make-up. Alone, she would sip tea, look at her ikons on the wall, murmur a prayer for Aunt Varvara, and above all think herself into the part she was about to dance. Louise was surprised to hear: "No, I'll make up first, all but the wet-white, and then put on my costume. I expect a visitor before the performance, I'll rest quietly before he arrives."

"Very good, madame."

When she made up for the double rôle in the *Nutcracker* Elena gave Snow Fairy an inhuman chill and sparkle, and Sugar Plum a sly sophistication which in fact suited Bronin's interpretation of the Prince. Tonight, as under her own fingers the whitened cheeks, the green-powdered eyelids and the pale pink mouth took on their stage shape, she saw that even Snow Fairy's other-worldly mask could not hide the restless warmth of a woman hungry for love. She ran the powder-puff over the rising blood in her cheeks several times after Louise had tightened the waistband of the beautiful new dress and tied the coronet of snowflake stars securely behind the glossy dark knot of Elena's hair.

"What time is it, Louise?" She twisted her head to look at the alarm clock.

"Thirty minutes to curtain-up, madame."

"Very well, you may go now, I'll ring when I need you."

"Will you try to rest, madame?"

But how to rest, how to make herself become Snow Fairy, when she could hear the galleries beginning to fill and the musicians gathering in their room on the floor below? She lifted herself on points and sketched an arabesque. He *must* come soon! She had heard nothing from him since he left her at Viborg! And then quietly and suddenly Louise was showing him in, and the door was shut, and she was in Karl Ericssen's embrace.

"Yelena Petróvna."

Elena put her arms round his neck—those slender arms which had so often mimed love—and felt him lift her off the ground as no stage partner had ever lifted her.

"You're such a little thing—so light," he said. "I thought you were taller when we danced in Petrograd."

"High heels." She felt like giggling, as he set her gently down. Like a schoolgirl with her first sweetheart, deliciously young and fresh.

"It's seemed a year since that night at the Astoria."

"Where have you come from, Karl?"

"Åbo. I went back to Finland from Reval, and came on to Denmark in the Baltic steamer. I only got in about two hours ago. I told you I'd be here to see you dance Snow Fairy. And you're beautiful!"

"Oh heavens, I hope it'll go well tonight!"

"Nervous?"

"Horribly. I always am."

"I'll be out in front, adoring you—"

"But did you get a good seat, so late?"

"A friend of mine got me an aisle seat in the third row of stalls. Man who lent me his house for the weekend. That's where I changed my clothes."

"In the city?"

"No, outside in the forest. In the royal park."

"That sounds nice."

"Not as nice as this." Ericssen looked round the little room with a smile. "I've never been behind the scenes before. Is that a make-up mirror? What are these?"

He was looking at the little gilt-framed pictures Elena called her ikons, hanging above the dressingtable.

"Those are my good-luck pictures, I always take them with me. That little painting was a present from my Aunt Varvara, I think

49

she found it in a Petersburg shop. It's supposed to be Carlotta Grisi, the first ballerina who ever danced *Giselle*."

"And the other?"

"That one really is copied from an ikon. It's my patron saint, Helena, with the Emperor Constantine as a baby in her arms."

"She has your beautiful eyes—"

"Karl . . . yes, who is that?"

"It's me—Bronin," said a voice from the other side of the closed door.

"Come in." She threw an annoyed glance at Ericssen. Vassily Bronin entered with his usual swagger. He was already dressed as the Nutcracker Prince, in the costume of white and silver which revealed every line in his slender but extremely powerful body.

"I beg your pardon, Elena Petrovna. I had no idea you were engaged."

"Let me introduce you to Mr. Karl Ericssen, Vassily Ilyich . . . Mr. Ericssen, this is Monsieur Bronin, the *premier danseur* of our company."

"I'm looking forward to seeing you dance tonight, monsieur." Vassily bowed. "I'm sure it's Tamirova you'll applaud, and rightly so. Elena, *dusha moya*, I didn't mean to interrupt you, but I thought you'd want to hear the latest news of the Zeppelins—"

"Oh, not another raid on London!"

"Yes, last night, a big one, but what do you think? Breithaupt is down!"

"Where?" said Ericssen sharply.

"In the North Sea, homeward bound, but the British picked them up. Isn't it fantastic? The first British success *and* Breithaupt safe—one doesn't know whether to laugh or cry."

"Is that a newspaper you've got?"

"A late extra." Vassily smoothed out the front page. The Danish headlines carried the story of Luftschiff 15, forced down in the Knock Deep, and a new photograph of her blond commander.

"He's very like you, Mr. Ericssen, isn't he?" said Vassily with his little giggle. "Why, you might be brothers!"

50

"Don't be silly," snapped Elena. "I told you, Mr. Ericssen is an American."

"You flatter me, monsieur," said Ericssen in his pleasant way. "Breithaupt is a good-looking fellow. However, he seems to be in custody at Chatham tonight; I don't feel inclined to change places with him."

"Well, you'll be happy now, Vassily Ilyich," Elena broke in again. "If Breithaupt's captured, he can't very well drop bombs on the Coliseum!"

Vassily looked slyly from one to the other. "I see I'm *de trop*," he said. "Again, forgive the interruption. Good-night, Mr. Ericssen. Au revoir, my lovely partner! We'll meet again in the Realm of Snow."

"Funny little man," said Ericssen, when the door closed. "Elena, darling, you're going to have supper with me tonight, aren't you?"

"I'd like to. Where?"

"Beside the fire, at my friend's house in Dyrehaven. In the forest. Wouldn't you like that?"

"But will your friend be there?"

"No, only the servants . . . Who the devil is that now?"

"Madame!" said Louise, with the door ajar, "ten minutes to curtain-up!"

Louise, unbidden, had brought a glass of tea. Elena held it in one hand, and sipped, while the dresser put the wet-white on her arms and shoulders. The door was ajar, to let her hear the overture and Act I, Scene I music; it was part of the ordeal of the *Nutcracker* that Snow Fairy had to wait through thirty-five minutes for her entrance. The wait increased Elena's nervousness at any time. Tonight, in the emotional turmoil of Ericssen's return, she found it impossible to sit still through the long sequences of the children's party. When she heard the music introducing Bronin's first entrance as the Nutcracker Prince, she left the dressingroom and went to the wings to watch.

Kamnov was standing opposite, between the heavy flats on the Prompt side. To her surprise—for the young manager disapproved of crowded wings—she saw Vera and several of the coryphées standing close behind him, while just ahead of herself, and dangerously close to the stage, stood Kolia and the other Cossack dancers, ready for Act II.

Kolia looked round and saw Elena. He giggled and whispered something to one of the other boys, who motioned him to silence. Then Kolia, apparently changing his mind, came on tiptoe to Tamirova and, still in a whisper, said "Have you seen Vassily, Elena Petrovna? Don't you think he's *naughty*?"

Precisely at that moment she saw him, as the grands jetés of the Nutcracker Prince brought him upstage, away from the footlights, and her gasp was gratifying to the malicious boy by her side. For Bronin, whose black head was always bare in this rôle, without even a fillet or an ornament, had chosen to wear a wig of pure gold, brushed straight back as Ericssen wore his hair, and he had changed his pale greasepaint for a golden brown like Ericssen's healthy tan. The faint sketching-in, with a dark stick, of a cleft in his chin, completed the weird and obviously deliberate resemblance to Ericssen, and also to the photograph of Breithaupt, the Zeppelin commander.

Elena's hands grew cold. She retreated, automatically on tip-toe, over Kolia's treble solicitudes: "What's the matter? Aren't you feeling well?" and ran back to her dressingroom, pushing through the corps de ballet coming up to support her as the Snowflakes in Scene II.

"*Mon Dieu*, madame!" exclaimed the dresser, "is anything the matter?"

"Get me a glass of water . . . Thank you!" She drank, touched her ikons, crossed herself.

"You're on in five minutes, madame!"

"Beginners for Scene Two, please!"—from the corridor.

"Are you all *right*, madame?"

Shivering: "I feel as if somebody . . . had walked across my grave."

You were wonderful, wonderful, wonderful. Exquisite, perfect, beautiful. The words washed over Elena in a great tide of comfort as she lay back, with her head on Ericssen's shoulder, in the motor carrying them out of Copenhagen. They were already among the budding lilacs of the suburbs, and an occasional street lamp caused bars of light and dark to move over Ericssen's intent face, his white tie, his starched shirt front.

"But I was terribly nervous at the start!"

"Yes, you were a little nervous in the first Act. Not in the second. Nobody had eyes for anyone but you."

"The audience liked me, didn't they?"

"They adored you. How many bows did you take—twelve?"

"Ten." And what a pleasure it had been, when the curtain fell for the last time, and the smiles were wiped at once off the stars' faces, to say casually to Bronin: "That blond wig suits you, Vassily. Try it again some time." She stirred luxuriously in the aftermath of a great stage triumph.

"One of the Danish critics said I was lacking in emotional depth."

"What a fool." The automobile was stopping. "Are we there?" Elena asked.

"Not quite. This is the Red Gate of Dyrehaven, and we change to a carriage here. They don't allow motors in the royal park."

A groom was standing by a horse's head near a gate in a high brick wall. "It's only a landau," Ericssen said, lifting Elena over the low step, "I know it ought to be a troika."

"And snowing. But it's springtime now. How quickly spring-time comes in Denmark!" There was a fragrance of snowdrops and wild violets from under the beech trees of Dyrehaven.

"The place we're going to is very rustic," Ericssen explained, caressing her. "One of the Danish kings built a retreat here, called the Hermitage. My friend rents a kind of hunting lodge belonging to the Hermitage, and it's as simple as can be. But I think you'll like it."

"It's like the first Act of *Giselle*—the cottage in the clearing," she said delightedly, as the landau drew up in front of a low brick building, shadowed by fine oaks, with the light of paraffin lamps shining from latticed windows. An elderly man in a striped waist-coat stood waiting by the open door. His wife, in country dress with embroidered linen sleeves and a red apron, conducted Elena through the panelled livingroom to a white bedroom where a log fire was burning. When she returned to Ericssen she was smiling. "What an enchanting place!"

"Come and have supper."

"I can't eat yet—I'm too strung up—may we wait awhile?" She moved about the room while Ericssen stood watching. Everything, as he had said, was of the simplest—heavy leather chairs and sofas, a few books and engravings of Danish battle scenes, bear pelts on the polished floor—the effect, by lamplight and firelight, was one of deep and drowsy comfort.

"That man and woman—are they the only servants?"

"There's a girl in the kitchen, and the groom, of course."

"Karl—the woman doesn't speak anything but German."

"Yes, well," he said, "a lot of Germans are employed in Denmark . . . I think we're expected to help ourselves, Elena." He lifted the lids off several silver dishes on a table set against the wall. "Here's caviar from the Volga, you like that, and some smoked sturgeon, and other things . . . No? A glass of wine, then?"

She drank to him and he to her, gravely; and Elena sat down on one of the huge sofas, with the lamplight full on her face and her slim body in the dark blue dinner dress. The sapphire brooch gleamed at the point of the low neck.

"You haven't asked me about Dr. Petersson, Karl."

"I've had better things to think about for the past three hours! But you did see the old boy in Stockholm?"

"Well, he came to see me. And I gave him the subscription lists, just as you said."

"Thank you, darling. That was a great help."

"But he came to see me dance, Karl, and sent me—*this*."

Ericssen came to her side, knelt down, and put a finger under the sapphire brooch. "What a pretty thing," he said casually, "I've been admiring it."

"Such a valuable present—just for taking him a letter?"

"That letter, darling? The letter can't have had anything to do with it! Petersson is a very rich man . . . a connoisseur of ballet . . . this is his tribute to the rising star."

"You're sure that's all it was?"

"Take my word for it." Ericssen stood up. "Look at you!" he said adoringly. "Do you know what you're doing to this queer old room? You're turning it into a magic place. I don't believe Copenhagen's only seven miles away. Presently we'll hear the *Giselle* music, and the huntsman's horn—"

"Enter the corps de ballet!" she said, and tried to laugh. But Ericssen, unsmiling, bent down again, and kissed her breast where the sapphire brooch held the edges of her dress together, and then her throat, and had her in his arms, captured, before he took her lips. And when she said Yes he had scarcely asked his question, because the entreaties and the promises came in the breaths between the kisses. Stay with me tonight, Elena, Love me, Elena, Yes, yes, yes.

IV

Tuesday, April 4, to
Saturday, April 8, 1916

Herr Hans Kolberg, president and managing director of the
Kolberg Steamship Line, was clipping the end off his first after-
lunch cigar when his confidential secretary came in with a
whispered message which made him sit upright in his swivel
chair.

"The *what* Fund? Bless my soul, what an ingenious devil he is!

". . . Appearing at the National Theatre? Of course I'd no idea,
I don't follow these things. Speaks French, does she? H'm.

". . . And where is *he*, pray? He was due back last week. Oh! I
see. Very well, Hoffmann, I'll see her in five minutes. No, don't
show her in; I shall come out."

Herr Kolberg laid down his unlit cigar. His desk as usual was
in perfect order, and the single correspondence file brought out
since his return from lunch was neatly laid in a leather portfolio.
He tossed it into a drawer and got up, his large stomach interfering
slightly with the movement. He was a man approaching sixty,
bald, but with a luxuriant moustache waxed and spiked in the
style made famous by the Kaiser, and impeccably dressed, with a
high stiff collar and white slips to his waistcoat. The grey spats
beneath his pin-striped trousers were less immaculate, and showed
traces of a wet day in Christiania.

The morning papers were lying folded on a side table. Hans
Kolberg glanced hastily at two of the theatre pages, assimilated the
contents, and went to look out of the wide window. The offices of
Kolbergske Dampskibselskab occupied an entire building on the
Stortingsgade, with K.D.S. in huge gilt letters across the front,
within sight of the ugly yellow brick National Theatre. Although
Kolberg wore gold pince-nez for reading, his long distance vision

was still excellent, and he could read the name on the billboards by the theatre door: TAMIROVA.

He found the owner of that name in his outer office, gracefully declining the coffee which two ecstatic young clerkesses were pressing upon her.

"Madame, this is too great an honour," he said, bowing low. "Pray forgive me for keeping you waiting, if only for a moment. Will you come this way?"

They went into the private room, warm with the heat from an old-fashioned porcelain stove, and Elena loosened her cloak. "No, I mustn't stay," she said, when Kolberg made to take it from her, "we have a stage rehearsal call at half past four."

"A rehearsal? After last night's tremendous success?"

Smiling: "Our ballet master is a martinet. Were you in the audience, Monsieur Kolberg?"

"Alas, no. Since Fru Kolberg died, I very seldom visit the theatre. Too much Ibsen about our national drama for my taste, madame! Too much doom and gloom! But I'll be there tonight, you may be sure!"

He eyed her gallantly. Kolberg, who thought of himself as a connoisseur, admired what he called "a fine figure of a woman", and this one was too skinny for his taste by far, but then her face was lovely, and she was a theatre girl! He said, "Will you be dancing 'The Red Sarafan' tonight? The papers are raving about your performance in that."

"No, not tonight—Mr. Kolberg, I really ought to have telephoned you yesterday. I'm at the Hotel Continental, five minutes away, and perhaps you might have come there to see me, as Mr. Ericssen suggested. But we had a dreadful day at the theatre. First my train was late, and that threw the practice out; and then there was some trouble about the scenery for *Prince Igor*—we were on call right through the afternoon. So I thought I had better bring you those papers about the Fund as soon as I was free today. I know Mr. Ericssen wants you to read them before he comes to Norway."

"You've seen him recently?" said Kolberg, turning over the envelope she laid on his desk.

"I had supper with him in Copenhagen on Saturday night."

The devil you had, he thought. And he began to talk about Karl Ericssen, whom he had known for years through his relatives in Norway—"he used to spend his school holidays at our saeter in the Dales"—and Karl's success and ambition, and while he talked he watched Elena's face. The muscles were under professional control, the smooth white eyelids never fluttered, but the smiling mouth gave her away. Elena's lips moved almost imperceptibly at every mention of Ericssen's name. Oh, he's her lover, not a doubt of it, Hans Kolberg thought. Fortunate and clever devil!

"Probably that's why he's so interested in helping the Norwegian sailors," she said, when Kolberg had finished the saga of the saeter. He was inspired to say,

"That of course; and then he was here last January at the time of the big fire at Bergen, when so many fishermen lost their little homes as well as their livelihood. They could ill afford that at a time when the North Sea is practically closed to them."

"Because of German submarines?"

"Because of the British minefields, *chère madame!* And the arrogant British assumption of the right of search!" Hans Kolberg had found the clue at last: he was able to launch without difficulty into an account of all the Neutral Mariners' Fund had done for the survivors of fishing-vessels which had struck mines, for crews deprived of their bonus when the British forced them into the Examination Base at Kirkwall in the Orkney Islands—a torrent of details for which he sometimes failed to find the words in French, and which Elena hardly understood in any language. But she was oddly reassured by the description of so many good works, which Kolberg afterwards described to his nephew as the most brilliant improvisation of his career.

"This has been a great honour, madame," he repeated when Elena rose to go. "May I ask for a further pleasure? My nephew and his wife would be charmed to make your acquaintance. If I could arrange a little luncheon party tomorrow, say at the Bristol Hotel, might I hope for the pleasure of your company? Say at half past twelve?"

"That would be delightful." The feel of the Kaiser moustache on the back of her hand was not agreeable. Kolberg told his

58

secretary to take Madame Tamirova downstairs in the lift, and took up his former position by the window. Very soon he saw her come out on the pavement, and cross the street into the park. The rain had stopped, but few people were strolling for pleasure; Elena was conspicuous as she went with her dancer's walk along the paths between the frozen garden plots. She paused to look at the two forbidding statues in front of the National Theatre: Ibsen in a frock-coat, Björnson in an Inverness cape. He wondered what thoughts were passing through her mind.

One who had been wondering the same thing for some time past was Lev Kamnov, who was in the lobby of the Hotel Continental when Elena came in from the park. He went up to the porter's desk as she claimed her key, and touched her arm.

"Elena Petrovna, I should like to speak to you."

"Yes, what is it?"

"Come and have a glass of tea with me, or a cup of coffee; you look very cold."

"If you wish." She let him guide her into the Theatre Café, that famous Christiania rendezvous for actors and literary men, where Ibsen had had his reserved table, and where even at that hour of the day, between the early luncheon and the early supper of the unsophisticated little capital, nearly every place was filled. Men and women were drinking coffee or beer, eating cream cakes, reading the papers and smoking, and waiters were hurrying between the tables. One took Kamnov's order as soon as he had seated Elena in a secluded corner. She began hunting in her bag.

"Will you give me a cigarette, please? I must have left mine at the theatre."

"You don't think these Norwegian people might be shocked?"

"Because I smoke in public? I see a fat woman smoking a cigar."

Kamnov smoked *caporal*. He lit a cigarette for her, and with pleasure heard her cough.

"The Director of the National Theatre has invited us to luncheon, Elena Petrovna. Tomorrow or the next day—I said I thought tomorrow would be best."

59

"I'm engaged tomorrow. If the Director gives us a choice, then why not Thursday?"

"As you please. I only thought tomorrow would be easier for you, with no rehearsal call in the afternoon." He saw that she was not paying attention to him. She was drinking coffee with her elbows on the table and her cup in both hands, and watching the waiter pulling heavy green café curtains over the uninspiring view of the misty Stortingsgade. Kamnov said sharply:

"Has your luncheon engagement anything to do with your late arrival in Christiania?"

"I don't think that's any concern of yours, Lev Yurievich."

"It'll be very much my concern if you're late for the performance."

Furiously: "I've never been late for a performance in my life!"

"You were twenty minutes late for practice yesterday morning."

"For *practice*—because the train was late."

"But you left Copenhagen on Sunday night, instead of with the rest of us on Sunday morning."

"Why are you bringing all that up now? Why not yesterday?"

"Because I didn't want to reprove the *première danseuse* in front of the whole company. I reserved judgment until I saw what sort of performance you gave last night."

"You heard the audience. You counted the curtain calls."

"I heard the audience. They clapped you as they clap performing bears in the circus, when they saw you throwing yourself about in 'The Red Sarafan'. God! what sentimental claptrap! You were dancing like a peasant girl at a village wedding." He hummed, deliberately dragging the beat: "'*Sew* not, *dearest moth*-er *mine*, the *scar*let *sarafan*—' It was very hard on Bronin."

"Has he complained? He's always complaining about something."

"*I'm* complaining, about a series of very uneven performances from the great Elena Tamirova. Brilliant one night, nervous the next, terrible *last* night—"

She gave a little flick of her expressive fingers, which showed what she thought of the shabby old café and the plain square faces of the Norwegian patrons. "For God's sake, Elena Petrovna!" he

60

said in an angry whisper, "these people are paying money to see you dance! You owe them as good a show as you'd put on at the Maryinsky! Where you will never dance again, unless this tour ends better than it began! You've been behaving like a prima ballerina assoluta, which you are not, and very likely never will be; and I advise you to mend your manners, unless you want me to make a report to the Director of the Imperial Theatres that'll finish you for good in Russia!"

The odd thing was that his threats had meant absolutely nothing. Lying on her bed, trying to relax before the 4.30 rehearsal, Elena tried to feel furious with Kamnov, and failed. She was glad that she had spat out one sentence picked up from the street boys in her old skating-pond days behind the Pushkin house, and left the Theatre Café; but that was all. The really important thing was to be alone and free to think of Karl.

He had promised to come to Norway at the end of the week, and go on with her to Amsterdam. He had talked about his work, and a job very nearly over; she had not dared or cared to ask what that might mean. Elena Tamirova was beyond thinking of the future. She was obsessed with the present. Her obsession took the form of a simple physical urgency: the longing to lie in her lover's arms again.

The tragedy of her Aunt Varvara's death, on that Bloody Sunday when she was fifteen, had so chilled and hardened Elena Tamirova that she had never been drawn into any of the affairs so common between boys and girls of the Ballet School. There had been episodes on the summer tours to be remembered only with disgust, and there had been some happy weeks with Fyodor Surov, when they were both twenty-one and wild with the excitement of the Russian Ballet's first success in London. She still remembered Fyodor's room beneath the chimney pots of Half Moon Street, where the London pigeons cooed on the windowsill, and the dawn smell of hawthorn drifted in from the trees in the Green Park. Then, much later, there had been Mikhail Mikhailovich, killed at Odensholm, not much older in years than Fyodor had been; young, clumsy and selfish even when he loved her most. No one had given her what Karl at once had given—the passion, full, complete and shared, of a very experienced man of thirty-three. The dancer turned restlessly upon her bed, and ached for him.

Three afternoons later she had her wish. In that same room, while the lights from passing cars on Stortingsgade wheeled over the darkening ceiling, Elena knew in the flesh those supreme moments which she had only mimed in the language of the dance. She had flung her cap over the windmill as far as Kamnov was concerned, sending a message over to the theatre excusing herself from the afternoon rehearsal, and she was quite prepared to face his wrath; yet when six o'clock struck the old discipline asserted itself, and she went into the sittingroom, where Karl met her with an adoring look.

"One forgets," he said, "in only twenty minutes one forgets how beautiful you are."

He was lying back in an armchair, with his fair head against the cushions, and his right hand, holding a cigarette, flat on the front of his white shirt. With his left, he tilted the reading lamp on a table by his side, so that beneath the amber shade the light fell upon the dancer. She was wearing a long white peignoir, with fan-shaped sleeves of broderie anglaise and a frilled hem, as immaculate as her white tutus at the start of each performance; her dark hair lay loose on her shoulders. When the spotlight fell upon her she automatically stopped, and smiled.

"Hold it!" said Karl. ". . . Confess now, Elena, in the very back of your mind, aren't you thinking it's only ninety minutes to curtain-up?"

"Eighty-five," she said, and Karl laughed. "What are you dancing tonight, my darling?"

"Oh—*divertissements*. A bit of this and a bit of that; you know. The pas seul from *La Esmeralda*, to begin with. And a lovely one act ballet called *Love's Trickery*—d'you know it?"

"Never heard of it."

"I saw Pierina Legnani in the première, just after I entered the Imperial School. I don't know how it'll please the Norwegians. They seem to like the acrobatic dances best."

Karl drew her down to the arm of his chair. "They like *you*," he said, "judging from the floral tributes." The sittingroom was full of bouquets and even azaleas and cyclamen in pots.

"Herr Kolberg sent most of these," Elena said. She felt warm, relaxed, light-hearted.

"He must have emptied his conservatories. *What* orchids! I'm glad I ordered pink carnations for your theatre flowers tonight."

"The orchids were very special. They were at my place at table when we had luncheon at the Bristol."

"You and old Kolberg?"

"And Axel and Elsa Kolberg—nephew and nephew's wife."

"I know the young Kolbergs. Did you enjoy yourself?"

"Y—yes. Well, to be truthful, not very much. He ate and drank such a lot—especially drank; and he *gobbled* so, it wasn't very pleasant."

"He's a rough diamond, Kolberg. Have you seen him again?"

"He insisted on giving me champagne in the Theatre Café after the show last night. I think he enjoyed being seen out with a star."

"Of course. But tonight you're going to have supper in the restaurant with *me*."

Karl's eyes were shut, for Elena was stroking his brow, and lifting his heavy blond hair strand by strand. She said diffidently, "Karl, Mr. Kolberg asked me to have dinner with him tomorrow night. He wants to show me the Fairy Tale Room at Holmenkollen, and the view over the fjord from the mountain, before we go."

Still with his eyes closed, Karl said lazily, "Dinner? But you'll be at the theatre."

"Why, that's just it, he knows I won't. I'm dancing the entire *Nutcracker* at a children's matinée, and Bronin and Vera will dance at night. Then they strike stage and go straight to the Rotterdam steamer."

The grey eyes were wide open, cold and alert. "Oh," said Karl Ericssen. "Oh well, that puts a different complexion on it. The Fairy Tale Room at Holmenkollen—I can't think of anything more respectable than that! Why don't you do it, darling—you could be back here by ten o'clock."

"But I don't *want* to, Karl!"

"Listen, Elena. Hans Kolberg is a very important business associate of mine, and I want to keep him pleasant and co-operatively inclined. Naturally he admires you; naturally he likes to be seen in public with the great Tamirova. Also he's a lonely old chap; both his married daughters live in Sweden. Do you really mind spending two hours with him at the Fairy Tale Room before you leave Norway? Remember you're out of a fairy tale to him—as you are to everyone who sees you on the stage."

He thought he knew so well how to persuade her by flattery that it was startling to hear Elena say: "How do you find him an important associate—to your munitions firm, or to the Neutral Mariners' Fund?"

"To both, my dear."

"Do little neutral countries need to buy munitions?"

"It's called defence, Elena. They're even better customers than the Great Powers." He drew her down into his arms. "Don't look so sulky, darling. Do this to please me; it isn't very much to ask. Remember, we're going on the boat together, and I'll be with you all the time in Amsterdam . . ."

"But when you go back to your own country, Karl?"

"I think I'll have to take you with me when I go."

"Are you quite warm enough, *chère madame*?" asked Hans Kolberg solicitously, and Elena nodded. Rather to her surprise he was driving himself, and instead of being sheltered behind the plate glass of a limousine she was sitting beside him on the front seat of a heavy Benz motor, climbing the steep unmetalled road outside Christiania. It was not really cold, though Elena's thin cloak was only of silk-lined green chiffon, with a long scarf of chiffon which could be worn as a hood. The April evenings were growing lighter. There was still colour in the sky, although down in Christiania the lamps were lit, and Vassily—supported by Vera Polidova as the Young Girl—well into his show-piece, *The Spectre of the Rose*.

"We have to stop here at the level crossing," Kolberg said. They had come to a little wayside station with an open wooden shelter on each side of the track, serving one of the outer suburbs of the capital. The simple timber houses and gardens, with one or two shops and a post office, were scattered along the slope of the mountain.

"It isn't a main line, surely?"

"No—dear me, no; this is Holmenkollenbanen, it was only opened three years ago. Very convenient—"

"To reach the hotel where we're dining?"

"Holmenkollen Sanatorium—yes, and further; it goes from the National Theatre right up to Frognersaeter. That's a very rustic restaurant, for skiers and walkers: you wouldn't like that."

Kolberg had turned towards her while they waited, and she caught a sickly odour of caraway on his breath. She remembered how much kümmel he had drunk at the Bristol lunch, and opened the window on her side of the car. A fresh scent came in from the snow still lying in patches on the wild heaths and bilberry bushes, the young birch bark, the sap just rising in the larches. Like a breath from Russia, it assailed Elena's heart.

"Here comes the train," she said unsteadily. It was a down train, sparsely filled, of two coaches filled with wooden seats; they saw children's faces at the window, and then the red tail light disappeared round a curve. It was very quiet in the little suburb.

"Now we can go on." The Benz was put in motion, the road lay steadily upward through the trees. "Is it far to your Fairy Tale Room, Mr. Kolberg?"

"About two miles more. We're at Vettakollen now; one of our new developments, alas! And another level crossing to negotiate."

"Why 'alas!'"

"Because I built my own villa here twenty years ago, never dreaming the hillside would be built up so soon. The railway is to blame for that."

"And the prosperity you've brought to Christiania." It was a mechanical compliment, the sort of thing Karl would have liked her to say, but it pleased Kolberg. He drew off one glove and twitched the spikes of his absurd moustache. Elena tried not to laugh. A train came up from the city, halted at Vettakollen station, moved on a little way, and stopped again.

"It's on the turntable," said Kolberg, listening. "We can cross safely now." He accelerated; the Benz shot across the track, and a man in a peaked cap came out of the little station and shouted after them.

"I gather a motor car is a rarity in these parts."

"They should know mine well enough by now," growled Kolberg, "seeing I live five minutes' drive away. Madame Tamirova, I want to show you my conservatories before we go on to Holmenkollen. You don't mind, do you? They've got some rather strict licensing laws at the Sanatorium, and I want to offer you a really good glass of champagne before we dine."

"Oh, but . . . we mustn't be late, Herr Kolberg. I'm leaving tonight, you know."

"I do know it, to my great regret. You won't be late. And here we are!"

Herr Kolberg's villa stood a good deal higher than the nearest of the new houses in Vettakollen, with a large garden behind a brick wall separating it from the rough country road. The gate stood open, and there was an electric lamp halfway up the drive. By its light, and that of another lamp above the door, it was easy to see that Herr Kolberg had added ideas from the Old Norway school to his modern villa, for hideous carvings, imitating the prows of Viking ships, sprang from the ox-blood painted roof, and imitation Runic stones peppered the wellkept lawns. Indoors, the décor was a medley of stuffed bears, Tiffany glass, and copies of medieval Norwegian furniture. The owner proudly led Elena into the drawingroom.

"What a delightful room," she said faintly, and Kolberg beamed. "My poor late wife's taste—just as she left it." Fru Kolberg's taste had run to an alcove in the Moorish style, to Delft-blue plates arranged on a walnut overmantel and to what Kolberg called "the largest private collection of Edvard Munch's paintings in the world".

"Cosy—not?" he asked. "There is really no word for it in French, chère madame! Gemütlichkeit—the real German cosiness was what poor Greta insisted upon everywhere we made our home. That is her portrait—painted by Munch, of course. These are my

daughters and their families. And this is my little sweetheart—
my little niece, Ingrid."

The family photographs, in heavy silver frames, were set out on
a side table. The picture he held out to Elena was only postcard
size, the product of a country photographer's studio, set in a
plain wood frame. It showed a young girl in a velvet party dress
with a lace collar, holding a bunch of Christmas roses in her hand.

"What a charming child! Your niece, you said?"

"My sister's daughter, Ingrid Sabiston. My only sister married
a Scots minister, and lives near Kirkwall in the Orkney Islands . . .
Now what would you like to drink—champagne?"

"Oh, not champagne, please." She was a little anxious, now,
about embarking on a bottle of champagne with Kolberg in that
silent house. "A glass of sherry—anything; and then we really
must be going." They would have reached the first interval at the
National Theatre, and Bronin's dresser would be sponging him
down before getting him into his costume for *Scheherazade*.

"Do please sit down, then, while I fetch it. The servants have
the evening off." But Elena remained standing, between the grand
piano and the photograph table, studying the postcard picture of
Ingrid Sabiston. Too tall for a dancer, the shoulders far too broad,
but the young body slim inside the clumsy dress, and the face so
lively and eager to please! A long braid of fair hair had been pulled
over one of Ingrid's shoulders, fastened with a large ribbon bow.
How old—seventeen, eighteen? Elena loosened her chiffon cloak
with a sigh. She had not removed it, nor her gloves, though the
room was warm, and her green chiffon dress had a high neck. She
had no desire to give Herr Kolberg the impression of being prepared to settle down for the evening. The clink of glasses sounded
in the next room, and Kolberg entered carrying a tray. His face
was very red and he had obviously had another drink of kümmel.

Elena declined sherry and moved into the middle of the room.
The place was like a furniture warehouse; it was impossible to take
three steps without touching a desk, a sideboard, an outsize sofa,
and the tables were littered with bric-à-brac—cloisonné boxes,
Benares brass ash-trays, a parade of ivory elephants.

"May I have a cigarette, please?"

"In the alabaster box behind you." Kolberg came forward, flicking his cigar-lighter, and Elena saw that there was sweat upon his brow.

"What beautiful flowers—just like those you sent me." It was the only thing she could think of to say, and she stooped over the sweet-scented azaleas in an effort to end the tension in the room. Kolberg's head swam. That pliant body in the green draperies, the lovely head bent above the flowers, excited him beyond control.

"My God!" he said, "you're beautiful! Give me a kiss." And he seized her roughly by the waist.

"This is ridiculous, Herr Kolberg—"

"Now don't try to make a fool of me, my dear—"

Elena wrenched herself free. The touch of his body had been horrible—that great paunch swinging against her slimness—but she kept control of herself, and said,

"It was very foolish of *me* to come here alone with you. I wish to leave now; will you drive me back to Christiania, or can I send for a taxi?"

"You're not on the stage here, Madame Elena," said Kolberg. He was more flushed than before, if that were possible, and one of his white waistcoat slips had come undone. "Come on, don't be so theatrical! Just be sweet to me—just give me one hour, that's all I ask! *Kiss* me—" And this time he actually succeeded in smearing a kiss over her averted cheek, pressing her up against the table until she got one arm free and pushed him away.

"You must be mad, Herr Kolberg. I am not your kitchenmaid, to be mauled and degraded, I am Elena Tamirova—"

He stepped back then of his own free will, and there was a furious glitter in his small eyes.

"Mauled and degraded—delightful language, I must say! You set too high a price on being Elena Tamirova—the ballet girl—the mistress of a German secret agent!"

"Are you . . . out of . . . your senses?"

"Come, my dear, don't go on acting with me. You know what your precious Karl is, whatever name he passes by—Ritter, Ericssen, I don't care; you wouldn't be his courier otherwise.

68

We're all in this together, so why should he grudge me a lick out of his plate—"

Her hand closed on the heavy alabaster cigarette-box, and as Kolberg's thick arms opened once more to embrace her, Elena struck him full across the chest.

Kolberg staggered. His face was suffused with blood. His heel caught in the heavy bearskin rug which lay above the carpet, and he fell to the ground backwards, at full length, while Elena, as slowly as if the weapon weighed a ton, laid the alabaster box behind her on the table.

Two or three cigarettes had fallen on the floor. She put them back in the box, mechanically, and went to kneel beside the fallen man. He was breathing rapidly and stertorously and there was froth upon his lips. Elena screamed then in the reaction of frenzy, and ran to the bell-pull. Far away it jangled in the depths of the villa, and then there was silence. It was true the servants had been sent away.

She ran into the hall, among the stuffed bears and suits of armour, looking for a telephone, with some wild idea of calling Karl at the hotel. There was not one to be seen, and the thought of hunting through the house was terrifying, even if she had felt sure of being understood by a Norwegian operator. She ran out of the house, closing the door behind her, and down the brightly illuminated drive.

No other dwelling overlooked Herr Kolberg's villa—so he had boasted on the way there; and yet she knew there were houses quite near, where help could be sought for one who was perhaps a dying man. Elena ran on in her satin slippers, all the faster as her eyes became accustomed to the starlight, and steadily downhill, but without ever seeing a gateway or a drive. She paused to catch her breath and collect her wits. In the silence of the woods she heard the creaking of the railway turntable at Vettakollen.

Immediately she knew that she was near the station. Elena put her dress straight, wound the chiffon scarf round her head and walked quickly on. The lighted station came into sight. The lamps were on the Up side, the shelter on the Down side was quite dark. She thankfully crossed the track and stood in the shelter, waiting.

In a few minutes a train came down from Frognersaeter. It was crammed with noisy boys and girls, singing student songs after a day's ski-ing in the Nordmark, and the driver hardly looked at Elena as she whispered "National Theatre" and offered him a coin from her evening bag. She stood jammed among the students, swaying with the train, until the song of the wheels began to remind her of the train from Petrograd, and two words Ericssen had spoken on the way. He said *Der Tag*, the wheels reminded her. He said *Der Tag, Der Tag, Der Tag.*

It was strange to come out of that dark tunnel of pain and into the lighted streets, where the good folk of Christiania were enjoy-ing Saturday night. The National Theatre corridors and foyers were brightly lighted, on the stage *Scheherazade* would be in full swing, and Bronin exulting in his rôle as the Favourite Slave. Elena entered the Continental Hotel. She was past hurrying now; it was an immense effort to lift each foot as she went down the long corridor to Ericssen's room and knocked.

"Come in!"

He was sitting at the writingtable in shirt and trousers, with his sleeves turned back over his starched cuffs, and the lamplight burnished the gold hair on his forearms as he jumped to his feet.

"What, back already! . . . Elena! Darling! What's the matter?" But she was beyond speech; Karl Ericssen helped her to a chair, and snatched up his silver travelling flask from the dressingtable. She noticed dully that a revolver and a shoulder holster lay beside it.

"It's brandy, drink it, and now try to tell me—"

Gasping: "I think—I may have killed him—Karl."

He seized her wrist in a painful grip that stopped her from fainting, and made her speak, listening—after one oath—without interruption, with the close concentration she knew so well, and going smoothly into his interrogation when her voice failed.

"How did you get back?"

"By the little train."

"So all this happened half an hour ago?"

"At least. Oh Karl, what shall I do?"

"And you're sure there were no servants in the house?"

"Yes."

"The lecherous old devil. I knew what he was, but I never imagined he would dare—Elena, listen to me. Are you sure you brought all your belongings away with you—bag, cigarettes, powder-puff, everything?" He looked her over. "Dress not torn, and gloves—you kept your gloves on? Good. You put the box back on the table, and you didn't drink out of the second glass? . . . Now tell me again how he fell. On the rug—where there was nothing for him to hit his head on? Right. Now I'm going to telephone—"

"To the police?"

"With any luck we'll get through without the police. No, to his nephew first—"

While Karl talked, he had been putting on his collar, tie and waistcoat, slipping in his cuff-links, slinging the holster underneath his arm before he put his jacket on. The thick notebook in which he was writing when she came in was thrust into his breast pocket. "Don't leave me Karl!" But she knew he had to telephone from the box downstairs; though there were no bedroom telephones in the hotel as yet, there was also no delay in getting through from the switchboard to a local number. Karl was back in the room within ten minutes.

"What did you tell him?"

"Told him his uncle phoned me and said he was feeling ill. Suggested we should both go out to Vettakollen and see how the old boy is. Now don't start crying, Elena, it's the only thing to do. I don't for a moment think you killed him, but something's up, and he may very well be dying, if not dead—I told them to get me a taxi, and another one for you."

"For me?"

"Yes, darling, you can't stay here. Your friends will be coming across from the theatre in less than an hour, and they mustn't see you in this state. Louise is looking after your baggage, isn't she? You go straight on to the boat. Go to your cabin and lie down, and wait for me. It's going to be *all right*."

He kissed her colourless face. Limp in his arms, Elena Tamirova looked up at her lover.

"Is Axel Kolberg in this thing too?"

"What do you mean?"

"This plot . . . this conspiracy . . . whatever it is a German secret agent does."

He released her. "What are you talking about? What absolute lunacy is this?"

"Kolberg told me you're a German spy, and your real name is Ritter."

"And you believed him?"

"Yes."

"Why? Because of my chance resemblance to a certain German flyer?"

"No. Because of what you said in the train three weeks ago . . . about *Der Tag*."

Karl's eyelids flickered. "It's an expression anyone might use, these days. But my dear girl, if you thought it so sinister, why did you promise to—see me again? We could have parted forever at Viborg; why were you willing to go on?"

With shame: "You know why," she said, and Karl laughed. "Yes, I know why; because we fell in love. And that's the only thing that matters—"

"Tell me the truth," said Elena Tamirova, "or *I'll* send for the police."

He seemed, all at once, to make up his mind. "Very well, then," he said, "if you must have it! My name is Karl Richard Ritter. I am an officer of the Imperial German Navy, seconded for special duty by the Admiralstab. In which, my dearest Yelena Petróvna, you have recently been good enough to act as my assistant."

"*Russia!*" she said. "Oh, what have I done?"

Karl saw that she was on the edge of hysteria, in another moment would be over the edge, and yet he could not bring himself to strike the blow in her face which would bring her back to sanity. He tried shock tactics in another way.

"Please," he said, "don't try to impress me with your Holy Russia; you told me yourself you were no patriot."

"But why did you try to make me into a traitor?"

"Elena, listen. The night I met you, I knew that you were restless, discontented, devoured by jealousy. I watched you, remember, while Kirillovna danced! You soon revealed that you were a woman with a grief, and grievances. People like you can easily be recruited to do the sort of work we want—"

"So it was all lies?" she said. "All a calculation, based upon my weakness? Even last week at Dyrehaven, when we were first together, you were lying to me then?"

"Could I lie to you with my body, Elena Petrovna?" It was the lover's tone, but Elena only laughed. "Easily!" she said. "The simplest way for any man to lie to a woman! How can I ever believe in you again?"

Karl looked at his watch. "Well," he said coldly, "you've suggested a possible line of action. Only I don't advise you to send for the Norwegian police; they might start investigating the Kolberg affair, which, let me remind you, is a long way from being settled. Here's what you should do. Either keep silent, go to the steamer and get out of Norway, or else go to the British Ministry and tell them Korvetten-Kapitän Karl Ritter is in town. They can't very well arrest me on neutral territory, but they'll be glad to know my whereabouts, and of course they'll welcome *you* with open arms." He slung his coat over his arm. "But take my advice and don't go to the Russians. They might ask too many questions —for instance, how you came by that sapphire brooch in Stockholm—"

"The brooch!" she said with her hand at her trembling mouth, "I knew I should have sent it back!"

"Ah," he said at the door, "that was the acid test—you kept it."

The wharves by which the steamers to Denmark and Holland lay were down by the East Station. In the haste of her arrival at Christiania on Monday morning, when the Copenhagen train was late, Elena had not noticed the legend "Kolbergske Dampskibselskab" in letters three feet high. Now the words picked out in black on a white ground, with K.D.S. repeated over the entrance to each quay, were lit from underneath with powerful electric lights, and could be seen all over the harbour. She realised that the *Kronprins Olav*, the Rotterdam steamer, was a Kolberg boat.

73

Carrying her cloak and morocco bag, the only possessions left in her room at the Continental, Elena picked her way along the quay. A steward met her at the *Kronprins Olav*'s gangway.

"I am Madame Tamirova. I am travelling to Rotterdam—"

"Your ticket, madame, if you please."

"Ticket? I have no ticket."

"Will you step this way and see the purser?"

The purser, all affability, came out of his office, and declared that a block reservation for the ballet company had been made by Herr Kamnov. Madame Tamirova had a first-class cabin—certainly; it was made up now, and the lady might occupy it at once—of course. Her baggage was already there. Björn, the key to Number Four! Supper would be served before sailing, at eleven o'clock. Or would the lady care for some refreshments now?

"Some tea, please." The cabin was narrow, very clean and primitive; her own bags took up most of the space. A ten-watt lamp without a shade hung from a cord in the ceiling. When Björn brought her tea it came on a tray with boiled milk and white sugar, while Elena longed for cut lemon or raspberry jam, but it was hot and strong, and she drank some while the Norwegian steward brought soap and towels and tried to rearrange the luggage.

"I hear the British subs are on the hunt tonight," he said in English before he took the tray away.

"Subs? Submarines?"

"*Ja.* They're hunting in the Skagerrak. The British are coming far west now, madame. Trying to tempt the *Hochseeflotte* out."

"Yes," Elena said. "Thank you, steward. Good-night."

"Good-night, madame."

When he had gone she bolted her cabin door, kicked off her satin slippers stained by the Vettakollen road, and pulling the fur cloak around her laid her head down on the pillow. She felt as if she would never be warm again. What she experienced was the chill of terror—the inherited, atavistic, Russian fear of the police, ten times intensified in her childhood by Aunt Varvara's tragic death. At any moment she expected to hear the tramp of Norwegian policemen coming aboard to arrest her for Kolberg's death. That was the dominant fear, stronger by far than the shock of

Ericssen's confession. Deep in her heart she had expected that confession, all along.

There was now a good deal of movement aboard the *Kronprins Olav*. Porters were coming aboard with baggage, passengers finding their cabins; there was the rattle of winches and shouting on the quay. Presently, in a great burst of talk and laughter, she heard the Russians arrive, and footsteps halted at her door.

"Are you there, Elena Petrovna?" Kamnov! She forced herself to rise and open the door a chink. "Yes, thank you, Lev Yurievich. I'd a headache and thought I'd turn in early. How did the ballet go?"

"Bronin was very fine. Sleep well; we'll see you in the morning. Quiet, you two!"—for Vassily and Kolia could be heard giggling and saying "Sh! Sh!" as they affected to tiptoe past Elena's door. There was one more interruption; Vera of course, who was always solicitous, with an offer of headache cachets, and then they all went off to supper in the ship's saloon, where somebody was playing a melodeon. "Sew not, dearest mother mine, the scarlet sarafan—" A clock across the harbour showed a quarter to twelve.

Out there lay the fjord, and then the Skagerrak, and beyond that the North Sea, the British subs are on the hunt tonight. Elena longed, and yet dreaded to hear the gangway taken up. There were orders being shouted now on deck. There was a new voice, speaking in Norwegian but perfectly recognizable, in conversation with the steward. She heard her own name, and footsteps coming towards her cabin.

"Elena?"

Karl was there in the darkness, with damp on his coat and in his hair.

"They've taken him to hospital. He's going to be all right." And then, as the breath left her body in a long sigh. "You chose me, Elena Petrovna! You chose *me!*"

V

Thursday, April 13, 1916

Mr. Cornelis Timmermann, theatrical costumier and jeweller, descended from a street car at the stop on the Leidseplein, and was at once swallowed up in a crowd of Amsterdammers viciously closing their umbrellas and scrambling aboard. He peered about him nervously. After leaving his house on the Herengracht he had had a guilty sense of being followed. When the street car moved on and the crowd thinned he bolted across the tracks to a corner café from which he could keep an eye on the square, and the members of the administrative staff emerging from the main entrance of the Municipal Theatre.

He ordered a cup of coffee and a glass of peach brandy, paying with a number of very small coins from a large leather purse, and settled down to watch. The wind was blowing off the North Sea and driving sheets of rain against the café windows: thanks to the rain and the thick crochet curtains it was not easy to distinguish between the men leaving the Stadsschouwburg at the end of the day's work. He saw the business manager and the chief cashier come out together and get on a street car, and the head electrician go pedalling by on a bicycle. Then a worried glance at his watch told him that by dodging the Dutch he might also miss the Russians. Mr. Timmermann put on his overcoat, which was steaming in the warm café, picked up the leather box he had kept beside his chair, and made his way through the fleet of home-going bicycles to the Municipal Theatre.

Underneath the arches the billboards announced:

For a Limited Season
The Maryinsky Ballet Company
Tamirova. Surov. Bronin. Lensky.
The Scandinavian Repertory
Lindgren. Sparre. Bang.

Mr. Timmermann allowed his eyes to travel down the playbill:

Wednesday, April 12: *The Sleeping Beauty*
Thursday, April 13: *Hedda Gabler*

He nodded with satisfaction. Then, as quickly as his height, his weight, and the leather box would allow, he moved away from the great glass doors and round the corner to the familiar stage entrance.

"'Evening to you, Mr. Timmermann," said the doorkeeper, looking out of his little hutch, "what's that you've got there? Something fancy for our Russians?"

"Bit of glitter for Madame Tamirova. She in her dressing-room?"

"On stage, more likely. The new star arrived last night, name of Surov; they've been working like madmen all afternoon. Why don't you go backstage and ask for Mr. Kamnov?"

Mr. Timmermann willingly obeyed. For all his size he could move unobtrusively, and he slipped behind the canvas flats of the vast proscenium almost unnoticed by the corps de ballet, who had just come off, panting and perspiring, after rehearsing the Dance of the Wilis for the fourth time. From far back in the wings, where the Dutch stage hands were grumbling that rehearsal time was up half an hour ago, he saw the ballet-master standing alone, his lips moving in the endless One and—Two and—Three, up-stage in the fantastic set designed for Act II of *Giselle*. Fyodor Surov was dancing a pas seul. He was wearing a practice costume of shabby black tights and tunic above which his ash-blond hair, worn rather long, gleamed like a point of light on the darkened stage. All costumes were alike to Surov. Whether in Albrecht's mourning black, or Prince Siegfried's silver, he was always the *danseur noble*, masculine in his interpretations, muscled with authority for the most exacting part. The solo variation he was dancing was famous for its frenzy and its vigour: the Tartar, with his astonishing elevations, soared above the merely acrobatic technique which Bronin brought to the same part. The surly stage hands broke into a spatter of applause.

Mr. Timmermann tiptoed off down the gas-lit corridor. There

77

was a door with a star on it; he knocked confidently, and heard Tamirova's voice say "See who that is, Louise!" The door opened a crack. He introduced himself: "Cornelis Timmermann, madame. May I come in?"

"Timmchik dear! Of course you may!"

He entered beaming, a tall, ruddy, Dutch St. Nicholas, holding the leather box as if it contained crackers and bon-bons for a good girl. His face fell at the sight of Tamirova. She was lying back in an ugly wicker chair, muffled to the throat in a white towelling wrapper, and the dresser was powdering her bare feet. An enamel basin filled with water stood on the floor.

"But I'm intruding, madame!"

"No, no, you're not. Louise has finished. My toes were nearly bleeding, isn't it absurd? After all the care I take—but Kamnov worked us rather too hard this afternoon. Fyodor is absolutely tireless."

She motioned to the dresser to pick up the sweat-soaked pink silk practice tights and tunic and bundle them into a hamper, and clear a chair for Mr. Timmermann to sit down. He looked round the dressingroom with pleasure. It was the third time Tamirova had danced in Amsterdam, and everything was familiar. The little pictures which she called her ikons were hanging beside the mirror. the inevitable glass of tea was on the dressingtable, and a half-smoked Russian cigarette in the ashtray. The bouquets she had received the night before as Princess Aurora were pushed anyhow into jars and vases; there were Dutch tulips, prim and parti-coloured, and pots of hyacinths, their sweetness overpowering the smell of sweat and effort in the room. And the star was as fascin-ating as ever, with her husky French and her expressive hands, and the beautiful hazel eyes softer than he remembered them. Certainly she was very kind, making Louise bring him tea, and asking, with a flattering recollection of details, about his business in theatrical jewellery and costumes.

"Have you been in front yet, Timmchik?" she wanted to know.

"I saw *Coppélia* on Monday night, madame. You were a brilliant Swanhilda."

"I thought Lensky did very well as Coppelius. He's good in

character parts. He's going to dance Von Rothbart in *Swan Lake*."
Elena looked at Timmermann expectantly, and the old man
smiled:

"Yes, madame, I brought it." He stooped to unstrap the leather
box, and the dancer clapped her hands. "You hear that, Louise?
My new crown for Odette!" To the rustle of many sheets of tissue,
the little crown was produced and set proudly before the mirror.
It was a ring of strass set on a base of swans' feathers, white,
narrow and glossy, and had six points of glittering rhinestone, each
tipped with an iridescent artificial pearl.

"It's beautiful, Timmchik. You must be a magician, to have
guessed what my new Odette dress is like. Louise, do give me my
slippers!"

They were behind the screen, clumsy carpet slippers such as a
charwoman might wear, and in them Elena shuffled forward to the
dressingtable, and sat down. Mr. Timmermann put Odette's
crown on her head. She pushed the wrapper off her shoulders until
only the ribboned straps of her camisole were showing, and picked
up the hand mirror, lifting her chin and arching her long neck in
the true ballerina's pose. "*C'est magnifique, madame,*" the dresser said.

"Let me show you how it fastens," Timmermann said to her.
"The elastic band passes under the hair—so, and is attached to a
hook hidden in the feathers, here. It will be absolutely secure on
madame's head—"

"And Odette can leap to her doom without a hair out of place,"
said Elena. "Thank you, Timmchik, it's the loveliest thing you've
ever made for me. But now take it off, Louise, we mustn't keep
Mr. Timmermann too long—"

He cleared his throat. "As a matter of fact I would like to have
a private word with you."

"Certainly, if you wish. Has Monsieur Kamnov seen the crown
yet? Then, Louise, you might take it along for his approval, and
remind him that Odette's old diadem nearly fell to pieces on my
head in Christiania. Then go to supper—I can finish dressing by
myself."

When they were alone she offered Timmermann a cigarette and
let him light her own. He twitched his chair forward. He had

79

been listening to the sounds of the theatre and was fairly sure that none of the Dutch staff was in the star's corridor. Somewhere near by he heard Surov singing and shouting as his dresser sponged him with cold water.

"What is it, Timmchik? Are you in any trouble?"

"Well, yes and no. That is, it's not my trouble, exactly. In fact . . . there's no performance tonight, is there?"

"The Repertory people are playing *Hedda Gabler*."

"Yes, of course. So that you could perhaps spare a little time . . .?"

"If you would tell me why, perhaps."

Whispering: "I have an escaped British officer hidden in my house."

"*Hidden!*"

"He got away from one of our internment camps in northern Holland and was smuggled into Amsterdam aboard a barge two days ago. You know I live on the Herengracht. It was quite simple to put him ashore near my house—"

"Why your house?"

The jolly Santa Claus face looked sly. "Well . . . I've helped British prisoners of war on their way before. Escapees from Germany, crossing Holland to get to the coast, that is. The authorities have been known to turn a blind eye in such cases. But this young man broke out of a *Dutch* camp, which means I could get into bad trouble for harbouring him."

"Is he an Army officer?"

"Navy. I assure you, madame, he dropped in on me without warning before dawn on Tuesday. Literally! He fell down like a log in my showroom, as soon as I closed the door behind him. He was fainting with hunger, wet to the skin and in pain from a wrenched shoulder. It was an hour before he could climb up to my attic. If I'd had word of his coming I might have been able to pass him on down the canals yesterday and get him off on a British trawler; but he was too feverish to risk it, and now—"

"Yes. Is he *fit* to travel?"

"He's young and willing, at least, and—I hardly dare to keep him longer."

"But why do you come to me with such a story? Why don't you go to the British consul?"

"The consul would send him back to Groningen. And Russia is Britain's ally."

"Yes . . ."

"And besides . . . with your help . . . I know a way to get him safely out of the Netherlands. Aren't some of your company crossing to Harwich tonight?"

"Yes, Bronin and five of the boys, they're going to dance at the London Coliseum."

"Couldn't Mr. Flett go over with them? As one of the dancers? Couldn't I bring him to your hotel this evening—?"

"No, absolutely not!" Elena said. She had been listening very quietly; now she started to her feet. "I don't see how we can possibly pass your man off as a dancer, or even how it can be done without a passport and travel papers, but I'm sure the fewer people who see him the better. He mustn't come to the American Hotel. . . . You're asking a great deal of me, Timmchik! Give me time to think it over! Give me half an hour!"

"I'll wait in front," said Mr. Timmermann quickly, and slipped out of the dressingroom. Elena sat down again, with her hands pressed to her throbbing head.

Since the night of her terrible fear in Christiania she had fallen into a new frame of mind, of self-hatred mingled with self-justification alternating with the physical passion she felt for Karl Ritter. As "Ritter" she found it difficult to think of him, and as "Ericssen" he was of course registered at the American Hotel, but Karl, he assured her, was his baptismal name, and much of what he had told her about himself was also true.

"You mean all you told me at Dyrehaven about your boyhood in Milwaukee, that was true?"

"I did spend a year in Milwaukee, when I was about sixteen."

"But your grandparents weren't Norwegian immigrants?"

"Certainly not!"

"And you really did visit Herr Kolberg's saeter, when you were a little boy?"

"My parents used to take me there on holiday."

81

"Are your parents living?" But that he refused to answer; he would implicate nobody but himself in what he was doing, any more than he would ever—did she understand, *ever* again—employ her to further any of his plans. "I've never worked with women before," he said, "and I was a fool to use a girl like you, especially with Kolberg. But naturally I thought as a woman of the world you would be able to handle an old goat like him."

The millionaire shipowner was a man of sufficient importance in Europe to rate a line in *De Telegraaf* for the first few days after what had been described as his slight stroke. Herr Kolberg was out of danger. His condition was improving. There was no reason to fear permanent disablement, and so on. Karl translated these for Elena carelessly, but she knew that he was vitally concerned. After all, he had called Hans Kolberg essential to his business.

Elena had lived for too long inside the world of ballet even to imagine how a Norwegian shipowner could further the aims of Germany. She had tried guessing, she had tried begging Karl to tell her, under the most solemn promises of secrecy, what had been the real contents of the two sets of "subscription lists" she had carried to Stockholm and Christiania. He had laughed at her, of course. All she could remember of what she herself had read was that the town most frequently mentioned in both lists was Bergen.

How Ritter spent his days in Amsterdam was also a matter for guesswork. He had hired a motor car and a chauffeur on Monday to drive to Rotterdam, but he returned in good time for the ballet, and on the following days she believed he had remained in the city. Sometimes she admired his daring in masquerading as an American businessman in Russia, especially when she remembered Nelidov had been hoodwinked by him; at others some glimmering of what his daring might have cost in terms of Russian lives came as a grim reproach for her own folly. The theatre was her escape. In a Cecchetti "class" carried out alone for one hour each day, in the regular practices and now in the extra rehearsals with Surov she strove to exhaust her body; in the two performances so far given in Amsterdam she had found a welcome escape into the only reality she knew.

Korvetten-Kapitän Karl Richard Ritter, that shrewd psychologist, had made only one mistake in his estimate of the dancer. He had correctly assessed the vanity and egotism of the ballerina *manquée*, but he had been misled by the story of Bloody Sunday into believing Elena utterly indifferent to the fate of a régime which permitted such tragedies. Clever and perceptive though he was, Karl was too entirely a German to understand that beneath Elena Tamirova's sophistication there was a depth of peasant belief in Holy Mother Russia; that when she touched her little ikon of St. Helena for good luck before a performance, she had an obscure recollection of the great ikons of St. Andrew and St. Catherine in the Kazansky Cathedral at St. Petersburg and even of the tomb of Kutuzov, Russia's defender, inside the cathedral door. It was to this deep spring of feeling that the Dutchman's sudden appeal had reached. To help a British naval officer to freedom would be a subtle vengeance on Karl Ritter, who never once since she stumbled on his true identity had said he was in love with her.

Elena completed her dressing hastily. Mr. Timmermann had told his story better than he knew. His description of the young man who had broken out of prison and was now in hiding, who had collapsed in pain and weariness as soon as he found shelter, had reached Elena Tamirova as a series of ballet sequences, bearing a distant resemblance to the libretto of *A Life for the Czar*. She could almost hear the orchestra playing the introduction to her own entrance, on points, as she put on a dress and long fitted coat of wallflower-coloured cloth and slipped her feet, wincing, into bronze kid shoes. Picking up her mink muff and a gold mesh bag which Karl had bought her on the Kalverstraat, she went out to join Mr. Timmermann, who sat nursing his empty box in the front row of the stalls. The stage was now almost in darkness. The rehearsal set had been struck, and the scene shifters were taking a break before beginning the transformation to Doctor Tesman's drawingroom. Only *Giselle*'s stark white cross remained on stage, and the heaped canvas painted to resemble the turf of her suicide's grave.

"Thank heaven the rain has stopped," said Mr. Timmermann, with a glance at Elena's fashionable shoes. The north wind was drying the pavement cobbles quickly, and ruffling the olive-green water of the Herengracht. He had stopped the taxi, out of prudence, where one of the many bridges crossed the canal not far from his own front door. Elena, who had never been there before, looked up with interest at Mr. Timmermann's house when he pointed it out. He had lowered his voice to a conspiratorial whisper, although there was nobody about in that quarter of the Herengracht. It was the hour when most of Amsterdam took its evening meal, and through several lighted windows could be seen Dutch family groups and Dutch interiors which deserved to be hanging in the Rijksmuseum.

Mr. Timmermann's house, like all its neighbours, had a hook in its attic door for the raising of furniture and chests on a pulley, but there the resemblance ended. On either side the seventeenth-century façades rose up with a splendid display of polished windows and weathered brickwork, while Mr. Timmermann's dwelling, although on three floors beneath the attic and the crow-stepped gables, was as narrow as a handsbreadth, with a front door that opened in two parts like a stable door, an understatement of a house, a gay little comment on all that was solemn and grand in the Herengracht of Amsterdam.

Mr. Timmermann slid his key into the lock and unbolted both halves of the front door. "Excuse me, madame," he whispered, "let me go first and show you the way." The lobby, scarcely three feet wide, was lit by a paraffin lamp set on a bracket just within reach of a stretching hand. When the wick was turned up Elena saw a little showroom through an open door on the right. The single window was thickly curtained in net, to preserve the fiction that there was no commerce in the Herengracht, but by the light of a street lamp could be seen a number of wax models in rigid attitudes, wearing uniforms or the court dress of past centuries. A policeman, a postman and a member of the fire brigade seemed to be keeping order in the silent group.

"The stair is rather steep. May I go first again, and light the lamp in the livingroom?" asked Timmermann. He mounted laboriously, with a heavy breath at each steep step, for the staircase rose like a ship's ladder and had a ship's rope instead of a banister, looped to the wall by iron rings. Elena lifted her skirt high and went up quickly. She seemed to rise through a gap in the floor, for landing there was none, into a livingroom lit only by the red glow behind the mica window of a porcelain stove, and the match Mr. Timmermann was striking.

"Don't move, madame, until I bring a light." Elena stood still until a lamp glowed at her left hand, revealing a kitchen with blue and white Delft tiles above a small cooking stove and sink, and copper utensils hanging on the walls. Mr. Timmermann, at the kitchen table, was lighting a second and much larger lamp, with a glass globe. He carried it into the livingroom, of which the kitchen was only the rear part, with a small window opening on a strip of courtyard. The livingroom ceiling was supported by timbered beams and had the panelled walls of the seventeenth century. A Javanese screen, carved and gilded, stood in front of a highly efficient modern safe, and beside the comfortable chairs stood low tables, each covered by what appeared to be a rug and holding bowls of soleil d'or narcissus.

"But where is the young man?"

"In the attic," said Mr. Timmermann. "My bedroom and the washing-place are on the next floor, and then there's a ladder to the attic. I'll go and let him out."

Elena sat down beside the stove. She heard the jeweller's heavy steps ascending another perpendicular staircase, then the scrape of a ladder dragged into place and a trapdoor lifted. There was a murmur of conversation, and then the footsteps came back followed by a lighter tread.

"Madame Tamirova, may I present Mr. Flett, of the Royal Navy?"

She had expected to be confronted by a desperate, perhaps by an injured man, a British Ivan Susanin, ready to give his life for the Czar. There was no sign of weakness in the solemn but confident face before her, as Mr. Flett made an awkward bow, and muttered "Pleased to meet you." He was a big young man, not quite as tall as Karl Ritter but with the heavy shoulders and chest of a prize-fighter; one shoulder was clumsily bandaged beneath his navy-blue turtle-necked jersey. He was wearing navy-blue serge trousers, which had been torn down one leg and roughly mended, and was in his stocking soles. His dark hair was long and rough, but he was closely shaved.

"How are you?" She remembered the English form of greeting.

"I'm not so bad," he said eagerly, "but I'm fair desperate to get out of here! Mr. Timmermann says you'll maybe give me a hand to win away—"

"Oh please!"—in smiling dismay. "You talk too fast. *Vous ne parlez pas français, monsieur?*"

"Sorry," he said, "not a word."

"Madame Tamirova is a Russian lady," said Mr. Timmermann. "She can only understand if you speak slowly."

"I've been in a Dutch internment camp since August," Flett tried again. "My ship was torpedoed by a German submarine. Torpedoed. Camp. Escape. *Compree?*"

"Excuse that I speak French." Elena turned to Mr. Timmermann. "He is very difficult to understand."

"He is a Scotsman, from the north," said Timmermann. "I also find his accent difficult."

"Has he no coat or boots?"

"His shoes were torn to shreds when he got here. He had no coat. He slept in a ditch one night and two under tarpaulins in the barges. It was raining all the time."

"He must be very strong." Elena smiled at the young man. "You want—to go home, no?"

"I want to get on with the war," he said. "I couldna stick the camp."

"But Mr. Timmermann!" she said hopelessly, "whatever made you think we could pass him off as a *dancer*? Even if the boys understood what he was *saying*—"

"Now, now," soothed Timmermann, "I think we should all sit down and have a little sip. There is coffee on the back of the stove—"

"He makes a great cup of coffee." The The Scotsman grinned. "It was very good of you to come, Miss—Mrs.—"

"Tamirova. Elena Tamirova is my name."

"Mine's David Flett. Are you living in Amsterdam, then?"

"I am a dancer," she said very distinctly. "I am here with the ballet company from Petrograd." She watched him taking that in, while she adjusted herself to a world in which nobody had heard of Tamirova, and Mr. Timmermann came back with the coffee tray, to which he had added a bottle of orange curaçao and three glasses.

"Your very good health," said David Flett, lifting his glass to them both.

"To your safe return to England," said Mr. Timmermann feelingly.

"There is only one way to get this gentleman out of Holland with the Coliseum party," said Elena firmly, "and the man to do it is Vassily Bronin. If Kamnov were crossing with them it would be hopeless. But Bronin can help if he wants to; we shall have to get him here and persuade him, if we can."

Timmermann started up. "Shall I take a cab to the American Hotel, and fetch him?"

"Vassily? He checked out of the hotel at noon. But I think I know where to find him . . . Do you know a theatrical boarding-house at the corner of the Singel, just beside the Flower Market?"

"Certainly."

"He will be there with Nikolai Levin."

"Why, that's only a few minutes away! I'll go there at once—"

"What time does the boat train leave Amsterdam, monsieur?"

"At seven seventeen, madame. The steamer leaves The Hook at eight fifty-two."

"Hurry then."

"Where's he away to?" asked David Flett, as Mr. Timmermann hurled himself down the steep stair.

"Gone to find—another friend—for you."

"Another Russian dancer?"

"Yes."

"Mercy me." David settled himself luxuriously in the plush-covered chair. He had been prepared for every kind of encounter since his escape from Groningen—with the guard who took his bribe, the farm wife who gave him food, the bargemen, the jeweller, and he had expected to finish up shaking hands with the skipper of a British trawler; but Russian dancers were more than he had bargained for. He decided to make the most of a few minutes of comfort. Old Timmermann had kept him close to the so-called attic, in which David had to bend almost double; he was terrified that the neighbours would know he had a British officer in his house. The attic was perishing cold. Similarly old Timmermann had kept him short of food, explaining that to increase his usual modest purchases, especially when buying meat, would cause comment in the neighbourhood. David looked longingly at the coffee pot. He didn't care for the curaçao, it was sweet sticky stuff; but would it be bad manners to fill his cup again?

Elena leaned forward and filled it for him. "Cigarette?" He took it gratefully, a black cigarette, but still better than cheap Dutch cigars. "Did you bring this from Russia with you?" he asked carefully. She said yes, a large supply. He liked her voice. He thought she was a bonny creature, far bonnier than any of the Dutch *meisjes* who came to the camp concerts at Groningen.

"Are you going back to Russia soon?" He tried to keep the conversation going, though the room, with the thick brown curtains drawn against the windy night, and the yellow flowers shining against the Russian's amber dress, was turning into a cavern of warmth and comfort which lulled his taut nerves into languor.

"Going back to Russia? I don't know."

"Do you come from Petrograd? Is that where you live?"

"I *came* from there, but I am not born there. I am born in the north, in Arkhangelsk, on the White Sea."

"Is that a fact," said David, deeply interested. "I've never been there myself, but I've heard old trawlermen speak about Archangel. Fine fishing there, they say."

"In summer yes, and also my father he—is hunting—the seals."

"There's grand fishing where I come from too," said David. "A town called Aberdeen."

"You have papers so?"

"What sort of papers?"

"To say where you are born, and if you are married—"

88

"I'm not married. A passport, do you mean?"

"Something to prove to the British captain that you are British too."

David produced a battered wallet from his hip pocket. "Here's my camp identity card," he said, "and here's letters from my father and my sister—she's a clerkess at the Admiralty in London. Here's some snapshots taken on board the *Yelverton*—it was the *Yelverton* I was in when she was torpedoed—and that's a girl I know in Orkney—"

Elena was leaning forward to look at the snapshots as he laid them on the coffee table. He could smell the scent she wore, like roses or sweet-peas, and see the faint dusting of powder on her pale matt skin. He could hardly take his eyes off her. But she took up the postcard photograph he laid down last, and looked at it almost with horror—at the tall child, the lively eager face, the braid of thick blonde hair on the clumsy party dress.

"But I have seen this picture!"

"Ye can't—it's just not possible!"

"Ingrid—Ingrid Sabiston," she said in a strained tone, and then they heard steps on the floor below, and the voice of Vassily Bronin protesting at the steepness of the stair. David gathered up his snapshots quickly as the Russian reached the livingroom.

"How cosy you look!" Bronin said gaily, as he took in the scene. David got up and awkwardly held out his hand. "My name's Flett," he said, and Bronin bowed.

"Flett, how perfect!" He kept his hold of David's hand. "*Dushenka*," he said admiringly to Elena, "you really do know how to pick them. First that gorgeous American, and now—this!"

Bronin dressed for travelling was an even more striking figure than Bronin as the Nutcracker Prince. He diffused a strong odour of sandalwood. Beneath a thick overcoat, which came nearly to his heels, he wore a light grey suit with a flowing tie of violet silk, with a matching handkerchief tucked in his cuff. He received Elena's "Don't be silly, Vassily Ilyich, we have a problem to solve!" with his sidelong smile, and a sly "Yes, *dusha moya*, so your Dutch friend tells me, but you've cut it rather fine—the boat train leaves in three-quarters of an hour."

David Flett, who had understood nothing after "Flett, how perfect!" freed his fingers from Vassily's, and in obedience to a warning look from Timmermann, listened patiently while the two Russians argued. He wondered if they were dancing partners. It wasn't that they jumped about, but they conveyed so much with their hands and arms—like a pantomime—he was prepared to bet they would dance well together. The girl was doing most of the talking, but in the end she said,

"Mr. Bronin is speaking much better English than I am, Mr. Flett. He will explain to you what you should do."

"Look here," said David, "if it's a matter of money I'm just about broke, but I can easy pay for my own ticket—"

"The ticket is the least of it, dear boy," said Vassily. "There's only one question—how to get you from the station to the steamer without discovery. We can't pass you off as a dancer, though personally I'd *adore* to—I think you'd be utterly fabulous in our Cossack dances—but it's no use, you're just not the type. Would you be too proud to be a railway porter, for an hour or so?"

"I'll be a scavenger if it means getting out of here," said David grimly. "But what if the other porters go for me? They'll know I'm not the real thing—"

"We'll have to risk that. Just do what I tell you when you get to the train—and *on* the train—"

"Mr. Timmermann, you'll have to find clothes for him," said Elena. "A porter's hat and smock from your stage costumes—oh, and a proper shirt and boots—"

The jeweller was beaming. "If they don't look too closely at the smock—"

"Hurry, man!" said Vassily. His idle mocking manner had suddenly become more purposeful. "Flett, do you think you can really get away with it? Bluff your way through if anyone accosts you?"

"If I can't, I'll just need to say '*Engels matroos*' and wend my weary way back to Groningen under arrest."

"It won't come to that. Now about papers. The British examine passports on the boat, so that's all right; the Dutch usually check papers on the train."

"But I've no passport, I told Miss Tamirova already."

"Neither have we, but we have travel papers. And Elena Petrovna has something she wants to give to you."

Elena was feeling in her gold mesh bag. She had a small sheaf of papers in it, bound with an elastic band. From this she selected one, with the Russian double eagle and an impressive series of stamps over the Cyrillic letters, and handed it to David Flett.

"I think, if they don't look for the date, that will do," she said. "There is no photograph, and they can't read the writing. It is an old travel permit of my own."

"Nothing that you'll ever need again?"

"No, never. It is only luck that I kept it so long. I hope it will bring luck to you."

David took the paper. In the golden lamplight the dancer's lovely face was alive with sympathy. With an unaccustomed, awkward gesture he bent and kissed her hand.

"You're an angel," was all he said.

"There, Elena Petrovna!" said Vassily. "How does it feel to be on the side of the angels—at long last?"

Lev Karnov, making himself responsible for the departure of part of his company to London, was struck by the energy displayed by Bronin at Amsterdam Central Station. The *premier danseur*, who usually expected others to wait on him, personally checked the disposal of all the costume hampers by an army of Dutch porters, who carried them to the train from a fleet of taxicabs, and handed his own valise to a tall man in a smock who went off alone, with the valise on his shoulder, to Vassily's reserved compartment. In the excitement and confusion inseparable from any Russian journey it was not noticed that the man then locked himself in the lavatory, emerging after the train had started with the smock in a brown paper parcel and wearing a homburg hat and a blue jacket, too thin for the windy evening.

David took his seat in the first-class carriage and looked through the window at the rushing landscape of Holland. Vassily had bought his ticket, and French newspapers for himself, David, and Kolia, who was twittering nervously in the corner opposite his friend. Vassily told him roughly to start reading. David's copy of *Le Figaro*, of which he understood not one word, lay open on his lap. He dared not look at the Russians. He had never known fear on the long way from Groningen to Amsterdam, not even in the first hours of his escape, when he dislocated his shoulder in a heavy fall down a canal embankment and had it jerked back into place by a friendly bargeman; but he was close to panic. Freedom was so near, not much more than an hour away. He knew he would resist violently if the Dutch officials tried to take him off the train.

The first of them pushed the door open. "Tickets, please!" Three first-class tickets, single, punched and collected. A polite salute, and the door closed. Ten minutes more; another town with lighted windows, the train stopping. Rotterdam. Dutchmen with gladstone bags looking for empty seats, glowering at the "Reserved" signs on the three compartments of the Russians. And on again. Doors thrown open, with an official sound, further down the corridor. "Here they come," said Bronin quietly. "Now Kolia, don't play the fool!"

Two men this time, in another uniform, even more correct in the matter of salutes. "Travel documents. *Vous parlez français, messieurs? Vos papiers, s'il vous plaît.*" Bronin took three stiff pages from his breast pocket and handed them over. The double eagle, the red seals, the blue overstamping gleamed in the light from the carriage roof. "This is all you have? No passports?"

"*Non, monsieur.* Here is a general exit visa for our entire party, issued by your Passport Office—"

"Check with Passport Control when you reach The Hook."

The noise of the wheels filled the silent carriage. Sparks flew past the dark window as the train rushed on to The Hook of Holland. David found his voice.

"What happens when we go through the barrier?"

"*I* go through Passport Control, with Kolia. You, my excellent porter, will be carrying our bags aboard the boat. Straight down to cabin ten, and wait for me."

"We'll never get away with it." The strain was telling on David now; he felt exhausted. But the look in Bronin's slanted, mocking eyes spurred him on to a last effort. Among the crowd in the corridors when the train stopped was one zealous porter, who appeared to have swung aboard ahead of the others, and who was heartily sworn at by one of his colleagues as he dropped to the platform. David had picked up a few Dutch oaths at Groningen; his reply as he lurched off with the baggage was entirely convincing. The British packet was at the wharf with steam up. He plodded on in a crowd of those who were only carrying hand-luggage, and made his way up the gangway. " 'Urry along there, you porters, 'urry along!" He had never been so glad to hear a Cockney voice.

". . . I told you it could be done," said Bronin, unscrewing his silver flask in cabin 10. There were only two thick glasses on the washstand; he poured brandy into these for David and Kolia, and used the silver top himself. "Congratulations, Mr. Flett!"

"It was done thanks to you," said David, raising his glass in salute. He felt weak. His shoulder hurt abominably, and he longed to lean his head against the velvet cushion and close his eyes. But the picture of a lovely face and expressive hands came behind his eyelids, and he added:

"And the lady—Miss Tamirova—it was her that planned it, wasn't it?"

"Well, partly. Mr. Timmermann was quite a help."

"I'm very grateful to you all . . . Will she be coming over to London, too?"

"Elena Petrovna? No, not this time. She has some very important engagements in Amsterdam."

"Is she a famous dancer?"

"Well-known, at least."

"If you get the chance, will you give her my thanks again?"

"We're sure to be in touch," said Bronin. "Have some more brandy."

"I'll need to report to the Captain now."

"Better wait until we're out of the harbour. Just in case there's any trouble at the Pass Control."

"But we're under the British flag now—"

"Don't let's take any chances!"

"We're moving!" Kolia squeaked.

The British steamer began her cautious departure from The Hook of Holland. She went out in darkness, for the German submarines were very active; it was not many nights since they had sunk "by accident" a great Dutch liner. Nobody spoke in cabin 10 until the pierhead was cleared, and left as a winking light astern.

"Now do you want me to ring for the steward?"

"If *you* please."

Vassily paused. "This is only a two-berth cabin," he said "but I daresay we could make room for you, couldn't we, Kolia?"

"Thanks again," said David. "Maybe they can fix me up a shake-down somewhere, after I've seen the Captain. I could sleep lying on the deck tonight, and thankful."

Vassily rang for the steward. It was the same Cockney who had been hustling the porters. "Will you take this gentleman to see the Captain?"

"Captain, 'e's very busy at present, sir—"

Vassily gave him a gold piece. "This officer has urgent business with your Captain, steward."

"Come this way, sir!" The steward grinned. He had seen officers dressed as civilians more than once since the prisoner of war camps were opened.

"Well, so long, Mr. Bronin," said David, offering his hand. "I'll never forget all you've done for me tonight. So long, Mr. Levin."

"Come and see us dance in London," said Vassily lazily. "Come round after the show. We'd like that, wouldn't we, Kolia?"

"*Oh oui!*" said Kolia, licking his purple lips.

David followed the steward up on deck, and stopped. It was raining again, and the wind blew the rain across his face, blew away the perfume of cabin 10, and the miasma of fear which had hung over his escape from Amsterdam. "This way, sir. You all right, sir?"—"Coming, steward. Just need—a breath of fresh air—" The engines were thudding, the bow wave curling and spreading on the surface of the sea. The steamer set her course for Harwich.

94

VI

Friday, April 14, 1916

David Flett's sister, Liz, said good-bye to her father and hung the receiver back on its hook. Then she called the exchange, asked the charges for her trunk call to Aberdeen, and put the money punctiliously into the box Mrs. Macandrew kept for that purpose in the back pantry of the boardinghouse near Regent's Park. Liz hurried off to get ready for the office.

Everything in her small back bedroom was in apple-pie order. The dishes and remains of breakfast, the only meal supplied by Mrs. Macandrew, were on a tray ready for removal; the bed was stripped. Presently Nora, the little Irish maid-of-all-work, would make the bed and clean the room; all Liz Flett had to do was put on her hat and coat and leave for the Admiralty.

I knew this was my lucky day, she thought. The evening was already set for dinner with Adrian Combermere at the Trocadero, the first important outing he had suggested, and now morning had brought the relief of knowing that poor old Davie was out of his Dutch internment camp and safe in Harwich. Liz whistled a tune as she pinned on her new three-cornered hat. A blackbird was singing the same tune in the poplar tree at the foot of the garden, bright with sticky new leaves, and the London sparrows were raiding the saffron-coloured crocuses pushing up through the city soil. It was wonderful to be Liz Flett, to have new rooms, a new hat, a new costume with a skirt which came only to the tops of her glacé lacing boots, and best of all to have been given the kind of looks new and right for April 1916. The statuesque, languid beauties so much admired when Edward VII was King had vanished from the London scene, and taken their swelling flanks and bosoms with them. The vogue was now for small girls like Liz Flett, with pert lively faces and short hair, trim and ready for action, the war-time girls.

David's call from Harwich and her own call to Aberdeen had occupied so much time that Liz decided to take a taxi from the rank at Baker Street Station. She sat back and enjoyed London, watching the shops opening and the people going to work, without paying too much attention to the newspaper posters. They said Vilna, Verdun, the Salient, said Passenger Steamer Torpedoed in the North Sea—there was always a lot of news, and always bad; but who knew it better, right from the start, than the clever girl who worked at the very heart of the machine? Liz hugged the thought of her special knowledge as the taxi swung round Piccadilly. She dismissed it in Trafalgar Square. It was better not to drive up in state to the very door of the Admiralty. Once she had done that at the same time as the First Lord, the Honourable Arthur Balfour, and a glance from his dark eyes showed what he thought of a girl cryptographer, paying off her taxi and fumbling for change, who blocked the way of his own limousine. Besides, the last part of the way was the best of all, she liked to do that on foot with a long look at Nelson on his column and all the proud buildings of Whitehall. Liz Flett had been employed at the Admiralty since October, but six months had not taken the edge off her final pleasure: the right to walk into the cobbled courtyard beneath the winged seahorses, between the dolphins sporting on the Adam screen, into the hall which might have been part of a gentleman's country house and from which Nelson had gone out to fight Trafalgar.

"Room 40," she said, showing her pass.

"Right, miss."

This was where the ripples that first broke over Odensholm had stopped. Those ripples which the little Swedish children saw before the Russian sailors tore the German signal book from the dead hands of the *Magdeburg*'s Yeoman had lapped slowly and inexorably round the seas of northern Europe, carrying the messages from Russia to Winston Churchill which ended in the surrender of the great prize found. The brief action in the Gulf of Finland, the insignificant skirmish in which Elena Tamirova's Russian lover died, had put into the hands best fitted to use it the key to all the naval dispositions of the enemy. The movements of

96

the High Seas Fleet and the German Naval Airship Service were known in London almost as soon as they were ordered in Germany, for the careful Germans—totally unaware that the *Magdeburg's* signal book had been captured—continued to use the code of August 1914. In that month there was one man connected with the Admiralty whose hobby had been cryptography. He was given a desk in Room 40, Old Building. Then there were two men, then ten, then more, until the locked door of Room 40 led to a warren of other rooms, most of them small and cramped, in which a band of men and women worked whose activities were top secret, unknown to any Department of the Admiralty except Intelligence, Operations and the Board itself. It was the triumph of Liz Flett's life, as far as she had lived it, to be one of them.

The room where she worked had four desks, two of them occupied. The head of the room, whose desk was nearest to the window, looked up and nodded as she came in, and then looked pointedly at the wall clock. Liz murmured,

"I'm very sorry to be late. I was detained this morning. My brother's got away from the internment camp."

"Good! Tell us about it at the tea-break." The Commander R.N.V.R., and the little old gentleman who had been a Fellow of All Souls', and Liz, bent over their work together. Liz's "In" basket was full. The signals confidently made by the German Navy and picked up by Direction Finder stations in Britain were passed on by private wire to the telegraph office in the basement of the Admiralty, and sent up by pneumatic tubes to be decoded in Room 40. The thud of the shuttle as it dropped into the waiting basket in the main room was heard on an average two thousand times a day. The German naval units, which had never heard of wireless silence, chattered obligingly to each other all day long.

Liz Flett worked diligently and well. She had what the Head of Room 40 called "a language brain", with first-class honours in French and German from Aberdeen University, and a very good knowledge of commercial Russian, but she also had the brain of a cryptographer, for whom codes revealed themselves easily in blocks of words or sentences, or in the simple substitution tables of the *Magdeburg* signal book. But while Liz went through her "In" basket she looked once or twice beneath her eyelashes at the fourth and vacant desk in the little room, which was Adrian Combermere's. A packet of cigarettes, a pair of gloves and a hat were lying there, as if Adrian had been summoned elsewhere when he was preparing to go home.

"Was it a rough night, does anybody know?" she enquired in a general way, when the tea-break came at ten, and the head of the room unbent enough to light a pipe. It was the little old don who answered, he who as a younger scholar had contradicted Heinrich von Treitschke's doctrine of Germany's expansion in every learned journal known to man:

"If you mean a *late* night, Miss Flett, my answer must be in the affirmative. The night watch were still here when we came on duty, but as to the degree of roughness or smoothness, the failure or success of their endeavours, I regret I—"

"Yours, Miss Flett," said the head of the room. A messenger had entered with a new batch of intercepts: there was a rapid sharing-out, and Liz uncapped her fountain pen. Poor Adrian, she thought, he'll be so tired. I wonder why he didn't go home, and where he is?

In a few minutes she looked up again, deliberately composed. "Commander, I think you should have a look at this one. It's an H.V.B."

"May I see it?"

Liz laid the intercept on the desk of the head of the room. It was a Zeppelin signal, made to Cuxhaven headquarters by a German naval airship, announcing its orders to leave the sheds at Tondern behind the island of Sylt. It contained the words "only Handelsschiffs Verkehrs Buch on board." This, meaning that only the mercantile marine code book would be carried in case of capture, was nearly always the prelude to an air raid on England.

"Where did this one come from, Miss Flett?"

"From our D/F at Hunstanton, Commander."

"Right. I'll take it to Liaison myself." Liz went back to her desk. There were moments when her place at the heart of the machine was not so pleasant, and this was one of them. She was terrified of air raids, and had been ever since being caught in

Breithaupt's famous raid on the London theatres. The thought of a possible air raid on London that night made her tremble. However, it was early in the day; the Zeppelins might either be on their way to France, or would be recalled to Tondern in the course of the morning. In any case they took five hours to cross the North Sea. Their signals, so lavishly passed, would be picked up by all the D/F stations which a year earlier the Director of Intelligence Division had established along the East Coast, and it might well be that their target was the Midlands, or even Liverpool. In any case there was nothing she, or the Commander, or even the Head of Room 40 himself could do about it. The H.V.B. signal would be passed on to Captain Hope of Admiralty War Staff Liaison and, with his comments added, sent in a red envelope to the Operations Room. The relations between Ops and Room 40 were so bad that Liz knew nothing would be heard of the decisions taken to deal with the H.V.B. Only the Zeppelin signals, coming in as intercepts, would tell Room 40 of the threat to England.

She looked up eagerly as Adrian Combermere entered and hoped she wasn't blushing. They were at the enchanting start of a love affair, when merely to meet unexpectedly made them both self-conscious, and Liz had not expected to see him that day until they met at the Trocadero. She thought he looked very tired. He was twenty-seven, the same age as herself, and looked older, especially when, as now, the night shift and the search for the enemy's cypher key, always changed at midnight, had been long and trying. He said impersonally:

"Good morning! The D.I.D. would like to have a word with you, Miss Flett."

The head of the room nodded dismissal, and then Liz was in the corridor with Adrian, alone except for the naval messenger who went stumping past with his box of decoded signals. He touched her hand, quickly, and she said, "I thought you were back at Chesterfield Gardens and sound asleep hours ago. Was it a terrible night?"

"Terrible. Jerry was thoroughly bloody-minded, he's getting far too clever when he changes keys. Elizabeth, there's a flap on in Intelligence—"

"But not about *my* work?"

99

"Of course not. It's about your brother—"

"David! I was just going to tell you, he's got back to England—"

"Don't I know it! Come on, dear, or Blinker'll have a fit."

There was no sign of a flap in the Naval Intelligence Division. The filing clerks were silently at work, as usual, and Mr. Hoy, the principal secretary, smiled as he motioned them into the private room; but in I.D. the calm often presaged a storm, and Liz Flett's knees shook as she greeted the Director. What has that miserable boy done now, she thought.

"Sit down," snapped "Blinker" Hall. Until early in the war he had commanded the battleship *Queen Mary*, and retained the crisp manner of the quarterdeck. Behind it was the most incisive brain in the Admiralty, a capacity for sizing up a situation immediately, and an almost hypnotic power of persuasion. Still in his early forties, Captain Hall was almost completely bald, with tufts of snow-white hair over his ears, and steely eyes with lids which fluttered so constantly as to give him his nickname, Blinker.

"Have you heard from your brother this morning, Miss Flett?" he said.

"Yes, sir. He telephoned at eight o'clock to tell me he'd arrived in Harwich."

"Your father know?"

"We thought he'd be on the Market by that time, so I waited until after nine and called him at the office. David said he would telephone later in the morning, as soon as he knew if he would get leave."

"He'll get some leave all right. Did he give you any details of his escape?"

"No, sir. Not over the telephone."

"Quite right. However, before he spoke to you he gave a full account of his movements to the interrogating officer at Harwich, who sent it on to me without delay." He tapped a file of papers at his elbow. "There are some interesting points about his story." Liz waited, trying not to glance at Adrian. "Just possibly we might be able to bring off something very useful indeed to this Department . . . if your brother can give us the kind of help we want."

"I'm sure he'll do his best, sir." Liz looked so unlike her usual competent self that Adrian Combermere came to her rescue:

"The Director would like me to meet your brother this evening, if you don't mind, Miss Flett."

"At the station?"

"At Liverpool Street," said Blinker. "He'll arrive at nine fifteen. They're going to keep him in Harwich today—the doctors want to have a good look at him—"

"He isn't ill, sir?"

"He's done some damage to his shoulder, nothing serious. But I want you both to meet him, so that Mr. Combermere can have a word with him before he reports to me tomorrow. Can you put him up at your rooms for the night?"

"I could if necessary, but Mrs. Macandrew always keeps a room vacant for her own sons when they're on leave."

"Arrange that, then. I don't want him roaming round London by himself."

"I'll look after him, sir."

"I'm sure you will. Is Mr. Flett older or younger than you?"

"Three years younger, sir. He'll be twenty-four in July."

Blinker turned the pages of the brief file on David Flett, Sub-Lieutenant, R.N.V.R. "Miss Flett, I want you to understand that this is a very important matter. In normal circumstances I would ask for a report from your brother's captain, but as you know Captain Willis-Turner went down with his ship when the *Yelverton* was torpedoed, and I can't wait for a report from Base at Scapa Flow. I want you to answer some questions instead. Your brother was born in Aberdeen?"

"Well, at Footdee, that's the old fishing village, but it's part of the city now."

"And was educated—where?"

"At Gordon's College, but he left when he was sixteen. He was always daft about the sea!"

"And the sea meant the Aberdeen herring fleet, I suppose?"

"No, sir, the white fishing. My father works for Garden and Company, and Mr. Garden took David on when he left school. He was mate in the *Moss Rose* when the war broke out."

"When did he join the R.N.V.R.?"

"About 1912, I think it was. He was taken straight into the Navy from the *Moss Rose* in 1914."

"Was he happy in the Navy?"

"You'll just need to ask him that yourself, sir."

Adrian Combermere smiled. He came very close to loving Liz when the Scottish turn of phrase, the Scottish truculence, broke through her carefully acquired speech and manner. Captain Hall blinked furiously.

"You're employed here subject to the provisions of the Official Secrets Act," he said. "Would you answer for your brother's discretion, as you would answer for your own?"

Hesitating: "That's a big responsibility."

"Don't take too much upon yourself, Miss Flett, it'll be Mr. Combermere's responsibility tonight, and mine tomorrow."

"Well, then!" said Liz Flett, stung. "If you want to know what *I* think about my brother Davie, all I can say is he's very stubborn, but he's very determined too. He's a faithful sort of a boy . . . and if he takes in hand to do anything, he always sees it through."

"I'm terribly sorry, Elizabeth," said Adrian Combermere. "The Great Eastern Hotel isn't as smart as the Trocadero, I'm afraid. We'll go there some night next week, when the present flap's all over."

"They gave us a jolly good dinner, anyway," said Liz. If not smart, the Great Eastern was certainly busy, for the restaurant was crowded with naval officers on their way to and from the East Coast ports. Adrian was the only young man not in uniform. Liz, jostled by waiters and men hurrying to the trains, thought with regret of the red charmeuse dress hanging in her back bedroom, which she had bought for the outing cancelled by Captain Hall's decision.

Adrian paid the bill. He looked less tired than in the morning, having had two hours' sleep in the afternoon, and had changed from the tweeds of the night watch into a dark suit. It was Liz who looked weary, for the sequel to the Zeppelin H.V.B. signal had meant a busy afternoon, and her fresh white silk blouse now looked limp and wilted. Adrian helped her into the jacket of her suit.

"Nine o'clock," he said. "We'd better get down to the arrival platform. We don't want to miss him in the crowd."

But when they reached the station level the 9.15 up from Harwich was posted fifteen minutes late.

"Blast," said Adrian. "I'd like to get out of here before Jerry comes over; if he comes, that is. And Jerry's usually a punctual fellow. You're not worried, are you, Elizabeth?"

"They say lightning never strikes twice in the same place." It was only seven months since the Zeppelin *blitz* had struck, in the form of high explosive, at Liverpool Street Station: there were still barriers up where the north-bound line was under repair, and ominous gaps in the houses round Broad Street. Adrian took the girl's arm, and pressed it to his side.

"Let's get out of this mob, shall we?" he suggested. The area between the news stand and the information board was erupting with bluejackets and their sweethearts and there was a surge of thirsty humanity round the swinging doors of the railway bar. Adrian steered Liz towards the end of the platform. "If David's train gets in after closing time there'll be dry throats and hell to pay. Lucky I got the bottle, to wet his stripe."

"He'll be pleased about the stripe. He didn't care much about being a Sub-Lieutenant."

"He was a bit too old to settle down easily in the Gunroom."

"He was two years older than the Senior Sub! Oh, Adrian, when Blinker asked me this morning if Dave was happy in the Navy, I nearly *died*—"

"Yes, I saw that worried you. You gave him a very good answer, though." They had walked as far as a barrier of milk cans, turned, and began to walk back. "Elizabeth dear, can't you tell *me* what the trouble was?"

"Well—it was partly that he was too *old* to be a junior officer. In a way he knew more than the others did, for after all he got his Master's ticket six months before the war broke out, and I think Mr. Garden would have given him a command quite soon. But then he didn't know a lot of the things they'd been brought up knowing—they'd been through Osborne and Dartmouth together, or 'shipmates in the old *Britannia*'—those were the seniors, of course. He fairly hated that. They chaffed him about being R.N.V.R.; 'Fred Karno's Navy', they called it, and 'the backdoor entry' and Davie gave them as good as he got, you may be sure. He used to imitate the way they spoke, as if they had a hot potato in their mouths. He said they were always yapping about 'dear old Mouldy, we were on the China Station together', or 'good old Bunjy, we were shipmates in the Med. back in the Naughty-Naughts', and of course all Davie knew about was fishing off the Faeroes.''

"Doesn't sound too cheerful," said Adrian. "Didn't he make any friends at all?"

"Yes, Magnus Sabiston, the Orkney boy, I told you about him. He declares that David saved his life when the *Yelverton* was sunk, and that may be true, because whatever else David is, he's brave enough! Sabiston was a Lieutenant R.N. when Davie joined the ship, but he's very much 'New Navy'—very democratic, I suppose you'd say, and he was interested in Davie's name, because Flett's really an Orkney name—"

"Did you know that?"

"Never. My grandfather Flett came from Portsoy," said Liz briefly. "Anyway, the Sabiston family were very nice to David, and when the *Yelverton* was at Scapa they invited him to the manse with Magnus, he enjoyed that. There's a schoolgirl daughter he was rather taken with, I think."

"David repaid young Sabiston well for his kindness."

"Yes, didn't he?"

Adrian turned Liz gently round until the dimmed-out light of a station lamp fell on her pretty face. Her eyes were troubled.

"Was that all there was to it, Elizabeth? Simply that he found it hard to adapt himself to the—traditions of the Royal Navy, and the discipline of the Service, or was there something more?"

Reluctantly: "Well . . . he was always in hot water with his Captain. There was one terrible row when Davie altered the disposition of the boats on his own initiative, because he said it was an emergency, and Captain Willis-Turner was furious—"

"They're not keen on initiative in the Navy."

"No. And then . . . the truth is, Davie has a violent nature. When I was living at home before the war, we never had a moment's peace when the *Moss Rose* was in harbour. He was always skylarking with the deckies, or getting into fights with foreign seamen . . . I hate to be telling you all this about my own brother, Adrian!"

"I know it isn't easy. But it helps."

"And about this job that Blinker has in mind . . . Look, if Blinker wanted Davie to take on some chap and lay him out cold, he would be great, but I honestly can't imagine him as a secret agent!"

"The train's signalled," said Adrian. Liz had an inspiration. She said, "Did you ever hear the story of the old Scotswoman who was told her son had been taken prisoner by the Moors, or maybe it was the Spaniards, I forget, and he'd been put to rowing as a galley-slave. Everybody expected the old wifie to burst into tears. But all she said—and it just describes my brother—all she said was, 'God help the man that's chained to our Davie!'"

The Harwich train came in with a gush of steam. Doors banged open, and a crowd of bluejackets jostled their way out to the platform. Adrian hurried Liz down the coaches. He was relieved to hear her cry "There he is! David!" A big young man, forging ahead of them through the crush, turned at once and waved.

"Hey, Lizzie, this is great!" Adrian was amused to see the cool Scots handshake, and the abrupt pat on Elizabeth's shoulder which indicated pleasure and affection.

"Davie, how *are* you?"

"Fine, lassie, fine! Is this somebody with you?"

"This is Mr. Combermere, from the Admiralty."

"Pleased to meet you."

Adrian, shaking hands, took stock of him. At Harwich David had been issued with a new uniform, a second-hand blue Burberry and an imitation leather valise to hold a few necessities. He looked exactly what he was, a shipwrecked mariner, staring round a little stupidly at the roaring station.

"Come on, Flett," said Adrian, "we didn't plan to greet you like a reception committee. Let's get a taxi."

"I've got a room for you at Nottingham Terrace," said Liz.

"That's great," David said again, feeling for his ticket as they neared the barrier, "but could you hold on half a tick? My shoulder's been annoying me, and a good rub with Elliman's Embrocation'll just do the trick. Would there be a chemist open?"

"There's a Boots not far from the station." First things first, thought Adrian, following the brother and sister up the ramp. He heard David say "How's my father?" and Liz, "You spoke to him, didn't you?"—"Aye, but how's he keeping, he'll never say!" and then they were out in Liverpool Street, with barely illuminated bottles of red and green showing the whereabouts of a chemist's shop. They had just crossed the road when the heart-stopping whine of an Air Raid Warning rang out across the darkened City.

"Hell!" said Adrian. "We'll never get a taxi now."

"We'll take the Tube," said David. "Aren't your new digs at Baker Street, Lizzie? Wait till I get my Elliman and we'll be off."

He came out of the shop cramming the bottle of embrocation into his pocket, shepherded them back to the station, dodged a policeman ordering all pedestrians to take cover, and told two Boy Scouts on bicycles, enjoyably shouting "Air Raid! Air Raid!" not to make such a bloody awful row. The Navy was very much in charge, but Adrian barked irritably, "For God's sake let's all hurry up! Liverpool Street got a hammering last September, we don't want to get caught again tonight."

The platforms of the Underground were crowded with people, some singing defiantly but most pale and tense enough to look as if they remembered the previous hammering of Liverpool Street Station, and diving thankfully into the train as it came in. They had to stand all the way to Baker Street, Liz partly protected from the press of people by the two young men. The searchlights were stabbing the sky when they came up to street level, and a zealous policeman refused to let them go any further.

"But officer, I live in Nottingham Terrace, it's right beside Madame Tussaud's," protested Liz. "We can be indoors in three minutes."

"Could 'ave your head blown off in one," said the policeman. "Stay right where you are, miss, till the All Clear sounds." The noise of anti-aircraft guns, beginning far down the Thames, was coming steadily nearer. The searchlights, criss-crossing, lit up the Borough of St. Marylebone. The house where Charles Dickens had lived and worked, the church where Robert Browning and Elizabeth Barrett were married, the streets with the historic names, the Nash terraces, the mews behind the poplar tree outside Liz Flett's window—the great and the small lay beneath the menace of the enemy as yet unseen and challenged only by the distant guns. "They generally come up the Thames, or right along a straight line, curse them," said Adrian Combermere. "Mathy did his Railway Raid like that, just as Breithaupt bombed the theatres. I can't believe there's more than one in the area tonight."

David looked over his shoulder. Most of the people who had come up from the Tube were a little way away, arguing with the policeman. Still, as Adrian noted, he lowered his voice to say, "When I was here on leave last summer, the Kaiser had some sort of rule that the Zepps could only go for London at the weekends —what happened to that?"

"He chucked it," said Adrian, "after the R.N.A.S. boys went over and bombed his Zepps on the ground at Fühlsbüttel and Nordholz. Anything goes now."

David nodded. He had moved a step or two on to the pavement, just beyond the station entrance, and the searchlights showed his gaunt young face, with the dogged jaw, raised enquiringly to the sky. "What are we flying against them?" he said.

"The R.F.C. flies the Blériot Experimental, the BE2C. Mounted with a Lewis gun and incendiary darts—it was the darts that did for Breithaupt over the North Sea."

"There's been a lot of changes since I've been away."

"Oh, I'm sure of it."

"*There he is!*" The shout came from a hundred throats. In the sky, where all the chimney smoke of London seemed turned to coils of silver by the searchlights, appeared a monstrous cigar-shaped object, the port and starboard lights clearly seen as it moved west. The guns in the Green Park and Regent's Park burst into a frenzy of anti-aircraft fire. Liz put her fingers in her ears. Across the glowing sky an object fluttered, tiny by comparison with the Zeppelin but harassing it like a gadfly, above and below, throwing its puny darts at the leviathan's skin. It was speedily joined by another insect of the same sort. "Two of the Blériots— from L.G. One or Two," said Combermere. He had put his arm round Liz, regardless of her brother's presence, and she pressed close to him and shut her eyes.

They heard the crump of the first bomb, far distant in the City, and then the Zeppelin seemed to shudder in mid-air and change its course. Still on the line of the Thames, which had led it into London, the enemy airship with the Blériots in pursuit turned eastward in retreat. A cheer went up from the crowd at Baker Street Station.

"That bobby's got his hands full now," said David. "Come on, run for it, Lizzie!"

They ran together, followed by a blast on a police whistle, away from the station, past Madame Tussaud's, and through the carriage entrance in a white wall which divided Nottingham Terrace from the pavement of the Marylebone Road. Liz, gasping with relief, put her latchkey in the door of Number 7.

"I feel so much safer when I'm home," she said, and led the way into her front sittingroom. David and Adrian hung their coats up in the hall and followed her.

"You don't think they'll come back?" she asked as she applied a match to the gas fire installed in front of the Regency basket grate.

"I think that Zepp was a stray," said Combermere. "He may have got detached from a strike further north. He'll run out of fuel if he turns back now, and he's probably over the Essex marshes by this time. Sorry Jerry treated you to such a welcome home, Flett!"

"Jerry?"

"That's right, we used to call him Fritz. Well, Fritz or Jerry, we won't let him spoil the evening; Elizabeth and I want to drink to your promotion. Shall I get the glasses out?" He turned to the cupboard where Liz kept the china for the tea she made on a gas ring. But Liz herself stopped him; she said "Oh wait a minute, Adrian, I want to show David his room first, and I'm sure he'd like a wash."

When they were alone in the room at the top of the house which Mrs. Macandrew kept for her sons in the Army, it occurred to Liz to ask if he was hungry.

"No thanks, I got my dinner on the train. It was nice, sitting at yon wee tables with the lamps all lit."

"They're going to take the dining-cars off for the duration, in a few weeks' time. Well, will this do for tonight, David?"

David sat down on the bed and lit a cigarette. "It's a treat compared to the old Dutchie's attic I was hiding in at Amsterdam. The ceiling was four feet high in the middle at its highest, and I lay on a flock mattress on the floor."

"Oh, Dave, you've had an awful time! Does your shoulder hurt you much?"

Impatiently: "It'll be all right in a day or two. Tell me about this Mr. Combermere. Is he your lad, Lizzie?"

"*Don't call me Lizzie!*"

"Well, Elizabeth, then. 'Ee-lizabeth and I wawnt to drink to yaw promotion'," said David affectedly. "You and him seems to be very well acquaint."

"We're in the same office, so of course we have a lot in common."

"Seems like a cushy job for a man that age. What is he—thirty? I thought the Military Service Act would take care of lads like him. Unless he's a married man, of course?"

"He is *not* married," said Liz hotly. "He has defective eyesight, and he's doing an important job. Any more questions?"

"No."

"The bathroom's on the half-landing."

"Wait a minute, Lizzie, don't go away in a huff. Have you any news of the Sabistons?"

"Magnus came to see me the last time he had London leave. You knew he was in the *Excellent*, on a course in director firing?"

"Aye, I knew that. And what about—his sister?"

She thought his awkwardness was shyness, and laughed

tauntingly. "The fair Ingrid? She left the Ministers' Daughters' College at the Christmas holidays, that's all I know. Are you interested? *Is she your lass, David?*"

"Get away!" He said it in the right jeering tone, the required mockery of gentle feelings, but as he listened to his sister running downstairs David lay back on the hard bed, hearing a sweeter voice than any he had ever heard say wonderingly "But I have seen this picture!" and then "Ingrid—Ingrid Sabiston!"

He returned to Liz's room as the "All Clear" sounded. The whisky bottle and glasses were on a tray with a jug of fresh water from the pantry tap, and Liz had taken off her hat.

"Mighty, what have you done to your hair?"

"This is what they call the Castle clip."

"Castle?"

"Irene Castle, the American dancer; she started the fashion. I don't suppose you ever heard of *her*."

"Don't you think it suits Elizabeth?" said Adrian, pouring drinks.

"It's not so bad," said the brother grudgingly. In fact the bobbed hair, swept back from her brow and flicked into a deep wave at the neck, suited Liz's pretty narrow face, with the neat nose and chin, very well indeed. He observed, when they sat down, that his up-to-date sister had also taken to smoking, and in a style he thought ridiculous, holding the cigarette between her thumb and forefinger, and puffing out the smoke like a tea-kettle. He remembered a slender hand holding a black Russian cigarette with a gold eagle, and a perfect smoke ring rising through the umbered shadows of a room on the Herengracht.

He forced himself to admire his new surroundings. The most attractive feature of Liz's sittingroom was the wallpaper, a William Morris design of green leaves and red berries left over from the days when 7 Nottingham Terrace was a private residence. His sister had not done much to improve the boardinghouse furnishings, except by putting her own books on the white-painted shelves—French novels in yellow on one side of the fire, English novels in a famous red sevenpenny edition on the other.

A bunch of daffodils in a green glass vase was carefully placed to give the maximum effect.

"This is a bit of all right," said David. "A lot better than yon bed-sittingroom you had in Bloomsbury."

"I've a much better job now, Davie."

"What is it you do, exactly, at the Admiralty?"

"Translations, from the German mostly."

"How did you come to land a job like that?"

Liz laughed. "I got it thanks to you! When women were being recruited for my Section, all the applicants had to be the daughters or sisters of naval officers. So you helped me qualify."

"But how did you come to apply at all?"

"I heard about the job after I came to work at Mr. Neroslavski's offices in London."

David laughed. "I wish my mother had lived to hear about this. Do you mind on the row she raised when you told her you weren't going to come out for a teacher? She thought a herring merchant's office in Market Street was a terrible come down for a university graduate! But my father's as proud as Punch. He was full of it this morning—our Lizzie working at the Admiralty."

"You're going to the Admiralty yourself tomorrow, aren't you?" Adrian said.

"Aye. Some Captain Hall I'm ordered to report to . . . would you have any idea what about?"

"Probably about your escape from Groningen, and how you managed it."

David's face closed. "Aye, well, there's not much to be said about that business. I know two lads ready to go down the route I took, and I wouldn't want to do anything to spoil their chances."

"Of course not," said Adrian. He leaned over and refilled David's glass. "I wish you'd begin at the beginning and tell us the whole story. Start at the wreck—"

"But Liz—Elizabeth knows about all that already."

"Only from your letters, Davie. You didn't write often or tell me much."

David flexed his shoulders in the narrow fireside chair. He was too big for it, and the wood cracked ominously as he tilted it backwards on two legs. "It was the fifteenth of August," he said. "We sailed from Scapa Flow on the twelfth. Our usual cruise was south to Kinnaird Head, and then east through the Long Forties to the Jutland Bank. However, this time we were patrolling in the Broad Fourteens, heading north by nor'east off the Dutch coast when Fritz's tin fish struck."

"Without warning, I suppose?"

"No nonsense about giving us a chance to take to the boats for Fritz—or Jerry. We never even saw the bloody submarine! Just the big explosion when the torpedo hit amidships, and then the poor old *Yelverton* gave a great lurch to starboard and went down stem first. Willis-Turner was yelling 'Abandon ship! Abandon ship!' and the lads all jumped for it. There wasn't time to lower a boat. We got away two Carleys and a barrel raft, but the raft was sucked down when the ship sank—her stern rose till it was just about perpendicular and down she went . . . Aye, poor old Willis-Turner! He was a right bastard, but he died the way he would have wanted—on the bridge, with the Colours flying."

"And you were on one of the Carley floats," said Liz.

"Well, I was just paddling about, d'you see, trying to find out where everybody was. I knew that if Fritz—if Jerry didn't surface and give us a blast with his guns, we'd a pretty good chance of being picked up, like both the Carleys were—"

"But you gave up your place to Lieutenant Sabiston."

"Did Magnus tell you that?" asked David easily. "He's a great hand at spinning a bender! I just changed places with him, that was all; Magnus was never much of a swimmer, and I thought I had a better chance than he had, in the drink. And to make a long story short I was doing great, I could even see the dunes, when the Dutch fishing-smack came up and took me on board. Then the skipper told me I was inside the two-mile limit and would need to be interned."

"So they took you off to Groningen?"

"They had me in a *Kazerne* for about three weeks, but it was due to close, so I was put in with the Royal Naval Division chaps, them that was interned after Antwerp."

"And when did you start planning your escape?" said Adrian casually.

"As soon as I got there." David sat up straight, and put his glass down on the floor. "I never gave my parole to the Dutch Commandant—never once; not even to go into the town! I knew fine that if I just stayed behind the barbed wire and kept my eyes open to see who would take a bribe and who wouldna, and got the map of Holland clear inside my brain, I had a fair chance; and besides, there were two of the senior officers that had tried to escape and been brought back. It was them that told me about the barge route and Mr. — the man to go to in Amsterdam."

He reflected. "Mind you, I'm not saying a word against the chaps at Groningen. The only thing was, they had it a lot better in Holland than the R.N.D. men in Germany—the real P.O.Ws.; we used to save our bread ration to send on to Döberitz. And they'd been there over a year when I was taken; the huts in Timbertown were up and the whole thing was organised: camp concerts and gardening and knitting classes and sports—God ha' mercy! I never meant to finish out the war whittling model yachts and raising poultry in a Dutch backyard."

Adrian nodded slowly. From all he had heard that day about David Flett, ex-mate of the trawler *Moss Rose*, insubordinate junior naval officer—and from all that Elizabeth's pride had left unsaid—he had expected something different from his encounter. He had visualised a Tony Lumpkin of the fishing fleet—a rough diamond, to put it at the best, whom to employ upon a delicate secret mission might well be hopeless. He had watched and listened; he had noted coolness and caution, heard a story of courage and personal initiative, doggedly pursued, and had even seen the Scotsman's expression change from the rather embarrassed, bewildered look of the station platform to one of confidence and remembered daring. He got up to go.

"Jolly good show," he said. "Congratulations, Flett! Now I'll be on my way; you and Elizabeth must have a lot of family news to catch up on."

"Why don't I make tea for all of us?" suggested Liz. "I'm sure I've some digestive biscuits somewhere."

"I could go a good cup of tea," David confessed. Adrian declined, shook hands with David and wished him good-night, and went to find his overcoat. Liz followed him silently into the hall.

"Look," he said quietly but more impatiently than he had ever spoken to her, "You're the landlady's star boarder, aren't you? Why don't you go down to the kitchen and make Dave a ham sandwich, or something a bit more appetising than digestive biscuits? And then rub his shoulder with his precious embrocation and give him a chance to get a good night's rest? That kid in there is very nearly at the end of his tether—and he's got to face Blinker in the morning."

"You're going to tell Blinker—"

"I'm going back to the office," said Adrian, with his hand on the front door knob. "Blinker said he would be there till midnight. I'm going to tell him that in my judgment it's a big gamble—but I think it may come off."

VII

Saturday, April 15, to
Thursday, April 20, 1916

The Director of the Intelligence Division was at his desk in the
Admiralty at nine o'clock next morning, and at once took up the
matter of the single Zeppelin which had dropped one bomb on
London on the previous evening. All the D/F intercepts in the
later afternoon had shown that the Zeppelins were heading north,
and Ops had duly relayed warnings by wireless to the Grand Fleet
at Scapa Flow and the Battle Cruiser Fleet at Rosyth in the Firth
of Forth. The lone Zeppelin attacking London, presumed to be
part of the northward strike, had not been accounted for until it
was actually sighted by ground observers near the Wash, and this
strict guard on wireless silence by the enemy was something new
and disquieting. For his own satisfaction, Captain Hall sent signals
to Scapa and Rosyth requesting a check on the whole file received
from the Admiralty after the first H.V.B. was picked up at
Hunstanton. That Intelligence and Operations were completely
independent of each other had led to a good deal of friction,
especially where Room 40 was concerned, and Captain Hall was
anxious to know that all information passed on to Ops did in fact,
and in its completest form, reach the Commands.

"Give Sir Alfred my compliments, and ask him to come to my
room," he told his secretary when the half hour of dictation was
over. "And if the Flett file has come back from his office, send it
in to me."

It was on his desk two minutes before Sir Alfred Ewing was
announced. The D.I.D. rose to greet the dapper little Scotsman
who as Director of Naval Education had played an important part
in shaping the "New Navy", and who from being the sole decoder
of German intercepts in August 1914 had risen to be the Head of

Room 40 and all the cryptographers and encypherers which it contained. Sir Alfred wore, as always, an imaginatively conceived outfit, this morning a grey suit, mauve shirt, blue bow tie with white polka dots under a butterfly collar, in striking contrast to Blinker's uniform.

"You've had a look at this?" said Blinker, indicating the Flett file.

"I have indeed. An interesting story, especially when supplemented by Combermere's acute comments and your own suggestions."

"Rather too far-fetched, the latter?"

"That depends entirely upon Mr. Flett."

"Quite so. How long would your people require for the encyphering of a fake British signal book for Flett to take to Amsterdam?"

"Three of them could do it in twenty-four hours, if they had to. I mean Fleet Paymaster Rotter and Commander Denniston—"

"Obviously."

"And Miss Elizabeth Flett. She isn't in their class, but she's better than any of the rest. A particularly quick and careful worker."

Blinker's lips twitched. "I like that," he said. "Room 40 at its best. The sister fakes the code and the brother carries it—quite a family affair. Good God, Ewing, what a master-stroke if it comes off! Talk about the double bluff! First, we get the *Magdeburg* signal book without any effort on our own part—simply because the Russians are in an unusually generous mood—and that helps us to win a near-victory at the Dogger Bank and save the East Coast towns from God knows how many German raids. Next, we have this heaven-sent opportunity to plant a fake code book on the enemy, and feed them misinformation which may mean all the difference between defeat and victory. If only we can bring it off—"

Sir Alfred coughed. "Should you have the young man in?"

Towards daybreak Liz Flett had suffered from a recurrent nightmare that David would greet the D.I.D. with his usual formula, "Pleased to meet you." But the impeccable young Lieutenant who

116

stood at attention before the Director's desk might well have been, in speech and manner, some senior officer's shipmate "in the good old *Britannia*, back in the Naughty-Naughts"; Captain Hall's steely eye surveyed him with a measure of approval.

"This is Sir Alfred Ewing, Mr. Flett," he said. "He's been reading the account of your escape from Groningen."

"Sir."

"You seem to have used the barge route very efficiently. How long were you with Mr. Timmermann in Amsterdam?"

"Two nights and three days, sir."

"An unusually long stay—or didn't you find it so?"

"I had a notion he was glad to see the last of me, sir."

"H'm . . . Mr. Timmermann is under constant surveillance by the Dutch police, on suspicion of receiving stolen jewels, specifically diamonds . . . So far we have persuaded them to give him the benefit of the doubt, because we find him a very useful fellow, but he does insist on sailing very close to the wind. Don't let any idea of gratitude send you to call on Mr. Timmermann when you return to Amsterdam."

"That's not very likely, sir."

"You were helped to get aboard the Harwich packet by two Russian male dancers, according to your statement?"

"That's right, sir. Mr. Bronin and Mr. Levin."

"*The Times* announces that Mr. Bronin and his group are going to dance for war charities at the Queen's Hall this afternoon. Would you be interested in being present?"

"I don't think so, sir."

"Did you share their cabin on the way to Harwich?"

"No, sir. The purser found a berth for me in the second class."

"You didn't care to continue in the Russians' company? H'm? Why not?"

"To tell you the truth I wasn't greatly taken with them, sir. They were both reeking with perfume, and the little one had his lips painted like a street-walker's."

"You found Madame Tamirova more attractive?" He watched the tightening of David's face. "This is the transcript of what you said at Harwich. 'There was a Russian lady there who sent for

Mr. Bronin. She said her name was Elena Tamirova, but I heard them calling her Elena Petrovna too. She gave me a paper that helped me to get through when the immigration officers came along the train.' "

" 'Petrovna' only means her father's name was Peter," said Sir Alfred. "The patronymic is general Russian usage."

"That's what my sister said last night when I let her see the paper," David said.

"Does Miss Flett understand Russian?"

"She was three years in a Russian herring merchant's office in Aberdeen and one in London. She can read Russian fast enough! She said the paper was an expired travel permit from Kiev to Petrograd, dated the seventeenth of March, but the stamps and all that fairly took in the Dutchman on the train."

"Wonderful what a bit of bluff will do," chuckled Sir Alfred.

"May I have that paper, Mr. Flett?" The Director added it to the file. "Now let us go back to the transcript. 'There was a Russian lady . . .' Begin at the beginning and tell me exactly how Madame Tamirova came into the picture."

He listened to David's halting narrative, told with the suppression of only one detail, and at the end he turned to Sir Alfred with a shrug. "The eternal feminine!" he said. "What will they think of next?"

"Mr. Flett has told his story very clearly," the older Scotsman said. "Perhaps we should now tell him what we know about Madame Tamirova."

"Certainly . . . Mr. Flett, the woman who befriended you, for heaven knows what reason of her own, is the mistress of a German secret agent named Karl Ritter, who has recently been masquerading as an American salesman of munitions called Karl Ericssen. He was in Petrograd last month in the company of Grigori Nelidov, one of the key men in Russia's war production. He may have met the woman Tamirova there, or earlier, but they were not known to be together until the first of this month, when our agent in Copenhagen received a tip-off from a reliable source telling him that they had left together for a country residence rented by the German Embassy, where they spent the weekend. After that they appear to have been quite open about their liaison. They stayed in the same hotel in Christiania, and are now together in Amsterdam. Further, when she was dancing in Norway Elena Tamirova was seen in the company of Hans Kolberg, a shipowner who has been on the British Black List since it was introduced last November. What's the matter, Mr. Flett? Does the name of Kolberg mean anything to you?"

"N-no, sir. You mentioned the Black List—I don't know what that is."

"A list of neutral shippers suspected of carrying goods presumably destined for Germany, which under an Order in Council the Royal Navy has the right to seize. You had no experience of the right of search in H.M.S. *Yelverton*?"

"No, sir."

"You will in your next ship. Well, there you have some of Madame Tamirova's background; what do you think of her now?"

"I don't believe a word of it."

"Mr. Flett!" said Blinker in a terrible voice. "Are you calling *me* in question?"

"I don't believe she's a bad woman. Not a girl like her."

"We're not a court of morals. Though incidentally she has an interesting record: she was previously the mistress of a minor Romanov princeling who was killed in action at Odensholm in 1914."

"Odensholm!" said Sir Alfred, and the eyes of the two Directors met.

"Sir, it can't be right," said David urgently. "If she was working for the Germans, why would she want to help somebody like me?"

Blinker shrugged. "I'm only the Director of Naval Intelligence; I must confess the vagaries of the feminine mind are quite beyond me."

David scowled. "Could she not just . . . be acquainted with this fellow Ritter and know nothing of what he was doing in Petrograd?"

"Let me tell you more about Karl Richard Ritter, alias Ericssen. My Section 14 has a very complete dossier on the gentleman. He's

119

a Lieutenant-Commander in the Imperial German Navy, in which his late father held the rank of Engineer Rear-Admiral, retiring in command of the Imperial Dockyard at Wilhelmshaven. His mother is—or was—an Englishwoman, the daughter of a doctor in Shanklin, where her brother still runs the family practice. Her sister married an American and lives in Milwaukee. Ritter spent a year in her home when he was a boy and went to high school in Milwaukee. He had the background and the aptitude to do exactly what he's doing now, which is why Admiral von Tirpitz had him seconded from his ship for special duty, but the thing to remember is that in spite of his mixed blood—or because of it—he's one hundred per cent German. He's one of the new breed—the fanatics, soaked in all that beastly blood and iron mystique of Bismarck's, dedicated to the All-Highest and the Fatherland; and to take the way he fooled the Russians as only one example, he's already worth a Dreadnought to his country's cause. Any woman he takes for his mistress is in my opinion automatically his accomplice."

He flicked a photograph across the table. "Have a good look at him. I want you to be able to recognise him if you see him."

David numbly took it up. He saw a keen face above the uniform wing collar, a cleft chin, steady eyes—almost the stereotype of a naval officer. "He seems quite a young chap," he said.

"He's thirty-three. That was taken three years ago, when he was one of Admiral von Tirpitz's naval entourage at the royal wedding in Berlin. Our reports indicate that he hasn't changed very much."

"Do you think there's any chance of me seeing him, sir?"

"Yes, I think it's very likely you'll see him," said Blinker, "about a week from now—in Amsterdam."

"Amsterdam!"

The D.I.D. rang for his secretary. "Have you that copy of *De Telegraaf* I asked for? Ah, with a translation too—thank you." He turned the pages of the Dutch paper rapidly.

"Madame Tamirova's season continues in Amsterdam next week," he said, "the ballet alternates with a repertory company. Now let's have a look at the programme. Monday the seventeenth, repertory, *A Doll's House*. Tuesday, ballet, *Giselle*. Wednesday, repertory, *Ghosts*—dear me, what a week of doom and disaster the Dutch are going to have! Thursday, ballet, *The Sleeping Beauty*. Friday, theatre closed, and Saturday, *Swan Lake*. That looks promising, Ewing, don't you think? The closed theatre, and then *Swan Lake*?"

"Remember it's the last night of her season," Ewing said.

"All the better." The Director looked up at David. "Yes, I want you to go back to Amsterdam," he said. "And there isn't any need to look so worried. You'll go back as a civilian, protected by full diplomatic immunity, and you need have no fear of being arrested and returned to the internment camp."

"You want me to get a hold of this man Ritter, sir?"

Blinker's hand smacked down hard on his desktop. "No, certainly not! Nothing like that at all! If we wanted Ritter behind bars we could pick him up tomorrow, even in a neutral country, but he's a great deal more valuable to us at liberty. We want certain information conveyed to him—and to his masters in the Fatherland—by way of you and the lady."

"I'm to go to Madame Tamirova?"

"Yes. Now think very carefully before you answer. Madame Tamirova knew you were a naval officer: did she learn your actual rank?"

"Not unless Mr. Timmermann happened to mention it. I just told her my name—no other details."

"Nothing at all? So far as she knew you might well have been a very important person, whose escape to England was a matter of national urgency?"

The slight note of mockery in the clipped incisive voice brought the colour to David's face. He looked sullen to the point of insubordination. Then he replied, "I don't know what she thought of me. She doesn't speak good English, and we didn't spend much time alone together."

"But you understood each other?"

"Oh yes, we understood each other fine. And I'm very grateful to Madame Tamirova; if it hadn't been for her I might still be in Timmermann's attic, or on the way back to Groningen under guard."

"So you don't relish the idea of using her to set a trap for her German lover?"

David was silent, and Sir Alfred again intervened with "I understand that you feel grateful to the lady, Mr. Flett. But remember, if she is innocent, the operation we have in mind will simply misfire, and you will return to England with no one a penny the worse for your trip to Amsterdam. Everything depends on Elena Tamirova. If she passes on to Ritter the information we intend to give to you, then you'll be convinced that she is in the service of the enemy, won't you?"

"I suppose so."

"And in that event," said Blinker briskly, "she should be very thankful to be operating in a neutral country. In England she would be tried in camera as a spy and imprisoned; in France she'd finish up before a firing squad. The French aren't as squeamish as we are about imposing the death penalty on female spies. Very well then, Mr. Flett, you'll be given your movement orders in due course; just at present one of my secretaries will take you along to E.1 and introduce you to Lieutenant-Commander Strawbridge. He's going down to Harwich tonight and you can travel with him."

When David left the room, as formally and precisely as he entered it, the Director of the Intelligence Division shook his head and sighed. "God knows," he said, "Combermere warned me it would be a long shot, but this is a longer shot than I expected."

"Would it be possible to send Combermere himself to Amsterdam? He's far more plausible as a Foreign Office messenger than this poor boy."

"Yes, certainly, he has the style and the background, *and* the brains, but Flett has one advantage—he has a reason for going straight to Madame Tamirova."

"I wonder if you're wise in leaving it to the last moment," Sir Alfred persisted. "Ritter may be across the border and back at the Marinamt before our man arrives in Amsterdam."

"I think he'll stay in Holland as long as the lady's there. He won't be the first agent to risk ruin for the sake of a petticoat! So, once again, it all depends on Madame Tamirova. If she can keep Ritter infatuated, we may just possibly have the biggest bit of luck that's come our way since the Russians handed over the *Magdeburg* signal book!"

The Section classified as E.1, David learned as he was conducted through the corridors of the Admiralty, handled reports of German U-boat movements coming from British and neutral sources. Braced for a briefing on submarine warfare, he was agreeably surprised when Lieutenant-Commander Strawbridge, who wore the ribbon of the D.S.O., hurried him out into Whitehall and into a passing taxi, saying earnestly that clothes were the first consideration, and that they'd better get up to Gieves as fast as possible. He made time, however, for a brief halt at Hatchards, and came out with a book parcel small enough to be put in his pocket as they drove on to Bond Street. There, at the naval outfitters', David was measured for his new uniforms, with the new stripe to be added, which was not at all disagreeable to a young man who had worn nothing but camp clothing for eight months past. The next visit, to a Regent Street shop specializing in men's ready-to-wear, was less successful, for the ready-made jackets wrinkled badly on David's powerful shoulders and upper arms, but there was no time for alterations, and finally a civilian suit of excellent dark material, a black overcoat and homburg hat, and an assortment of underwear were packed in a leather suitcase which a District Messenger would deliver at Liverpool Street Station at half past six.

David, on hearing these arrangements made, congratulated himself on his discretion. He was learning how to handle the English at last. The thing was never to ask questions (the Navy discouraged questions, especially from very junior officers) and let them do the talking until they revealed what one wanted to know, and he very much wanted to know why he was going back to Harwich several days ahead of the presumable start of his mission to Holland. At least he had found out the approximate time of their departure. When they left the outfitters' he suggested telephoning to Liz, who might be expecting him to spend the weekend at Nottingham Terrace. He was smilingly told that she would know, by now, that he was going out of London.

They had luncheon at the Berkeley, where David put another painfully acquired lesson into use by forbearing to comment on the grandeur of the restaurant and the elaborate dishes (now fewer than before) which appeared on the menu. The place seemed to be full of pretty girls lunching with officers. He had a good look at them out of the tail of his eye. Girls had played a large part in his plans for his first Saturday back in London, and there was a flat in Bayswater, accommodating quite a number of girls, where he had intended to spend the evening. Blinker's nonsensical plan had of course put paid to that. He thought of it as nonsensical, when he thought at all, but he had to give his mind to Lieutenant-Commander Strawbridge, who was asking amiable questions about friends of his own interned after Antwerp, whom David had known slightly at Groningen. After luncheon he proposed a matinée, and they started down St. James's Street to St. James's Theatre, where they were lucky enough to get two returned stall tickets for *A Little Bit of Fluff*. David was charmed with Miss Ruby Miller, whose infatuated admirers in the armed forces of the Crown were said to drink champagne from her slipper, but in the darkened theatre he was able to put the back of his mind to work on the one detail he had not passed on to the D.I.D.—the fact that the Russian dancer had recognised the photograph of Magnus Sabiston's sister. He was nearly sure that Hans Kolberg was the name of the young Sabistons' uncle in Christiania.

The two naval officers bought drinks in a bar after the theatre —for themselves but not for each other, since the "No Treating" law was rigorously enforced in the West End. They took a taxi to Liverpool Street Station where the District Messenger was waiting with the suitcase. In a reserved smoking compartment to Harwich, they settled down in corner seats, lit cigarettes and opened the evening papers.

"Loss of the *Hazelhead*."

The familiar Aberdeen name caught David's eye at once. He read on:

"There are no survivors of the Tarras Line passenger steamship *Hazelhead*, sunk by enemy action on Thursday night when three hours out of Aberdeen en route for Christiania. Two seamen, James Crichton (42) and Albert Dawson (44) both of Aberdeen, who were picked up by a trawler, died of exposure on the way back to port. They told the skipper that the *Hazelhead* was torpedoed without warning by a U-boat, the periscope of which was visible as it surfaced to view the wreckage." The passenger list was then given in full. There were several Aberdeen names—Taggart, Lewis, Rust—which were vaguely familiar, and then one which seemed to leap out at him from the page:

Sabiston, Mrs. Astrid Marie, Manse of Hamnavoe,
near Kirkwall, Orkney.

"God damn them!" he said aloud. "They've got my friend's mother now!"

"What's that?"

David passed the newspaper to Lieutenant-Commander Strawbridge, and explained his friendship with the Sabistons.

"Poor lady, she was a long way from home," said Strawbridge. "Have you any idea why she was en route for Norway?"

"She *was* a Norwegian," David said. And Mr. Kolberg of the Black List's sister, he added in his mind. "She was a very nice lady; she had me to my tea at the manse every time the *Yelverton* came off patrol when we were up at Scapa. Poor folk, they'll be in despair; I'll need to write to the minister."

"I don't think you ought to write to anybody for the next few days."

"Why not?"

"Just to be on the safe side. The fewer people who know your actual whereabouts, the better." Strawbridge studied David's sullen face. "Look here, Flett, I'm terribly sorry about your friend and all the other poor devils who were lost with the *Hazelhead*; but this sort of thing is just one more nail in Germany's coffin. Let me see, was the *Lusitania* sunk before you were interned?"

"Aye, surely, three months before."

"Then you remember the row about the American lives lost

in the *Lusitania*. There were Americans aboard the *Arabic* when the Germans torpedoed her in August, and after a stiff Note from President Wilson the Kaiser's government promised that no merchant ships would be attacked without warning or without giving the passengers a chance to take to the boats. But of course they haven't kept their word. Look at the Dutch liner *Tubantic*, look at the cross-Channel steamer *Sussex*, both torpedoed last month without warning! There were American lives lost in the *Sussex* too, and Wilson sent another Note to Berlin. Now it's the *Hazelhead*. I tell you, it only needs a few more such incidents, and the United States will enter the war on the side of the Allies."

"You don't think we can beat Germany without the Yanks?"

"Doesn't look very like it, does it? No, Flett, I'm not being a defeatist. In E.1 we're only concerned with U-boat warfare and the U-boats have become a greater threat to Britain than the High Seas Fleet and all the Zeppelins at Cuxhaven. I don't know what game *you're* in and I don't want to know, but my orders are to put you in the picture about one aspect of the submarine campaign, and this is as good a time and place as any."

It was certainly a good place, with the noise of the train drowning the tone to which Lieutenant-Commander Strawbridge lowered his voice as he moved closer to David on the opposite seat.

"You know already that the German High Command has refused to risk a pitched battle with the Grand Fleet in the North Sea. Admiral Ingenohl shirked it, Admiral Pohl shirked it, and although the new C.-in-C., Scheer, says he's anxious to bring us to battle, he keeps well behind the shelter of the Heligoland Bight. It's the submarine packs that harass us night and day, both in torpedo attacks and as minelayers. We're developing new forms of defence and reprisal against the U-boats, but as yet we're dependent solely on the movement reports my Section spends all its time sifting and estimating. Do you follow me?"

"Certainly."

"You were a fisherman before you joined the Navy, weren't you? Did you ever fish off the northern coast of Norway?"

"It was the Faeroes grounds we fished mostly, but I know the northern waters too. In my old ship, the *Canterbury Bell*—that's when I was a deckie—the skipper fished off the Lofotens."

"Then you know the area. We've had persistent reports, since the early days of the war, of a German submarine base in Norwegian waters; supposedly, in August 1914, located very near the harbour of Bergen. This base is said to have been transferred elsewhere after the Bergen fire last January. So much we've learned from sea reconnaissance, chiefly by the Northern Auxiliary Patrol. And according to our agents on land, the chief organiser of this base—I mean logistically—is a German naval officer who poses as a neutral businessman, and uses the name of Ericssen. Have I said enough?"

"That's up to you."

"Any questions?"

"Has a man Kolberg anything to do with the subs and their bases?"

Strawbridge's eyes sharpened. "What do you know about Kolberg?"

"Captain Hall mentioned his name and said it was high up on the Black List."

"So it is. His freighters have been hauled up half a dozen times under the Orders in Council which apply what's called 'the doctrine of continuous voyage'—carrying goods to neutral ports which will ultimately go to Germany. Oh, there's no doubt of Herr Kolberg's sympathies. He's one of the obliging neutrals who're doing their best to draw the fangs of our blockade of Germany. But we've had no reports connecting him with submarine activities—so far."

"I just wondered."

Strawbridge looked out of the window. "Not long now," he said. "I'm going to turn you over to the medicoes when we get to Harwich. Your shoulder's been giving you hell, hasn't it? I noticed you wincing when you were trying on your new togs at the tailor's."

"I don't know what Surgeon-Commander Black'll say when he gets me back on his hands again."

"Nothing, probably; it takes a lot to surprise those Harwich

127

fellows. Oh, there's just one more thing." Strawbridge lifted his overcoat down from the rack and took out the small parcel he had brought from Hatchards. "Here's some reading matter for you," he said, handing it to David. "Captain Hall's instructions. He wants you to be thoroughly familiar with the story and scenario of a ballet called *Swan Lake*."

The naval surgeon who had examined David Flett's shoulder on Friday morning promptly ordered the young man to bed when he reappeared at Harwich on Saturday night. "Give it a good rest now and you'll be all right," he promised, "but go on as you've been doing and you'll lay up rheumatics and arthritis and all kinds of devilment for yourself later on. Better try eating and sleeping for a bit, and get some flesh back on your bones."

After two days' bed rest the painful shoulder did feel better, which David attributed entirely to his own ministrations with what remained of his bottle of embrocation. Ten hours' sleep on two nights, alone in a clean bedroom with the North Sea air blowing through it, had been good medicine for a man cooped up for so long in the crowded huts of an internment camp. David was now billeted in one of the Harwich hotels, previously used by travellers to and from the Continent. It was now commandeered by the Navy and dignified, as a shore establishment, with the name of one of Nelson's frigates; and from its galley an obliging cook's mate carried to David's bedroom trays of the kind of food he liked best: strong sweet tea, beef stew and potatoes, and the fresh fried fish for which his palate had craved in Groningen. There were still fishing boats going out from East Coast ports south of the Humber, although none from Harwich: Harwich harbour and Harwich Roads were crammed with vessels of war and merchantmen, and the steam packets which were the chief links with neutral Holland came and went punctually on their nightly runs.

The doctor sent up an armful of newspapers, reviews and magazines, and David started catching up on the war news which had reached the naval internment camp so late, or so much censored, as to be rather worse than misleading. He attacked the publications in the same way as he had studied navigation for his Master's ticket, moving his lips and scowling over some unfamiliar words, but learning much more than he had cared to know before. Strawbridge's comments on the Black List and the Orders in Council had been stimulating to a young man who as a boy in the shadow of his sister's compulsive desire to excel had never made enough use of his brain. Now he learned about the war on the land fronts, the British under gas attack in the mud of the Salient, the Russians dying and surrendering under the tremendous German counter-attack at Lake Naroch, General Townshend besieged in Kut, the great name of Garibaldi living again in the Italian capture of the Col di Lana, the generalship of Philippe Pétain in the terrible battle of Verdun. He read with envy of the exploits of the Northern Patrol, that armada of yachts and trawlers; of the minesweepers; of the drifters which helped the Dover Patrol with their net barrage against enemy submarines. He saw that the whole of Europe had become a conflagration, which made his own troubles in H.M.S. *Yelverton*, even his internment, of little importance; and that in this epic condition it should surely be possible for him to deal justly with the problem of Elena Tamirova, *première danseuse* and potential enemy. That was the sensible way to look at it. Only a fool would feel joy, as he now felt, in the mere prospect of seeing her again.

On Tuesday he had breakfast in the mess, and from then on had no lack of company. He met all sorts and conditions of seamen, from the officers of Harwich Force, who under Commodore Tyrwhitt were taking part in continual and aggressive action whenever the cautious enemy dared to make one of his tip and run attacks against the North Sea ports, to the grey-bearded Cornish trawlermen with gold rings in their ears who had come with their grown sons to serve in the auxiliaries of the Dover Patrol. He heard yarns about Tenth Squadron, composed almost entirely of R.N.V.R. men and Newfoundland fishermen, the latter unbeatable at boarding suspected contrabanders in the teeth of the northern gales. He heard rumours of a new force to be called Q-ships, in which merchantmen with camouflaged armour would lure the U-boats to their doom. He took part in arguments about Winston Churchill, who after the disasters of

Gallipoli had ceased to be First Lord of the Admiralty and was now in France in relative obscurity, commanding the 6th Royal Scots Fusiliers. Admiral Jellicoe and Admiral Beatty were both reported to be disillusioned with the former First Lord, who had interfered too much in naval strategy, their own province. Many senior naval officers, brought up in a great tradition of understatement, disapproved of Churchill's intemperate language about the Germans—his "babykillers of Scarborough" speech after the East Coast raid was thought to be in bad taste. At the level of the Harwich transit mess the opinion was that Colonel Churchill was likely to be heard from again.

One of the great changes which had taken place during David's internment was not overtly discussed in the mess or in any publication. It was something he read between the lines for himself, and indeed had first sensed in London when the lone Zeppelin hung above the town. It was this, that whatever war might hold of glamour had passed from the Royal Navy into the the hands of the new air forces, the Royal Naval Air Service and the Royal Flying Corps. The Navy, which had been expected in August 1914 to fight another Trafalgar and end the war by Christmas, had not yet won its decisive victory. There had been a defeat at Coronel, redeemed by a success at the Falklands. There had been the insult of the sea bombardment of England's northeast coast at Scarborough, Whitby and Hartlepool, only partly avenged by the near-victory of the Dogger Bank in January 1915. Since then the High Seas Fleet had stayed behind the protection of Heligoland and Borkum fortress, the Grand Fleet in the northern mists of Scapa and Rosyth, and young men like David Flett who had joined the Navy in expectation of instant glory found that the glory had passed already to still younger men. The flyers had captured the popular imagination. Even the German aces, like Mathy, Breithaupt, "Kaiser" Strasser, were spoken of with some admiration, but the new idols of the British people were John Slessor the Haileybury schoolboy, Brandon the young New Zealander who had forced Breithaupt down, and all the other youngsters who took off in the BE2s down the tar-barrel flarepath from Hainault Farm and Sutton Farm to defend London.

On Wednesday night the entire transit mess turned out to visit a local cinema, requisitioned for a special showing of "Britain Prepares". This was a series of "film pictures" made with Admiral Jellicoe's approval to show daily life in the Royal Navy, and the men at Harwich enjoyed watching the familiar routine of coaling ship and swabbing decks from the comfort of plush tip-up chairs. It was when he returned from this outing, and was about to go into the anteroom for a drink, that David with his room key was handed a sealed envelope which contained a single line of typing:

"You are to meet the London train at Harwich Station at 1105 hours tomorrow Thursday."

He was there at half past ten. The laconic order had triggered off an accumulated restlessness: however much he loathed the job they had set him, he wanted to be getting on with it now. The morning train from London was seldom crowded. David spotted Adrian Combermere immediately, looking as he thought "artistic" in a brown tweed coat and silk muffler: Adrian was carrying a black brief-case stamped with a device in gilt. They shook hands and exchanged greetings.

"I wasn't expecting *you!*" said David.

"They could spare me better than someone in I.D.," said Adrian, "and I was pretty well in the picture already. Been bored, hanging about down here?"

"I was getting a bit fed up. Beginning to wonder if the whole thing was off."

"It's not off; in fact, tonight's the night. Shall we take a walk along the front?"

"We won't get far in any direction without a pass."

But there was a stretch of what had been a promenade before Harwich became an armed camp, with one or two seats still intact, and a little wooden shelter with side windows which offered some privacy for their talk. Overhead three aircraft of the R.N.A.S. went roaring out to bomb German targets in Belgium. The smoke from their exhausts lingered on the grey sky long after the noise of their engines had died away.

Elizabeth was well, Adrian said, in answer to a query. She'd been on a special job this week and he hadn't seen much of her. The "special job" was inside the brief-case he carried, although he didn't tell her brother so; Adrian put on his spectacles before he opened it. The prim gold rims made his thin face look elderly and donnish.

"You're to carry this when you cross to The Hook tonight." he said. "Here's your diplomatic passport. Here are letters to our Naval Attaché at The Hague—he's been recalled to London—just the usual contents of a diplomatic bag. And here's a book we've had prepared, printed and bound since you saw Blinker. It's a fake signal book which we want conveyed to the Germans. We want them to use this code to break signals to be sent from our W/T stations, and we hope this will bring the submarine packs to points where the Navy can deal with them. So the object of the exercise is to give Mr. Karl Ritter access to this book, either to copy the code or photograph the pages."

"Can that be done—photographing, I mean?"

Adrian recalled that the precious *Magdeburg* signal book, damaged by sea water, had been photographed at home by Russell Clarke, one of the best men in Room 40. He said, "Oh yes, it can be done. We got the whole thing on to twelve pages, with photography in mind."

"Well, that's all very fine, but what exactly have I got to *do*?"

Adrian told him.

"But good God, man, it's just not possible! I couldna act a part like that to save my life."

"You're not expected to be acting, just to be yourself."

"She'll see through me in five minutes."

"She'll be absorbed in herself and her own performance, if I know anything about dancers. How did you get on with *Swan Lake*?"

"Oh, man," said David, "that's the worst thing about the whole bloody business. How can anybody take that rubbish seriously?"

"You thought it was rubbish, did you?"

"Well, for pity's sake! There's this Prince Siegfried, looking for a wife, and he takes up with Odette, but she's a swan, and there's Von Somebody but he's an owl, and his daughter, that's Odile—Odette and Odile, I had to read the damned thing twice before I got their names sorted out—and they're all bewitched or enchanted or something . . . I don't know why folk pay money to see a thing like that!"

"Even so, you'd better take another look at the scenario. Blinker thinks that *if* Ritter goes after the code book, it'll be while you're at the ballet."

"Yes, you told me, I understand that. But he'll only know about it if *she* tells him, and what if she doesn't tell him?"

"Do you think there's any doubt of that?"

"I don't know."

"In any case your orders are absolutely final. One: you're not to get into any sort of fight with Ritter."

"What if he tackles me?"

"Keep away from him—that's important. But in case of trouble remember you won't be entirely on your own. There will be two of our men in the neighbourhood of the theatre, playing a barrel organ—they'll keep an eye on you. And the second order is that you *must* return to England on Sunday night. We've had to get Foreign Office approval for this stunt, and they won't stand for our Ministry at The Hague being disrupted for longer than three days."

"You said 'we' an awful lot this morning, Combermere. Who's 'we', exactly? Would you be in the Secret Service by any chance?"

"Good Lord, my dear fellow, whatever put that in your head? I work in the same Section as your sister, you know that; but sometimes I run errands for the D.I.D.; this happens to be one of them."

"What was your job before the war?"

"I taught French and German to junior boys at Eton."

"Will you go back to that again?"

"Yes, I think so. I'd rather like to have a House at Eton, one of these days."

Oh, the very thing, thought David joyfully. Oh, Lizzie, you've got to hook him! A House at Eton, I can't think of anything to suit you better. He turned a smiling face on Adrian, and Adrian thought what an attractive fellow he was after all, now that he'd had a few days of rest and decent food, and didn't think it necessary to scowl.

"Have you any idea what ship I'm to be posted to?"

"I don't suppose even Blinker Hall knows that. You're keen on getting back to sea, aren't you?"

"Of course."

Adrian sighed. "You're a lucky chap, Flett. Off on a big adventure tonight, and then a new ship, and adventure of another sort. You've no idea how I envy you. At least you haven't got what I've got—the finest collection of white feathers in the whole of London."

"I've been envying the chaps out there." He nodded at the turquoise horizon, plumed with the smoke of three torpedo boat destroyers of Harwich Force.

"Yes, that's the way it goes," said Adrian Combermere, rising, "everybody wants to be doing somebody else's job in this bloody awful war."

"Lizzie seems pleased enough with hers," said David.

"Elizabeth's the lucky one," said Adrian.

VIII

Friday, April 21, and
Saturday, April 22, 1916

"Good-afternoon. My name's Flett, I believe you have a room for me?"

The reception clerk of the American Hotel bowed in recognition of a reservation made by the British Ministry, and turned the register towards David. "Yes, most certainly, Mr. Flett. Very welcome! We have a nice room with bath on the second floor—"

"I'd like to be a bit higher up. Say on the third. And I want a room with a telephone."

"Quite so, sir. Not all of our rooms have private telephones as yet, but if you don't mind being on the street side of the hotel, I could give you a very suitable corner room on the third floor."

"That'll do fine." The telephone beside the huge brass bed with the frilled pillowcases and the white crochet spread seemed, when David had locked his door behind the polite clerk and the luggage porter, to bring his mission from the merely fantastic to the real. Once he lifted that Continental handset, so different from the wall fixtures of Britain, he was committed; and he dared not delay too long, for he had arrived four hours late in Amsterdam. There had been a warning from the Admiralty that the Germans intended to lay mines outside Harwich dock gates in the course of Thursday. This of course was a Room 40 intercept, and might have been a false alarm, but the British minesweepers were at work for hours before the harbour-master received permission to let the Dutch packet sail. None of the passengers had had much sleep that night.

David inspected his bedroom, to put off the evil moment. It was extremely comfortable in the Dutch style, with a big rug on

135

the floor and little rugs on the low tables, just as in Mr. Timmermann's livingroom. There was a balcony with white summer furniture, supposing summer ever came to Amsterdam, over which an orange awning was already lowered in case the sun should penetrate the clouds. David stepped out and surveyed the busy street, the canals and a vista of public gardens. He saw the ugly brick mass of the Municipal Theatre on his left, and a glimpse of the busy Leidseplein beyond. For what he had come to do, it was a well-placed room. He turned back, sat down on the edge of the bed, and felt the sweat break out on his face as he picked up the telephone. The quick question in Dutch was only the first of the difficulties he had to overcome.

"Can you put me through to Madame Tamirova, please?"

"I'll connect you with her suite, *mijnheer*."

The line went dead. David looked at his wristwatch. Two o'clock. She might be lunching anywhere. That damned delay at Harwich! Then he heard her speak, he was too excited to know in what language, but the sweet dragging voice was unmistakable.

"Madame Tamirova?" he said stupidly.

"*C'est de la part de qui, monsieur?*"

"Madame—excuse me—this is David Flett. F-l-e-t-t. We met last week at Mr. Timmermann's, remember?"

"But how is this possible? How is it you have come back to Holland?"

"Ah, that's a long story," he said, "I was sent back on a . . . special mission, by my . . . superior officers. They were all very grateful to you for what you did."

"It was nothing," said the charming voice. "It was Vassily, really, who did it all."

"I hope you'll let me express my thanks in person." He plunged. "Will you have dinner with me tonight?"

"Dinner with *you*? Oh, but I'm afraid I have another engagement."

"Surely you can spare a little time for me? I'm free all afternoon—the man I was to have seen at our Ministry has gone back to London—"

"I'm leaving in ten minutes to go to rehearsal."

136

"But it's Good Friday, I thought the theatre was closed."

"We'll rehearse in a practice room, not on the stage . . . Mr. Flett, would you like to have tea with me here later on?"

He felt an immense relief. "That's very kind of you. About what time?"

"Five thirty—five forty-five. About then?"

"Yes, and many thanks." He waited to hear her say good-bye and then hung up. A great fatigue had suddenly possessed him.

The afternoon seemed long in passing. David had been told to show himself with his official brief-case in the hotel, so he carried it down to the big café, where he ordered beer, rye bread and cheese. Sitting over coffee, reading the day-old English papers he had already seen at Harwich, he became aware of a Dutch Army officer eying him speculatively from an adjacent table. Was it possible that the man had seen him at Groningen, where the Dutch Commandant, Colonel Termaat, had often entertained Dutch officers? He paid his bill without hurrying and left the café on the theatre side. A long mirror in the entry assured him that he ran little danger of being recognised as Sub-Lieutenant Flett, R.N.V.R., who had worn the jersey and shabby trousers of the naval internment camp. In his dark clothing and black homburg hat he looked like a young Presbyterian minister in holiday attire.

He walked into the arcade in front of the Municipal Theatre, and gave silent thanks that a ticket for *Swan Lake*, bought and sent to London by the British Ministry, was already reposing in his wallet. In front of the theatre, locked and darkened for Good Friday, "Sold Out" stickers had been pasted over the billboards which announced the Last Performance of the Maryinsky Ballet Company.

Saturday, April 22, 1916.

SWAN LAKE
In Three Acts

Odette/Odile	Tamirova
Prince Siegfried	Surov
Von Rothbart	Lensky

David continued round the theatre. He noted that the narrow Marnixstraat separated the building from the American Hotel, and that a way in to the hotel kitchens lay exactly opposite the side exits of the theatre. Then he returned by the arcade and made the circuit of the Leidseplein. It was garish even at four o'clock on a dull afternoon, with the braziers of the chestnut vendors glowing, and flaring lamps on the stalls where women tall as guardsmen, with gold earrings gleaming beneath lace caps, were beating batter and selling hot *poffertjes*. The bars and cafés were full of girls and sailors, and two men, one to turn the handle and one to collect the money, were operating a huge barrel organ grinding out the dated strains of "Ta-Ra-Ra-Boom-de-Ay!" In a short walk down the Leidsestraat David saw two more street organs. It was impossible to tell if any of their crews were the men he might have to call upon for help.

And how soon he might need help David only realised later, when he was going down the corridor to Elena Tamirova's suite. He had been told Karl Ritter occupied the room next door. Supposing Ritter were with Elena already, sipping tea and waiting to meet the British naval officer so eager to return to Amsterdam. Would he, David, be able to keep his own head and avoid a row? Even without Ritter, would he have self-control enough not to arouse Elena's own suspicions by mentioning the name of Kolberg? He knocked and was admitted. Elena was alone. He laid his brief-case on a chair and let her lead him forward, in her graceful way, to the bay window, where a tea table had been arranged between two sofas without interrupting the view of the olive-green canal. A pair of swans was circling slowly beneath willow boughs just tinged with green.

Tamirova was not quite as he had remembered her. The clothes were different, for one thing. Instead of the golden brown dress and furs which he had vainly tried to describe to Liz, she wore what he believed ladies called a tea-gown, the colour of smoke, and her hair was out of the tight ballet knot and piled in loose coils on her little head. The whole effect was softer, and made Elena appear younger, but she looked tired and far less gay and eager than when they were planning his escape at Mr. Timmermann's. David hardly knew what to say to her. He had never acquired the small talk necessary for "poodle-faking", as it was called in the *Yelverton*'s Gunroom, but Elena made conversation for them both as she served Russian tea and tiny sandwiches. How pleasant it was to see him again and how surprising; how agreeable London must be in the spring; and had he been to see Bronin dancing at the Coliseum?

"I'm afraid I hadn't time. Running up and down between the Admiralty and the Foreign Office," he added on an inspiration.

"He got an excellent notice in *The Times* on Tuesday. Of course he's only appearing in variety in London. Imagine, there are actually performing seals on the same programme!"

David nodded, he hoped sympathetically. From his reading of *Swan Lake*, he judged that a few performing seals would improve that work considerably.

"I know your season here is a great success," he said. "I was quite surprised you had to rehearse this afternoon."

"We work with the ballet-master every morning, and very often we rehearse in the afternoon as well. Every afternoon, since Surov joined us. Surov is never satisfied. He wasn't happy about Act II of *Swan Lake* when we gave it last Saturday night, so we worked on that again today. After all, it's the last performance of the tour. We shall have to do our very best tomorrow night."

"And then you go back to Russia?"

"I myself? I'm not quite sure. The ballet season is almost over in Petrograd, so I may stay with friends in Denmark for a little while."

David remembered Blinker's story of the house in the forest, rented by the German Embassy, and the chilling thought came over him that Elena Tamirova was truly committed to the enemy. He said lamely:

"I'm looking forward to seeing you dance."

"Are you really?" Elena had been looking away from him, down at the two swans circling in the watery sunlight which at last had broken through the clouds. Now her extraordinary hazel eyes, made more brilliant by the black rims round each iris, were turned sceptically to his. "But you didn't come back to Holland just for that, did you?"

"I told you on the telephone," he said. "I had to come back

here on a special mission." He looked quickly at his brief-case on the chair.

"Who are you, David Flett?" said Elena Petrovna. "What sort of a young man is it who is crazy to escape from Holland in one week, and comes back to Amsterdam again the next?"

"Somebody doing a special job, maybe?"

"What kind of a job?"

His laugh, through sheer nervousness, succeeded in sounding foolish. "I shouldn't be telling you this, but I'm a government courier. I came over with despatches for our Naval Attaché at The Hague, but somebody forgot in London that the Ministry would be closing for the Easter break, and so I'll have to hang about over the weekend until my man comes back."

"I see." She accepted his explanation in good faith. It was just the sort of muddle in which all Russian government departments specialised.

"Madame Tamirova—if you can't have dinner with me tonight, would you have supper with me tomorrow, after the ballet?"

"Supper?" Elena looked genuinely surprised. "But we'll be very late. *Swan Lake* is a long performance, and then we have to pack and get out of the theatre."

"We could come back here. It's just across the street, and there's a nice restaurant as well as the café."

"Yes, I know. But really, I can't promise; I'm always exhausted after dancing Odette and Odile."

"It must fairly take it out of you, to dance two parts."

Elena smiled. "Two parts if you like, but only one character. That's how Borelli, my old teacher, taught me how to interpret *Swan Lake*. I dance Odette and Odile as one person—in whom the good and evil strive."

It was after half past six when David Flett went back to his room. Beginning by acting a part, reciting words prepared in advance and memorised, he had ended by feeling as if he could stay for ever in the window bay, listening to Elena's voice and looking from the white swans on the darkening water to her lovely face and eloquent white hands. He left without her promise to see him again, driven away by the thought that Ritter might appear; but once back in his room, where the chambermaid had already turned down the bed as if the day were over and nothing remained to him but sleep, he was devoured by restlessness. The thought of them together became too much to be borne.

He had already studied the layout of the American Hotel. On the ground floor, near the entrance on the canal side, was the luxurious small restaurant he had mentioned to Elena, and David thought that if on this free evening she intended to dine in public this might well be where her "dinner engagement" would take place. He doubted if he could sit through a meal in the same restaurant where she and Karl Ritter were dining tête-à-tête. But from the street level there was also a staircase, leading direct to a mezzanine floor with a little bar and gallery lounge which gave a clear view of the lobby. About half past seven David took the lift to the ground floor and walked upstairs to the bar. It was a cosy place, more like a taproom on the Kalverstraat than the bar of a fashionable hotel, panelled in polished wood, and with the golden drinks of Holland winking on bevelled glass behind the counter: orange curaçao, orange bitters, apricot brandy. The sound of clinking tumblers was deadened by thick tapestry covers on the tables. In this hushed calm David ordered a Bols, and drank it standing, ordered a second and carried it out to the gallery. Nearly all the tables were occupied by men, some of whom glanced at his brief-case with its gilt crest, and then at him, over their cigars. He heard some German, and more Dutch, spoken around him.

About a quarter past eight he saw Elena and a man come out of the lift, and a liveried chauffeur, who had been chatting with the porters, sprang quickly to attention. The man was wearing a black evening overcoat, and his blond head was bare. It was not possible to see him full face, but there was no mistaking Ritter's clean-cut Saxon profile and deeply indented chin. David was looking at the enemy.

Elena was clinging to Karl Ritter's arm. She wore a black velvet dress with a little cape and many jewels. The people in the lobby turned to look at her; there was a whisper of "Tamirova!" and the little murmur of admiration she loved. Even from his place in the gallery David could see that she had eyes for no one but

Ritter: the beautiful calm face which he had seen looking down at the swans was transformed by a sexual infatuation so intense that his own body was shaken by an agony of sexual jealousy. He heard the chauffeur repeat "Amstel Hotel, *jawohl!*" and saw him hold the swinging door open for their departure. David went back to the bar. Another genever, another cigarette. Presently he went down to the flower stand in the lobby, scribbled his name on the card the flower-girl gave him, and told her to take a basket of forced lilies of the valley to Madame Tamirova's suite.

He was having breakfast in his room, still in pyjamas, when the telephone rang.

"This is Elena Tamirova speaking. I want to thank you for the lovely flowers."

"I'm glad you liked them. I noticed you had flowers in your sittingroom."

"Those stiff Dutch tulips! Yours have such a delicious scent . . . Did I wake you up, Mr. Flett?"

"No, not at all, I'm delighted you called—"

"Your voice sounds sleepy." A little laugh, intimate and beguiling.

"*You* sound very wide awake."

"I? I'm on my way to the theatre."

"I hope you've thought again about having supper with me after the show?"

"Yes—I think it could be managed, if you promise not to keep me up too late!"

"I promise. I'll reserve a table in the restaurant here. And—thank you, Elena Petrovna."

The little laugh again. "What is your father's name?"

"Alec."

"Then goodbye, David Alexeivich. Come to my dressingroom about twenty minutes after the curtain falls."

"I will."

Fyodor Surov, the *danseur noble*, had his own views on how to dress for the rôle of Prince Siegfried. Leaving the satins and the

142

glitter for the ballroom scene in Act II, he liked to wear a stage version of hunting costume in Act I, to contrast the robust masculine character of the prince with the spellbound girl who was Odette by night and a white swan by day. In russet-coloured tights and tunic, he had himself made up with a healthy tan greasepaint, against which his Tartar eyes glittered strangely beneath the silvergilt wig he wore as Siegfried.

So arrayed, and with fifteen minutes to go till curtain-up, Surov left his dressingroom, and stopping for a word of encouragement to Lensky, who thought himself miscast as Von Rothbart, he went to call on his partner, Tamirova.

He found her exactly as he had expected: dressed in white as Odette, with Mr. Timmermann's new crown on her head, beautifully made up, and trembling with the nerves which always afflicted her when, as in *Swan Lake* and the *Nutcracker*, her entrance was delayed until the second scene of the first Act. She was holding her St. Helena ikon in both hands when Surov entered, and murmuring what might have been a prayer.

"Fyodor, my dear! Not still worried about the adagio?"

"Not worried about anything at all." It was not true, he was worrying about her, but Surov knew better than to say so at such a time. He took possession of one of her nervous hands and pretended to nibble the fingers, while being careful to keep the wet-white from his painted mouth.

"Elena, we're going to dance better tonight than we've ever danced together before!"

"I wish I didn't feel so tired. You've made us rehearse *so* much—"

"You'll forget all that when you lead out your Swan Maidens and float into my arms."

"Thank God it's *your* arms, Fyodor." It was such unexpected encouragement that he went down on his knees beside her, and pretended, with his broad Tartar hands, to span her tiny waist.

"You didn't say that when you left me all those years ago, Elena Petrovna."

She laughed down at him. "Think how well you've employed

those years, my Fyodor. The most happily married man in the Imperial Ballet!"

"But then Alyssa never had your ambition, darling. She was ready and willing to retire from the stage when we got married."

"*My* ambition!"

"Yes, Elena. And what I came to tell you is that your greatest ambition may soon be realised. And to *beg* you—to travel back with us direct to Petrograd."

"What are you hinting at?" Elena tried to rise, but Surov's strong hands held her fast. He said, "It seems almost certain that you'll be classed as a ballerina when we return to Russia. Kamnov has recommended it, on the strength of your great performances in Amsterdam. And our old maestro, Borelli, has been very active back in Petrograd. Dearest Elena, aren't you pleased?"

She closed her eyes to savour the moment. She murmured, "I thought the great honour was to go to Katia Kirillovna!"

"Never! It was never even thought of—not for one moment, whatever some newspaper hack may have been paid to say. No; you are the Director's choice. I shouldn't wonder if Kamnov told you so himself tonight."

"I'll like hearing it from Kamnov. But it was sweet to hear it first from you."

"Did you hear all I said, *dushenka*? I begged you to travel back to Petrograd with the company. One never knows what may go wrong with these promotions, and I want you to be on the spot to receive yours."

"I rather thought of spending a few days in Denmark first."

"Only a few days, Elena Petrovna? Or—forever?"

"I don't know yet."

"You're very much in love with this man Ericssen, aren't you?"

"Please, Fyodor!"

"I know you were very lonely when Prince Mikhail died. But don't go away with a stranger—not to stay! You have so many friends in Russia—many more than you realise. Alyssa wants you to come to us in the country for a long rest, as soon as the new baby arrives in July; and then we can make our plans for the future. Elena Tamirova, ballerina; some day prima ballerina assoluta, with every theatre in the world opening its doors to her! We'll dance in America together when the war is over—"

The call-boy was heard shouting in the corridor.

"Don't cry, Elena Petrovna. It's all before you still! Don't cry as if the world would end tonight! You'll streak your make-up, silly girl! Now dance your best for me and Russia, and give me your blessing before I go on stage."

She made the sign of the Cross above his head in the old Russian way, and blessed him in a whisper drowned by the call-boy's voice:

"Overture and beginners, please! Overture and beginners!"

The Amsterdam Municipal Theatre was very large. Immediately behind the orchestra were the *fauteuils*, reached by staircases on the right and left, then rows of less expensive stalls and then the back stalls in the *parket*, behind and slightly above which were three rows of loge seats. The circle and two galleries rose above the *parket*. On each side of the stage were two boxes, those on the upper level being very ornate and supported by caryatids. Marble, mahogany, gold leaf and red plush had been used profusely throughout.

David Flett's seat was on the aisle in the second row of the circle. Most of the men around him were in dark suits like his own, and their women in highnecked velvet dresses, or fussy lace blouses and old-fashioned princess skirts, but in the stalls everyone was in evening dress. The last night of the Maryinsky Ballet Company was an important social event. Prince Hendrik and a party of his friends were in the royal box, and courtiers and leading citizens were scattered through the *fauteuils*. Some of them, close observers of the Czar's blundering with Sturmer and Sazanov and the Duma as well as of his terrible losses at the front, had the private conviction that this was the last time for many a day that they would applaud Russian dancers who came direct from Petrograd.

David had hired a pair of opera glasses, and while the house filled to capacity he kept them trained on the stalls. It was some time before he saw Karl Ritter, because he had expected to find

Elena's lover in the centre of the front row, but just before the overture began he saw the blond head at the far end of the third row of *fauteuils*, close to the left-hand staircase. Ritter appeared to be alone. He wore a white camellia in his dress coat, and had no programme.

The concentration of the audience was almost tangible as the conductor took his place on the podium, and the house-lights dimmed. Many of the spectators had seen Tamirova and Surov in every ballet since the Tartar came to Amsterdam, and as many more had seen their first presentation of *Swan Lake* on the previous Saturday night. It was already an item for connoisseurs of ballet to remember, full of grand effects of dramatic power which had almost eclipsed the virtuosity of the dancing. "It was when she put her hands over his eyes," said a young man in the seat behind David, "that I got the most shattering *frisson!*"

It was a Dutchman who was speaking, but he and his friend, who had the musical score of *Swan Lake* lying open on his knee, were showing off their English, peppered with a few French words. "I only wish darling Vassily was here to dance Von Rothbart," said the youth with the score. "I can't *imagine* Lensky in the part." "My dear, it's only Surov's jealousy, he absolutely *insisted* on having Lensky." An older man asked the chatterers to be quiet. In a solemn hush Tschaikovski's overture to *Swan Lake* began.

Almost at once David Flett was overcome by the desire to yawn. He had slept badly for two nights running, and the warmth of the crowded theatre was an encouragement to sleep; but the yawning, which he tried to stifle, was a sign of nervous strain as the dénouement of his mission began to come near. Also he had already made up his mind not to enjoy the ballet for its own sake. The Gothic castle set was heavy and depressing. As they appeared, he found the Princess Mother and the Tutor boring, the miming of drunken gaiety by the corps de ballet artificial, and Prince Siegfried, even when danced by Surov, a posing and ineffective ass. *Swan Lake* fell far short of David's previous high-water mark of entertainment, which was Harry Lauder singing "It's Jist like Bein' at Hame".

The first scene came to an end with Prince Siegfried and Benno leaving the castle to shoot the wild swans. The affected young men behind David fluttered the pages of their score and twittered about the pas de bourrée and the pas de quatre. Ritter was still in his stall, impassive, his arms folded. And then the curtain rose on another scene, quite different from the Gothic castle and the formal park: a desolate landscape and a lake over which a flight of swans was gliding, led by one with a crown on its head. From a ruined chapel, at first almost invisible among the rocks, a soft radiance began to pour as Odette, the Swan Queen in her human form, came forth to lead the Waltz of the Swan Maidens and dance with Siegfried the grand adagio which explains that she can only be freed from the enchanter's spell if she is loved completely and for ever.

What was now created for the audience was a scene of pure beauty. Surov and Tamirova, so perfectly matched, went into their pas de deux in spinning pirouettes and the fantastic elevations in which Surov excelled, while behind them the Swan Maidens, moving in double diagonal lines, imitated the graceful movements in which Odette's white slender arms mimed the beating wings of the royal swan. The apparition of Von Rothbart in the guise of an Owl, to change the maidens back into their swan form at dawn, gave the ritual of the ballet a moment of frightening truth, to which the audience responded by a tribute worthy of the Maryinsky—a rapt and absolute silence after the curtain fell.

The new experience through which he had passed kept David Flett motionless in his seat for several minutes. He only remembered his reason for being there when some of the people around him rose to leave for the interval. He reached for his opera glasses and levelled them on the third row of *fauteuils*. Ritter's seat was empty.

David left the circle hastily. He checked the bars, the cloakrooms, the corridor on the Marnixstraat side of the theatre. He waited until the bell rang for Act II, and satisfied himself that Ritter was not returning late to his place in the *fauteuils*. Then, to the surprise of the attendants in the foyer, he had himself let out to the arcade and turned the corner to the Marnixstraat.

Before he left his hotel room the chambermaid had been on her

147

rounds, and David had had time to make some preparations inside the chest of drawers where his brief-case now lay behind a simple lock, the key to which was in his pocket. He had also drawn the curtains closely. Looking up at his window on the third floor of the American Hotel, he saw that the curtains were still closed, but now at the edges nearest the window frame the faintest thread of bluish light was visible. That was all, but as he shivered in the cutting wind from the North Sea, David was certain that Ritter had taken the bait so ingenuously offered by the foolish young "courier"—the bait passed on by the girl who had just danced Odette as the personification of faith and purity.

He fought one of the hard battles of his life on that street corner, while a barrel organ manned by two tall fellows in clogs and round fur hats ground out "Tipperary", and a vendor of salt herrings shouted his wares from a pitch outside the service doorway of the American Hotel. The desire for violence, instinctive in his nature, was urging him to dash across the street, through the hotel, and attack Ritter with his naked fists. Only the Navy discipline, which he had resisted so sullenly in his first ship, kept him on the damp pavement with his jacket collar turned up and his hands thrust deep into his pockets until he had self-command enough to return to the theatre.

The attendant at the door of the dress circle indignantly refused to let him return to his seat until the second act was over. The ballet was approaching one of its climactic moments. In the gorgeous ballroom of the Princess Mother, Siegfried—believing the enchanter's daughter, Odile, to be his beloved Odette—was dancing his exultation, and Surov in white and silver mimed his wild joy in a brilliant series of grands jetés and a fantastic accelerando. David Flett stood watching by the circle door. He saw Tamirova, in black gauze, execute to gasps of admiration the thirty-two fouettés which Pierina Legnani first made famous, and it seemed to him that the floating black tutu was edged with a blue glimmer of betrayal, like the light which edged his window in the hotel across the street. The moment came for which the connoisseurs were waiting, when the face of the betrayed Odette appears at the ballroom window while Siegfried is pledging his heart to the false Odile. It was a moment dreaded by the dancers as risking an element of bathos in the ballet—another such risk was the possible breakdown of the golden barque in the final scene—and even the ballerinas who had danced Odile sometimes tried to avoid the risk by a too-dainty mime of covering Siegfried's eyes. Tamirova rose to the moment like a tigress. As Odile she literally flung herself upon her Siegfried, muffling his sight with a fierce gesture which only the masculine authority of Surov could match. They danced the triumph of evil while a long shudder of pity and terror—the undeniable *frisson*—ran through the house.

David bought a drink at the interval. Adrian Combermere had told him that the ethereal stars of the ballet sweated copiously while they danced, and he was sweating too as he wondered how to face Elena Tamirova when the show was over. Ritter had not returned to the theatre. He wondered if the German had copied the fake code in the brief-case or photographed it and if, with such a prize in his possession, he would have the nerve to spend another night in Amsterdam. In the third act, Tamirova was dancing Odette again, betrayed and forlorn, and condemned by her evil genius to spend the rest of her existence in the form of a swan. In Surov's arms, raised high on Surov's shoulder, she danced renunciation and forgiveness until her Siegfried, knowing that only his sacrifice would save her, joined her in the dance of death which ended with their plunge into the lake. While the light of paradise streamed up and over the stage, illuminating Elena's tragic beauty and the Tartar's stern profile, the lovers began their voyage to eternity in the barque drawn by a crowned swan.

Then the ovation began, the applause of a frenzy not often heard in the sober Municipal Theatre of Amsterdam, the homage of a ballerina's dreams. Surov led out Tamirova again and again, while the bouquets piled up across the footlights; Lensky brought out Vera, who had danced the Princess Mother. Even the leaders of the corps de ballet received their tribute, and Tamirova graciously led out the ballet-master. Kamnov, bearish in dress clothes, bowed repeatedly, smilingly refused to make a speech, and finally bent his bullet head low over the trembling hand of

Tamirova. It was a triumph, said the sated audience, filing out; a night to remember, unforgettable.

David, when at last he found his way behind the scenes, waited in a wilderness of canvas flats and piled dress baskets for what seemed to him far longer than twenty minutes. He found himself constantly dodging beneath the first spiral of an iron staircase leading to the upper regions as the Dutch scene-shifters and stage cleaners came and went, while still trying to keep his eye on the door of the star's dressingroom. It remained closed. From the large rooms where the boys and girls of the corps de ballet were changing there came shrieks of laughter and triumphant chatter, and once even an outburst of hysterical sobs. Presently, the dancers began to emerge in their street clothes. David failed to recognise Lensky, who had been made up to look thirty years older as Von Rothbart, going off with Vera Polidova to celebrate at a night bar on the Rembrandtsplein, but soon after Lensky left the door of Tamirova's room was opened, and a grey-haired woman put her head out.

"Monsieur! S'il vous plaît, monsieur!"

He followed the dresser thankfully. Inside the overheated room, where flowers were piled on the table and chairs and massed on the floor along one wall, Elena was talking to Surov and the ballet-master. She had been sponged down by Louise, standing in the tub of tepid water hidden by the screen which divided the dressingroom in two, and was belted into a gown of coarse white towelling like a boxer after a successful bout. Her face, wiped clean of all the paint and mascara, was glistening with cold cream. Surov was still in his costume as Prince Siegfried, but he was wrapped in a flannel dressing-gown and had a towel tied closely round his neck. Runnels of sweat, starting beneath his wig, gleamed darkly on his pale make-up for the last act.

"Mr. Flett, I'm so sorry to have kept you waiting!" Elena said remorsefully. "May I introduce you to Monsieur Kamnov . . . and to my princely partner, Fyodor Surov?"

Kamnov, who knew little English, gave an awkward nod. Surov at once shook hands. David turned to Elena and said:

"You were sublime."

Sublime—he didn't know where he'd picked up such a word: perhaps in church. It was the right word, though, for Surov laughed and hit him a friendly blow between the shoulders. "Well spoken, sir! Very good! Sublime Elena Petrovna, we shall drink to you!"

"Fetch a glass for Mr. Flett," she told the dresser.

He now saw an open bottle of champagne before the mirror, and when he was given his full glass and the others refilled their theirs he waited for Surov to give the toast. But the *danseur noble* lifted his glass to "The future!" and to the future Elena with a grave face drank.

"Now we leave you," Kamnov said. "Fyodor, no chills, please!"

"I'm coming, Lev Yurievich." Surov stopped at the door and said something in Russian which made Elena smile and nod. "Good-bye, Mr. Flett!" he added, and the door shut. Elena lifted her arms to the ceiling and stretched her whole body like a cat.

"Tired?" said David.

"Tired, but oh! so happy!"

"You've had the triumph of a lifetime, haven't you?"

"Yes, I think I have." She seized him by the hands. "David Flett, I think you brought me luck. I'm so *glad* that you came back to Amsterdam!"

He saw that she truly meant it, that any awareness of having betrayed him to her German lover had passed from Elena Tamirova's mind. She was inside her own glass bubble, the dancer's paradise, enchanted by the spell of her own success.

"It's late," he said. "Get your dress on, you're exhausted."

"Not really. Louise!" The woman went with her behind the screen. There was a rustle of taffeta, and Elena called: "Do have some champagne. Open the other bottle!"

"No, thanks, we'll have some more at supper. I say! What happens to all the flowers?"

"They'll be taken to the hospitals tomorrow. But not yours, of course—"

She came out smiling, in the black velvet dress she had worn to dine at the Amstel Hotel, but without her fake diamonds, and wearing a spray of David's lilies of the valley. It might have been guile, it might only have been her instinctive desire to charm; he realised that he would never know. Elena touched her lips with geranium salve before the mirror and took up her powder-puff.

"Elena Petrovna, will you tell me something?"

"If I can."

"What did Surov say to you just now, before he left?"

"Oh! That! He asked me to promise again to go straight home to Russia."

"And will you?"

"Yes. Yes, I think so. I've had a wonderful experience tonight, David Alexeivich. A—sort of new beginning. The promise of much better things to come."

"I'm very glad."

"Now we must really go. Louise is waiting to pack up. Oh! My ikons! They always come with me." She unhooked two little pictures from the wall and picked up her gloves and velvet bag. "Good-night, Louise!" The corridor was deserted. "I always leave by the side exit," Elena explained. "We can go out through the theatre."

The stage was now in darkness. Men in overalls were pulling canvas covers over the seats, taking them methodically from a pile in the corridor beside the door, while another team swept up programmes, silver foil and chocolate papers from the red carpet. "Lady forgot her fan!" a hoarse voice said from underneath a seat. "Forget their own heads next, I shouldn't wonder!"

The side exit door was still unbarred. The keen night air blew into their faces, and Elena pulled her cape tight at the neck. David looked about him quickly: there was no sign of Ritter on the Marnixstraat. The barrel organ was still playing, the herring merchant closing up his cart. One or two motor cars went by.

He cupped her elbow with his hand. "We can cross now." He looked down at the beautiful faithless face. There was a sharp scorching breath on his cheek, the delayed sound of one crack, and then another, and Elena Petrovna fell against him with a choking cry.

"Elena! Dear! What is it?" But he knew what it was: the blood was welling from her throat, and the man turning the barrel organ had flung himself across the street at the fellow behind the herring cart. That much David saw as he lifted Elena up into his arms and carried her back into the theatre.

"Surov! Surov!" It was the only name he could think of to shout as he laid her down on the pile of canvas covers, and undid her cape, and stared in horror at the blood pouring over her breast. But it was Kamnov who came, quicker than the stunned theatre cleaners, quicker even than a man in a fur cap and clogs who ran in from the street: Kamnov, whom she had never liked, who knelt down by her side. It was Kamnov who held her hand, and spoke to her in their own language, when Elena Petrovna's head dropped low on David's shoulder, and she died.

IX

Monday, April 24, 1916

The city of Wilhelmshaven, having the second most important war harbour in Germany after Kiel, was always busy, day and night, in the month of April 1916. Lying on the north-west shore of Jade Bay, an anchorage even bigger than the British base at Scapa Flow, it was connected with the North Sea by the Jade Canal, from which locks led to the New Harbour and shipyards. The Imperial Dockyards, of which Karl Ritter's father had once been Engineer Rear-Admiral Commanding, were working three eight-hour shifts a day on refitting and repairs and munitions factories had been opened on both banks of the Jade. In spite of this activity, and the migration to little Wilhelmshaven of labourers from all over Germany, it remained a pleasant town, with wide tree-shaded streets and green spaces. In the late evening when the streets farthest away from the town centre were deserted the air was as fresh as in a seaside village.

This, at least, was an article of faith with Karl Ritter's mother, an Englishwoman who had managed to create something like a garden in every naval base where her husband had seen service. At Wilhelmshaven, the base of his last command, they had set up house in an apartment building, chosen by Frau Ritter for the fine lime tree in the middle of the cobbled courtyard and the possibility of digging flowerbeds against the walls. In twenty years, overcoming the prejudices of her neighbours, she had made a very pretty place of it; nearly all the apartments had window boxes now, and clematis and ivy had covered the courtyard walls. On the Monday night when Karl Ritter returned to Wilhelms-haven he was met inside the entrance gate by the scent of narcissus and the sight of the lime tree with its new green leaves like a flock of tropical birds, floodlighted by the old gas lamp with three jets which stood in a corner of the yard.

It was late. So late that most of the windows in the building were in darkness, but the porter's lodge was lighted, and both Herr and Frau Schmidt looked out to see who was coming in after ten o'clock at night. They were ready to offer their servile compliments to the Herr Korvetten-Kapitän, and to tell him unasked that the Frau Konteradmiral was at home. Quite well, poor dear lady, but so very lonely! Ritter nodded curtly as he went upstairs. There was no lift, but the stairs and halls were spacious and there was only one apartment on each floor. His father's name and rank on a brass plate, worn with polishing and almost unreadable, confronted him on an oak door on the second landing. He rang the bell with his old schoolboy ring and heard light footsteps hurrying to the door. His mother, small and grey-haired, blushed like a happy girl as she let him in.

"Charlie, darling!" As usual when she was excited Muriel Ritter spoke in English, and her son silenced her with a quick kiss.

"How are you, mother? You look very well," he said in German, as he followed her into the long narrow hall. It exuded a familiar smell of vegetable stock and furniture polish and the worn plush of the portières which hung over all the doors. Near the entrance stood an immense mahogany hall-stand, on which Ritter laid his gold-braided hat, the boat-cloak which was part of his full dress uniform, and finally his sword-belt and sword.

"Darling, how grand you are!" his mother exulted. "Did any of the neighbours happen to be about when you came in?"

"None of the neighbours, only our inquisitive porter, and Frau Schmidt."

"She'll tell the others," said Frau Ritter hopefully. "I just wish they could all see you now! Have you been at the Marineamt?"

"At the Admiralstab. I had an interview with Admiral von Holtzendorff this afternoon."

"And have you been posted?"

"Yes, and promoted. Are you pleased?"

"Kommandant Karl Ritter! How proud poor Papa would have been! Come into the parlour, dear, and let me look at you."

The parlour was exactly as he remembered it from his Christmas

155

leave—from further and further back, to the time when he came home from his school year in Milwaukee; it was surely a sick fancy to think that two nights ago when shots were fired in the Marnixstraat everything in this familiar parlour must have changed. An oilpainting of his father in naval uniform hung above the draped overmantel, along which his own silver cups for athletics stood in a polished row. Beside his mother's easy chair stood a revolving bookcase with her sewing-box and a bright tangle of silks on top of it, and her English novels on the shelves —Wells, Bennett, Galsworthy; the sets of Goethe and Schiller were behind glass doors in the bookcase. Watercolours of the Isle of Wight and of Norwegian hills and meadows hung on the crimson-papered walls. It was all unchanged and changeless; surely here for a short time he could find rest.

"But you look so tired, Karl!"

"I've done a lot of travelling just lately. The trains are terribly crowded nowadays."

"You haven't been to sea?"

"No."

"Well, you must have something to eat and drink before you tell me everything that you've been doing."

"I've had supper, mother. But I'm very thirsty."

"Do come with me, my dear, and see what we can find to tempt you."

Karl Ritter followed to the kitchen rather unwillingly. It was a big, dismal place with a coke range and a mousetrap set ready in one corner, and the cupboard, when Muriel Ritter opened the door, was bare indeed. A piece of cold pork and a bowl of apple sauce in the meat safe, a pat of butter, two eggs, a small cream cheese and half a loaf of rye bread seemed to be all the food available. "If I spread cream cheese on buttered bread, Charlie, would you enjoy that? With a bottle of your father's wine?"

"Really, I'm not hungry, mother . . . Is this all you have to eat in the house?"

"If I'd known you were coming, I could have got a chicken. But the British blockade is terribly efficient, of course . . ." It was said with a spice of malice, and Muriel Ritter, not waiting for Karl's comment, went off to the stone-floored larder where the wine was kept and came back with a bottle of Steinberger Kabinett.

"Only the best for you tonight! Will it be cool enough?"

"Sure to be. It's not exactly warm, even in here." Karl stood in the chilly kitchen waiting, like any German male in a woman's province, for her to hand him the corkscrew, wipe the best glasses, set them on a silver tray. She watched him draw the cork expertly. "If you're thinking about breakfast, Karl, I know a shop where one can generally get bacon. I'll run round first thing in the morning."

"I don't like you running out to the shops yourself. Let What's-her-name go—young Anna-Luise. Where is she tonight, by the way?"

"She left at the beginning of March to work in one of the munitions factories. That's where all the servant girls are going nowadays."

"But then who does the housework?"

"Frau Schmidt does the rough twice a week, and I can manage the rest quite well by myself."

"I don't like to think of you here all alone."

Muriel Ritter made no reply. She picked up the tray and they went back to the livingroom, where the flowers in her window boxes nodded against the broad panes which would be opened wide, in June, to let the scent of lime blossom fill the room. The wine was poured and she drank to his promotion, watching while Karl Ritter drained two glasses as if Steinberger Kabinett, the noblest wine of the Rheingau, were tap water. Now that he was sitting at ease, but still with his shoulders braced in the dark blue uniform of his Service, she saw that her son was not so much tired as worn and driven to the knife-point of fatigue. I'm sixty-five, so he must be thirty-three, she thought. He looks fifty tonight, with those terrible lines between his nose and the corners of his mouth. As if he hadn't slept for days.

"How long leave did they give you, Karl?"

"Only twenty-four hours, I'm afraid."

"Oh dear! And then you join your new ship, do you?"

"Eventually. She's in dry dock, at Kiel."

"The *Lützow*? I know you were hoping for the *Lützow*."

"It's the *Pommern*, Captain Bölken. One of the Deutschland class. In Admiral Mauve's Division of the Second Squadron."

"But Karl, the Deutschlands? Didn't they have a nickname —I remember Papa telling me—didn't they use to be called 'the five-minute ships'?"

"They're pre-Dreadnoughts, mother. Not the fastest ships afloat, but a long way from being obsolete."

"Five-minute ships, because they won't last much longer under fire—oh, Karl!"

"Listen, mother. I know my father used to discuss a great many Navy matters with you, so you should be able to understand. I can't expect my own career to go quite as planned, since Admiral von Tirpitz left the Ministry of Marine last month."

"He was a very good friend to you, I know. But if you had an interview with Admiral von Holtzendorff today—"

"Holtzendorff is only the Naval Secretary, not the Minister. And the new Minister, von Capelle, is a nonentity. He's just as eager as von Holtzendorff to play the American game."

"What do you mean by that?"

"I mean that since Chancellor von Bethmann-Hollweg and the politicians got rid of Tirpitz, there's no one left at the Marinamt with the authority to insist on the total, all-out, maximum use of naval power, including submarine power. Take this silly affair of the Channel steamer *Sussex*. President Wilson threatened to break off diplomatic relations with Germany simply because two or three American citizens happened to be aboard when she was torpedoed. And now this great Holtzendorff, who said last January that our submarines would break the British inside six months, gave orders this very morning to stop the U-boat campaign against merchant and passenger ships until further notice. If that's not playing the American game, what is?"

"Aunt Evelyn writes from Milwaukee that she expects President Wilson to declare war on Germany any day now."

"Aunt Evelyn had better stick to the Ladies' Garden Club, that's all she knows anything about."

Sharply: "She's not as limited as all that, Karl. And *I've*
expected action by America, ever since the *Lusitania* was sunk last
year."

"The *Lusitania* was carrying arms for the Allies, and the German
Embassy gave her passengers printed warning not to sail."

Karl Ritter had poured his third glass of Rhine wine, and this
he was drinking slowly, admiring the golden liquid and turning
the green-stemmed glass approvingly in his hand. Something in
his calm superiority annoyed his mother beyond discretion.

"You're so very well-informed, darling boy; do tell me what they
say in the Köningin Augustastrasse about Sir Roger Casement?"

"What do *you* know about Sir Roger Casement?"

"Oh, we hear a lot of things in Wilhelmshaven! Herr Blum
brought the story back from the Dockyard at noon today, and
Frau Blum came downstairs to tell me about it, after he went
back to work."

"You know I don't like you to be intimate with Jews."

"How ridiculous, Karl, the Blums have been our good neighbours for the past ten years. But about Casement—it is true, isn't
it, that he was trying to subvert Irish prisoners of war into
fighting on the side of Germany?"

"He was trying to form an Irish Brigade, auxiliary to the
German Army."

"With any success?"

"Not much."

"Naturally the crack Irish regiments would remain loyal to the
Crown."

"Whatever the men in the P.O.W. camps thought, Casement
has a great Irish following. He volunteered to lead a rising which
would detain British troops in Ireland and relieve the pressure on
the Western front. So he was landed near Tralee, on the west
coast, last Thursday . . ."

"From a German submarine, of course?"

". . . and captured almost immediately by the English police.
So now he's in jail, and his excitable friends in Dublin started
the rebellion prematurely. There's been fighting in the city since
Good Friday."

159

"But is it true that a German ship was carrying arms to the Irish rebels—under the Norwegian colours?"

"The *Aud*? Herr Blum is very well informed! Her Captain ordered her blown up after he was challenged by a British warship near Queenstown."

"Well, well!" said Muriel Ritter with a smile. "I wish the All-Highest joy of his Irish allies. They've made a wonderful beginning."

Two spots of pink had appeared in her thin cheeks beneath the flyaway grey hair. Her son reminded himself, with an effort, that she was an old woman as well as a foolish one. He changed the subject.

"How are you getting on with your welfare work, mother? The Naval Ladies' Circle and the Fleet Comforts Fund?"

"I haven't been at any meetings since the New Year."

"But you used to work for them both so faithfully."

"I tried to, Karl, if only for your dear Papa's sake. But it's no use: the other ladies don't think of me as Admiral Ritter's widow any more. Since the British blockade began they ostracise me at the meetings, and some of them even cut me in the street. I'm *die Engländerin* now to all of them—their country's enemy."

"What rubbish! You've been a German citizen for more than thirty years."

"But people don't change, Karl. I've always been English in my heart."

"You're a great anxiety to me," he said.

"Is an English mother such a handicap to a brilliant naval officer's career?"

"Not to *my* career, I assure you. I mean I shall be more anxious about you than ever now, living in this huge flat alone without a maid, and cut off from all your women friends."

"I don't think you worry about me overmuch, Karl. Since your tour of the dockyards started two months ago, I've only had one letter from you—a scribble from Lübeck in the last week of March . . . Oh, that doesn't matter, I'm sure you were very busy in the service of your Fatherland. I don't complain. I've so many happy times to remember—all the good years when your father was alive; and I know this curse that has fallen upon Germany was not the work of men like him. But now I think the time has come for me to leave Wilhelmshaven for good and all."

"But your home is here!"

"Not any more, Karl. This place means nothing to you, I know. When you marry, your bride will want something more up-to-date—"

"I have no plans to marry," he said stiffly. "Mother, where would you go? You never liked Berlin."

"I want to go *away from Germany*," she said.

"Not back to England?"

"As you just reminded me," said Muriel Ritter, "I'm a German citizen. I doubt if the British would admit me while the war goes on. And there's something more: I long to see your Uncle Richard again, and I think he would welcome me. But one of his sons was killed at Gallipoli and the other at Neuve Chapelle. Don't you think their mother might refuse to see me? Or if she, if poor Aunt Betty were generous, how would her friends in Shanklin feel about meeting me? I'm *die Engländerin* here, I'd be the German woman there; I'm nobody . . . I'd like to go to Switzerland, Karl. To one of those little towns along the Lake of Zürich, where I could live quite cheaply and trouble nobody . . . least of all yourself."

"I doubt if you'd be issued with a passport," the man said.

"Why not?"

"For the very reason you've just given—your British birth."

"But Karl, surely you could arrange it for me. You've got such powerful friends at the Marinamt! My application would be approved without question, with backing from that quarter . . ."

"Impossible," he repeated. "I can't possibly approve of such a crazy scheme . . . Come, mother, don't start crying, you know I hate hysteria. I'll go to the bank tomorrow and arrange for you to draw an increased allowance from my pay, so that you can be more comfortable here at home. And then we must both make the best of a bad job, that's all."

"I don't want your money, darling—" Her tears could not be held back now.

161

"If you'll excuse me, mother, I think I'll go to bed. I've had all the scenes that I can stand."

Muriel Ritter slept indifferently, and woke when dawn was flooding her bedroom with a milky light. For some time she lay relaxed beneath the covers, enjoying the slim, light feel of her body, as girlish at twenty-eight as it had been at eighteen, and thinking what she would wear that afternoon when Engineer Captain Ritter came to take her walking in the park. Her pale pink muslin dress with the draped bustle, and the parasol—Hans loved her to wear pink, and said she was his English rose . . . Germans were so sentimental! But how she loved that sentiment, that protective love, after seven years as a governess, out on her own in the great world! Hans thought they could be married soon. He had nothing but his pay; they had waited long enough already, but he wanted to assure her of a good home when he was away at sea. Everybody said he would end up as an Admiral. Dear Germany! How good it had been to her, how much better it would be when the dear Crown Prince Frederick and his English wife, Queen Victoria's own daughter, were on the throne. Hansi, beloved bridegroom! Muriel opened her eyes on his photograph, which she always kept on her bedside table. What a brown, merry face he had! She stretched out her hand to bring the picture closer. Then she saw that not the face alone, but the figure in the old-fashioned uniform was brown, that the pasteboard behind the glass was brown with age, and that her own hand was liver-spotted and tremulous, the hand of an old woman.

Muriel Ritter's head dropped back on the pillow, and she remembered everything. Dear jolly Hans was dead, and the good Emperor Frederick and his wife had passed like shadows from the stage where their son the Kaiser now revelled in the limelight . . . and he had brought their simple pleasant world to war and ruin . . . and Karl had come home on leave, and was angry with her . . .

It was my fault, she thought remorsefully. I ought never to have argued with him about the *Lusitania*, and Casement, or told him I wanted to leave Germany, when he was so very tired.

Only he irritated me, looking so like my brother Dick dressed up in a German uniform, and explaining everything as if I were senile, or a child. He isn't happy about the *Pommern*, how could he be, he wanted to be under von Hipper in the flagship. I'll make it up to him today, she promised herself, getting out of bed. I'll be ready to go out with him if he should ask me, and I'll get Frau Schmidt to give me an extra morning, and do all the housework. Then I can tell her that Karl is now Commander Ritter.

The waking dream of youth and felicity made it all the harder to see her real self in the pier-glass, that bony figure, shrunken in the white cotton nightdress, with the grey hair done in two thin little plaits. Muriel Ritter hurried through her dressing. A long black skirt, a white blouse with a lace neckband held in place by tiny gold-tipped bones—she wouldn't give up that fashion, which hid a scraggy old neck so well! Grey hair brushed up into a pompadour. Now she was at least presentable—and it was still barely seven o'clock.

The shop where she intended to buy bacon would not be open for another hour. As she ground coffee in the kitchen, flitted into the diningroom to set the table, Frau Ritter counted over other treasures—a pot of greengage jam in the store cupboard, real cane sugar—to bring out for her boy. Would the greengrocer have any oranges? Karl liked a good American breakfast—always had, since his year in Milwaukee, and President Wilson's Notes had made no difference to *that*! He would be angry if he found her cleaning his shoes.

His uniform, though—that deserved a bit of valeting. Karl's boat-cloak on the hall table was white with the dust of the Wilhelmshaven streets. She took it to the kitchen for a good brushing. Would she wake him if she brought his other garments from the bedroom? She tiptoed in.

Karl had hung his uniform tidily over two chairs. Contrary to his usual neat habits, the rest of his clothing had been flung down anywhere—shirt, undergarments, socks in a heap on the floor; collar and tie, cufflinks, gold watch and chain, loose change, notebook and fountain pen all tangled on the dressingtable. The

163

fresh white linen cover, with her own drawn-thread work, was rumpled under a framed photograph of the Kaiser. It was one which Wilhelm II had autographed and presented to Karl's father at the time of the admiral's retirement. The spiked helmet, the spiked moustache and the neurotic glare seemed to brood over the younger Ritter's bedroom. Karl was sleeping heavily. The blond stubble beginning to appear had blurred his close resemblance to his English uncle: it was a Teuton who lay with one cheek crushed into the pillow and his lips swollen with sleep. His mother left the room as quietly as she came.

She brushed his coat and trousers as carefully as she had brushed the cloak. One of the waistcoat buttons was hanging by a thread. She carried it into the parlour where her sewing-box lay with her embroidery work, and opened the window on the bright April morning. Now the sounds of the docks and factories, beginning their day shifts, invaded the quiet courtyard of the lime tree and the lamp.

The navy-blue waistcoat was unexpectedly heavy in her lap. She ran her fingers round the lining and felt something hard and square. One of the pockets must be torn, she thought; he really ought to have an orderly. Perhaps as a Commander? Would a pre-Dreadnought, a "five-minute ship", carry sailor-servants? The place where the lining joined the serge had been roughly sewn with large black stitches. Muriel ripped them apart with one stroke of her scissors. Two documents bound in limp leather slid out into her hands.

One was a *Kaiserpass*. Frau Ritter had never seen one before, but she knew what it was, a kind of super-passport issued only to Germans on special government missions, and calling on all German embassies and legations abroad to help the bearer. Inside there was an envelope with the Admiralty crest, rubber-stamped with the previous day's date and addressed to the German envoy at Christiania.

The second appeared to be an American passport, the first four pages covered with visas, containing a photograph of her son and made out in the name of Karl Ericssen.

She laid them on the table beside the tray with the unfinished wine and glasses, and was sitting looking at them, with her arms crossed over her shrunk breast for warmth, when Karl Ritter came into the room.

"Good-morning, mother!" He was wearing an old tweed suit with a blue shirt, no collar or tie, and looked as if he had flung his clothes on, like a country lad going out to work in the fields. "You ran off with my uniform," he said good-humouredly, and then, coming up to kiss his mother, he saw his waistcoat on her lap and the passports on the table.

"You've been spying on me!" he burst out furiously, and she, as furious as he was, bade him not use that word to her, not spying—spying— . . . Ritter snatched up the documents and thrust them inside his shirt. "I should have locked my uniform inside the wardrobe," he said thickly. "I was fool enough to think my father's house was safe."

"You dare to bring your father into this! He would throw you out of his house without pity, if he knew you'd lowered yourself to be a common spy!"

Ritter told her she was raving, a crazy old woman, crazy *Engländerin*; it was the same hard bullying tone as he had used to Elena Tamirova when he dared her to denounce him to the British envoy in Christiania. But generations of Englishmen stood behind Muriel Ritter; she held her ground, and raged at him that he was worse than vile, had betrayed the honour of his Service, had made himself liable to be shot if he were captured out of uniform—

"Not in the neutral countries, mother. In Russia, yes."

"You've been in *Russia*?" she said, halted in spite of herself.

"I spent two weeks in Russia last month. There was no danger; those people are very easy to fool."

"Before you wrote to me from Lübeck?"

"I turned in my report at Lübeck on my way to Copenhagen."

"You were posing in Russia as an American?"

"That wasn't difficult, thanks to Aunt Evelyn and Milwaukee."

"And those Norwegian visas in the passport—you used our holidays in Norway to help you there?"

"Particularly in my dealings with my father's dear old friend, Hans Kolberg."

"He's in it, too? He would be, of course. Oh, my God, is there no end to the vileness? Karl, how could you do it? How could you use all our old happy times—all Aunt Evelyn's kindness —for some foul underhand espionage?"

Karl Ritter grew pale. "If you were a German woman," he said, "a true German mother, you would be proud of the special work that I've been given to do. I don't consider it either foul or underhand. I've been carrying out the orders of my superior officers, who found me well-equipped to perform certain duties, and that's all. You know what it means to be under orders. Surely my father taught you that."

"I learned duty and obedience in my own country, Karl. But you—you're going to continue with this 'special work'? The *Kaiserpass* and this letter mean you're going back to Norway? It was all a lie about your posting to the *Pommern*?"

"No, that was true enough. I told you I was joining the ship eventually. But yesterday I was ordered to go on another mission to Norway, before I go to sea again."

"And that'll be the end of it?"

Ritter walked restlessly to the window, and spoke with his back to his mother. "I wanted it to end—now—and be done with it forever. God knows I brought them a prize from Holland worth an army division! I had a success that may give us victory by Christmas; but they only made that a reason for ordering me to carry on."

His mother, who had been riveted in her chair, got up and took him by the arm.

"*Why* did you want to finish with it, Karl?"

"Because a girl I had grown to care for very deeply was shot dead in Amsterdam three days ago."

"Shot as a *spy*?"

"No, murdered. But murdered by my fault—"

"You shot her? You were there?"

"I was nowhere near her," Karl said roughly. "The last time I saw her she was on the stage, brilliant and beautiful—"

"An actress?"

"A dancer. A famous Russian dancer." And at his mother's

look he burst out with the old childish name: "*Mutti*, little *Mutti*, when you spoke last night of my future bride you had no idea . . . how you cut my heart. For Elena loved me, even though I used her in my work and frightened her, and I would so willingly have married her—she was the most wonderful mistress any man could have—"

Sixty-five years of Victorian prudery, of a governess's morality, of the unswerving standards of a German Lutheran household, stiffened Muriel Ritter's spine and made her draw back in horror from her son.

"You mean you were living together as man and wife?"

"I meant I was her lover, that she gave me three weeks in paradise. Does that shock you, mother? Don't turn away from me!"

"Turn away from you? I never want to speak to you again! A spy and a libertine—my only child! Go away, Karl. I can't even look at you any more. And don't send me more money, or any money, ever again. A spy's pay is tainted and hateful—like yourself."

X

Monday, April 24, to
Wednesday, April 26, 1916

When Karl Ritter presented the Imperial Naval Staff with twelve pages of carefully copied code, the contents of the "new" British naval signal book, Admiral von Holtzendorff did not think it necessary to inform him about all the aspects of the rising in Ireland. But the steamer *Aud*, carrying war material to the Irish rebels under the Norwegian flag, was not the only German vessel supporting the Easter Rising. The entire High Seas Fleet, under Admiral Scheer, was preparing on that Monday morning, April 24, to put to sea and attack the East Coast of England.

Scheer, the Commander-in-Chief since January, had been only a little more daring than his predecessors in his sorties into the North Sea. A destroyer sweep off the Dogger Bank in February had been followed by an expedition in the latitude of Lowestoft in early March, neither of which had been rewarding to the Germans, but had yielded some useful information to Room 40. The British cryptographers noted that when the new German C.-in-C. put to sea, he transferred the flagship's wireless call sign, DK, to the W/T station at Wilhelmshaven, and took another call sign as long as the fleet was at sea. When this change of sign was picked up by the British D/F stations it was reasonable to conclude, on the evidence of February and March, that the High Seas Fleet was about to sail against England. Such a change had appeared in the intercepts during the forenoon of the twenty-fourth, and had been duly conveyed by Room 40 to Intelligence and Ops. Before very long another set of intercepts revealed that ten Zeppelins were operational "with only H.V.B. on board". There was the usual caution until their destination was revealed, but no one doubted that the air arm would support the naval attack by bombing London. Meanwhile, the Irish rebels had barricaded themselves inside the Law Courts, besieged by English troops, and blood was flowing in the streets of Dublin.

Captain Hall, the Director of Intelligence, spent an anxious morning. Sir Alfred Ewing visited him more than once, for both men were increasingly worried about the use being made of the intercepts by Operations, and particularly by the Ops Director, Captain Thomas Jackson, R.N., who had the great responsibility of keeping the Chief of the War Staff, Admiral Sir Henry Oliver, advised of German movements. Further up the vital chain of command the Admiralty Board passed on its orders to the British Commander-in-Chief. As the forenoon hours went by Hall became increasingly anxious to know if Admiral Jellicoe, at Scapa Flow, and through him Admiral Beatty at Rosyth, had received orders to put to sea. When the High Seas Fleet left the Jade at noon, no British counter-move had yet been ordered.

It was nearly half past twelve before "Blinker" remembered that Lieutenant David Flett, R.N.V.R., involved in a minor incident in Amsterdam on Saturday night, had reported at the Admiralty nearly two hours before, and was waiting in an anteroom.

"Can you spare a few minutes more, Ewing? I'd like you to hear whatever Flett has to say."

"I'd like to hear it too."

David was sent for. His manner to his superior officer was as correct as at their first encounter ten days earlier; physically he appeared to be in even worse shape than when he arrived from the internment camp. Sir Alfred, always sympathetic to young people, noted how the young Scotsman's dark eyes burned in his pale face.

"Well, Mr. Flett, your mission to Amsterdam had an unexpected conclusion," Blinker began.

"Yes, sir."

"Do you believe that it accomplished its object?"

"Sir?"

"Have you reason to think that Ritter had access to the signal book, and time to copy it?"

169

"I thought so, sir; and the two British agents thought so too."

"Give me your reasons, please."

"There was the look of my room from the street while the—the ballet was going on. Then when they came back with me from the police station Lester and Amory said the lock of the drawer where I put the brief-case had been picked, though I couldn't have told that myself. Forbye, there were all the wee things I was told to do, like putting a hair inside the pages: we went through the list, and it seemed as if the book had been well handled, for all he'd been so careful—"

"This was at what time?"

"Half past three on Sunday morning, sir."

"You were able to check all the details carefully at that hour?"

"Lester made me."

Blinker smiled grimly. "Robert Lester is a first class man," he said, "as I believe you have good reason to know."

"I would never ha' gotten away from the police if it hadn't been for him, sir."

"Assaulting a sergeant in the execution of his duty," said Blinker thinly, "is not the best way to commend yourself to the Dutch police. You were very lucky to escape a night in the cells."

"Lester told them I had diplomatic immunity."

"And Lester got the British Minister out of bed at his country house and had him motor across Holland at two o'clock in the morning to back up your credentials. His Excellency was furious, of course—I'll never hear the last of it from the F.O. Good God, Flett, what possessed you? Your position in Holland was quite delicate enough without striking a policeman."

"He was rough with *her*," said David sullenly, and Sir Alfred, who had been studying his fingernails, looked up in surprise.

"Was she alive, then, when the police came?"

"She was dead, sir. She died in my arms, with Mr. Kamnov kneeling down beside her; and when the bobby came he—it was the unfeeling way he handled her that riled me—"

"Of course you were under a great strain," said Sir Alfred soothingly. "You're very fortunate to be alive."

"Me, sir?"

"Yes, you were fired at too, weren't you? Or do you think both shots were fired at Madame Tamirova?"

"I couldna charge my memory, sir."

"Would you tell us exactly what happened when you left the theatre?"

David went through it again: the shots in the Marnixstraat, Elena Tamirova mortally wounded in the throat, her body taken to hospital and then to the police mortuary, himself under interrogation at the police station, finally the announcement that the murderer, who had not long evaded capture, was a self-confessed Russian terrorist. "I killed the parasite Tamirova" (his statement had run after a sworn translator could be found) "to avenge the exploited working class."

"But in the head-hurry of the chase," said David angrily, "we all let Ritter through our fingers. *He* never came near to see what had befallen her. Mr. Amory went over to the hotel while Lester and me was still with the police, and he learned that Ritter had checked out of his room at midnight. He was over the frontier at Nijmegen as fast as his chauffeur could drive him— back inside Germany, and scot-free."

"But that's exactly what we wanted to happen, Mr. Flett," said Blinker reasonably.

"Did you want Tamirova killed?"

"Certainly not; her death was unfortunate, but we mustn't be sentimental about it. She passed the word to Ritter, just as she was meant to do; she was completely in his power, completely a traitor to the Allied cause—"

"She was very happy, just before she was killed. She said she was going home to Russia, to make a new start—"

"You think she was more sinned against than sinning?" said Sir Alfred Ewing.

"Yes I do, sir."

Blinker shrugged. "Let me add one detail to your Tamirova dossier, Mr. Flett. A Swedish shipowner called Petersson committed suicide in Stockholm last Wednesday. Before he died—he fell out of a window—he named Karl Ritter and Hans Kolberg as the organisers of a German submarine base in Norwegian waters, and Elena Tamirova as a courier who delivered an important message from Ritter to him exactly a month ago. As time goes on we'll no doubt learn more about the consequences of that, but it's highly probable that innocent people will die because of Tamirova's guilt."

"It was Ritter led her into it, sir," persisted David. His head was lowered; he looked like a young bull as he confronted Blinker. "He's got away with it this time. But some day him and me will meet face to face. And then I swear to God I'll kill him with my bare hands!"

Captain Hall stood up behind his desk. His spare energetic figure quivered with suppressed annoyance; his white tufts of hair shook like the ears of an angry cat. "I should content myself with the Dutch police sergeant, if I were you, Mr. Flett," he said. "Retribution will come to the Ritters of this world in less melodramatic ways! In about a week, when we start sending messages in the code he copied, we shall see if your venture was successful, and I think we will. Today I'm too much concerned with a wretched pederast called Roger Casement, whom we've got behind bars, and a bunch of Paddies playing the Germans' game for them in Ireland, to give more time to the Tamirova affair. You're to have a few days' leave before you join your ship. You've been posted to the *Hampshire*, Captain Savill, reporting at Base H.Q. at Scapa Flow on Sunday. I'll let your Captain know that you've rendered some service to this Department. There's no need to tell him about your fracas with the Dutch police."

"Thank you, sir."

"Good luck, Mr. Flett," said Sir Alfred Ewing. He too rose and offered David his hand.

"Could I ask *you* a question, sir?"

"What is it *now*?" said Blinker, with his hand on the bell-push.

"The man that shot her, sir—was he really a Russian terrorist?"

"What makes you think he wasn't?" snapped Hall.

"I thought it was queer when an attaché from the Russian Ministry at The Hague turned up in the middle of the night to look after a murderer. I thought the Czar's government weren't so keen on terrorists. Do you think there's a chance that the Russians will be able to extradite him?"

"I've no idea how the Dutch law stands on that," said Blinker.

"You know, I think we owe it to Mr. Flett to tell him the truth," said Ewing, and David turned back to him in relief.

"I think we may have underestimated the Russians," said Ewing carefully, "once, we thought them easy to hoodwink. Apparently the Russian Embassy in London has been aware of Madame Tamirova's folly—to rate it no worse—for some weeks past. She was denounced to them by one of their own best agents, whose suspicions of her were aroused at Copenhagen. The so-called 'terrorist' was merely a hired gunman paid to put her out of the way before she could do further damage. From the Russian viewpoint, it was a summary execution."

"Who was the agent?" David asked, and Sir Alfred looked at him sadly. "You know him," he said, "it was the dancer, Vassily Bronin."

David Flett drew in his breath. The two older men waited, while his whole body seemed to knot itself in rage, and then he gasped "Bronin? That rotten little painted faggot?"

"The Russians call him a valuable man," said Blinker. "I hope you're not thinking of going for *him*, Mr. Flett. He and his troupe left Newcastle for Norway yesterday. He must be halfway to Stavanger now."

"And they'll get over the North Sea safe and sound, no doubt. It's only the decent folk that meets in with the submarines." He shook his head. "I beg your pardon, gentlemen. I've had a nasty knock. Have I your permission to leave?"

Blinker Hall shook hands with him then, and wished him luck in his new ship. But when David saluted and went out the D.I.D. was scowling as he resumed his seat and rang for the latest file of decoded intercepts to be brought in.

"I don't want to say 'I told you so'," said Sir Alfred Ewing, "but in the light of events it does look as if you should have sent another man to Amsterdam, more experienced than that poor lad."

"Poor lad indeed!" said Blinker. "I'd like to have that young rough on the parade ground at Whale Island for an hour. I'd knock some notions of discipline into his thick head! That threat to go for Ritter with his bare hands, on top of what he did to the Dutch policeman, was quite intolerable. Sometimes I wonder what the 'New Navy's' coming to."

"The Old Navy had its problems too," said Ewing. "Do you remember a saying of Admiral Napier's—I think it was at the time of the Portuguese war—he said, 'we can manage the men very well at sea, but they're the devil in harbour!' Young Flett has been on the beach too long; he'll be all right once he joins his ship."

"Old Charley Napier!" said the D.I.D. "A real sportsman in his best days. I wish we had him on the Board now. He'd make mincemeat of those piddling fellows in the War Room . . . Do you suppose they've alerted Jellicoe and Beatty yet?"

In an outer office of Intelligence Division Lieutenant Flett found that all the papers relative to his new posting, including an open travel warrant, had been prepared, and there was nothing further to detain him at the Admiralty. The principal secretary thoughtfully asked if he would like to see his sister. Her Section was not open to visitors, but there was an anteroom where they could meet and talk. David muttered something about "not wanting to bother her . . . would be in touch with her later", and went away. He was in no mood to meet Lizzie, with or without her schoolmaster. From Harwich, early that morning, he had sent the suitcase with his civilian clothes by railway delivery to Lizzie's London address: if she cared enough to open it she might exclaim over the stained jacket, from which repeated spongings had not quite removed the marks of Tamirova's blood. That should keep Miss Lizzie's busy brain active for a while. Meantime he didn't want to face her battery of questions, what had Blinker said, when was he going to Aberdeen, how was his shoulder, all fired off in the tone of superiority which irritated him so much. So he left the Admiralty with only half a glance at the statue of Nelson in the hall, and certainly without half a thought of the national hero's departure for Trafalgar. His own goal was the Clarence public-house across Whitehall.

Standing at the bar, downing two straight whiskies, he began the process of numbing his mind with alcohol to the point where Blinker's eyes, steely beneath the fluttering lids, and Bronin's painted face, and Ritter's fair head seen across the theatre, should merge into a blur of temporary oblivion. There was only one thing he wanted to remember, that across the North Sea—and almost at this hour—the funeral of Elena Tamirova must be taking place. Kamnov had arranged it all. There would be a Russian Orthodox service, and no doubt a crowd of gaping Dutch spectators at the cemetery, while the "terrorist" sat in his prison cell, waiting calmly for the wheels of the extradition process to go round. Then Elena's executioner, like her denouncer Bronin, would disappear into the vast anonymity of Russia, and the Maryinsky ballet, like the Great War, would go on.

David left the Clarence and began to work his way north from pub to pub. Advances of various sorts were made to him, which he rejected. He spoke to nobody, drinking straight, a nip and a chaser, whisky more expensive now but the water still free. At one pub in the Strand he bought a ham sandwich, but the bread seemed to stick in his throat, and he left half of it uneaten. By closing time he had reached the Criterion bar, and when it emptied he picked up the first tart who accosted him on the pavement of Piccadily.

"I want another drink first," he told the girl.

"I know ever such a nice club, lovey, if that's what you want. Just round the corner!"

It was a drinking club near Soho Square. David was not too steady on his feet as they walked there, with the girl clinging, contrary to King's Regulations, to his arm, and he had a vague and angry feeling that there was some laughter when they went in. But soon enough all rational feeling ceased, for Lieutenant Flett passed out cold after drinking a tumbler of raw spirits, and was dragged, not unkindly, into a back bedroom to sleep it off.

"How about a nice cup of tea, ducks?" That was what he heard when he awoke, as the evening sunlight began to fill the grubby room. It was the Piccadilly girl who was bending over him. His uniform was hanging anyhow from hooks on the bedroom door, and he was in his underclothes, crumpled with sweat; the girl was in her cheap silk petticoat. "You come here," he muttered, and she came with a giggle, willingly.

At ten minutes to four, while David Flett was lying in his drunken sleep, the Admiralty had directed the Grand Fleet to be at two hours' notice for steam. At five minutes past seven the order was given to raise steam and proceed to sea. About an hour later an intercepted wireless signal, decoded by Room 40, revealed that one of the German objectives was Yarmouth, which could mean that another probable target might be Lowestoft. Of the ten Naval Zeppelins whose emergence from their sheds that morning had been noted by Room 40, six were ordered to support the battle cruisers by a strike at the East Anglian coast.

There was no air raid on London that night. No sirens broke in on the fierce scene of rutting and drinking through which David Flett tried to bury his guilt in more than one compliant body. While he writhed and gasped in the counterfeit of love he could forget, however briefly, that he had been one of the hunters of a lovely foolish creature—as helpless, in the end, as Odette beneath the spell of the enchanter—and that she lay now in her foreign grave under the rain he could hear lashed on the dirty window by the rising wind.

The wind whipped up the heavy head seas against which the Battle Fleet from Scapa and the Battle Cruiser Fleet from Rosyth struggled southward to confront the enemy. Admiral Jellicoe was in the latitude of Cromarty and Admiral Beatty in the latitude of the Farne Islands when Commodore Tyrwhitt and Harwich Force caught up with the German battle cruisers and tried to draw them away from Lowestoft. In this Tyrwhitt failed. Between four and five o'clock in the morning Lowestoft and Yarmouth were bombarded by the Germans with considerable loss of life and property. Where Tyrwhitt did succeed in his long-range action with Admiral Bödicker's battle cruisers was in chasing the enemy from the scene. The German C.-in-C., Admiral Scheer, gave no support with his Battle Fleet. By 6 a.m. the whole High Seas Fleet was running for Wilhelmshaven, and had reached a point over a hundred miles from Beatty's force, and three hundred from Sir John Jellicoe's. Once again the elusive enemy had avoided battle and retired to the shelter of the Heligoland Bight.

Lieutenant David Flett, R.N.V.R., on leave, knew nothing about the raid until the early editions of the evening papers appeared on Tuesday afternoon. By that time, after a series of moves from one point to another in the West End, he was on his way by taxi with two young women to their flat in a Paddington mews when the words *Where was the Navy?* smote his eye. He stopped the cab and bought the paper which had used this striking banner, and as best he could (for one of the young women insisted on sitting in his lap) read an expression of the national fury at the Lowestoft and Yarmouth raid. Goaded by the Irish rebels, who still held out in the Dublin Law Courts, the British raged that the enemy could attack the East Coast whenever and wherever he pleased. The invincible Navy, "the sure shield of Empire", had arrived on the scene too late to save Lowestoft, or give the German admirals the beating they deserved.

At half past seven on Wednesday morning the London train, running slightly late, disgorged its passengers into the smoky cavern of Aberdeen Joint Station, among them Lieutenant David Flett. It was the moment he had dreamed of in the internment camp, imagining a reception committee consisting of his father, his old friends of the Garden Line, and some of the pretty clerkesses from various fish houses whom he had taken to the variety shows at the Tivoli and the Palace when he was mate of the *Moss Rose*. Now he was coming home without even having sent one telegram to announce his arrival, and his blurred reflection in the window of the station buffet showed him haggard and pale, with a rip in the shoulder of the blue raincoat he carried over his arm, and a cut on his chin from shaving in the train. His hat was at the slightly raffish angle known as the Beatty tilt, which was not popular outside the admiral's Rosyth command. David put it straight angrily as he went out into the station yard and headed for Market Street.

For the first time since the tragedy of Elena's death, he felt his spirits rising. In the debauchery of London he had to some extent purged his grief and guilt, and like an animal had instinctively turned towards his home. This was the scene, between the filthy harbour water and the granite setts of Aberdeen, which David knew best in the world. He could name every vessel lying at the Regent Quay (far fewer foreigners than in 1914), and even every driver of the horse-drawn lorries now lining up outside the Fish Market to take the fish bought at auction to a special train. The familiar smells of fish offal and tar, coal smoke and kippering smoke, oilskins and seaboots in the ship's chandlers' shops, burning oak chips at the fish curers', herring barrels and drying nets on the banks of the Dee rose up around him in the busy street. In those few granite blocks where shipowners, bankers, ice merchants and foreign traders occupied a warren of small offices, Liz Flett had taken her first bold step on the path to success. He could see the signboard of her first employer, "N. M. Neroslavski: Moscow and Petersburg" still in place above bolted and blinded windows. Here David himself had gone every week to draw the increasingly large pay of a trawlerman, and here their father had spent more than thirty years of his working life.

The offices of the Garden Line, which employed the elder Flett as a fish salesman, were directly opposite the Commercial Quay side of the Fish Market. They were already open, but David knew better than to look for his father there. He knew the old man's timetable to a minute: at half past seven Alec Flett, a widower for five years past, would have started breakfast at Maggie's Diningroom opposite the Albert Quay. It was not much more than an eating shop, with a fly-blown card in the window announcing Skate Tonight, and there was also a mention of Hot Pies and Bridies, Chips, and Potted Head. A bell rang loudly as David pushed the door open. Maggie's establishment was divided into two: the outer room was patronised by the boys who would presently be "booking" on the Market, able to afford only a cup of tea and a roll. They looked up and stared as the naval officer came in. The older customers ate in an inner sanctum where Maggie herself, fat and jovial, presided over a stove behind a screen and three oilcloth-covered tables set all day with cruets, forks and knives. At one of these sat David's father, with a Fish Market crony on either hand.

"Well, well, look at Admiral Jellicoe!"

The greeting, from an elderly cashier called Veitch, got an ill-natured laugh from all Maggie's customers. Somebody at the table next the screen called out "The Navy's here!" and someone else retorted "High bloody time too." David saw several grinning faces through a thick haze of smoke. He hung his hat and raincoat on a peg, and reached across the table to shake hands with his father.

"Aye, Dad, you're there," he said laconically. "Aye, Mr. Veitch. How are you, Mr. Bannerman?"

The third man at old Flett's table, who was the accountant at Garden and Company, said kindly, "Welcome back, Davie!" But old Flett himself, screwing up his pale blue eyes to see his son better, said sharply:

"You're not looking well, man. What hindered you?"

What he actually said was "Wot 'indered yeow?" for Alec Flett had once been employed by a fish merchant in Billingsgate Market, and had grafted a Cockney accent on to his native Aberdeen. The result was fearful and wonderful, as his outspoken friends often told him, although without denting his self-esteem at all. He was a little man with a large bald head for which the neat features Liz had inherited seemed much too small. At the moment of David's arrival he had a newly lit pipe in his mouth filled with his favourite tobacco, Mitchell's Three Star Bogie Roll.

"Nothing hindered me, Dad," said David. "The surgeons wouldna let me away from Harwich for a day or two."

"Is your arm not better?"

"Aye, it's fine now."

"How's our Lizzie?"

"Doing great."

Veitch said, "It'll be a clerkin' job she's at in London— typewritin' and sic like?"

"She does a lot o' translation work, she says."

"Not much of a job for the great university don." But here

Veitch's malice was interrupted by Maggie herself, who came screeching from her stove to give the newcomer the most enthusiastic welcome he had had so far.

"What are you for, Davie lad?" she asked. "A Finnan haddick? Ham and an egg? Or herrin' in oatmeal—ye was aye fond o' that?"

David felt a tide of sour whisky and bile rising in his throat. The atmosphere in the diningroom, of strong pipe tobacco and the men's Market clothes, was as ripe as the fo'c'sle of a trawler homeward bound after the catch. The very mention of ham and herring, in his present state, made his stomach heave.

"It's ower early for a herrin', Maggie," he said. "I never fancied a herrin' till the month o' June . . . Gie's a sup tea and a buttery rowie," he added while Maggie cackled her pleasure, and Veitch sneered, "I thought a Navy lieutenant would be speakin' pan-loaf now. You haena lost your fisher tongue, Davie!"

The buttery roll, warm from the bakery and spread with sharp marmalade, tasted fine with the strong sweet tea. I kept it down, thought David. He turned to Mr. Bannerman.

"I was terrible sorry to hear about Bob."

"Aye," said the accountant, "your Dad would tell you in a letter, nae doubt . . . Died of wounds at twenty, poor lad. It's just about killed his mother."

"I'm very sorry," David said again. He had hardly known young Bannerman; the boy had just started "booking" in the summer of 1914.

"You were a lucky lad last night, Dave," said his father. "Gettin' out of London before the air raid started."

"Was there a raid last night?" He reached for the folded copy of the local paper, creased at the Stop Press. The blurred type announced that five German Army Zeppelins had begun bombing the outskirts of London shortly before eleven o'clock, being driven off by fierce gunfire and attacks from the BE2s. They had jettisoned their bombs over the naval camp at Shotley, Deal Harbour and the open countryside. The continental quay at Harwich had been severely damaged in the course of the raid.

"My God, what a night," he said. "Fancy Parkeston Quay!"

He remembered leaving from that quay four hours late, on his way to see Elena Tamirova.

"Ah, but that's nothing, man!" All the three elderly men seemed to speak at once. Separately and together they described the sufferings of Aberdeen, the trawlers sunk by mine and torpedo, the discontent among the crews and the paralysing strikes of January, the good work done by the Royal Naval Reserve Transport Section ("knockin' the Navy intill a cocked hat") the bravery of a local man, Chief Skipper Peter Yorston, the dangers of the black-out and whisky up to sixpence a glass. Nobody in the diningroom (though one or two men shook David's hand as they went out) asked about the loss of the *Yelverton* or his escape from Holland. He hardly expected it. He knew well enough that their whole world lay between Point Law and Pocra Quay, and all that was expected of himself was to say "Is that a fact?" or "Deil a bit!" at intervals in the saga. But he gave his father complete attention when the old man said,

"Did you hear about the *Hazelhead*, Davie?"

"I did that. It was an awful tragedy."

"Aye, it fairly shook the folk o' Aberdeen," said Mr. Bannerman. "I saw John Mitchell, the chief clerk at Tarras and Company, yesterday at dinner time, and he was sayin' the loss of the *Hazelhead*'s put ten years on to Mr. Endicott."

"He'll pull through," said Alec Flett oracularly, from a cloud of Bogie Roll. "They're a tough lot the Endicotts. I remember when I was a boy seeing John Endicott's grandfather, the American skipper, when he came over to start Mr. John in the Aberdeen office. He was a great chap, old Brand, there wasna much you could tell *him* about the sea."

"Brand Endicott married a foreigner, didn't he?" said Veitch.

"Aye, he fell in with a Russian lady at the time of the Baltic wars. Old Brand was half a foreigner himself it if comes to that; his father was a Yankee skipper too . . . Davie, man, it's time I was on the Market. Will you wait or I'm done and come back to the office wi' me? Mr. Garden said to tell you he would like to see you."

"It's your busiest time, Dad," objected David. "I think I'll go home for a while and come back again. We might try a round of the pictures at the Electric, and get something to eat down town."

"Ye've struck oil today, Alec," said Mr. Veitch. "Ye'll be getting late dinner at the Palace Hotel, nae less. Lieutenant Flett's too grand a lad for pie and chips at poor Maggie's."

"What's that you're sayin'?" Maggie poked her head round the screen suspiciously. Whereupon David kissed her greasy cheek and called her "ma auld sweethert" as he paid the modest bill for all of them, and the customers slinging on their coats laughed appreciatively. Make a goat of yourself and you're popular here, David thought savagely; but he was touched when his father remarked as they prepared to cross Market Street:

"Veitch is a sour old devil, you were a good lad not to let him rile you, Dave . . . By the way, there's a parcel and a letter you better read, at home."

With surprising alacrity, Mr. Flett then nipped across the street under the noses of two dray horses, and disdaining the steps jumped on to the high ledge surrounding the Fish Market, on which the fish boxes would be flung as soon as they were sold. He was now "on the Market", no longer a rather shabby old gentleman in a cheap eatinghouse, but a small autocrat in the domain in which the Fish was king.

The Market, a long low building on the north side of the Albert Basin, was open on the harbour side, where the trawlers had moored for unloading in the early hours of the morning. Between the water and the wall beyond which the fish-trucks waited, lay the Fish itself, naked in dead wet rows of turbot, halibut, cod, or in boxes of plaice, whiting, and lemon sole—the Fish caught at the risk of human lives, in defiance of the enemy's mines and submarines, ready to be despatched all over Britain as food for a nation at war. Alec Flett and the other salesmen quickly took up their positions, Mr. Flett owing to his lack of height perched on a fish box, each where his firm's catch was laid out. Watches were compared with the huge clock outside the Market Superintendent's office. At eight precisely a bell beside the clock was struck, and the auctioning of the fish began.

David looked on for a quarter of an hour. He had seen the

morning sale a hundred times, always admiring the speed shown by the old hands like his father who were attentive to every movement in the knot of buyers and sold almost faster than their young clerks could book the figures. As soon as each lot of fish was sold it was rushed away by fish porters armed with long metal hooks to seize the handles of the boxes or the heads of the larger fish like skate. With a rattle, a squelch and occasional curses, the day's catch vanished from the Market of Aberdeen.

David strolled down the wharf. Only two Garden Line trawlers were berthed, the *Honeysuckle* and the *Jessamine*; a deckie on the latter shouted in answer to his query that the *Moss Rose* was at sea. He walked past *Forward Pride, Silver Seas, Graceful, Fruitful* and *Lapwing*, and watched the men in oilskins, wearing stocking caps, sluicing down the scaly decks. He remembered the cabins which in the days before he became an officer and a gentleman he had shared with five others, cabins stinking of the engines, the stoke-hold and the main fish room. He glowered at a youngster who looked up from the deck of the *Bon Accord* at the naval officer and said something to his mates which made them laugh.

David Flett had never thought of the Fish Market as a beautiful scene. A Moray Firth sunset or the Northern Lights dancing above a frosty landscape had been his concept of natural beauty, almost equally satisfied by grocery calendar art. Perhaps it was the new perceptiveness given him by *Swan Lake* which made him recognise the harmony in the low red brick buildings of the Market against the grey granite towers and spires of the city, gleaming beneath a sky of pearl. It was a Northern beauty with its own savage stripe of cruelty, as the gulls, perched in rows along the roof, swooped down to tear the red entrails of the monk-fish almost from the hands of the women gutting them into barrels. The shrill cries of the birds rose above the noises of the Market.

"Hey, Davie! Are ye too grand to speak to an auld friend?"

He was back at the *Honeysuckle* again, and Pat Downie, once a deckie in the *Moss Rose* but now the *Honeysuckle*'s mate, had come out of the wheelhouse and was looking up at him. David gave him a cheery greeting. No, he wasn't for a cup of tea, and it was too early for a dram, but how's yourself, Pat, and how's the wife?

183

What like a shot had they brought in, and what like was their trip?

"Rotten, man, fair rotten," the young mate said of catch and voyage. "The *Canterbury Bell* reported a sub hangin' aboot, so we made off for the North Pier before we had time to winch the trawl in twice. It's a damned shame, ye ken. If the Navy can't give us right protection, why can't they arm the fishing fleet? I'll swear if I had a gun on board I would blow a Jerry or two out of the water . . . I say, Dave! Was't Jerry or the Dutchmen had a grip o' you?"

"It was the Dutch, Pat. Eight months, I was in."

"But you got clear of them, good for you. It would be worse for them that's out-and-out prisoners o' war, eh?"

"That's right."

"Are ye game to come down to the Cross Keys about six o'clock and celebrate?"

"I'll need to bide with the auld man tonight, Pat."

"Maybe we're not swanky enough for a Navy gent like you. If you change your mind ye know where to find your old shipmates. Ta-ta!"

Pat Downie drew himself up in his seaboots, and gave a mocking parody of a Navy salute.

When David reached the house where he was born the little village of Footdee was very quiet. The fishermen's children had straggled off to school, and Mrs. Main, the neighbour's wife who "redd up" the widower's house every morning had been and gone. In the neat small squares, built about the time of Waterloo at the meeting of the River Dee and the North Sea, there was no human being to be seen. This, after his chilling reception in his old haunts, Lieutenant Flett regarded as a blessing.

Footdee had been for many generations a closed community of fisherfolk. There had been some change in the employment of the men, due to the introduction of steam trawling, but the one-time "white fishers of Fittie" were fishermen still; deeply religious and rugged individualists, marrying only within the confines of their own village. David's father, who had not the physique for a trawlerman, had been exceptional in going to work in London, but he had come back to Footdee to take a wife from Middle Row, and settle down with her in North Square for the rest of their married life. The little house, with its back wall to the sea, had been bought by David's grandfather when the Footdee houses were put up for sale in 1880. He had increased its two rooms by an attic, not much larger than Mr. Timmermann's in the Herengracht, which later became David's bedroom; Liz, before she went to London, slept on a sofa-bed in the parlour. David looked in there and saw the parcel his father had mentioned—a large box from Gieves in Bond Street, no doubt containing his new kit. The other room where Mr. Flett now slept alone in the bed recess hidden by a curtain was as always very tidy, though before David pushed the window up there was a powerful smell of Bogie Roll. It was warm, for Mrs. Main had put enough dross into the small range to keep it alight for hours. David's first act was to shake down the dross and stoke the fire with a shovelful of best Haighmoor, so as to get enough hot water from the little boiler to take the chill off a cold tub. He felt a great desire to be physically clean.

David had taken his uniform jacket and waistcoat off before stoking the range. Now he sat down in his father's armchair and lit a cigarette. His head was clearing. He felt better than he had felt since he left the police station at Amsterdam.

Who are you, David Flett? That was what Elena had asked him, as they watched the swans sailing on the Dutch canal; this was what he now, and for the first time, asked himself. His belief in the identity of David Flett had been severely shaken. That competent young fisherman, the mate of the *Moss Rose*, had been a social misfit in H.M.S. *Yelverton*, and now, as "a Navy gent", appeared to be a social misfit at the harbour of Aberdeen. If he had roots anywhere in the world, they were here; but he realised that the war would not leave Footdee or even the city of Aberdeen unchanged. Liz as usual had been the smart one; she had seen the changes coming and struck out on her own. What sort of life did the future hold for David Flett?

He looked round the kitchen uneasily, seeking for any peg on

185

which to hang his past. Since his mother's death many of her favourite knick-knacks had been removed, condemned by Liz as in bad taste and later by Mrs. Main as dust-catching. The shell boxes, lumps of coral, cowrie strings, green glass balls and other sea treasures had disappeared into the parlour sideboard—or possibly the ash-cart—and only one of Mrs. Flett's possessions remained in its old place. This was a chromolithograph of Lord Kitchener—not the Kitchener of the recruiting posters, with the pointing finger and the fanatic's eyes—but Kitchener as a Field Marshal, the soldier supreme, in whose fortunate star the British people had an almost mystical belief. David's mother had had a great admiration for "K. of K."

The letter his father thought he ought to read—at least, the only letter to be seen—was stuck behind the frame of the Kitchener picture. David recognized the postmark and the clear schoolgirl hand as soon as he took it down. He read:

> Manse of Hamnavoe,
> By Kirkwall.
> April 21st, 1916

Dear Mr. Flett,

My father bids me thank you for your very kind letter and your expression of sympathy in our great bereavement. We can hardly realise yet that my mother is with God.

She was very anxious about my Uncle Hans, who suffered an attack on April 8th, and insisted on going to Christiania to nurse him. That is how she came to be aboard the *Hazelhead*.

We try to think of the many, many other families who are sorrowing like ourselves. In such a time of grief it is good to know there is some happiness somewhere in the world, so thank you for telling us that David has got back to England. Let us pray that he and Magnus will come safely through the war.

> Yours sincerely,
> Ingrid Sabiston

David read the letter twice, and the ingenuous words, the simple piety, were like a cup of cold water in his rage and pain.

So his impassive little father, after all, not Liz or clever Combermere, or brilliant Blinker Hall, had been the one to unravel another strand of the thread that bound Elena to Kolberg, and Kolberg to the Sabistons! Not for the first time David had the glimmering of an idea that the Sabistons might lead him to his revenge on Ritter.

He supposed there would always be gaps in the story. Some of them might be filled in unexpectedly, like the revelation that Bronin was the man who had denounced Elena Tamirova, and others he hoped to find out for himself—if he could do so without hurting Ingrid Sabiston. She had come to mean a great deal to him. She might even be the one who could help him to realise his own identity.

He fell in with a Russian lady. The words, as spoken by his father, had wrenched David's heart. He was not sure of their accuracy, for he remembered having heard as part of harbour gossip that old Mrs. Endicott had been a Finn, but that made no difference to a young man who had fallen in with a Russian lady too. A lady who had good and evil in one nature, like Odette and Odile.

Through the open window of the little back scullery, where his tin bath hung on hooks from the ceiling, David heard the sound of the North Sea, the suck of the tide on the Footdee pebbles which had been the melody of his childhood in this house. It gave him strength to say aloud "I must forget her!" and get up to fetch from his jacket pocket something he had brought from Amsterdam.

It was one of the little pictures Tamirova had called her ikons. He had picked it up, when the police took away her body, from the pile of canvas covers where he had laid her down to die; the other had probably fallen from her hand in the Marnixstraat. It was the picture of a dancer, with a dark stain on her long graceful ballet skirt.

David took the poker and made a cavern in the heart of the fire. Then he dropped the frame and broken glass into the ashpan beneath the grate, and looked at Elena's luck-bringer for the last time. If it had been a portrait of herself, of Tamirova in her glory, he would have kept it as a treasure, but he had no idea who the dancer might be. He had never heard of Carlotta Grisi, but there was a name written beneath the figure which he had heard connected with the murdered woman:

Giselle

David Flett dropped Elena Petrovna's ikon into the red heart of the fire. The slender arms, the wreath of flowers, the smiling face, flared up for an instant and were gone.

XI

Wednesday, May 3, 1916

The parish of Hamnavoe in the Orkney Mainland lay with its church and manse on the northern shore of Scapa Flow, between the larger parishes of Orphir and Kirkwall. Dr. Sabiston, who had been minister of Hamnavoe since 1888, preferred his small charge to a great city church, for though a fine preacher he was an even more distinguished scholar. His work on the antiquities of Orkney had brought him fame abroad, and he frequently acted as an external examiner in Church History at the Scottish universities.

When the Reverend Henry Sabiston (his doctorate in Divinity still some years away) brought his Norwegian bride to Hamnavoe in 1890, it occurred to neither of them that they were making their home in a lonely place. There was a tiny hamlet beside the pier at Scapa, another at Kirbister, yet another at Houton, and even a general merchant's shop within easy walking distance of the manse gates. All of these were centres of news and interest for the Orcadians, an original and self-sufficient people, and when the Sabistons wished to take part in town life there was Kirkwall, not much more than three miles away. In the early days they kept a pony and a "machine", for Astrid Sabiston had brought a handsome dowry from the Kolbergs, and life was very comfortable at the manse.

What was lonely in those days was the great expanse of water called Scapa Flow. Sheltered from the Atlantic gales by the hills of Hoy, it was sometimes used as an exercise ground by the Home Fleet, but for most of the year it lay vast and empty, a mirror for the splendid colours of an Orkney sunset, or the silver and pearl of the white nights of June. The manse children, when they were taken to play on the beautiful shore of Waulkmill Bay, tumbled in and out of the water, ran races with their dog, and saw no other faces than their parents' through the long summer afternoon.

When Ingrid Sabiston, who was eighteen years and three months old in May 1916, began going to school in Kirkwall she had walked the shore road in all weathers, meeting nobody but farming folk until the red tower of St. Magnus' Cathedral rose above the roofs of Kirkwall town. Two years of war had so completely changed the Mainland that to the girl it began to seem as if the Grand Fleet had always been at Scapa Flow.

From the manse windows they could see the battleships anchored north of Cava Island, in the Bring Deeps, and the outline of Flotta, beyond which the smaller craft and base ships like H.M.S. *Victorious*, which in March 1916 arrived as an accommodation ship and workshop for the dockyard staff, lay in Long Hope Sound. The destroyers and auxiliaries lay in Gutter Sound and Wedell Sound. Twenty months of all-out effort had transformed Scapa Flow into a city of ships, a series of anchorages within an anchorage which was at the same time an exercise ground and a base for the aircraft carrier *Campania*. On all the shores and islands of the Flow naval establishments proliferated. Scapa itself was being transformed into a seaplane base. The Clestron Barrier had been erected against the attacks by submarine which were Sir John Jellicoe's waking nightmare. Sunken ships and net-boom drifters supplemented the Barrier. Depot ships, like H.M.S. *Imperieuse* and *Ghourko*, with the repair ships *Cyclops* and *Assistance* and colliers and oilers without number were attached to Admiral Miller's Base at Long Hope. Ingrid Sabiston, using a pair of binoculars given her by her brother in the Navy, could identify most of the capital ships from her bedroom window at Hamnavoe.

Ingrid was not at her window on the afternoon of the third of May, but working in the back yard. Less than a month before, she had waved good-bye when her mother sailed for Aberdeen aboard the *St. Sunniva*, on the first lap of the fatal journey to Christiania; since then she had found that in work, physical work which used her hands and her whole body, lay her immediate salvation. It kept at bay the horrible imaginings, which she knew tormented everybody at the manse, of the way her mother had met her death at sea.

Like some of the gardens in the treeless island, the manse had a plantation of low-growing trees like elder and mountain-ash. There were a few wild cherries among them, just breaking into blossom along with the creamy sprays which would become rowans and elderberries in the autumn, and beneath the trees, against a stone wall, a row of black-currant bushes. Ingrid was on her knees, weeding and loosening the soil round the currant bushes, when Agnes the manse servant, a stalwart fifty-year-old, shouted to her from the gate:

"There's a gentleman visitor, Ingrid."

The girl stood up at once, and called back:

"Tell him Daddy's gone to Kirkwall."

"It's you he's come to see," the maid said, and stood aside to make way for David Flett.

There was the beginning of a song, heard several times since he joined the *Hampshire*, which David thought exactly suited Ingrid at this moment when he saw her again. She was still dressed like a schoolgirl, in a white silk blouse and an old black school skirt not much below her knees, but the schoolgirl plait had gone, and her very fair hair, cut short, swung in a bell round the nape of her neck. One hand, stained with weeding, was half-way to her mouth in an arrested gesture of surprise and joy.

"She is standing by the poplars,
   Colinette with the sea-blue eyes—"

It was ridiculous, of course. Her name wasn't Colinette, and there wasn't a poplar on the Mainland as far as David knew, but the sea-blue eyes were brilliant as Ingrid ran up the garden to his arms. He ran more than halfway to meet her. It was as natural as that, though he had never taken her in his arms before, far less tried to kiss her. But now he held her fast, she smelt of sunshine and blackcurrants, and when he kissed her Ingrid said "Oh Davie, thank the Best you're safe!" and he saw tears in her eyes.

"Ah, Ingrid," he said, touched to the heart, "dinna greet. Wee lassie, dinna greet,"

She was not a wee lassie, but a tall girl who would some day be a big woman in the style of her Norse-Orcadian race. But

David Flett had a limited stock of pet names, and the diminutive was his only expression of tenderness, although Ingrid was tall enough to lay her head on his shoulder and rest it there for a long moment before she drew away. He kept hold of her hand as they turned towards the gate from which Agnes had tactfully disappeared.

"Oh, Davie, it's been such an awful time!"

"I know, Ingrid. I've been terribly, terribly sorry for you—"

"Your father wrote, so very sweetly. And your sister too."

"I thought I would just wait till I could come myself."

She looked sideways at him, not flirtatiously, but with a speaking gladness. "When *did* you come, Dave?"

"I joined the *Hampshire* last Sunday. This was the first time I could get ashore, and I mustn't bide: the picket-boat's due to leave at six o'clock."

"From Houton?"

"No, from Scapa."

"That's not so bad, then, we can have some tea. Do come in!"

They went round the gable-end of the little whitewashed manse, which looked no different from any Orkney farm, and in at the front door. "Daddy will be so sorry to have missed you, he won't be back till seven."

"How *is* your father?"

"He tries so hard to be brave, and carry on. But then he misses her so much—" They sat down in the livingroom, where the blinds were drawn halfway down the windows. Hamnavoe manse was so small that as one room was required for the minister's study the livingroom was used as a diningroom, but Mrs. Sabiston had never allowed it to deteriorate into a place for relaxing and romping, even when her boys and girl were small. In fact it contained some valuable things, brought from the house in Christiania where her family lived before Hans Kolberg exercised his rogue fancy on the villa at Vettakollen. The furniture was First Empire, dating from the Bernadotte era, and on the walls were contemporary prints of Oscarshall, Frogner Manor and the Royal Palace at Christiania. The whole effect, unfortunately, was rather grey and chilly, and the room had always intimidated David Flett.

"You know, if she had had a long illness, or an operation, and we had been prepared for the worst . . . But just to happen like that, without warning! Never to see her again! Daddy read the funeral service in church, the Sunday after it happened, and one old man came up and said to him as we were going home: 'Aye, minister, it's queer not to be wending our way to the kirkyard!' . . . Oh, Davie, it's such a comfort to talk to you about it!'

"You'll be a great comfort to your father, Ingrid."

"I try to be, because he's so worried about poor little Olav. All Olav wants to do is join the Army and kill Germans, because they killed his mother—"

"How old's Olav again?"

"Fourteen."

"I hope to God we finish off the Germans before Olav's turn comes."

"Daddy's trying to take his mind off it. That's one reason why he's in Kirkwall today. There's a Presbytery meeting, and he's going to meet Olav after school and take him to the tailor to be measured for his first long trousers. Daddy's going to the General Assembly this month, and Olav's going with him to see Edinburgh."

"What about you?"

"I had three years of school in Edinburgh. I don't mind being left alone. It'll give me time to get my breath back."

"It was just a terrible pity your mother took the trip at all."

"We didn't want her to go, but she worried dreadfully about my uncle Hans in Christiania. He'd been ill since the beginning of April, and she insisted on going over to see him. If only Magnus had been here! If *he* had told Mother it was too dangerous a trip she would have listened. She never paid any attention to Daddy and me . . . Davie, if it hadn't been for you we would have lost Magnus too."

"You mean when the *Yelverton*— Nonsense, lassie! You all make far too much of that. There's nothing special in hauling a chap aboard a Carley."

"What *was* special was going over the side yourself." Ingrid paused. "There's something I wanted to ask Magnus about that

193

time, and I didn't dare. Will you tell me? Is drowning a very dreadful way to die?"

David Flett thought of the maelstrom as the *Yelverton* was sucked down, the torn bodies, the faces black with oil, the faces and flailing limbs burned beyond recognition, and he heard again the screams of dying men.

"No, not drowning," he lied, "it's the canniest way there is. Magnus would tell you—the poor lads just lay back on the water and drifted off. There was no suffering."

She put out her hand to him, and at that moment Agnes, a cyclonic mover, burst into the diningroom and exclaimed:

"I say, Ingrid! Will you manage the tea if I run down to the shop for a minute, before the minister comes back?"

"All right, but don't be too long—" The girl turned to David when the door closed noisily. "Agnes's minutes have turned into hours since there was only me at home. Down to the shop, over to Scapa, across to Houton—and that does take time, because her sister at the farm's expecting her first baby—oh well, I suppose we're lucky to have her, really. Let's go into the kitchen and see if she actually *infused* the tea."

The kitchen, with the maid's bedroom above it, was built at right angles to the main part of the manse, and thus got all the afternoon sunshine through a window cut above the sink. The kettle was boiling on the peat fire, the teapot and caddy were in readiness, and everything else was on a tray with an embroidered cloth, ready to be carried into the livingroom. David agreed enthusiastically when Ingrid proposed that they should have tea on a corner of the kitchen table. He thought the manse kitchen a splendid place, with its strawbacked Orkney chair, its cured hams and strings of onions hanging from the rafters, the meal ark in one corner, and the back door wide open on the yard where hens were clucking and a tortoisehell cat licked her kittens on a pile of sacks beside the peat stack. It was such a comfortable tea, too, with buttered oatcake and cheese as well as cakes and scones, and eaten sitting down. The Wardroom of the *Hampshire* had already presented alarming hazards in the way of afternoon tea taken while standing about and balancing a china teacup in a precarious saucer. David sighed happily and looked at the sun shining on Ingrid's hair.

"I like your hair short," he said. "Is that what my sister Lizzie calls the Castle clip?"

"This is the Agnes clip. When the time came to put my hair up I couldn't get a hat to fit, so Agnes took the kitchen scissors and chopped off my plait. Magnus says it's enough to scare the crows."

"It's bonny. It suits you better than it suits Lizzie Flett."

"Oh, brothers love to criticise their sisters, don't they?"

"Where's Magnus at now? I dropped him a line from Aberdeen, but there's been no reply as yet."

"He's still at Liverpool. His new ship, the *Chester*, was commissioned there yesterday."

"The day of the big air raid—you knew Aberdeen got a dusting too? I bet it shook them up at the Fish Market."

"Yes, well, the Zepps didn't get as far as Liverpool. But tell me about you, Davie. How do you like the *Hampshire*?"

She asked the question with some anxiety. David had never discussed his troubles in H.M.S. *Yelverton* with Lieutenant Sabiston's schoolgirl sister, but Ingrid knew that they were real enough, and once Magnus himself had gone so far as to say:

"I like Flett, and he certainly knows his seamanship, he'll be a good man at a pinch. But he got the Owner's goat right from the day he joined, and then he was too chummy with the crew. It's not his fault; he just wasn't properly trained to handle men."

"Don't patronise Davie just because *you* went to Dartmouth!" she had flared up, but Magnus refused to quarrel. He was a very good-tempered brother. And just how good a man Davie Flett was at a pinch Magnus had found out, the day the *Yelverton* was sunk . . . Ingrid waited eagerly for David's answer.

"I think I've landed lucky this time," he said without hesitation. "Captain Savill seems like a fine chap, and they're a nice lot in the Wardroom. Oh—you can tell Magnus when you write—my Captain's put me on to searchlights. Magnus'll maybe not think much of that now that he's a Lieutenant of the Turret."

"I'm sure he'll be impressed. But what about your Morse?"

195

"I worked at it real hard at Groningen."

She asked more questions, and listened devotedly while David told her about his life in the internment camp and his escape, up to the moment of his arrival at Mr. Timmermann's door. There were questions in his mind too, but for the life of him he couldn't ask them then. Looking at Ingrid's candid face, where the astonishing sea-blue eyes burned against a skin of cream and roses, he found the very name of Kolberg stuck in his throat. How to suggest to this gentle girl, her mother killed so recently, that the submarine which sank the *Hazelhead* might well have come from the secret base in Norway which her uncle and Karl Ritter had helped to organise? There would be another time for questioning, and meanwhile the thought of the picket-boat forced David to look at his watch.

"I'll need to run," he said, "the Commander-in-Chief dines aboard us tonight."

"Admiral Jellicoe? Does he really? Oh, Davie, aren't you glad you got your stripe?"

"I suppose so; but he won't pay much attention to the likes of me . . . Can I come and see you again soon?"

"Of course, but if you come in to Houton next time, telephone, it's much too far to walk."

"Have you the telephone, Ingrid?"

"We put it in at Christmas, the lines are being extended all round the coast. It's an easy number to remember. Hamnavoe 1."

"That's great. I'll let you know next time I get ashore—"

"And then I can pick you up with the motor-bike."

"The motor—the Harley-Davidson? Magnus's bike?"

"Yes, why not? Magnus taught me to ride; it wasn't difficult. I often take Daddy about in the sidecar now."

"But how do you manage—?"

"Don't be a Mrs. Grundy, Dave! I wear breeches and boots, of course. But to spare your blushes, I've a most concealing coat which I put on as soon as we get into Kirkwall."

"You girls!" said David. "What will you get up to next?"

He looked at Ingrid as she rose, imagining those long legs in khaki breeches, and a boy's cap with goggles on the flying cornsilk hair. You couldn't picture her as a ballet dancer in a hundred years, but how strong she looked, and in her own way how enticing! She kept the table between them. He guessed that she was embarrassed to remember that headlong, childish run into his arms.

But Ingrid's mind was not on kisses. She thanked David gravely for his visit of sympathy, and said again that her father and Olav would be sorry to have missed him. "Daddy often mentions you at family prayers," she said. "I'm sure he'll pray for you in your new ship tonight."

"Does he find comfort in praying, since your mother died?"

"At first he *couldn't* pray," said Ingrid simply. "He couldn't accept that an enemy submarine might be the instrument of God's will . . . Do you know what helped him after the first few days as much as anything? Just an old ballad about Sir Humphrey Gilbert that I learned at school.

> "He sat upon the deck
> The Book was in his hand;
> 'Do not fear! Heaven is as near'
> He said, 'by water as by land!'"

David was not the last of the officers on shore leave to reach the *Hampshire's* picket-boat at Scapa Pier, but as one of the most junior he was accommodated with a seat on the cabin roof while the midshipman of the boat and his crew of three took them across the Flow. The *Hampshire* was swinging to the tide at a single anchor, and as the picket-boat came up to the starboard gangway she loomed above it, a tremendous hulk. She was one of the older cruisers, Tyne-built in 1903, of over 10,000 tons burthen and carrying a complement of six hundred and fifty men. Before the war *Hampshire* had been on both the Mediterranean and the China stations. She had certain defects, which the younger members of the Wardroom assured David he would discover as soon as she put to sea, but under the command of Captain Herbert Savill, R.N. she was a taut and happy ship. David, as he saluted the quarterdeck and went off down the after companionway, already had the feeling of returning home.

The officers' cabins flat was sufficiently commodious in

H.M.S. *Hamshire* to give even a newly joined Lieutenant a small cabin of his own. Lieutenant Flett had a bunk with four drawers, a fold-up wash basin, a single-leaf table against the bulkhead, and a flat tin bath screwed to the deckhead by clips, very much like the bath in the scullery of his home. He had no watch to keep until the graveyard watch began at midnight. It was not disagreeable to have time to dress for dinner in the new mess uniform, and to see in the small looking-glass a very presentable young officer, with dark hair properly cut and brushed, and dark eyes less troubled since the afternoon hour with Ingrid Sabiston.

It was also pleasant, as David made his way later along the main deck, to be no longer a one-ringer. His promotion had got him out of the Gunroom bear-garden for good, although he imagined it would be a very decorous bear-garden on this particular evening, when the Commander-in-Chief dined aboard. The Senior Sub would prohibit horseplay, and the cracked records of "Keep the Home Fires Burning" and "Roses of Picardy" would remain inside their tattered sleeves. David entered the smokingroom. On such a fine May night it was brighter than usual, for Scapa Flow was bathed in evening sunshine, which filtered through the skylight to supplement the electric light. It was furnished in club style, with signed photographs of King George V and Queen Mary, and groups of *Hampshire* officers taken at various periods of the cruiser's service. In one of these, taken in the Mediterranean in 1912, Lord Kitchener, looking as stern as in the chromo admired by David's mother, sat with Captain Savill and his officers, stiff in their tropical whites.

The officers of 1916, while not effusive, were far from stiff in manner, and Lieutenant Flett was greeted pleasantly by those of his seniors who were not immersed in the new magazines. He was of course too recent an addition to the Wardroom to address any of them by their nicknames, although as "Soldier", "Pilot", "Padre" and "Pills" the group of men standing under the skylight with pink gins in their hands were known to one another. David was joined by another Lieutenant, by name Ramsay, and the two young men took their gins and bitters into a corner and discussed football. Captain Savill was not so fanatical about organised

198

games as the unfortunate Captain Willis-Turner of H.M.S. *Yelverton* (David Flett had particularly disliked medicine ball, never featured aboard the *Moss Rose*) but football was part of the life of a ship's company, and pitches had been laid out on Flotta Island where twelve Navy teams could play at one time.

"I dare say you know we're on two hours' notice for steam now," commented William Ramsay. "That means patrol tomorrow, I suppose. Unless good old J.R.J. takes us all off on another bloody useless sweep."

David nodded. Ever since he joined H.M.S. *Hampshire* he had heard someone, at some time every day, use the same words about the abortive expedition to Lowestoft, when the Grand Fleet had missed contact with the enemy by something like four hours. "Another bloody useless sweep" was how disillusioned junior officers, who had long since given up any hope of fighting another Trafalgar, viewed the Commander-in-Chief's cautious sorties.

"What area will we be patrolling?" he enquired.

"The Faeroes probably. You know that run, don't you?" David said Yes. One element of his acceptance in the *Hampshire*'s Wardroom was that he was no longer a raw recruit, in the Navy by "the back door entry", but "an old Scapa hand" who had known the Flow in the early days, when the *Hampshire* was based on Cromarty. Even the fact of his internment and escape was an asset in the eyes of contemporaries like Bill Ramsay.

"Some of the trawler chaps were saying in Aberdeen last week that they were having a rough time off the Faeroes," he observed.

"*Hampshire* to the rescue!" Ramsay grinned. "We've nursemaided the trawlers often enough. But wait till we're ordered back to protect the White Sea trade. You haven't lived till you've experienced the pleasures of coaling in a White Sea port, under the auspices of our gallant Russian allies."

"Archangel?"

"Alexandrovsk. We were up there last December. Coming back to Scapa for turkey and plum duff when we were whipped off to hunt for the *Porpoise* and the *Morning Star*, two of our destroyers who'd contrived to get mislaid somewhere off Fair Isle."

"Find them?"

"We picked 'em up all right, but God! what seas we shipped on the way back to Scapa! Shan't forget last Christmas Eve in a hurry . . . How about another pink gin?"

"Not for me, thanks."

"Smart fellow, all set to be keen and alert for our guest of honour. Have you ever met him before?"

"Jellicoe? Lord, no! Never seen him any nearer than standing on the bridge of the old 'Tin Duck', once when she was coming in through Hoxa Sound."

"Nor have I," confessed Bill Ramsay. "Of course you realise what tonight's tamasha is all about? Building morale, they probably call it in the flagship, or restoring confidence, or some such rot. The Fleet morale is fine, if we could ever see some action! I wish I could say as much for all the rest of it."

David construed All the rest of it to mean the general conduct of the war, and agreed—as no sensible man could fail to do— that it had been a bloody awful week. The Germans had been prevented from giving the promised help to their Irish allies, and the Dublin rising had been put down with a firmness which promised a harvest of hatred in the near future. Roger Casement and the ringleaders would stand trial for treason, though one of them, De Valera, might cheat the gallows on account of his American citizenship. But this equivocal success in Ireland was all that Britain could boast of in the dark beginning of May 1916. On April 29 General Townshend had been forced to surrender Kut-el-Amara to the Turks, who thus acquired ten thousand British prisoners of war. At the same time the same number of Russians surrendered to the Germans when the month-long battle between Lake Naroch and Vilna ended; but in that battle the Russians had one hundred thousand dead. In France, caught between the stalemate of the Salient and the slaughter of Verdun, Sir Douglas Haig and General Joffre were quarrelling over the intended joint offensive on the Somme. At sea, German mines had taken a heavy toll of British shipping. By May it was clear that already the losses since the New Year would be not far short of 100,000 tons. In the North Sea, where the old battleship *King*

Edward VII and the light cruiser *Arethusa* had been mined and sunk since the New Year, the Grand Fleet had already been saddened by the tragedy of the cruiser *Natal*, which blew up in the afternoon of December 30, while a party of Cromarty children was being entertained aboard.

It was against this gloomy background of bad news and loss that Admiral Sir John Rushworth Jellicoe, K.C.B., the Commander-in-Chief, left the Fleet Flagship *Iron Duke*, otherwise known as the Tin Duck, to dine in H.M.S. *Hampshire* on the evening of the third of May. He was piped aboard while Captain Savill and his officers stood at the salute, and on the short walk to the Wardroom, where he was welcomed by the Commander as Mess President, he contrived to give the impression that he was seeing into and round and through everyone and everything in his path. Admiral Jellicoe was fifty-seven years old. He was a little man, only five foot six, but a terrifyingly trim and fit little man with a gimlet eye. At Scapa he played as hard as he worked: golf on the newly laid-out Flotta links, medicine ball on deck each evening. Jellicoe had held all the key appointments in the Royal Navy. On becoming Commander-in-Chief in August 1914 he had issued three pages of Grand Fleet Battle Orders, and it was one of the changes David Flett had noted with dismay that the G.F.B.O.s now ran to seventy pages. These covered—though with a few omissions—every contingency the Fleet might encounter if and when it met the enemy.

"Sir, may I present Lieutenant Flett, who has recently joined us from an internment camp?" said the Commander, when nearly all the smokingroom introductions had been made. David, six inches taller than the little admiral, looked down at a spare, self-contained face with a hint of humour in it.

"Where were you interned, Mr. Flett—Holland or Denmark?" said Jellicoe.

"At Groningen in Holland, sir."

"Ah! with the Naval Brigade. So you met my old acquaintance, Commodore Henderson?"

"He was the Senior British Officer, sir."

"A valuable man. Had you any companions on your escape?"

"No, sir."

"And how long did the homeward journey last?"

"It took me near seven days, sir, from Groningen to Parkeston Quay."

"Very good!"

"Mr. Flett was one of the few survivors of the *Yelverton*," the Commander interposed.

A shadow crossed the Admiral's face. "How many men were lost with the *Yelverton*, Mr. Flett?"

"Over three hundred, sir. Right near the whole ship's company."

"You were very fortunate."

"Sir."

It wasn't so much what he said as the way he said it. So interested, like. David, as he brought up the rear of the procession into the mess, thought he might "drop a line" to his father and tell him about the Commander-in-Chief's visit: it would be a great tit-bit for the Fish Market. But now his attention was riveted by the Wardroom as he had never seen it before, with all the ship's silver trophies out of their glass cases and ranged along the dinner table, where candles burned in silver sticks beneath pink fluted shades. The mess waiters wore white gloves and the white napery was as stiffly starched as the white shirt-fronts of the *Hampshire*'s officers. There was an alarming array of forks and knives and wine-glasses, but Lieutenant Flett was getting better at forks and knives now, and also at keeping his voice lower than a trawlerman's normal pitch. In subdued tones he made conversation with his neighbours.

At the head of the table Jellicoe sat between Captain Savill and the Commander. David looked along the glittering expanse from time to time: he didn't want to stare, but it was something to realise that there sat the Commander-in-Chief, the man who had the greatest responsibility in Britain on his shoulders. He had always respected the C.-in-C. as a man who had risen to the top on his own merits, for John Jellicoe did not belong by birth to the hierarchy of the Old Navy. The son of a master mariner, he had pulled himself up the ladder of promotion by sheer merit.

Jellicoe was talking about the notorious German raider *Moewe*, the minelayer which had sunk the *King Edward VII*. Much of what he said was drowned, for the young men at the foot of the table, by the music of the Royal Marine band, playing softly in the flat outside.

The dinner proceeded with grave formality from course to course. It was a study in black and white, with the candle shades the only note of colour, for no roses were obtainable in an Orkney May to fill the brightly polished silver bowls. The dark blue uniforms were almost black by candlelight, and the burgundy flowed black-red into the crystal glasses. It was also a study in civilisation: in the social tradition of a great Service, refined through years of respect for rank and etiquette into a style as formal as a ballet, and as such it finally impressed the unimpressionable soul of David Flett. I wish that lot in Maggie's Dining-room could get a look at this, he thought. It did not occur to him to think "I wish they could see *me* now," because in the presence of so much human power and might he was beyond thinking of himself. Where was the Navy, the sneering bill-boards asked. In a new surge of pride he felt, The Navy's here!

The dinner moved to its climax. The cloth was drawn. The decanters of port and marsala went clockwise round the table. The Corporal of Marines whispered to the Commander, "The wine has passed, sir." The Marine band ceased to play. The Mess President rapped on the table.

"Gentlemen, the King!"

"The King." It was the Navy's privilege to drink the King's health seated. Outside in the flat, the Royal Marines began to play the National Anthem.

At this emotional moment David Flett watched the Commander-in-Chief. Jellicoe's head was slightly bent, and his fingers gripped the stem of his wine glass. Against his will David remembered Winston Churchill's often quoted opinion, that Jellicoe was the only man who could lose the war in one afternoon.

XII

Thursday, May 4, to
Thursday, May 11, 1916

Before the Admiral's barge took Sir John Jellicoe back to H.M.S.
Iron Duke, every ship in the Battle Fleet had received orders to
put to sea. By the time Lieutenant Flett, out of mess uniform
and into seaboots and a duffel coat, arrived on deck to keep the
middle watch, the *Hampshire* had sailed from Scapa Flow by Hoxa
Sound and embarked on the long passage through the Pentland
Skerries towards the North Sea.

David wore seaboots on the advice of his brother officers, and
as soon as the *Hampshire* reached the open sea he understood all
he had been told about the old cruiser's defects. For if H.M.S.
Hampshire lying at anchor was an imposing sight, at sea she
wallowed and waddled desperately, with her decks awash, when
the slightest sea was running. For this and other reasons she was
sometimes jovially referred to as a death trap. She was an armoured
cruiser, but her six-inch armour plating was not strong enough to
resist heavy attack by modern guns. Her own guns were numerous
but not impressive. She carried twenty three-pounders but only
ten of larger calibre—four 7·5-inch and six 6-inch, and she was
not equipped with director firing. A relic of King Edward VII's
peaceful reign, *Hampshire* ploughed gamely after the Dreadnoughts
at a rate of speed which, if the black squad called on everything
they had, could be raised as high as 23 knots.

The object of the exercise, as Captain Savill told his assembled
officers at first light, was the perennial one: the enticing of the
High Seas Fleet from the shelter of the Heligoland Bight. A
preliminary attack was being mounted on the Zeppelin sheds at
Tondern from two British seaplane carriers supported by elements
of the Battle Cruiser Fleet. The Battle Fleet from Scapa took

station off the Skagerrak, with the battle cruisers to the south, minefields laid and British submarines on watch, and there they all waited for Scheer until two o'clock in the afternoon of May 4. Then the Commander-in-Chief ordered a return to base, and "another bloody useless sweep" was over.

One reason for the withdrawal was obvious: the difficulty of maintaining the Grand Fleet at sea without refuelling. Only certain officers of the flagship *Iron Duke*, with Admiral Beatty and his officers in H.M.S. *Lion*, knew that an Admiralty signal had informed the C.-in-C. at noon that the enemy appeared unaware that the British Fleet was at sea. It was, therefore, particularly galling that about one hour after the Grand Fleet altered course for home the German battleships should have come demurely out from cover, to hang round the site of the raid on Tondern for nearly twelve hours before returning to Jade Bay.

H.M.S. *Hampshire* passed May 6 at coaling, with Number Threes the rig of the day for officers and coaling rig, composed of anything that came to hand, for men. A crew of six hundred and fifty men like the *Hampshire's* could handle over 300 tons an hour, from the collier's hold into the bunker, but it was gruelling work, and so was the swabbing and holystoning of the decks which followed. Saturday in a ship's time-table was the day for cleaning ship, when the sailor's personal belongings were scrubbed, including his bag and ditty box: it always meant a heavy day when coaling coincided with ship cleaning. Saturday night had its own ritual in the Wardroom mess, with the toast of "Sweethearts and Wives" to be honoured, and some mild ragging; Captain Savill judged that few of his officers, after two abortive sorties in ten days, would be in the mood for merriment. He decided to invite them to sherry in his fore-cabin, as a change from the usual gathering in the smokingroom.

Lieutenant Flett walked along the Captain's flat, to where the Royal Marine sentry guarded the Captain's outer door, with feelings not far short of satisfaction. The abortive sortie to the Skagerrak had not enraged him as it had the young men who had already spent more than twelve months on manœuvres and sweeps which always just missed a confrontation with the enemy.

After the internment camp it had been like living in a new world, which was at the same time his own, old world, to be beating across the North Sea in the *Hampshire*, with his eyes screwed up and watering, his face beginning to smart and crack in the teeth of a gale which blew away all the doubts, the degradation and the pain of the past month. He passed into the fore-cabin, made pleasant by Captain Savill's chintzes and family photographs, and said, "Good-evening, sir," to his host.

Captain Savill was chatting with the chaplain, who appeared to have something on his mind about the Presbyterian religious services held aboard the *Ghourko*, an auxiliary which served the Grand Fleet for all purposes from refrigeration to theatricals and boxing tournaments. Savill excused himself politely to the padre, and taking David by the elbow led him to the table where a mess waiter was serving drinks.

"Sherry, Mr. Flett? Or do you prefer gin and bitters?'

"Sherry, thank you, sir." The Captain's attentiveness was slightly alarming. David had only had one conversation alone with Captain Savill, on the day he reported for duty, when his new Captain had alluded briefly to a very favourable letter he had received from the Director of the Intelligence Division about Mr. Flett. Now, with David's glass filled, Savill dropped his voice to say:

"There was an allusion to you in a despatch I received from Captain Hall today."

"To me, sir?"

"Quite a brief message. I was asked to pass the word to Lieutenant Flett that the first results are satisfactory. Those were the actual words, 'the first results are satisfactory'. That means something to you, I suppose?"

"I think so, sir."

"Very good. Ah, padre! I hadn't forgotten you. Mr. Flett may be the very man you're looking for—"

The Captain returned to his other guests. The chaplain was delighted to discover that Lieutenant Flett was a member of the Church of Scotland and therefore highly eligible to escort the Presbyterians to worship in the *Ghourko* next day.

"The reason why I'm making such a point of it," said the chaplain with the anxious courtesy of the Church of England towards all other denominations, "is that most of the men prefer to attend Divine Worship aboard. However, a local clergyman, the minister of Hamnavoe, is taking tomorrow's service in the *Ghourko*. I do think as many Presbyterians as possible should turn out, don't you?"

"I'll look after it, padre. Dr. Sabiston and me are quite well acquaint already."

"That's splendid, my dear lad; I'll leave it all to you." It was merely a matter of falling out the men and laying on the boats; there were not many Scots in the *Hampshire*, though probably the non-conformists would swell the congregation in the *Ghourko*. The padre happily changed the subject to the forthcoming sports at Long Hope on Hoy Island, and David had only to offer a few remarks, such as Jolly good show and Tophole stunt, which he had already learned in H.M.S. *Yelverton*. He was free to think, then and later, of Blinker Hall's message about the satisfactory results. That meant, of course, that the enemy had begun receiving—and acting upon—signals based on the fake codebook allowed to fall into Karl Ritter's hands. David wondered, as he wondered every day, where Ritter was now. Back aboard a German battleship, snug in Jade Bay, or still employed as a secret agent, somewhere in the Norwegian fjords? He wondered if his English mother was proud of her clever son.

The Flow lay bright and peaceful next morning, when David took his party of worshippers, immaculately groomed and with cap ribbons pressed, to the service aboard the s.s. *Ghourko*. Out on the water he could see the white-harled front of Hamnavoe manse, and wondered who was preaching in Hamnavoe kirk while Dr. Sabiston was ministering to the Navy. It was a great relief to David to meet Ingrid's father for the first time since his bereavement in a crowd of officers from all through the Fleet. A few awkward expressions of sympathy, a clumsy turning aside of any reference to the sinking of the *Yelverton*, could be resolved by a cordial handshake in such company. But the stern, sad face of the minister in the black Geneva gown relaxed pleasantly when David said,

"We're off to the Pentland Firth for a three-day exercise, Dr. Sabiston. Will it be all right if I come up to the manse when I get shore leave?"

"Any time, David, you know you're welcome any time."

"Will Ingrid be at home on Thursday, then?" persisted David.

"I think so; but she's a busy girl these days. There's the Red Cross at Kirkwall, and the cliff patrol, and I hear talk of a job at a Y.M.C.A. canteen at Long Hope too . . . I'll tell her to expect you on Thursday anyway. Will that do?"

"Thank you kindly, sir." David had to give up the minister to a superior being with three gold rings on his sleeve and an Edinburgh accent, and to content himself with the half-promise of Thursday, always provided the *Hampshire* returned to base in time.

The 2nd Cruiser Squadron of the Battle Fleet consisted of H.M.S. *Minotaur*, the flagship of Rear-Admiral H. L. Heath, and three other armoured cruisers, H.M.S. *Hampshire*, *Cochrane* and *Shannon*. It was the custom for the Squadrons to leave Scapa Flow in turn for battle practice, and so on Monday morning the 2nd Squadron steamed out of Hoxa Sound, the principal entry to the Flow and guarded by gun emplacements, into the 14-knot tide-race of the Pentland Firth.

Battle practice, of course, had to be carried out according to the principles laid down in Grand Fleet Battle Orders by the Commander-in-Chief. Jellicoe, himself a gunnery expert, adhered strictly to long-range firing, although this had not been too successful at the Falkland Islands battle or the Dogger Bank. Ships were always to be manœuvred on a single line and a parallel course, and while it was unlikely that H.M.S. *Hampshire* could ever successfully take the offensive it was nevertheless frustrating to be committed always to the defensive mentality of the Commander-in-Chief. Within these limitations the armoured cruisers worked hard in the Pentland Firth. On the first day (as on so many other days since August 1914) they took turns in long-range shooting at a towed target during many hours of grey and rainy weather. No provision had been made in the G.F.B.O.s for night action, for the good reason that the last British admiral to fight a night action had been Sir James Saumarez in 1801, but the early darkness of the eighth of May gave an opportunity for lamp-signalling practice. This soon reduced the 2nd Squadron to a state of chaos.

The position of the Signals Officer was in May 1916 not very well defined. Jellicoe had a Signals Officer in the Fleet Flagship, but Jellicoe was known to distrust wireless telegraphy, and to depend on visual communication by means of linking cruisers. When Lieutenant Flett told Ingrid Sabiston that he was "on searchlights" he meant that Captain Savill was taking the visual link problem seriously—more seriously perhaps than some of his fellow captains. He had put David in charge of the hand lamps, worked by men trained as flag-signallers, and now the deficiencies in searchlight control became obvious as the hand lamps wavered and failed to hold the target. Mercifully, the ships of 2nd Squadron were three miles apart and there was no collision, but angry yells rang across the water and the final signals were profane. David spent all his watch below next day working out corrective angles and shutter speeds, wishing that he had gone further in mathematics and paid more attention to his school text-books. He had heard in the internment camp about a device called the iris shutter which the Germans were fitting to their searchlights, but it was not available in the Royal Navy and he decided not to mention it. He had learned in H.M.S. *Yelverton* what befell the brash profferer of unsolicited advice.

"Ingrid," said Dr. Sabiston, as father and daughter sat at their one o'clock dinner on Thursday, "do you think that young man of yours will be here this afternoon?"

Smiling: "There hasn't been any word to say he won't. And the *Hampshire's* back in the Flow again—Agnes heard it at the shop."

"The shop runs a wonderful intelligence service. Well, if the excellent David does appear, how do you propose to entertain him?"

"Why—to tea, I thought!"

"Could I persuade you to take yourselves out of the way for

an hour or so first? I've an article for *Chambers's Journal* that I want posted in Stromness, and four sets of examination papers to draw up before bedtime—"

"You'd like to have the house to yourself. If David gets here early enough we might have a little picnic by the Loch of Skaill and Agnes can give you your tea whenever you want it. Would that do?"

"Perfectly. I'd like you to have a happy afternoon, Ingrid; you deserve a change. Wear your white dress, and look nice."

"Shouldn't I wear black to go to Stromness, Daddy?"

"No," said the minister decidedly. "I should be sorry to see you in bright colours, but white is different. Your mother never liked to see young people in deep mourning."

But that made Ingrid pick up the dessert plates hurriedly and take them straight out to the kitchen, so that her father should not see her tears. She had been feeling guilty all the morning, as if it were wrong, in her sad home, to be so happy about David's coming. And yet as she changed into her white dress she caught herself humming a tune as she remembered that her father had called David "that young man of yours".

"David was delightfully definite about wanting to see *you*," her father had said, when he came back to the manse on Sunday afternoon. "Delightfully definite"—that was the way her father talked; but how it had soothed the searing recollection of the way she had rushed headlong into Davie's arms! It was seeing him so suddenly, she defended herself, instinctively recognising that the young man's physical presence had given reality to all the vague romantic feelings she had built around him for so long. At her boarding-school it was the height of fashion to have "a crush" on some young soldier at the front. A naval officer in an internment camp was almost as good, especially if he were by schoolgirl definition a hero, and after the sinking of the *Yelverton* Ingrid had willingly transferred her hero-worship from a cinema star called Dustin Farnum to Sub-Lieutenant David Flett. She had written to him, saved up to send him a Christmas parcel, sent him her photograph and showed the other girls a blurred snapshot taken of him with Magnus. It had been a matter of paper and pasteboard—but now he was back, and it was real.

David came to Hamnavoe manse in one of the "machines" which plied for hire between Houton Pier and Kirkwall, disentangling himself from a noisy group of young officers on their way to spend the afternoon in the town. He was enthusiastic about the plan for the afternoon: the Fleet was at four hours' notice for steam, which allowed time for an excursion, and he wheeled the motor-bicycle from its shed while Ingrid filled a Thermos flask and put on a hat and gloves for the visit to Stromness. She was rather doubtful about her white dress. It had been new for her school prizegiving in the previous June, and seemed too short and too skimpy now. But she had one of the jersey coats which were coming into fashion, and David looked at her admiringly as he settled her in the sidecar with the picnic basket.

After two abortive attempts at starting, the Harley-Davidson roared off, with an encouraging shriek from Agnes. David was not an experienced driver. He made heavy weather of the shore road, once so lonely, and now crowded with traffic of all descriptions from the horse-drawn machines to the builders' motor lorries, for construction work never seemed to end at Scapa Flow. Ingrid sat holding on to her black straw hat. She would have liked to draw David's attention to the distant hills of Sutherland, visible on such a brilliant day across the Pentland Firth, but he was grimly preoccupied with the traffic, and she dared not speak. Soon they reached Stromness, and David pulled up at the entrance to the main street, so narrow that at some points two vehicles could not pass.

"Will we walk up to the post office?" he asked. "There's an awful lot of staff cars round the entrance to the hotel."

"Yes, we'd better leave the bike here," Ingrid agreed. The congestion of traffic in Stromness was even worse than on the shore road, for the charming little port had become the headquarters of Western Patrol, and the Stromness Hotel, a favourite resort of officers joined by their wives for short leave, also housed the offices of the Civil Engineer of the naval base. Even the pavements were crowded as Ingrid and David walked along. She was glad that the Stromness folk, many of whom she knew, should see her walking with her handsome sailor.

"Look at the flag," she said. "That's Sir John Jellicoe's car!"

A limousine, with the Commander-in-Chief's flag flying on the bonnet, was backing away from the staff cars and turning round.

Admiral Jellicoe, with the Civil Engineer in attendance, came out of the Stromness Hotel with his usual quick, brisk step. Several staff officers followed him. His blue uniform, with six rows of medal ribbons, was immaculately pressed but far from new. Lieutenant Flett came smartly to attention and saluted his Commander-in-Chief. It was no perfunctory salute he received in return, for Jellicoe's courtesy was legendary, and it was said that he would acknowledge the salute of the youngest boy in the Fleet as gravely as the salute of an admiral. Ingrid Sabiston was thrilled.

"Isn't he a darling," she said when the limousine drove away. "Was he nice when he dined aboard the *Hampshire*, Davie?"

"Very nice."

"I wonder what he was doing at the Engineer's office. Probably blowing him up about the new wharf at Lyness, they say it isn't nearly finished yet."

"He has a lot on his mind, all right."

"Oh, but," she said, recollecting. "I haven't told you the good news. We only heard this morning—Magnus's ship is coming up to Scapa on the fifteenth."

"Great!" said David. "It'll be grand to have a news with old Magnus again. I thought the *Chester* was to be at Rosyth with the Battle Cruiser Fleet."

"It's an exchange of Squadrons—the 3rd B.C. is coming north for gunnery exercises."

"We'll be hearing all about director firing."

They reached the post office, where Dr. Sabiston's learned contribution to *Chambers's Journal* was duly weighed and posted. The subject of Magnus and the *Chester* was not resumed until they found themselves down at the harbour, where David cast an expert eye over two steam trawlers moored at the little quay.

"I'm right pleased Magnus is coming north," he said, "it'll do your father good."

"Yes, it will. It's something for him to look forward to, instead of looking back."

"I thought when I saw Dr. Sabiston on Sunday he was very

come-at about your mother's death." It was the strongest expression for affliction David knew.

"It's terrible in the evenings when we're alone," Ingrid sighed. "When Olav goes to bed, Daddy wants to talk about her—to remind me of all the little things, as if he thought I could forget! Last night he told me all about their first meeting—it was heartbreaking to hear him."

"Aye, where did they meet, Ingrid? Was it in Norway, or was it here?"

"It was in Norway. Daddy was on a walking tour with another young man. Mummy had gone to spend the summer at a saeter her family had in the Dales, with one of her girl friends from college, and when the two boys stopped to beg a drink of milk the girls pretended to be real saeter girls—you know, like dairymaids, they were in peasant dress—and they made Daddy and his friend milk the cows themselves, and it was all sort of silly, and good fun."

"That was a nice beginning to remember."

"Yes, they liked to keep the anniversary, it was the sixth of July. Daddy didn't find out for ages how rich the Kolbergs really were—"

David's hands clenched in his jacket pockets. "What about Mr. Kolberg in Christiania—your Uncle Hans? Wasn't he in a terrible state when he heard about your mother?"

"Cousin Axel was afraid to tell him at first."

"What was the matter with him, like? A heart attack?"

Puzzled: "We never really knew. Axel just called it 'an attack'. I think it must have been a slight stroke. Uncle Hans was very stout and heavy when I saw him last."

"When was that?"

"The summer before the war—1913. We used to go to Norway for a holiday every second year."

"And is he keeping better now, your uncle?"

"He's well enough to be back at business. Axel wrote to say they were both going up to the Bergen office next week."

"Your uncle does a big trade with Germany, doesn't he?"

"Dear me, what an inquisition!" Ingrid spoke lightly, but David saw that she was not pleased. He was adroit enough to change the subject.

213

"I hear there used to be a lot of Norwegian trawlers at Stromness before the war," he said.

"Yes, for the herring fishing. Mummy used to love to talk to the crews. They always said they felt at home in Stromness."

"It's an awful nice place."

The little town, with its single street straggling under Brinkie's Brae, was looking its best in the May sunshine. The threats of war were always present, one of them implicit in the Clestron Barrier protecting the entrance to the Flow by Hoy Sound, but the great hills of Hoy stood up against Stromness like timeless guardians. They had seen many sailors putting into the harbour to water their ships—Captain Cook and Sir John Franklin, and the captains of the Hudson's Bay Company: now the great hills kept the ring for the new champions of Scapa Flow.

"If I get half a chance when the war's over," David said, "I would like fine to buy a share in a boat up here and trawl out of Stromness for the herring."

"Davie! Would you really?" It was the first time she had ever heard him speak of that mythical future when the war was won.

"There's big money in trawling," he said seriously. "Twenty pounds for every working day was our gross earnings when I was mate in the *Moss Rose*. Of course I was a fool and spent it as fast as I earned it then, but I know the money's waiting to be made."

"But would you not want to live in Scotland, Davie?"

He laughed. "We're *in* Scotland, you daft lassie."

"In a sort of way," said the Orkney girl.

"Come on and let's have our picnic. Unless you would rather have tea at the hotel?"

"Davie! When I made tomato sandwiches!"

They decided to go up the Atlantic coast to Birsay. The Loch of Skaill, David declared, would be "crawling with the Navy". He had seen the *Hampshire's* cutter, towing a skiff and loaded with intending picnickers, leaving for the West Mainland ahead of the picket-boat.

The Harley-Davidson roared north along a deserted road. Past Yesnaby, past the beautiful Bay of Skaill, through Sandwick, into the Barony of Birsay. They left Skara Brae behind without stopping, although Ingrid shrieked above the wind of their

progress, "That's a Stone Age settlement, Daddy writes about it"
—driving headlong into their own future, without a thought for
the Stone Age or any day and generation but their own. They came
to Birsay, a small jewel, with orange lichen glowing on the roofs
of the little hamlet and the ruined walls of Earl Robert Stewart's
palace, and yellow celandines gleaming by a little burn that ran
down to the sea. Wallflowers and pansies were coming into bloom
at the cottage doors.

"What a rare place!" said David, helping Ingrid out of the
sidecar.

"Isn't it?" She pulled her hat off, and waved to a man in
Territorial uniform standing at the door of the little post office.
"That's one of the cliff-watchers, Dave . . . Oh look, the tide's
coming in, we can't cross over to the Brough."

She pointed to a long causeway, running from the beach
below the hamlet to the Brough of Birsay, the fortress island;
there sheep were calmly cropping the grass where an ancient Celtic
church had stood. Already the incoming tide was swirling over
the causeway, which now appeared like stepping stones, as the long
Atlantic rollers broke on the white sand of the Mainland. "You
can be marooned on the Brough for six hours if you forget about
the tide," said Ingrid. "Daddy was once, when he was studying
the site of an old Norse hamlet. He was so cold and hungry when
he got home."

She looked like a young Valkyrie herself, with her flying fair
hair, and the short white dress moulded against her long legs as
she led the way down to the beach. There was a stiff breeze from
the Atlantic, but they found a sheltered place between the couch-
grass and the rocks, where Ingrid poured tea from the Thermos
and they ate the tomato sandwiches and chunks of cake.

"Mummy used to bring Olav and me here when we were little,
after Magnus went to Dartmouth," the girl said as they packed
the mugs back in the basket. "We had Thermos tea then too. But
Mummy was so sweet, she used to make a little fire, just as if we'd
had to boil a kettle, and we played at being Cornish wreckers, and
shipwrecked mariners, and I don't know what all—"

"Let's have a fire now," suggested David. There were wood

chips in plenty on the beach, and he had matches. Soon a tiny fire of salty wood, sparkling blue-green in the sunshine, flickered between stones in the white shale sand.

"This is great," said David. He lit a cigarette, and leaned back lazily against the tussocks. The causeway to the Brough was entirely covered now, and the birds of Birsay, the fulmars and the kittiwakes and the Tammie Norries, circled and called from cliff to cliff. Once or twice the brown head of a seal appared far out in the bay.

"That's Marwick Head, isn't it?" said David, nodding at the great precipice beyond Birsay to the south.

"Yes. And those two headlands are the Yamnas. Didn't you go out kuithe-fishing here with Magnus, one night last summer?"

"Not me."

"Oh, I remember now, it was Lieutenant Robertson he took. Well, anyway, if you're fishing off Birsay you have to take your bearings by the Yamnas. 'Steer by the Yimna Yamnas' that's what old fishermen say. When they get both the Yamnas in line they can bring the boat straight in from Birsay Bay and draw it up here on the shingle."

"There's somebody prowling about above the Yamnas now."

"Oh, Dave, he isn't prowling, that's one of the Territorials on cliff patrol."

"What's he looking for—a German submarine?"

"It *could* happen," she said with dignity. "I'm a watcher myself, down on the Black Craig cliffs at Stromness. I go there twice a week—"

"You're taking on too much war work. What's this about the Y.M.C.A. hut at Long Hope?"

"They're going to need a lot of extra helpers there."

"Maybe, but why *you*, doling out tea and fags to the Navy?"

"Why *not*?"

"Because I want to keep you to myself, that's why."

He hadn't meant to say it. Already he knew in his bones that Ingrid Sabiston was the right woman for him, that she could live life at his own tempo, that with this kind and simple girl he would have his best chance of happiness. But she was very young, and his mind was not quite free of a ghost in white tulle and Odette's crown, nor of darker thoughts still, and he had not meant to speak until the way was clearer, but . . . She was so near, and so lovely, with the white jersey discarded on the white sand, her lips parted as she looked at him, and the sea-blue eyes wide. The skimpy dress was strained over the splendid curves of her young breasts. He wanted to lay his head there and make her his for ever.

"Because you're *my* girl, Ingrid, aren't you?"

"If you want me to be."

He took her in his arms then, and kissed her, lying in the sand, feeling her whole body against his own, no ghost, but a living and passionate woman. She gave him kiss for kiss, she sighed her happiness; but Ingrid's gentle strength was never overborne, and it was she who first released herself from their embrace.

"Don't, Davie, we mustn't. People can see us from the cliffs."

He damned the cliffs and the cliff patrol and kissed her till her cheeks were burning. But Ingrid broke away from him and said breathlessly, "*Please*, Dave! I want to talk."

"What about?"

"Something that's worrying me."

"Well?"

"Why did you ask all those questions down at the pier about my Uncle Hans?"

David groaned and sat up. There it was again, unending, the Kolberg shadow.

"Why did you ask me about his business with Germany?" she went on. "I don't know anything about it."

"I never thought you did, Ingrid."

"But there is *one* thing," she hesitated, "that I think I ought to tell you. Only you must promise never to mention it to Daddy." She laid two or three more splinters of wood on the tiny fire, and watched the flame.

"I think you ought to know the real reason why my mother went to Christiania . . . She *was* upset about Uncle Hans, of course. But she'd been worrying because we hadn't been to Norway for so long, and she was afraid Axel Kolberg—he's Uncle Hans's nephew, not his son—would get the company all into his own hands.

And Mummy wanted to make sure of a place for Olav there."

"For Olav? But he's just a kid!"

"Well, yes, but he doesn't want to go into the Navy, as Magnus did from the time he was ten, or to the University; and K.D.S. is a very big business, Dave; Mummy was only thinking about Olav's future."

David was silent. He thought, as he had thought in Aberdeen, that there would always be gaps in the story. Here was another detail: his kind friend Mrs. Sabiston had her own share of the Kolberg strain of greed and self-interest. That was what had driven her to risk her life on the submarine-infested sea.

"I don't mean Mummy would have approved of trading with the enemy," Ingrid went on. "But how do you know Uncle Hans does anything of the sort?"

"He's pretty high on the Black List, Ingrid. I heard that at the Admiralty."

Contemptuously: "Some of your sister's gossip?"

"The Director of Intelligence told me himself."

"Oh." Ingrid was visibly dismayed. She drew her hand away from David's.

"When you used to go to your uncle's," he said, "did you ever meet a German chap called Ritter?"

"Not that I remember. Who is he?"

"He's an officer in the German Navy. He's been friendly with Mr. Kolberg for a long time."

"Magnus may have known him, but I never did. Davie, what's all this *about*? Why are you being so mysterious? Do you mean this Ritter and my uncle are mixed up in the war in some wrong way?"

"I think they are. In fact I know they are."

"And how do *you* come into it?"

"Through the girl who helped me to get out of Holland."

"You didn't tell me about any girl."

"I'll tell you now." He described his meeting with Elena at Mr. Timmermann's, her ready sympathy and quick wits, and the paper she had given him to escape from Dutch control. The sea-blue eyes were steady on his own till he ended the story with his return to England.

"Was she very pretty?" It was Ingrid's first question, and David answered briefly, "Yes, she was lovely."

"A Russian dancer." Then, inconsequently, "I never got to see the Russian ballet. At school they only took us to see Shakespeare plays, and once Martin Harvey in *The Only Way*."

"Elena was a famous dancer in her own country."

"Was? Where is she now? And what had she to do with this man Ritter?"

"He was her lover, Ingrid. That's why she was shot and killed in Amsterdam on the twenty-second of last month." He dared not add, "And I was there." He saw that the girl was deeply shocked. She drew the white jersey round her shoulders as if a shrivelling wind from another country had brought her the intimations of a darker world.

"The twenty-second," she said slowly. "Why, that's not three weeks ago."

"It seems like a long time to me."

"Someone like that . . . can't be easy to forget. If she was beautiful and famous . . . and on the stage, that's always glamorous—"

"Glamour's not the right word for Elena Tamirova. It was just something she had in herself—I don't know what it was—"

"Fascination?"

"Aye, maybe."

Ingrid was pouring sand over her little fire. The dregs of the Thermos, a damp turf, the stones of the miniature hearth were piled on the last embers; nothing was left of the flame they had kindled on the beach between the Brough of Birsay and Marwick Head.

"It's time to go," she said. "Davie, I'll have to think about all this. Perhaps I'll talk to Magnus when he comes home, and find out what he knows about Uncle Hans and Ritter."

"You do that." He offered his hand to help her to her feet. But Ingrid got up in one swift movement, and shook the sand from her white skirt.

"There's just one thing," she told him bravely. "When I said . . . I'd be your girl if you wanted me to be . . . I didn't know about Elena Tamirova."

XIII

Friday, May 12, to
Saturday, May 27, 1916

On the day after the picnic at Birsay H.M.S. *Hampshire* left Scapa
Flow on one of the routine patrols in which that versatile cruiser
was an auxiliary to the 10th Squadron. She was accompanied until
next morning by her sister ship from the 2nd, H.M.S. *Cochrane*,
so that searchlight drill between the two ships could take place
during the hours of darkness, which in those northern latitudes
lasted from eleven at night until two in the morning. From
eleven until one o'clock, somewhere north of the Shetlands, the
hand lamps winked their messages between *Hampshire* and
Cochrane.

"Much better, Mr. Flett," said Captain Savill when the
exercise was over.

"Thank you, sir."

"Too bad it's such a fine clear night. We didn't have much of a
chance at approximating to battle conditions."

"The stokers did their best to give us coal smoke, sir."

"So they did." The Captain dismissed the signals officers and
their crew. "It's the devil of a problem," he said to the Commander when the signallers had dispersed. "The day may come
when we depend entirely on the searchlights for communication.
You know what the message capacity of our W/T is like. The
Minotaur wasn't receiving us last time we were in the Pentland
Firth, neither were we reading them. What if the hand lamps turn
out to be useless in the smoke of battle? The lamp crew is a long
way from being expert yet."

"What if we go to action in a fog, sir?"

"Don't even hint at such a thing."

"Flett is turning out quite well," said the Commander, "but I agree with you about the men on the lamps. They still need working up."

"I sometimes wonder," said the Captain thoughtfully, "if any ship's company can be worked up beyond a certain point. These chaps have been at the peak of preparedness for the better part of two years now; it isn't easy to keep them there indefinitely."

"Scheer is bound to make a move next month, sir."

"He may, but will we?" Captain Savill retired to his quarters in poor spirits. The strain of the long wait was telling on him as much as on his officers. But the new day dawned, with the bo'sun's mates shouting "Rise and shine!" along the lower decks, and the timeless routine went on—Divisions, drills, defaulter's parade, grog issue, dinner. The *Hampshire*, detached from her Squadron mate, went off on her own on a familiar beat. Due north to the Faeroe Islands, where a few Aberdeen trawlers were hailed, and north-west to the coast of Iceland, and all the time no blockade-runners were encountered, no merchantment even, except a Dane out of Greenland with a perfectly innocent cargo for Copenhagen, who made the usual expostulations at the British search.

"You haven't seen much of this kind of thing, have you, Flett?" asked the Commander as he stood watching, with his glass at his eye, the return of the search party from the *Dannevirke*. Lieutenant William Ramsay's red head could be seen in the stern-sheets of the boat. Captain Savill occasionally gave a junior officer command of a search party; and in this case he had been reasonably sure of the Dane's innocence.

"Not a great lot, sir. The *Yelverton* was never auxiliary to the Northern Patrol. Her beat was usually east to Jutland Bank or south-east to the Frisians."

"So it was. Well, by the time you were shut up in Groningen, my lad, Northern Patrol was stopping sixty vessels a week, and even as late as last March I think they averaged about thirty. We've wounded the tender feelings of every shipowner in the three Scandinavian kingdoms, while the Russians are doing damn-all in the Baltic to stop the contraband trade with Lübeck."

Boldly: "Is it true that the C.-in-C. thinks we should risk

going to war with Norway and Sweden, to enforce our blockade of Germany?"

"That sounds like a choice quote from a Wardroom cag to me . . . As a matter of fact I hear the C.-in-C. is quite willing to take on the United States as well, if they kick up another row about our right of search."

There was a suspicion of a grin on the Commander's face, and Lieutenant Flett thought it wiser to say no more. The *Danne-virke's* indignant plume of coal smoke was vanishing astern, and the *Hampshire* resumed her course towards Iceland. They skirted the east coast as far as the Arctic Circle, and shivered in their duffel coats; the watches below screened the scuttles in a vain attempt to sleep through the dazzling Arctic nights. Three times on her way back to base, H.M.S. *Hampshire* spoke to British cargo steamers making gamely for Trondheim or Bergen. The freighter captains always had great tales to tell of hairsbreadth escapes from German submarines and minelayers. Each claimed to have seen the notorious *Moewe*, wearing her favourite disguise, the blue and gold of Sweden, and performing one of her most impudent tricks —filling her own bunkers from some captured British collier, before proceeding on her lethal way. All were indignant about having to go about their business unprotected. There was an increasing demand in the merchant marine for a return to the convoy system of the Napoleonic Wars.

Through these five days of routine patrol, unrelieved by any incident, and thanks to the *Hampshire's* W/T capacity, limited to short wave, without much news of the outside world, David Flett worked harder than he had ever worked before in a ship of the Royal Navy, and not only at searchlight signal drill. He became particular to a fault in all the set exercises of each day. In his watch on deck the lifeboat's crew had to fall in at least once, and go through their evolutions at top speed. The ship's boats had to be swung out on their davits with equal speed. The order "Clear Ship for Action" had to be carried out at the double. David "worked up" his watch beyond the knife-edge of preparedness which Captain Savill thought they had already attained, and in the process he worked himself up too. He deserved, but of course did not receive, higher praise than the Commander's moderate verdict that he was turning out quite well, for he was on the way, at last, to becoming an excellent sea officer. No longer, as in the *Yelverton*, was he too friendly with the crew. He had got the measure of them now, and they respected him.

Half the trouble David met head-on in the *Yelverton* had been the fault of Captain Willis-Turner, himself a product of the New Navy, socially insecure when he came up against senior officers from the Old, and only too ready to bully the entries from the R.N.V.R. Captain Savill was an officer of another stamp. David admired him, and even began to realise the importance of the despised team games in welding the crew together. When he took part in Divisions at nine o'clock on Sunday, with the whole ship's company forward in the waist and on the fo'c'sle, with the White Ensign at the peak, the Marine bugles blowing, and the order "Off hats!" obeyed in one motion by six hundred and fifty men, he felt the satisfaction of being a useful cog in a machine greater than he had understood before.

As soon as they returned to Scapa Flow and the drudgery of coaling, Bill Ramsay—one of the officers who were first to start a "buzz" in any Wardroom—came back from a trip to Base at Long Hope on the island of Hoy with the news that the C.-in-C. had been at Rosyth with his Chief of Staff. Admiral Sir Henry Jackson, the First Sea Lord, had travelled up from London with his own entourage, and the debonair Admiral Beatty, commanding the battle cruisers at Rosyth, had of course been present too. A top-level conference was an excellent topic for a "Wardroom cag", and gave rise to speculation on the prospect of "another bloody useless sweep".

The frustrated officers at Scapa might have felt more hopeful if they had known that only a few days after Jellicoe met the First Sea Lord in Scotland an even more important conference was taking place at the Marinamt in Berlin. Admiral Scheer was determined to fight at last. He was weary of the tip and run raids, and the criticisms of the All-Highest, Kaiser Wilhelm II. On May 18, Scheer issued an Order of the Day which read: "The bombardment of Sunderland by our cruisers is intended to compel the enemy to send their forces out against us. The enemy's ports of sortie will be closed by mines."

The German submarine minelayers, to the number of eighteen, had already been ordered to sea. One had a special mission. It was the result of an earlier conference, in another part of the Marinamt, where certain anonymous individuals whom Blinker Hall would have liked to meet considered a report from an American businessman in Norway, who called himself Karl Ericssen. Decoded, the report turned out to be a rather hysterical summary of various successes, ending with an impassioned request that the writer might now be allowed to return to active duty and join the ship to which he had been posted, the *Pommern*. The faceless men decided on one more mission for him first.

On the morning of the day when David Flett met his old friend Magnus Sabiston again, there was a major flap at Scapa Flow. Reports that a U-boat had penetrated the booms of heavy nets across Hoxa Sound sent every vessel in the Flow to panic stations. All guns were manned. Torpedo nets were placed in position, and battleships without nets were protected by the colliers and store ships which at once laid themselves alongside the giants of the Fleet. All small craft available patrolled the harbour in search of the invader. It was a manœuvre fairly quickly executed, the only alternative being to send the whole Fleet out into the Pentland Firth, which took an hour and a half. When the flap was safely over the minesweepers had to set to work and sweep all the channels down which the suspected invader might have passed.

In nearly two years of war, no satisfactory method of counterattacking the U-boats had been put into general operation. A Cambridge professor and a naval officer had invented the hydrophone to detect the beat of a submarine propeller at a distance, but this had not yet come into production, and although depth charges had been invented their supply in May 1916 was strictly limited. So the capital ships at Scapa were still dependent on the smaller craft to act as buffers in the event of a torpedo attack, and when Ingrid Sabiston looked out that morning she saw the Flow in the same state of agitation as her own poultry yard when a rat's gleaming eye was seen among the Buff Orpingtons and Rhode Island Reds.

Ingrid herself was restless and unhappy. In the week since the Birsay picnic she had passed through every degree of heat and cold, and every variety of emotion with regard to David Flett. Sometimes she had an hour of purely sensuous enjoyment, recollecting those first wild kisses while the Atlantic rollers surged around the base of Marwick Head; sometimes she wove innocent fantasies about the future. She would be married to Skipper Flett, of the grand Orkney name, and they would live in one of the houses on the shore at Stromness, built out over the water, where she would watch from the window for Davie's trawler coming home from sea. In another mood Ingrid felt only cold anger that he could speak so tenderly of the dead ballet-dancer so soon after he had held Ingrid Sabiston in his arms. To the Orkney girl, manse-bred, Elena Tamirova was nothing more or less than an immoral woman.

She was beginning to wonder if her coldness had driven Davie away for good, when she came home from a Red Cross meeting in Kirkwall to hear that he had telephoned. "The worthy David", as her father called him, had been in touch with Magnus and would meet him at the manse that afternoon.

H.M.S. *Chester* had duly arrived at Scapa Flow early on May 15, and Lieutenant Sabiston had at once been granted shore leave on compassionate grounds. He was a master at swinging the lead, and the Captain who sent him ashore to visit his bereaved family might have been surprised to hear the gales of laughter to which he had reduced two of them within twenty minutes of entering the manse. Magnus was an incurably cheerful fellow: he had been stricken to the heart by his mother's death and the manner of it, but Magnus's wounds had never taken long to heal, and he belonged to a profession trained to take death in its stride. His return to Scapa, and his breezy nonchalance, had done more to calm young Olav than all the minister's fatherly care.

"Ingrid!" Magnus's shout came vigorously upstairs in the

middle of the afternoon. "Come on down and pour the tea. What are you prinking up there for anyway?"

"Getting a handkerchief!" she called back, and banged her bureau drawer shut. She was looking out for David, and there at the last moment she saw him—not driving from Houton, but coming on foot from Scapa pier, with his head down and his shoulders forward in his characteristic thrusting walk. She ran downstairs past the hum of voices from the livingroom and pulled open the front door.

"Ingrid!" As soon as she saw his delighted face she knew it was all right. There was only time for a quick handclasp in the hall. She whispered "I haven't said anything to Magnus!" and took him into the livingroom, where the survivors of the *Yelverton* exchanged shouts and blows of greeting. Magnus had brought with him two new friends from the *Chester*, Lieutenant-Commander Gibbings and Assistant Paymaster White, to whom Dr. Sabiston had been discoursing on the Broch relics of Orkney; the dim silver-point of the Norwegian livingroom was relieved by the stronger colours of navy blue and gold.

The room seemed full of large young men. Magnus Sabiston, like Ingrid, had inherited their mother's very fair hair, but he was otherwise a true Orcadian—even taller than David Flett, and heavily built. One day he would be fat and florid, but at present P.T. and football were keeping Magnus in good hard trim. Young Olav, who had been allowed to miss school to see his brother, was an ordinary bullet-headed boy in the glory of his first long trousers.

They had a splendid sit-down tea in the livingroom, with boiled eggs, brown bread and freshly-churned butter from a nearby farm, oven and girdle scones made by Agnes, and a Victoria sandwich filled with raspberry jam which was Ingrid's own handiwork. She presided rather nervously over the tea table, in a new black dress of fine wool which set off her dazzling complexion and the brightness of her hair, and three of the young men could not take their eyes off her, while her father was piercingly reminded of the pretty Norwegian girl he had met long ago at a saeter in the Dales. It was a very decorous tea party, for the guests remembered that they were in a house of mourning, but the noise that four young officers, a pretty girl and a schoolboy could make was enough to amuse and at the same time sadden Dr. Sabiston. How quickly we're forgotten, he thought. Only a few weeks ago my poor Astrid was sitting at the head of the table, pouring tea from that same silver teapot; and now it's Ingrid's hour to receive the compliments and have her head turned by these good-looking fellows. What said Oliver Edwards? "Cheerfulness was always breaking in!" The minister felt he threw a shadow on their cheerfulness. He was Orcadian by long descent and some of the superstitions of the Islands lingered in his blood. It seemed to him that a premonition of death was in the room. Rising with an excuse of work to do he went into his study and sat down at his desk with his grey head in his hands.

Magnus was singing the praises of the newly commissioned *Chester*. With another light cruiser, the *Canterbury*, she was attached to the 3rd Battle Cruiser Squadron at Rosyth, which the 5th Battle Squadron had been sent to replace temporarily, and according to the young Lieutenant of the Turret her ship's company was composed entirely of eccentrics or exceptional men.

"I've never been down at Rosyth," said David, "but some of the *Hampshire* chaps liked it better than the Flow."

"Handy for Edinburgh leave," said the young A.P.M.

"Nice if you happen to belong to the Band of Brothers," said the Lieutenant-Commander. "Personally I think it's a bit late in the day for the Nelson touch."

There was a general laugh. Admiral Beatty, whose admirers in the Battle Cruiser Fleet had revived Lord Nelson's idea of a Band of Brothers in the Navy, had also his detractors: his flamboyance was not to everybody's taste.

"Give me J.R.J. any day," said Magnus, lighting a cigarette.

"J.R.J. dined aboard us a couple of weeks ago," David said. "He was great; but my word! he got his kail through the reek when he had us off to the Skagerrak in the dead silence of that same night, and all for nothing."

"We missed that particular abortion," said the Lieutenant-Commander thankfully.

"But you admire Sir John Jellicoe, Davie," Ingrid protested. "Remember how beautifully he acknowledged your salute outside the Stromness Hotel last week!"

"Funny you should say that," Magnus tilted backwards alarmingly on his antique, spindle-legged chair. "I was talking to one of our kids yesterday, thrilled to death because the C.-in-C. had returned *his* salute, in a very grand style—"

"Here at Scapa?"

"No, at Plymouth, when the kid was training. I had to referee a football match our second eleven was playing, and this young Cornwell was walking alongside me up to the Flotta pitch. The P.T. bloke says he's a good little footballer, and you can see he's as keen as mustard on the Navy. He told me he'd been a delivery boy on a Brooke Bond Tea van in London, and seeing Jellicoe was the biggest thing that ever happened to him. Pretty good for a little Cockney vanboy, eh?"

"What a nice lad," said Ingrid. "What did you say his name was?"

"That was funny too. This kid's not in my Turret, so I asked his name—we've only been in commission two weeks, and I don't know all the names yet. You could tell by the way he answered he was as proud as Punch he'd been promoted. 'Boy First Class John Travers Cornwell, sir!' he said. He made it sound like Horatio Viscount Nelson."

The cigarettes had to be stubbed out then, for the inexorable notice for steam hung over all the sailors.

"Thanks for a wonderful tea," the visitors said to their young hostess, and the Lieutenant-Commander added, "Sabiston, can't we arrange a Ladies' Day aboard, and invite your sister?"

"A tea fight, or a sherry party, or something, to wind up the Long Hope sports?" suggested the A.P.M.

"We'll be at sea on Sports Day, what d'you bet?" said Magnus . . . "Davie, we've ordered a machine to take us back to Houton; if we all pack in we can give you a lift."

"That would be great, but our picket-boat comes in to Scapa and I can easy walk it. Ingrid, will you put me ben the road a bit?"

"Oh, come now, Miss Sabiston, no fair!" said the smitten Paymaster. "Why should the *Hampshire* have the honour?"

There was more laughter as the good-byes were said, and Dr. Sabiston came out to see the young men off. Magnus told his father he hoped to get shore leave on Sunday and attend the service in the kirk of Hamnavoe. But his farewell was said to David Flett as White and the Lieutenant-Commander climbed aboard the machine. It took the form of a hard slap on the back, and the words, "It was grand seeing you, Davie!" to which David replied merely, "Good luck, lad!"

"Same to you. And—thanks again for last August. So long!"

Ingrid and David went down the front garden and turned left to Scapa past the church and along the shore road. It was nearly six o'clock, and the traffic had thinned out. They could walk quite comfortably side by side, between the Orkney fields now a patchwork of green and violet-brown, and the waters of the Flow.

"Magnus is looking well," David began.

"So are you, Davie. Much better than when you came back to Orkney."

"Must be the Iceland air."

"Did you have a good cruise?"

"It was quiet enough, after we left the Faeroes."

They walked on in silence. It was a beautiful evening, and the larks were singing high above the Mainland farms. To Ingrid it was her dear native place; to David, a strong bare landscape so like East Aberdeenshire that it seemed like home.

"So you decided to say nothing to Magnus about—what we discussed last week?"

"I didn't see why Magnus should be worried too."

"I'm sorry if you've been vexed about it, Ingrid."

"Just tell me one thing." She turned and faced him. "What are this Ritter and my Uncle Hans supposed to have actually done? Please give me some facts, Dave. I don't like hints."

"I'll tell you what I was told at the Admiralty," he said, "and I doubt you're not going to like it. Ritter and your uncle are said to have organised a secret base in Norwegian waters—for submarines raiding the North Sea."

He saw her face grow pale as the hideous association of ideas took shape in her mind.

"You mean—the *Hazelhead* might have been sunk by a submarine that my uncle had—protected?"

"If it's true that such a base exists—it's possible."

"If I thought that . . ." Ingrid drew in her breath. "I'd make sure that my brothers and I had nothing to do with any of the Kolbergs, ever again—"

"There's only one way to be sure if it *is* true—"

"You mean find the base?"

"I mean find Karl Ritter."

"But that's impossible!"

"I'm not so sure."

They walked on quickly, past the shop where Agnes went so often for groceries and gossip, and Ingrid mechanically greeted two women carrying shopping baskets, each with two or three children at her skirts.

"It came into my head when we were on patrol," said David, "that some day soon Ritter might make for Orkney. The biggest prizes in the war are here at Scapa Flow." He had no need to indicate, even by a jerk of his chin, the battleships lying at anchor in the late afternoon sunshine of the Flow.

"Make for Orkney in a submarine?"

"Aye, very likely, if their base exists, he could do that."

"But he couldn't wander round the Islands all by himself! The police would find out about him inside twenty-four hours!"

"So they might—unless he had some local body helping him."

"It's all like a bad dream," said Ingrid miserably.

David stopped where the road began to wind around the last bay on the way to Scapa Pier. "You know we're off to sea again tomorrow?"

"I heard you saying so to Magnus."

"Before we go, I want to tell you something, Ingrid. There was never anything between that Russian girl and me. She was Karl Ritter's, body and soul. Have you any idea what I mean?"

"But you admired her, didn't you? How did you come to know

230

about her death? How many times were you with her, Dave?"
David took off his hat and ran his hand over his dark hair.
"Can't you just let it be, dearie? It's too long a story, and there's
a lot of it I'm not allowed to tell. Will you not believe that you're
the only one for me, and trust me still?"

The dread which every sailor's sweetheart knew, that this might
be their last parting, fell like a blow on Ingrid's heart. She clung
to him, regardless of anyone who might be watching, and begged
him to come safely back to her. She stood there waving when he
left her, and turned again and waved his hat on the road to Scapa
Pier. It was not until she had reached the manse gates that Ingrid
remembered something: David Flett had not named the local
person who might give aid and comfort to a German spy.

H.M.S. *Hampshire* resumed patrol on May 20, as a mounting
tension developed in the Grand Fleet. There was a persistent
"buzz" about a plan called Operation M, an attempt on the
grand scale to lure out Admiral Scheer, and Wardroom strategists
who had all along advocated carrying the war into the Baltic
predicted a speedy departure for the Kattegat and the Great Belt.
This had been so often discussed in the *Hampshire* that there was a
flicker of excitement when the cruiser was ordered, not back to the
Faerocs as had been expected, but to set a course south-east,
and a corresponding depression when the patrol limits were set
in the Long Forties, from forty to one hundred miles seaward of
Aberdeen. Here the *Hampshire* spoke a Tarras Line steamer, the
Ferryhill, heading east to Christiania along the seaway where her
sister ship the *Hazelhead* had been torpedoed. The British minesweepers were out in force, and the *Ferryhill's* captain was calmly
confident of making port.

Encounters with the neutral passenger steamers were what the
Navy captains dreaded. It was not easy to enforce the right of
search aboard a vessel which declared itself to be carrying nothing
but coal, ballast and the passengers' baggage, and neutral suscepti-
bilities were always easily inflamed by insistence. Yet the
passenger ships of neutral countries carried special risks to Britain.
Sometimes there were Germans aboard, who insisted on sending

231

off wireless messages to their "firm"—the firm being the head-quarters of the High Seas Fleet, and the code messages conveying news of the whereabouts of British ships. Unfriendly neutral vessels often acted as look-outs for the Germans, and when not equipped with W/T used carrier pigeons for the same purpose. On the second night of the *Hampshire's* eastward patrol the middle watch had a sight of the Norwegian-American liner *Kristiansfjord*, which persistently tried to elude the British blockade, steaming west out of Stavanger with all her lights extinguished. There were huge seas running, and the *Hampshire's* watch on deck clung to every handhold as Captain Savill, hastily summoned to the bridge, appeared in oilskins pulled over his pyjamas and damned the Norwegian captain who would risk a collision at sea or armed attack by any one of the belligerents while he had passengers aboard.

That stormy night marked the end of the fine May weather. Across the North Sea, Admiral Scheer cursed his meteorologists, who had not forecast the bad visibility which prevented airship reconnaissance. He decided to postpone the attack on Sunderland, although he was already committed as regards his submarines, which could only remain at sea until May 30 without refuelling. Aboard the *Hampshire* a wireless message was received from Base at Long Hope ordering the cruiser to coal at Cromarty, which meant that after coaling, when they were back at four hours' notice for steam, most of the crew could be set ashore for exercise. This necessarily took the form of a route march through the charming scenery of the Black Isle, on that day blurred by a wet thick mist, and not appreciated by the sailors. David Flett went on the route march with them, slogging out his exasperation at missing Scapa and another sight of Ingrid Sabiston.

The new patrol took them north again through rain squalls and heavy head winds to Latitude 66 degrees, and then south again hugging the Norwegian coast by Trondheim and Kristiansund. Here on May 26, the day before her orders were to head west for Scapa Flow, H.M.S. *Hampshire* intercepted, and after investigation sent off under armed guard to Contraband Control, two Nor-wegian freighters carrying iron ore from Narvik to Rotterdam. Two furious skippers were reminded of the rule of "continuous voyage", by which the British could seize anything which might be conveyed on to Germany, and advised to tell their story to the examining officers at Kirkwall. It was not a bad haul for a short cruise. It even had its sporting moments, for the two freighters had done their best to avoid capture, giving the slow-moving *Hampshire* a fair run for her money until she was within range, when one warning shot across the bows pulled the Norwegians up. Not so the cargo boat they intercepted next morning, in a livid daybreak when the skies were streaming rain. It was in the latitude of Bergen, just before *Hampshire* began her run to the west. Through their glasses, the British officers could see the Bergen registration clearly, with the freighter's name, *Thorfinn*, and the company's: K.D.S.

"One of the Kolberg boats," said the Commander, who was on the bridge. "Straight off the top of the Black List, eh?"

"She's making no attempt to run for it, sir," said somebody.

The *Thorfinn* was lying low in the water, and proceeding south at a slow speed. The *Hampshire*'s officers waited while Captain Savill was summoned to the bridge, and the signal "Heave to!" made to the Norwegian.

"Proper sitting duck, this one."

"Nothing to hide, innocent as a new-born babe—maybe?"

"It's probably the *Moewe*," said someone with a nervous laugh. It was a relief to hear the order given to run out the *Hampshire*'s guns. The gunnery officers went to action stations with their crews.

The *Thorfinn* lay in the trough of the heavy seas, broadside on, a sitting duck if ever there was one, obediently hove-to. There was no sudden hoisting of the German colours, no flash from concealed guns. The *Thorfinn* was just what she appeared to be, a neutral cargo vessel, prepared to submit to the cruiser's enforcement of the British blockade.

David Flett kept his binoculars on the *Thorfinn* as the *Hampshire* came up astern. He could see the bearded captain, wearing oilskins, on the bridge. Another man, probably the first mate, was by his side. On the deck below a little group of men were standing by the port-side rail. He counted heads, three, and a fourth man half hidden at their backs . . .

Three men in stocking caps, and one bare-headed, very fair . . .

There was rain on the glasses of his binoculars. David wiped them dry and focussed them with care. The man on the *Thorfinn's* deck was not in uniform, but wearing a dark sweater with a thick turtle neck and a short raincoat. But there was no mistaking the face of Blinker's dossier, the profile seen in the American Hotel: the man on the Kolberg freighter was Kolberg's accomplice, Commander Karl Ritter.

XIV

Saturday, May 27, 1916

"Request permission to command the boarding party, sir!"
"You, Mr. Flett?" Captain Savill checked his surprise. The request was not only unorthodox; it seemed out of keeping with the personality of the reserved young officer who had joined the *Hampshire* only a month ago. He remembered Captain Hall's two brief communications on the subject of Lieutenant Flett.

"Permission granted," he said, and watched the quick reaction in the young man's face. "Pass the word for Chief Petty Officer Faraday." The very experienced C.P.O. was an insurance, he thought, against any mistake young Flett might make aboard the *Thorfinn*.

"He can't go far wrong," said the Commander, reading his Captain's unspoken thought. "We'll have the Norwegian Government at our throats over yesterday's doings anyway; we may as well throw in the *Thorfinn* for good measure."

"In for a penny, in for a pound, eh?" said Captain Savill, watching the boat on its way to the freighter, rocking in the heavy swell. "I was just wishing we weren't minus two detachments of Marines already, if we have to send this sportsman in."

The search party made a neat job, in the very high sea, of boarding the *Thorfinn*, where surly seamen eyed them from the rail. The watchers aboard *Hampshire* saw the meeting between Lieutenant Flett and the freighter captain, and the two men disappearing inside the *Thorfinn*'s housing. Twenty minutes passed before the boat was seen on the way back.

"Flett looks like the cat that swallowed the canary," the Commander observed. "Must have found some very juicy contraband aboard."

But David had himself well in hand when he reported to his Captain. With an impassive face, he said that the *Thorfinn* was

235

bound for Germany, carrying a small cargo of iron ore, zinc and copper to the port of Lübeck. Captain Savill whistled.

"Another one for Kirkwall," he said. "Lucky we're on our way home."

"Sir?"

"I mean we'll be able to shepherd this one right into the Examination Base, Mr. Flett. What d'you say her skipper's name is—Monrad?"

"That's right, sir, Erlend Monrad. He's a native of Bergen. Man about fifty-five. Been with the Kolberg Line for thirty years." He was talking too much now and showing his excitement, laconic though the short sentences were. David took the bull by the horns.

"May I request further permission to command the armed guard aboard, sir, when you send the *Thorfinn* to Contraband Control?"

Captain Savill had expected this. His long experience of men told him that in David's pertinacity there was more than a junior officer's keenness and ambition. Normally he would have refused such a request from an officer of David's rank, or only granted it after consulting the Captain of Marines. Here the circumstances were exceptional. The Marine force had been depleted by the two previous arrests, for one thing, and for another Captain Savill hoped the young man's previous sea experience might make him a good guard officer for a disgruntled merchant skipper. He said,

"If I put you in command of a guard aboard the *Thorfinn*, you'll have to keep close station with me until we reach the Orkneys. With any luck we should make port before dark. I'll send a message to Contraband Control as soon as I'm in wireless radius, and let them know the *Thorfinn*'s coming in. 'Fraid you'll have to sleep aboard her, though; they won't examine tonight, and possibly not till Monday morning. I'll see that you're relieved tomorrow. Is that understood?"

"Aye, aye, sir!"

Captain Monrad, now that his fate was sealed, seemed determined to take it philosophically. While his first mate was on the bridge, where one of the *Hampshire*'s men stood guard over the helmsman, he invited the young naval officer into his cabin for a drink. David refused the fiery akvavit; he was very much on his dignity, with all the might of the Royal Navy behind him. But he was interested in observing the Norwegian, whose old-fashioned frill of beard surrounded a red face, determinedly jovial, in which intelligent grey eyes were set close together.

"Tha''s all right, Mister," said the skipper, whose fluent English was marked by an excess of glottal stops. "Have a cigar? . . . I know you Bri'ish have your own pro'lems, I don' blame you for kickin' up a row. We let your Con'raband Con'rol sort it all out, eh? My gover'men' pro'est, for sure; maybe you pay an indem'ity, maybe you don'; we leave it, eh?"

"I'm required to remind you, Captain, that the armed guard under my command does not constitute a prize crew. Your cargo will be examined by the authorities at Kirkwall and referred to London. If the decision goes against you, the British Government reserves the right to purchase your cargo at a valuation, and repatriate yourself and your crew to Norway."

"Very goo', very well spoke'," said Captain Monrad approvingly. He bit the end off a cigar. For two pins this old goat would call me "sonny", David thought. "You know the drill, I see, skipper," he said. "Been in British hands before?"

"Not me, Mister. But we hear a lo' abou' your Mi'istry of Blocka'e, and the way it runs."

"I'll bet you do." He went out on deck. The C.P.O. had posted the guards as ordered. They had all been issued with rifles before leaving the *Hampshire*, and carried the Navy issue ·455 Webley pistol.

"What do you make of it, Chief?"

The C.P.O.'s opinion was that it was a rum go, and no mistake. "The skipper's a cool hand, sir. We caught him red-handed with war materials for Germany and he's smiling away as if we'd picked him up with a boat-load of Bibles for the Salvation Army."

"The crew's not quite so merry."

"They'll be thinking they've lost their bonus, sir. Besides, you don't get much change out of them Norskies."

"Anything more I can do for you, Mister?" said Captain Monrad, coming quietly up behind them.

"Answer one or two questions, please. Have you any German citizens aboard?"

"All my men are No'wegians, Mister."

"And you carry two mates and a wireless operator. I'd like to see the tally of your crew."

"Tha's not necessary, Mister—"

"Not carrying stowaways, are you?" David regretted the jeer as soon as it was uttered. The false joviality drained from Captain Monrad's whiskery face, and the little eyes became coldly alert. "The tally, skipper," he repeated. "Chief Petty Officer, come with me!"

They went in almost unbroken silence through every deck of the *Thorfinn*. The quarters aft were not extensive. The two mates shared a cabin, and next to the captain's there was a small berth with bunks for two passengers, both stripped to the planking, and with no sign of occupation. They inspected the fo'c'sle, the engineroom, the galley, and had the cargo hatches lifted for a second look. It was not necessary to tick off the names on the manifest reluctantly produced by Captain Monrad, for the numbers tallied: every crew member was accounted for, with nobody over, and nowhere from stem to stern of the *Thorfinn* did they encounter the fairheaded man with the dark sweater whom David had seen through his binoculars from the *Hampshire*'s deck.

The last visit was to the wireless operator in his little shack. He turned out to be a square-headed boy from Christiania devotedly reading a wireless manual with a crime novelette beneath it.

"You've reported your position to the Kolberg Line by W/T, skipper?"

"Na'urally." The secret amusement was back on Captain Monrad's face. David left him in the wireless shack and went back with Faraday to the streaming deck. The high seas were still running, but he noted that the battered old freighter shipped less water, under the same conditions, than H.M.S. *Hampshire*, which could be seen, a majestic grey presence, holding her parallel

238

westward course. He knew Captain Savill would not let the *Thorfinn* out of his sight until both ships were off the Orkneys. Walking up and down the deck, with his step unconsciously imitating Savill's measured tread as he paced the starboard side of his own quarterdeck, David reflected that his Captain had no idea of the real war material carried by the Norwegian cargo boat.

He was absolutely positive that Karl Ritter was aboard. He also had a good idea where, as he studied the *Thorfinn*'s boats, swung outboard in a far from shipshape manner. Ritter had been watching from the port bow as the *Hampshire* came up, and it would have been quite easy to cross to starboard and climb into one of the boats before the search party arrived. Under a tarpaulin, lying on the floorboards between the thwarts, and no doubt provided with food and drink, he would be no more uncomfortable than David himself in the Dutch barges when he escaped from Groningen. The whole thing had been prearranged. Ritter was going to Orkney intentionally, although not, as David had predicted to Ingrid, in a submarine. The "sitting duck" freighter, actually a decoy duck for the British cruiser, was Ritter's chosen means of transportation to the prizes of Scapa Flow.

Lieutenant Flett knew where his duty lay. It was to search the boats, discover Ritter, challenge his identity and report by signal to the *Hampshire*. Ritter, of course, might come out shooting, and in a battle with Monrad and the two mates on his side he might put up a very good show indeed before the *Hampshire* could come to their assistance. But David thought a fight on board was hardly likely. Ritter was too sure of his ground. Aboard a Norwegian vessel he was as firmly on Norwegian soil as in the Continental Hotel at Christiania, and even if taken off by force he would no doubt be able to talk his way out of any legal consequences worse than a spell of internment in the Isle of Man.

In the surge of his desire for vengeance on Karl Ritter, which had grown stronger every day since Elena's murder, David still felt an unwilling admiration for the nerve of the man. This attempt to land in Britain was by far and away his most daring exploit since his impersonation of an American businessman in

Russia, where one false step meant certain death. He deserved a chance to bring it off. He deserved to become the hunted, not the hunter—to give away, as the hunting proceeded, information useful to his enemies. Just as a puppet called David Flett, manipulated by the skilful hands of Blinker Hall, had been made to deposit information in Karl Ritter's path.

Those daylight hours on the *Thorfinn* were not easy for Lieutenant Flett. He was certain of the presence of his enemy, but did the enemy know the identity of the British officer who had headed the search party and now commanded the guard on the *Thorfinn*? He was fairly certain Ritter had never seen him in Amsterdam: he had scarcely left his room at all before the performance of *Swan Lake*. But there was his name, which by naval etiquette he had announced to Monrad: had the skipper passed it on to the man in the starboard boat while David was presenting his report in the *Hampshire*? If so, it could be dangerous. A man like Ritter would certainly remember the name of the silly young officer who had turned up so opportunely in Holland with despatches for the Naval Attaché. David turned over those problems in his head during a midday meal which he was compelled to share with Captain Monrad, while Faraday fell out the guard by twos, and they were given food and beer in the galley by the Norwegian cook. The mates were the least friendly of any aboard this willing captive, the K.D.S. freighter *Thorfinn*. The first mate, on the bridge most of the afternoon, spoke not one word to David as he stood near the helmsman, making sure that the freighter kept station with the British cruiser.

In the late afternoon they had not one chaperone but two, as a cruiser of the redoubtable 10th Squadron appeared out of the mist on her way back to Scapa Flow. The heavy rain stopped about five o'clock, but the mist thickened to fog patches which reduced visibility, and the new arrival communicated with the *Hampshire* by signal lamps. David, watching the lamps spell out their messages, could not fail to see how often these were lost in the fog, repeated, and then lost again. But the 10th Squadron cruiser was a practical comfort. She kept company with the *Thorfinn*, at Captain Savill's signalled request, until both cruisers set course for Holm Sound, to enter Scapa Flow between Burray Island and the Mainland.

It was nearly nine o'clock when David told Captain Monrad to order the Norwegian helmsman to steer for Shapinsay. It was a relief to see the Orkney skerries, and then the cliffs where the guillemots and puffins were crying in the wet mist, and presently, as they entered the Wide Firth, the lights of Kirkwall harbour and Kirkwall town. The Examination Base was in an area of the bay already occupied by several blockade-runners, including the two sent in by *Hampshire* on the previous day. To David's huge relief, the Contraband Control cutter came out from port immediately, and hailed the freighter.

"Bu' this is ou'rageous! I shall complain to my Gove'ment! You have no ri' to take me off my ship!"

Captain Monrad's angry bellows were to be heard far beyond his cabin. Out on deck, the junior Control officer shrugged his shoulders and looked at David Flett.

"You're absolutely certain of your ground, Lieutenant?" he said.

"Positive."

"Because the practice is to allow no one ashore until a ship has been examined, and often not even then."

"You're not allowing them to go ashore, Mr. Kidd, you're taking them into protective custody."

"In that case we ought to have a police warrant."

"Get one, then,"

"But what's the charge to be?"

"Offences against the Official Secrets Act."

The Control man whistled. "I hope you can make it stick, Lieutenant Flett."

"I'll make it stick all right. But let's see what your superior officers think about it first." He was lucky that both Kidd and his colleague, Mr. Johns, were decidedly junior in Contraband Control: a senior man might have refused point-blank to take the Norwegian captain, his two officers and the wireless operator ashore. But Captain Monrad's violence succeeded in annoying

Mr. Johns, and in no time the four Norwegians were being assisted, not too gently, over the *Thorfinn's* side and into the waiting cutter.

"You'll have to come along with us, Lieutenant," Kidd said. "The duty officer will want a full report of this."

"Certainly." David took C.P.O. Faraday aside.

"I don't know how long I may be detained ashore, Chief Petty Officer," he said, "I want the crew confined to quarters while I'm gone. Get them all inside the fo'c'sle if possible and put two men on the door. Do any of them bunk along the alleyway?"

"Young Sparks has a berth of 'is own, sir, like the mates."

"Young Sparks is out of the picture, so that's all right. About your own quarters: you and Morrison take the passenger berth and the rest bunk down as best they can. It's only for one night— I hope."

"What about yourself, sir?"

"I'll sleep on the captain's sofa."

"And what about a guard on deck, sir?"

"Post a guard at half past ten, if I'm not back by that time."

Into Faraday's face, apparently carved out of seasoned teak, there came the faintest flicker of surprise at his young Lieutenant's proceedings. Thank God the pubs will be closed by now, thought David. I wouldn't like Faraday to think I'm staying ashore for a drink.

"Carry on, Chief Petty Officer."

"Aye, aye, sir."

. . . "You young de'il," spat Captain Monrad, when David took his place in the cutter. "I'll see you're broke' ou' of the Navy for this!"

"Break away," said David. Thinking of his night in a Dutch police station, he wondered if he could incite the angry man or one of the mates to assault a sergeant. He had no hope of young Sparks, the wireless operator, who looked bemused by the whole thing. But as it happened the duty officer at Contraband Control was a Londoner, anxious to assert his authority without reference to the local constabulary.

"But no charge is being made against you, Captain Monrad,"

he said when he had talked to David in a private office. "We merely think that you can assist us in certain enquiries we're making, more conveniently here than on shipboard. You are not prisoners. You will be given comfortable quarters in our own hostel, and you'll be seen by the Chief of Control at nine o'clock tomorrow morning. Then of course you will be taken back to your ship before the cargo examination takes places."

It all sounded eminently reasonable. So reasonable that David, when he left the office, began to hope that he might dodge the "bottle" he would certainly deserve from Captain Savill when his high-handed conduct aboard the *Thorfinn* came to light. The wrath of Willis-Turner about altering the disposition of the *Yelverton*'s boats would be as nothing to the rage of Captain Savill at this latest example of David Flett's initiative, but then, if it turned out well with Ritter—! He had a new problem now, and he walked briskly off up Shore Street to a point where he could see the lights of the *Thorfinn* lying in the Examination Base.

It was nearly ten o'clock, and in the foggy weather already dark. There were lights in the Kirkwall Hotel and also in the Ayre Hotel, from which came the sound of a piano and voices singing "If You were the only Girl in the World", a hit from a new London show. There were always officers on weekend leave at the waterfront hotels: the parties would go on till midnight ushered in the Sabbath day. David walked out on the Ayre itself, the old causeway used as a road which divided the Bay of Kirkwall from the ancient anchorage called the Peerie Sea. It was very cold. He had left his oilskins aboard the *Thorfinn*, and now turned up his collar, wishing that he had remembered to bring a peajacket from his cabin in the morning.

He had done everything he could to help Karl Ritter. As far as possible, he had made the *Thorfinn* a solitude: nobody, until the deck guard was posted at 10.30, would see the German's departure—if he took it—from the ship. David found to his annoyance that he was shaking "like a lassie" at the thought of hunting down Karl Ritter. It was one month, to a day, since he had stood at the corner of the Marnixstraat and watched the faint light from his room at the American Hotel. Karl Ritter doing what he bloody well pleased, and David Flett a poor tool, watched in his turn by two guardian angels playing the hurdy-gurdy! He drew a long breath, and prayed for a chance to level the score for that.

Straining eyes and ears it seemed to David that after about ten minutes he saw a slight alteration in one of the *Thorfinn*'s riding lights. It disappeared and then shone out again as if some object had passed in front of it. Say a human body, clambering stiffly out of a ship's boat and swarming down the davits to the bulwark before dropping quietly into the sea.

It was now too dark and foggy to distinguish anyone in the water, but surprisingly soon David heard the sound of a very strong swimmer, moving rapidly and quietly towards the shore. At once he threw himself down on the bank, on the Peerie Sea side of the causeway, and waited for the sound of footsteps on the little beach. They came. Raising his head cautiously, he saw Ritter pull himself up to the Ayre and stand feeling inside his clothes for something hidden there, while sea water poured from his body to the road. Apparently satisfied, he walked off confidently into the direction of the Ayre Hotel.

Ingrid Sabiston put the motor-bike away in its shed, crossed the dark yard, and let herself into the manse kitchen. They had not locked the back door when the emergency summons came for Agnes. Nobody locked his door in honest Orkney, but Ingrid thought she might bolt hers tonight, when for the first time in her life she was alone in the manse of Hamnavoe.

The peat fire, which hardly ever went quite out, had sunk to a rosy glow with a ring of white ashes round it. Ingrid put on fresh peats and glanced uncertainly at the kettle. A cup of tea would be reviving after the fast drive in the fog and darkness, but she felt too lazy to set about making tea at bedtime, and remembering a boiler full of hot water decided to take a bath instead. It was the first time she had driven the Harley-Davidson at night, and though only to Houton and back it had been an effort. Ingrid needed warmth and relaxation.

She took off her tweed jacket, damp with fog, and sat down

in the strawbacked Orkney chair, stretching her long legs to the fire. Ingrid wore over her whipcord breeches an old white sweater of Magnus's, with the Navy turtle neck and much too big for her, and an equally ancient pair of riding boots. "The Girl of the Future!" her father had said when he first saw her in that kit, straddling the motor-bike—she liked that, just as she liked the new length of her hair. She ruffled up her hair now—it was as damp as her jacket—and yawned contentedly.

The sound of bicycle tyres was so soft that Ingrid doubted if she really heard it. But there was no mistaking the quiet footsteps in the yard, nor the gentle tap at the back door. She started up, glancing at the window, where the blind had not been drawn: anybody could look in now and see her, quite alone, by the light of the paraffin lamp swung from the ceiling. She was not really frightened, for this was Orkney and she was in her own home, but in her heart she wished she had shot the bolt across the kitchen door.

"Who's there?" she said.

A voice with an indefinable accent said "Please . . . be-so-good!"

It was a phrase which reminded her of early lessons in Scandinavian good manners, and disarmed her; besides, she was the minister's daughter, and any person in trouble might come in search of her father's help. She opened the door on a tall man whose fair head was bare, and who smiled and bowed politely.

"Good-evening," Ingrid said uncertainly, "did you want to see the minister?"

"Do you speak Norwegian?" the man said in that language. Ingrid told him, in Norwegian, "Only a few words."

"But there *was* a Norwegian lady here?"

"That was my mother, she's . . . not here any more. Are you one of the sailors from Stromness?" Ingrid asked. "Come in! I didn't know the Norwegian herring fleet had started to come back to Orkney."

"Oh, there are always a few trawlers at work," said the man. He came in with an apology. His clothes were very wet, and drips began to fall on the brown linoleum which Agnes kept in a high state of polish.

"But you're soaking!"

"It has been a very wet night, miss."

"You look as if you'd fallen in the water."

"Well, as a matter of fact, I did," said the man. His English was quite fluent after all.

"How dreadful! Look, you must have a cup of tea," said Ingrid, testing the heat of the kettle on its crook, "and sit down beside the fire. If you don't mind the cat's mat" (indicating a large clean sack folded by the hearth) "you could put it under your feet to catch the drips!"

"You're very kind to a stranger, miss." A stranger certainly, but Mummy would have wanted me to be kind to a poor Norwegian sailor, especially a nice polite one like this, she thought. Such an attractive one, too, with good features and a strong indented chin. He had taken off a damp muffler and was wiping his face and hair with it.

"Surely you haven't cycled all the way from Stromness?" she said, taking up the heavy iron poker and stirring the fire to a blaze.

"I must explain to you, miss. I jumped my ship at Kirkwall—into the harbour, this is why I am so wet. I want to sign on with a trawler at Stromness . . . Is the Herr Pastor at home?"

"He'll be back soon, and the maid will, too," Ingrid lied. Even the manse tradition of giving hospitality to everyone was not strong enough to extinguish her little flicker of fear at being alone in the house, in the fog, with this foreign sailor. "I'm sorry the kettle takes so long to boil," she said. "How did you come to be in Kirkwall?"

"I was a deckhand on a Norwegian freighter, miss. Our captain, he was not a good man. I will not sail with him again. I will find another ship at Stromness, and go home."

"You're still quite a long way from Stromness."

"I have been hoping you would give me shelter for the night."

"Oh, but—we haven't got a room to spare," she said, and as an inspiration, "I'm expecting my brother in the Navy. He often brings a friend to stay with him."

The man smiled. "I am not a fit guest for your beautiful home,

246

Miss Ingrid. Any shelter will do—any shed—I can lie on sacks like this here——"

"How did you know my name?" whispered Ingrid. Her eyes dilated as the fairhaired man got up from the Orkney chair. His wet clothes were steaming. He looked very tall and menacing in the lamp light, but his voice was still gentle and reassuring.

"I was told if I needed help to go to Hamnavoe, where the kind Norwegian lady used to live, and ask for her daughter Ingrid—"

"Who told you that? What is your name, and who sent you to me?"

"Please don't be alarmed, Miss Ingrid. Believe me, I wouldn't hurt you for the world! But I need dry clothes, and the chance to lie up for a few hours . . . I stole a bicycle in Kirkwall, and the police will be after me—"

"You stole a bicycle!" she said contemptuously. "If that were all! You're Karl Ritter, aren't you? And your accomplice, my uncle Hans Kolberg, was the one who told you to come here!"

The mask of simplicity, of the bemused sailor in a foreign land which he had worn so well, slipped from Ritter's face at the revealing word accomplice. He made Ingrid a formal bow.

"Yes, I am Karl Ritter," he said. "I see you were expecting me."

Without a word she stooped and lifted the heavy poker from the hearth, turned, and crossed the kitchen to the door leading to the passage and the livingroom.

"What are you going to do, Miss Sabiston?"

"I'm going to telephone for the police."

"I shouldn't do that if I were you." Ritter had not moved or raised his voice, but the threat of violence hung between them now, a hairsbreadth from fulfilment.

"You've come to the wrong house, Mr. Ritter," said Ingrid with chattering teeth. "Whatever my uncle Hans may be, we're loyal here. We don't harbour German spies!"

"Don't be such a little fool!" He took two steps towards her. Ingrid gasped, and raised the poker high. "I didn't come here to frighten schoolgirls! What I want, and what I mean to have, is dry

247

clothing and a few hours in hiding, and then I shall be gone and never trouble you again. Now forget about the telephone and put that ridiculous poker down. I could take it away from you with one hand, only I don't want to hurt you—"

"You can kill me if you like," said Ingrid Sabiston, "but you won't get me to help you; and if I live I'll do my best to see you hanged—you murderer!"

"It's no use, Ritter," said David Flett from the yard door. "Ye'll not break this one like you broke Elena Petrovna."

The sound of that name, the last he expected to hear spoken in that place, struck Ritter like a physical blow. He swung round to face the newcomer. David's jacket was nearly as wet as Ritter's, and his trousers were splashed with mud above the ankles. He held his Service Webley in his hand.

"Davie!" Ingrid gasped. He looked away from Ritter for a moment, and with one quick glance took in the gold hair, the pale terrified face, the breeches and the boots.

"Aye, it's me," he said. "I would have gotten here sooner, but this chap nicked the only bicycle outside the Ayre Hotel—he had the start of me."

"Good heavens!" said Ritter, in complete command of himself, "it's the dashing Lieutenant from the *Thorfinn!*"

"Lay down the poker, Ingrid," said David, "Put your hand in his jacket pocket and take his gun."

She obeyed, shaking with aversion as she went close to Ritter. The weapon came out with something sticking to the butt. It was the envelope of oiled silk in which the spy had carried it during his swim ashore, and it clung to Ingrid's fingers like a serpent's skin.

"Bring it here to me." David dropped Ritter's gun into his own left-hand pocket, and kicked the yard door shut with his heel. "That's better," he said, "now we know where we are. There's nobody in the house, is there, Ingrid?"

"No."

"On second thoughts," said Ritter pleasantly, "I believe Miss Sabiston ought to call the Kirkwall police. I had rather rely on British justice than on you, Lieutenant—?"

"Flett. Did ye never hear Elena speak of David Flett?"

"You were the British officer at Amsterdam?"

"I was."

"My God!"

"She's not going to call the police," said David, "because a British prison's not a safe place for you. By the time the police took you out of Kirkwall, over the Pentland Firth and into the Tower o' London, you would manage to get round them some way or another. A German naval officer out of uniform, making on to be a Norwegian deckie, found near the Grand Fleet at Scapa Flow—man, there's only one sentence for that. But I some think ye'd dodge the firing-squad, Korvetten-Kapitän Ritter!"

"So what do you propose as an alternative?" jeered Ritter. "—By the way, my rank now is Kommandant; I was promoted recently."

"The reward of merit, eh? Was that what you got for bringing home the code book?"

The moment he flung out the words David knew that he had sealed the doom of one of them. For Ritter understood him in a blinding flash of clarity; it hardly needed the German's strangled cry, "So the code book was a fake!" to tell him that only he or Ritter himself could leave that place alive.

"Aye," he said, "you did a rotten job; it wasna worth a woman's life."

Ritter said nothing. He now had only one idea, to which even his mission to Orkney must take second place. He must remain alive long enough to reach his rendezvous, and send back word to Berlin that the precious code was false; that to use it to break the British signals would send German sailors to their death. He looked at the Webley in David's grasp. It was trained steadily upon himself. Ritter knew—among so much else that he knew about the Royal Navy—the defects of the ·455 Webley pistol. The handle was set almost square to the frame instead of sloping, so that the sights failed to align instinctively in the hand of all but an expert shot, which he was sure David Flett was not. The Webley gave that split second of delay which here and now might

249

save his own life. Life for life's sake was not precious to Karl Ritter. Elena's death and the load of guilt it laid upon him, followed by his mother's terrible rejection, had taken all the savour out of living; but he was above all a German naval officer, bound by the inexorable and sometimes insane demands of a great Service . . . He must live, and Flett must die.

"I waited long enough out there to hear you and Ingrid," David said. "I heard her calling you a murderer. *She* wasna thinking of Elena Petrovna. She was thinking about her own mother, murdered by your men at sea. Tell her—and let me hear you tell her—if the submarine that sunk the *Hazelhead* came out of the base you and her uncle set up off the Norwegian coast?"

Ritter fell into the trap. Some vestige of chivalry, some dismay at Ingrid's horror-stricken face, drove him to say, "*No*, for God's sake! U73 was never up at Namsos—it was a raid from Heligoland."

"So *Namsos* is the place!" said David, and then Karl Ritter risked everything and launched himself in a flying tackle at the Scotsman's knees. The pistol flew from David's hand as they went down together. It slid across the floor almost to Ingrid's feet. She looked down at it stupidly, and from it to the two men struggling on the floor. They scrambled to their feet, still locked together, landing heavy blows on each other's bodies, lurching up against the table, which was strong enough to withstand them, and knocking over the Orkney chair, which was not. They fell up against the fireplace, and knocked the kettle off its hook; the water, now boiling, poured into the fire and sent steam and a cloud of peat ashes billowing through the kitchen; and still the heavy body-blows, the grunts of rage and pain went on. Both men were in fine condition, and well matched in height and weight; Ritter was ten years older but the better boxer and all-round athlete, while David fought only with the power and fury of the old harbour brawls at Aberdeen. Gradually Ritter forced the younger man back to the floor and held him there with one hand. He drew a heavy knife from its sheath above his hip. Ingrid shrieked. David tore himself free and bit Ritter's wrist. He dropped the knife. David pushed it away with a clumsy movement of his shoulder as Ritter seized his throat.

He was completely pinned down by Ritter's body. They lay one upon the other in an awful travesty of an embrace. while Ritter's long hands circled David's neck and slowly tightened in a strangle-hold. Ingrid saw David's body slacken, his arms fall helplessly across the floor. Suddenly she awoke from her trance of horror. She picked up the knife and put it into David's hand. In a single movement, and with the last of his strength, he drove it deep into Ritter's side.

For a moment there was no sound in the kitchen but the German's dying gasp and the ticking of the clock above the fireplace. Then David Flett pulled himself free, and with one hand on the kitchen table dragged himself to his feet. His head was ringing, his body battered from head to foot. He did not look at Ingrid Sabiston.

"Go ben the house," he said. "Go into the parlour and wait for me."

She obeyed him. David bent over the body. The knife, driven in at haphazard, had entered Ritter's side with precision, between two ribs. Blood was beginning to soak through the dead man's coat and ooze round the haft of the seaman's knife. David turned the body over. Round the waist were two belts, one of oiled silk holding cartridges, the other, of suede, holding money in various currencies. These he left in place. He put Ritter's gun back in his coat pocket. The blood was beginning to drip on to the linoleum; he folded the sack and shoved it underneath the corpse. Then he examined his own face in the mirror beside the sink. It was not marked, for he had taken Ritter's assault on his body, and his heavy sweater concealed the marks round his neck. He turned on the single tap and washed with cold water and yellow soap until his face was stinging.

When he had done his best to brush the ashes off his uniform he went to Ingrid in the livingroom. She was flung over a big chair like a sprawling foal, with her legs limp, and her breath coming in long sobbing gasps. She looked up fearfully at David.

"Is he *dead*?"

"Aye, he's dead all right. Now stop that, Ingrid! Have you any spirits in the house?"

251

"Daddy got a bottle in for Magnus."

David turned to the beautiful Empire sideboard and brought out two glasses and the bottle, more than half full. It was Highland Park from the local distillery, and he had never cared for malt, but after he had made Ingrid drink a thimbleful he poured a four fingers' measure for himself and drank it gratefully.

"Davie, what are we going to do?" said Ingrid in the shadow of a voice.

"You leave all that to me. Just tell me—what are you doing here all by yourself?"

It steadied her to explain: "Daddy's still in Edinburgh with Olav. He's going to preach in St. Giles' Cathedral tomorrow. It was an old engagement and he didn't want to break it."

"What about the kirk here?"

"A divinity student from Kirkwall will take the service."

"And where's Agnes?"

"They telephoned from the farm. Her sister's baby started to come too soon, and Agnes was needed there. I took her over in the sidecar about half past nine."

Until then he hadn't realised how she was dressed. Now he looked at the long line of thigh, the slender legs, and saw the points of her young breasts through the thick shapeless sweater, more provocative than the most revealing decolletage. Over the stirring of desire he began to tell her about the seizure of the *Thorfinn* and his plan to let Ritter come ashore. He thought she hardly understood what he was saying, but when he described Ritter's theft of a bicycle, and his own hunt for another bike to pursue the German down the Scapa road, he saw that she was following him closely.

"Where did you think he was going, Davie?"

"I thought he would try for the seaplane base at Scapa, he could do a lot of damage there."

"What did you think when you saw him making for the manse?"

David was silent.

"Did you think one of Mr. Kolberg's relatives might be waiting to help him on his way?"

252

"Certainly not!" he said. But from his heart a shadow had departed when he listened to Ingrid's denunciation of her uncle's accomplice. It was not that he had suspected her, but that he had once believed in the truth of Elena Tamirova: if she were false, then anyone in the world could be false too.

"When I think of my uncle Hans I'm so ashamed," she said, but David was following another train of thought:

"There must be somebody in Orkney ready to work with him, unless he came on an out-and-out suicide mission. Let's see what his papers say." He had put the documents in the oiled silk case into his own pocket.

One was the *Kaiserpass*, which Muriel Ritter found at Wilhelmshaven, and which as neither could read German they failed to understand. The other was a Norwegian passport for Karl Ericssen, seaman; it was quite new and not stamped at all. The third was a half-sheet of stiff paper slipped inside the leaves of the *Kaiserpass*. There was nothing on it but a large diagram, set inside a very detailed road-map, headed "Jellicoe, 28.5.1916."

"What the devil's this?" said David.

"I'll light another lamp, so we can see better."

"Look at the numbers and the wee flags, what's that for?"

"I don't know, but I do know where the roads are. Round Stromness, and the roads to Skara Brae—not the way we went that day, but the back roads . . . David! The diagram must be the Stromness golf links! The flags are meant to mark the greens—"

"Five has a ring round it."

"And the twenty-eighth of May's tomorrow—"

"He came to assassinate Admiral Jellicoe."

"He wouldn't have got anywhere near him," Ingrid said.

"On the links he could. He could have done it, Ingrid! And then think what it would have done to the Navy—to the war—"

"And Ritter wanted to use this house to hide in," said Ingrid. She looked round the familiar room with disgust for everything connected with the Kolberg name. But the colour was coming back to her face, and her voice was stronger. David took her by the shoulders.

"You saved my life, Ingrid."

"Best be thanked for that!"

Then David drew her close and began to kiss her mouth, with both hands on her hips, pressing her against him; and immediately desire leapt from a stirring into a strong seeking column, and he wanted to tear off the tantalising sweater and kiss her breasts. The primitive lust to kill had been assuaged; now another lust, equally primitive, demanded its fulfilment. Ingrid drank his kisses, her strong young body moulded itself to his own. He knew that he could carry her upstairs to her bed now, and utterly possess her. He also knew, with his last vestige of sanity, that their life together might be ruined at the start if they became lovers while the man he killed was lying in the silent house.

With a great effort he released her, and put her tenderly back in the big chair.

"Oh Davie—Davie!" was all that she could say.

"I'll need to go," he said. "There's a lot to do, and not much time."

"But what will you do with—*him*?"

"I'm not going to tell you, Ingrid. The less you know, the better. All you have to do is say nothing. Not a word to your father, or Magnus, or anybody. If it comes out, I'll take the whole thing on myself. Now just bide there for a wee while till I get everything clewed up."

He went back to the kitchen. It was after eleven o'clock, and raining heavily. There was not much time to do all that must be done if he was to be back at Kirkwall pier by half past twelve. That was when the guard boat from Scapa Flow made a tour of Kirkwall Bay, and the Lieutenant of the Night Guard could be persuaded to take him out to the *Thorfinn*.

There was a good deal of blood on the kitchen floor. He found a pail and cloth and washed it off, and brought sacks from the pile that always lay beside the peat stack to wrap round Ritter's body. He left the knife where he had driven it in, and put the Norwegian passport, in the oiled silk case, in the corpse's pocket beside the gun. A foreign seaman, killed in a brawl—that was

254

how the Procurator-Fiscal might see it, if the thing came to an investigation.

Then David wheeled the Harley-Davidson out of its shed, and with a considerable effort took the body across his shoulders in a fireman's lift. He got it into the sidecar, where Ritter's fair head lolled over in the ghastly semblance of a drunken passenger.

"Ingrid!" She came at once to join him in the kitchen, looking fearfully at the empty floor and the extinguished fire.

"I've had to tak' the Harley. I'll bring it back and take the push-bikes in to Kirkwall. Don't wait for me. Lock your doors, back and front, and try to get some sleep. When's your father coming home?"

"Monday night."

"I'll try to get leave sometime on Monday. Good-bye, my dearie."

He could not touch her again, with hands that had been covered with Ritter's blood, but she understood, and even smiled, and whispered "Good-night, darling!" as if they were parting after some romantic evening in a world at peace. He thought of that as he started the bike with a roar that seemed to waken the sleeping countryside, and started for Deerness.

At first David Flett had thought of dropping Ritter's body in the Loch of Kirbister, to which a lonely path led from behind the manse. But he had no weights, and the thing might come to the surface and be discovered by fishermen or picnickers, and besides, the loch was far too near the manse of Hamnavoe. With his fixed intention of keeping Ingrid out of any investigation, he drove to the extreme point of the East Mainland.

To get there he had to drive across the peninsula from Scapa Pier, through highly cultivated farmlands, and he gave thanks for the wild weather, which had tempted none of the farming folk to spend their Saturday night in Kirkwall. He reached the coast without meeting anyone—reached the cliffs, fifty to a hundred feet high, against which the North Sea broke with the same fury as less than forty miles away by crow's flight the long Atlantic surges beat against Marwick Head.

There was a place in Deerness called the Gloup, which he had once visited on an idle sightseeing excursion with two young men from the *Yelverton*. It was a long chasm in the cliff, loud with the suck and surge of the sea far below; a place which few cared or dared to explore by land or water. A body might lie there for some time undiscovered. Or it might be carried out to the North Sea, and never found till it was unrecognisable.

David drove as near to the cliff edge as he dared, over the rough short grass. The wind was howling there, and the waves said "gloup, gloup" at the foot of the chasm as if invoking the demon of the place. He walked round the bike and looked down at the silent passenger in the sidecar.

As stunned and shocked as Ingrid, in his own way, David Flett felt no compunction for what he had done. It was him or me, he thought grimly, the devil got what he was working for. He remembered Elena Petrovna, and felt he had avenged her truly, as he had sworn before Captain Hall. But then he remembered the two of them, crossing the foyer of the American Hotel together —Elena in her beauty, and Ritter at the height of his power and confidence—and the dead man in the sidecar seemed shrunken by contrast, the body grown smaller already without its inhabiting spirit. It was no longer possible to think this helpless thing had been an enemy.

With a final effort David dragged Ritter's body free, and staggering to the verge of the Gloup of Deerness flung it into the abyss.

XV

Sunday, May 28, to
Wednesday, May 31, 1916

Ingrid Sabiston went to bed but not to sleep. In the chill which followed the deep shock of Ritter's intrusion and death she lay between the blankets, shivering and praying for daylight to come. This was the only prayer she was able to utter: the simple "bonie-words" of her childhood faltered before the stark facts of assassination and murder. At five o'clock she got up and, as always, looked from her bedroom window over Scapa Flow. The great ships swung at anchor under a mackerel sky. Light-headed for lack of sleep, Ingrid looked for the *Chester* before she remembered that her brother's ship was in the Pentland Firth for gunnery practice. It took her almost as long to recall that David was not aboard the *Hampshire*, but—if he were still at liberty—in a seized Norwegian freighter at the Examination Base. Of how his night ride might have ended she did not dare to think.

She went downstairs, wearing an old cotton dress, and set the yard door and kitchen window wide. Although it was so early she was in dread of Agnes's return by machine from Houton if the baby, a seven months' child, had arrived safely. Ingrid cleared the hearth, rekindled the peat fire, drew hot water from the boiler and set to work to scrub the floor. She found the stained cloth David had used earlier, washed it clean and used it with a brush to go over every inch of the linoleum, and when the floor was dry she polished it until it shone. Next, and before she drank a cup of tea and ate a slice of bread, Ingrid overhauled the Harley-Davidson. There were no traces of blood, for David had used the sacks carefully, but here again she washed and polished the leatherwork. There were blades of grass on the wheel rims, and she knew the motor-bike had been taken off the road.

Agnes telephoned before eight o'clock, bawling her relief and joy at the birth of twins to her sister. "Twa peerie laddies, but Best be thankit! the doctor says they're fine, and their mother too! Oh, what a night we had here, me brother-in-law was about out of his judgment, but I told him to cheer up and Mary would get through all right—" There was a good deal of this, punctuated by suitable replies from Ingrid, before Agnes said:

"And what like a night had you, all on your own?"

"Oh, a very quiet night."

"You werena feared with me not there?"

"Not a bit."

When she hung up the receiver after telling Agnes to spend all day with the new mother, Ingrid sat beside the telephone in deep thought. David's belief that Ritter must have had an accomplice in Orkney had powerfully impressed her. She pictured a second assassin, briefed to take over if the first did not appear, waiting for the Commander-in-Chief at the fifth green on Stromness links, and knew there was something she ought to do at once. She dreaded the enquiries which might result, but Jellicoe's life came first, and taking her courage in both hands Ingrid called the Kirkwall exchange, and asked to be connected with the admiral commanding at the Long Hope Base.

Sir John Jellicoe, the Commander-in-Chief, played golf as usual that Sunday afternoon. He seldom had time to play more than five holes—even that was frowned upon by some inhabitants of Sabbath-keeping Orkney—and for the short Sunday game which he enjoyed so much he preferred the little Stromness links to Flotta. His opponent on this occasion was a Surgeon-Captain, an old friend who went round with him in a companionable silence which did the overburdened admiral as much good as the game. No caddies were available on Sundays, and the two men usually had the little course to themselves. Today, much to Jellicoe's annoyance, several pedestrians seemed to be hanging about the pathways; he said they put his eye out, and wondered who the devil they could be.

"They're probably plain-clothes men, Sir John," said the surgeon. Jellicoe gave him one of his gimlet looks.

"Oh, you've heard that tomfool story too, have you? It's probably all over the Base by now."

"Far from it. It was passed on to me as a top secret—considering that I might be one of the interested parties."

"You think somebody might really take a pot-shot at us from behind those bushes? Be sensible, man! That telephone call came from some cranky old lady who objects to Sunday golf on principle, and made the whole thing up to stop our games."

"We can't take chances with your life, Sir John."

"Now who the devil would want to assassinate me?"

"I know it's not done in the Navy," said the Surgeon, "but you must admit Sarajevo turned all our minds to assassination. If some German agent were to kill Kitchener, can you imagine the panic in the Army and the Cabinet?"

"Kitchener is more than a hero, he's a kind of demi-god to the whole country," said Jellicoe dryly. "If an old sailor like me were forcibly removed tomorrow it would make little difference to the conduct of the war. Beatty would be C.-in-C. in my place, and run the whole thing brilliantly, with the Nelson touch and the Band of Brothers . . ."

He stooped and took sand from the sandbox, shaping it to make a tee.

". . . Or else he might find himself stuck up here at Scapa like myself, obeying the commands of the Admiralty Board while the months drag by . . ."

The admiral and his friend ended their game at the fifth hole and walked back to the waiting motor car. The specially recruited plain-clothes men went off duty, and the larks sang high above the deserted links. The assassin lay face down in the Gloup of Deerness, caught underwater between the rocks at the foot of the gully and not as yet carried out to sea. The crabs and other rock creatures had already begun work on the body, and the long fair hair of Karl Ritter moved with the lap of the water, as strange a seaweed as ever floated on the Orkney shore.

The dead man had indeed had one accomplice, but not, as Ingrid had dreaded, a second gunman posted to make sure of Jellicoe at the fifth green. He was the commander of a German minelaying submarine, one of the fleet of eighteen which Scheer had ordered to sea on May 17 to stop the British ports of sortie. Some of them had met with fatal accidents on their mission, or had returned to base, but U75 had successfully laid a minefield north-west of the Orkneys where from neutral sources the German Command had learned the cruisers sometimes went. It was now lying off the Atlantic shore of the Mainland, not far from Marwick Head. After darkness fell on that strange Sunday, the last day but one of calm before the storm, U75 surfaced several times to search, through her periscope, for the expected pin-point of light near the Yimna-Yamnas, just south of the Birsay shore.

"Kommandant Ritter is not punctual at the rendezvous, sir," said the First Lieutenant at five minutes to midnight, and the captain shrugged.

"He may have been captured at the golf links," he said, "or else he's lying holed up in—what do they call it—the ancient settlement at Skara Brae while the police and military beat the countryside for him. In that case he must take his chance alone, Lieutenant: I can't give him more than one hour's grace."

The hour from midnight to one o'clock passed slowly. At one there was still no sign of the man U75 had been ordered to meet and take back to Germany. Her commander gave orders to sail for home as soon as their mission off the Mainland was completed. The submarine rose to the required height, and as she left her station twenty-two mines were laid in the channel west of Marwick Head, not two miles from the beautiful bay of Birsay where David and Ingrid had walked together in a happier hour.

Tuesday morning

As the survivors of Scheer's U-boat fleet made their way home on Monday, May 29, there was a deceptive calm on the surface of the North Sea. The bad weather had blown itself out, and only a few wisps of mist trailed over a sea like blue satin, on which little fishing smacks put out from the Danish and Norwegian shores.

No British ships were reported attacked or sunk, no neutral vessel carrying contraband to Germany invited seizure. Only the fishermen were employed in the stretch of water called the Skagerrak, to the south of which lay Jutland Bank.

Soon after the morning shift came on duty in Room 40 on Tuesday morning, a major flap began to develop at the Admiralty. The intercepts from Hunstanton-on-the-Wash and other D/F stations, decoded by the cryptographers, showed that Scheer had ordered the High Seas Fleet to assemble in the Jade Roads outside Wilhelmshaven by seven o'clock that evening. This was duly reported to the Ops Room, and on this occasion Operations lost no time in alerting Jellicoe. By noon, the C.-in-C. at Scapa Flow was warned that the German Fleet might put to sea next morning.

"What do you think, Adrian?" asked Liz Flett as they walked round the lake in St. James's Park during their lunch hour. "Is it the real thing at last, or just another Lowestoft?"

"How should I know?" said Adrian reasonably. "It looks very like the real thing, but so it has before; the most important thing is for our side to get there first this time."

Liz agreed. She was as attractive as ever, spending a good deal of her salary on new summer dresses, displaying them before Adrian Combermere like a pretty little mating bird. Their affair had been hanging fire for some weeks past, and in her heart Liz blamed David, always her favourite scapegoat. Adrian never criticised me till the night Davie came back, she thought sorely: now he always seems to be analysing and disagreeing with whatever I say or do. In the tranquil park, where the flowerbeds were in full bloom, the irritating thought impelled her to say:

"I wonder what my brother Davie's up to now. He's been lying doggo since his trip to Amsterdam."

"I only wish I'd seen him when he came through London," Adrian said. He knew far more than Liz did about that trip to Amsterdam. "Doesn't he ever write to you?"

"He writes to Dad sometimes, and Dad passes on the news to me. Dave's been on patrol, but if he's back in the Flow today he'll be aboard his ship now, won't he, Adrian? Not ashore, I mean?"

"No; all shore leave is automatically stopped when the C.-in-C. is under warning. They'll be at two hours for steam already, I shouldn't wonder."

"Let's go back and see if anything more came in."

"You're a demon for work, Elizabeth." It wanted fifteen minutes to the end of their lunch break.

"But it's so exciting, knowing what goes on, Adrian! Isn't it amazing that the Germans still stick to the *Magdeburg* code book? That with all their cleverness they don't know it's in our hands?"

"Let's hope they don't try any new stunts today."

But the Germans continued to signal by the codes captured at Odensholm in 1914, as faithfully as they now decyphered and believed in the British code which David Flett had carried to Amsterdam. About five o'clock that afternoon the intercepts showed that Scheer had made an operational signal to his Fleet at 3.40 p.m. Exactly two hours later, forty minutes from the time the Admiralty War Staff knew about Admiral Scheer's signal, Sir John Jellicoe was ordered to take the Grand Fleet into the North Sea, eastward of the Long Forties, and rendezvous with Beatty and the battle cruisers.

Tuesday evening

The Grand Fleet leaving Scapa Flow was always a magnificent sight for the depot workers and Orkney people living near the great anchorage. They were accustomed to the movements of the Squadrons, as these left on exercises and patrol, but the departure of the entire Fleet was a rarity, and on the last occasion—the abortive expedition to Lowestoft—it had taken place under cover of darkness. On this night in May the stage had all the scenery of high drama. Summer Time, which had come into law in Britain a few days earlier, was an innovation not observed at Scapa Flow, and so at ten minutes past eight, when Jellicoe gave the General Signal, the vivid colours of an Orkney sunset were already in the sky. By half past nine, when the Fleet sailed, the sunset glow was fading through umber to violet and blue, later to be muted to the pallor of the Northern summer night. The low hills and farmlands on the shores of the Flow faded into the

262

dusk; and against this soft panorama the massive grey battleships passed out in a procession seven miles long.

It was Olav Sabiston, sent to bed but glued to the bedroom window with the binoculars, who came tumbling downstairs to tell his father and sister that the Grand Fleet had weighed anchor and was passing out of Hoxa Sound. They were in the livingroom, Ingrid thankful that her father had not asked for the lamps to be lighted but seemed content to sit in the soft Orkney twilight, telling her about the General Assembly and the rich experience of preaching in St. Giles' Cathedral. She knew that she looked ravaged by the strain of the past three days and the burden of the first great secret of her life, but her father's eye was turned inward, and she saw that he was over the worst of his bereavement. Whereas for me the worst is coming, she thought; and oh! what will it be?

"Daddy! Ingrid! They're going out!" screamed Olav, bursting in. There was no need to ask what he meant; Dr. Sabiston merely paused to say "Are you sure, boy? The Fleet, not just a Squadron?" and then all three were hurrying to the summer seat at the bottom of the front garden, from which they could look over the glebe field and the shore road by the Flow.

"They're on the move all right," said Olav assertively, and his father sighed assent. There was no mistaking that superb departure. Admiral Jellicoe had twenty-four battleships under his command, of which eight, forming the 2nd Squadron, were then at Cromarty. The sixteen led the van: the new Dreadnoughts which were Britain's pride—campaigned for, lobbied for, paid for at a great price—with the great old Navy names of *Benbow, Bellerophon, Temeraire, Collingwood, St. Vincent.* They were accompanied by twenty-two cruisers and fifty-one destroyers, with the new names soon to make naval history: *Tipperary, Acasta, Ardent, Shark.* One by one they slipped out of Hoxa Sound, passing by Swona Island to the Pentland Skerries, and from there were hidden in the tumbling darkness of the grey North Sea.

"It can't be just an exercise, can it, Daddy, when the whole Fleet goes out?" asked Olav.

"No, I don't think it's an exercise, my boy."

263

"I wish Magnus could have had shore leave today. I knew something was up, when he said he'd come, and didn't."

Ingrid was silent. The minister and the boy took turns at using the binoculars, trying to identify the ships in the gathering dusk. She, too, had longed for shore leave—for David; he had only been able to telephone from Long Hope on Monday afternoon:

"Not a chance of getting over to Houton today. I'll try again tomorrow."

"Yes, do."

"Are you all right, my darling?" (He was much less shy of endearments, Ingrid had noticed, when they could be spoken at a distance.)

"Yes, I'm fine, Davie. What about you? When did you get back aboard the *Hampshire*?"

"Sunday forenoon. A Marine guard relieved us, and the Norwegian skipper was let back aboard. There wasn't a yap out of him; I think he was feared to speak."

"That's good. David, I called the Base and warned them there might be trouble at the golf links—"

"Are you worrying about that?"

"N-no, not really. Not now."

"See you tomorrow, then."

"Yes, Davie."

An unsatisfactory conversation, trying to give nothing away— not even their feeling for one another—and Ingrid knew, as she watched the Grand Fleet fade into the night, that it might be their last on earth. She shivered, and her father put his arm around her.

"You're cold, lassie. We must go indoors."

"Let's wait a little longer, Daddy—please."

The lights of the last of that great armada dwindled and disappeared; the scent of wallflower in the manse garden grew stronger in the falling dew. The summer stars came out over Scapa Flow.

"Well," said the minister, "we've watched the passing of the greatest fleet the world has ever known. May God bless all who sail in her tonight!"

There was jubilation in Room 40 and the Intelligence Department at the Admiralty next morning, when it was learned that for once the Royal Navy had the advantage of moving faster than the enemy. Jellicoe and Beatty had put to sea two and a half hours before Admiral von Hipper and the German Battle Cruisers, four hours before Admiral Scheer and the German Battle Fleet left the Jade. They were steaming to rendezvous with each other at 2.30 p.m., at a distance of fifty miles apart in the latitude of the Skagerrak and Jutland Bank, while the Germans would presumably move due north past Heligoland, using the Amrum Channel which they kept swept through the British minefields. The scene was set for action in the early afternoon, and all along the East Coast of Britain preparations were made for the consequences of what, after nearly two years of anticipation, was expected to be the new Trafalgar. All the docks were cleared to take in home-faring or crippled ships, and tugs were ready to go to their assistance. The approaches to the Thames Estuary and the English Channel were covered, in case Scheer's northward sortie should be a feint to disguise an attack on the south-east, while Harwich Force and Dover Patrol were standing by. More ominously, hospitals along the East Coast were warned to expect the wounded.

No one in the whole Grand Fleet knew, as Liz Flett and Adrian Combermere did, of a tiny incident on which much of the coming action might depend. The Fleet Flagship, with Admiral Jellicoe aboard, was just in sight of the 2nd Battle Squadron which sailed from Cromarty and took station on the Grand Fleet in the middle of the forenoon, when Room 40 had an unexpected visit from Captain Thomas Jackson, R.N. This officer, the Director of Operations Division, had what one Lieutenant called "a supreme contempt" for the work of the cryptographers—that bunch of amateurs, civilians and women; and seldom if ever entered their domain. On this crucial morning, when the whole High Seas Fleet was operational and the intercepts coming in thick and fast, Captain Jackson's appearance was as brief as possible. He merely asked, without an explanation:

"Where do our D/F stations place the German call sign DK?"
Someone said, "In Wilhelmshaven, sir."

"Thanks."

The door slammed. Nobody spoke. Then one of the senior cryptographers said uneasily: "That was a funny question."

Pens were laid down. "It was," said Adrian Combermere. "He wouldn't by any unlucky chance be thinking about Scheer?"

"Scheer left Wilhelmshaven more than eight hours ago."

"Yes, and Jackson has been sent all the intercepts, of course."

They were all talking at once, Liz and the little old don, Adrian and the Commander R.N.V.R. who was one of the best men in Room 40, all beset by the sinking sensation that Jackson's impatient query might mean trouble for the Fleet.

"But he *knows*," said Adrian, "we explained it to Liaison at the time of Lowestoft, that when Scheer puts to sea he takes another call sign for the *Friedrich der Grosse* and transfers DK to Wilhelmshaven—"

"What if he doesn't know, or has forgotten?" someone said.

"*Bloody* pompous fool—"

"Shut up," said the Commander, "that won't do any good. I'm going to find Sir Alfred. He and Captain Hall ought to know about this at once."

But the brusque Director of Operations Division, who had not condescended to give any particulars about his query to the workers in Room 40, had already done the mischief. Ops had signalled to Admiral Jellicoe that the German C.-in-C. was still in his Jade base at ten minutes past eleven. He received this signal at about a quarter to one. By that time the High Seas Fleet had passed Horns Riff to starboard and was steaming north parallel to the Jutland coast.

Wednesday afternoon

When Admiral Jellicoe received this striking piece of misinformation David Flett was keeping the first dog watch below. Before going to his cabin he had smoked a cigarette with a group of officers who ranged from the taciturn (the Commander) to the jubilant (Lieutenant Ramsay), each in his own way convinced that today was *the day*, *Der Tag* as the enemy called it, when the great sea victory would at last be won. The *Hampshire* had been detailed by Jellicoe to act as the linking ship between his light cruiser screen and the advanced scout line formed by the 1st and 2nd Cruiser Squadrons. Earlier in the day, as she passed ahead of the Battle Fleet, the *Hampshire* had sighted the *Iron Duke*, though at a distance, and the crew had cheered the Commander-in-Chief, a small figure just visible on the flagship's upper bridge. Lieutenant Flett cheered with the rest. Maybe I helped to keep him alive for this day, he thought, and Ingrid did too.

But if this was *Der Tag* at last, he cursed himself for having now in his possession the two vital documents he had taken from Ritter's body. If I'm killed in action it won't matter, he thought, but if I'm wounded, and taken below unconscious, what'll happen if a German passport and a map of the Stromness links are found in my inside pocket? I might finish up in the Tower of London myself, who knows?

Of course he should have done something about Ritter's papers —he knew, too late, exactly what—when he was ashore at Long Hope on Monday afternoon. But on Monday he had still been walking on eggshells, obsessed by the idea that Captain Savill would ask for an explanation of his dealings with Contraband Control at Kirkwall and his prolonged absence from the *Thorfinn*, noted perforce in David's own report. Possibly the preoccupation of all senior officers with the intended sortie had saved him from interrogation; Captain Savill had had priorities on Monday which did not include the fate of a Norwegian freighter brought in, as a matter of routine, by one of his junior officers.

David felt a strong temptation to destroy the Ritter papers. But if he came through the day unharmed, they would be valuable proof—placed in the proper hands—that in destroying Karl Ritter he had destroyed a dangerous enemy agent: they might even save David Flett from appearing at a court martial on a capital charge. Court martial or Court of Session? He didn't know enough about the law to be certain where he would be tried if the death of Karl Ritter were brought home to him. Lying on his bunk, watching his clothes swaying on their hooks as the *Hampshire*

267

picked up speed, he went over in his mind for the hundredth time all the likely causes of discovery. Was it possible that nobody between Hamnavoe and Deerness had been interested in the comings and goings of a motor-cycle on that stormy Saturday? Would the Gloup keep its secret for ever, or was Ritter's body even now lolling in a much-frequented stretch of open sea? Did salt water completely erase the fingerprints from the haft of a seaman's knife?

He hadn't thought about fingerprints until too late. What David knew about crime came from lurid newspaper articles rehashing the story of Dr. Crippen and the trial of Oscar Slater, but he had a vague idea that finger-prints were considered important by the police. Had his own, when he grasped the knife and drove it home, been complete enough to obliterate all traces of Ingrid's when she picked it up and put it in his hand? Was there the remotest danger that she herself might be accused of being an accessory before the fact of murder?

All the latent chivalry in David's nature, stirred by Elena Tamirova's weakness, had now been fully awakened by the strength of Ingrid Sabiston. By allowing Karl Ritter to reach the Orkney Mainland, he had subjected the girl to a trial of endurance which, he knew only too well, was still a long way from being over. She had to wait and watch while he went into battle; he was, on every count, the lucky one.

He heard the footsteps in the alleyway, the knock on cabin doors, and knew it was a messenger from the bridge.

"Begging your pardon, sir, the Fleet's going to action stations in 'arf an hour!"

"Right!"

David swung his legs off the bunk, feeling a great relief. This was it at last, and all he had to do now was grab his gas mask and duffel coat and join the other men off watch in the smokingroom. He was sure there would be tea going, and there was. The officers drank it with one eye on the clock.

"Has anybody the faintest idea what's happening?" said a deliberately languid voice from the depth of an armchair.

"The buzz is, the battle cruisers have engaged the enemy.

Master Hipper was supposed to be in Jade Bay; quite a shock for Beatty's boys when he turned up off Jutland Bank."

"No!"

"Fact!"

Unconsciously everyone held his breath to listen. The Grand Fleet and the battle cruisers were now not fifty, but nearly seventy miles apart. There was nothing to be heard but the drone of the turbines and the rattle as the securing chains of the *Hampshire's* guns were released.

"There we go!"

The Marine buglers were sounding "Action Stations", followed by the "Double". In an instant the smokingroom was deserted. Six hundred and fifty men went through the drill practised times without number: the turret crews manning gunhouses, magazines and shellrooms, the fire and wreckage parties doubling to their posts. The seconds in command detached to replace officer casualties took their places in the lower conning tower. The stokers were throwing on coal to keep up the pressure as the screaming turbines sucked in the steam. The old cruiser had been ordered to increase her speed to 20 knots.

David Flett joined the senior searchlights officer at their post. The Fleet had altered course during his watch below, and was steaming to join Beatty. David noted that although the afternoon was bright, with a light breeze, the visibility was already decreasing, and that between ships spread over an enormous front of ocean visual contact would not be easy to maintain. He wondered inconsequently what Magnus Sabiston was doing, and where the *Chester* was.

Wednesday, late afternoon

When the Grand Fleet bugles sounded "Action Stations" H.M.S. *Chester* was already on the road to glory.

At about half past two the Commander-in-Chief learned from Admiral Beatty that the forward scouts of the Rosyth force had sighted the enemy—which the Admiralty's signal, not much more than two hours earlier, had placed in Jade Bay. In a cold rage, resolving to doubt all future tactical signals from London

269

and rely entirely on information relayed from his own ships, Jellicoe started steaming at full speed towards the battle cruisers. He knew that Beatty, engaging von Hipper, would entice Scheer and the German Battle Fleet towards himself. By way of immediate assistance to Beatty, he detached from his own force the 3rd Battle Cruiser Squadron, which was normally based on Rosyth, but which, being at Scapa Flow for gunnery practice, had sailed from Orkney with the Grand Fleet.

Attached to the three "Invincibles" of this Squadron were two light cruisers, H.M.S. *Canterbury* and the newly commissioned *Chester*, in which Magnus Sabiston was a Lieutenant of the Turret. *Canterbury* and *Chester* were in the van, ahead of the slower "Invincibles", and in company with four destroyers, *Shark*, *Acasta*, *Ophelia* and *Christopher*, which acted as the Squadron's submarine screen. All were racing south by east at a fast 25 knots, which brought them within earshot of the battle while still a long way out of range.

Terrible things had happened to Sir David Beatty's force as soon as he joined battle with Admiral Hipper. His ships, outlined against the western sky, presented a clear target for the devastatingly accurate German fire. At 4 p.m., fifteen minutes from the start of the action, Beatty's flagship, H.M.S. *Lion*, was hit by a shell on the roof of her "Q" turret amidships, and was only saved from the explosion of the magazine by the presence of mind of her mortally wounded turret officer, a major of the Royal Marines. Within two more minutes the *Indefatigable* was hit. She exploded and sank with fifty-seven officers and nine hundred and sixty men. In the same manner, by a German salvo which exploded her magazines, the great battleship *Queen Mary*, once commanded by Captain Hall of the Intelligence Division, went down with a total loss of twelve hundred and forty-six lives.

In this great gunnery duel the British scored a few successes. Hipper's rear cruisers, the *Moltke* and *Von der Tann*, received damaging hits, and the destroyers on both sides engaged in a mêlée of their own, in which the German battle cruiser *Seydlitz* was torpedoed. By the time the *Chester* reached the scene the fighting had spread over a vast front, so clouded by funnel smoke and brown cordite fumes that the range-finders of both forces could judge their distance only by the flashes of the guns.

The splinter mats were out, and the spray rattled like hail against the gun shield when Magnus Sabiston, as officer of the watch, made a round of the *Chester's* deck. The guns were ready for action, and the gunlayers rubbing the mechanism with handfuls of waste. He paused beside the forward 6-inch gun. The sight-setter, holding his telepad nervously in his hands, was the youngster who had been so proud when Jellicoe returned his salute at Plymouth, Boy First Class John Travers Cornwell.

Magnus had taken a kindly interest in this lad since the beginning of the football games on Flotta. He was the youngest member of the ship's company, sixteen years and four months old, and also one of the keenest, though the nine older members of the forward gun crew naturally treated him as an idle young rascal, which they called "training the kid up in the way he should go".

"You all right, Cornwell?" Magnus asked.

"Yes, sir, thank you."

"We'll be going to action in a few minutes."

"Yes, sir." The Marines had the bugles at their lips. Lieutenant Sabiston doubled to his turret as Captain Lawson, who had sighted gun flashes to the south-west, turned to investigate. At the sound of "Action Stations" his own crews stood to their guns, while down in the magazines and shellrooms the half-ton shells and cordite propelling charges were transferred to the lower handing room. From there the shell moved in an armour-plated cylinder to the working chamber from which it was delivered by hydraulic power to the open breech of the gun. When the gun was firing, the control officer in the fighting top passed on the deflection and rate of change of range to the sight-setter, standing to the left of the gun.

Jack Cornwell, sight-setter of the forward gun, put on the telepad which connected him by wire with the gunnery officer. In spite of having told Lieutenant Sabiston that he was "all right", the boy was badly scared, and the gunlayer and his mates gave him reassuring grins. He tried to grin back, but he had seen dead bodies in the water as they raced to join the action, and ships on fire, and he knew death might be near for all of them. He tried to think of pleasant things, like his home in Manor Park, and his Mum and Dad. Dad had been a soldier, over age in 1914, but still he'd gone back to the Army as soon as war broke out, and with a Dad like that what could a boy do but join up himself as soon as he had turned fifteen? Mum worried about them both, but she'd been ever so proud when her Jack did so well at Keyham Barracks, and got promoted to Boy First Class, with a whole shilling a week for pay. He tried to remember what the clergyman had said when he was confirmed at Keyham. Something about "be faithful unto death"—he couldn't remember, in this noise coming roaring all about them, how it went on, but he knew it meant the same as what the sergeant-instructor said again and again at Keyham: "The gun must be kept firing as long as one man is left who is able to crawl." But that was gunnery practice, this was the real thing, and a word of warning came through the wire to his telepad. Jack Cornwell raised his left hand to the disc which he must turn, at the word of command, till the notch was in a straight line with the arrow on the brass plate below. He saw a flash of gunfire leap out of the mist ahead.

The *Chester* had encountered not one but a group of the enemy's light cruisers, the nearest on the port bow being the *Frankfurt*. The flash which the gun crews of the *Chester* saw was the *Frankfurt*'s first salvo, which fell a good two thousand yards beyond the *Chester*. Fired very rapidly, a second German salvo fell five hundred yards short. Simultaneously the *Chester* opened up with all her guns, and fired for the first and last time at the enemy. The third salvo from the *Frankfurt* was dead on target.

Jack Cornwell saw his mates fall dead around him, and heard the crash of the turrets as the *Chester*'s port guns, like his own, went out of action. He felt pain everywhere, as if his body had been torn open—pain like a flame which sent him spinning up to some high point of endurance, into a great golden ball of light where he was only ears and a hand steady on a brass disc. His torn body began to sag across the gun, and he braced himself against it. *The gun must be kept firing*, he knew that all right, and he would stand there *as long as one man is left* stand there and wait for *who is able* wait for his orders God! oh God! *as long as one man is left who is able to crawl* . . .

When Captain Lawson had manœuvred his ship to safety, and the first aid party reached the forward gun, they found seven dead men sprawled on the deck, two severely wounded in the lee of the crumpled gun shield, and standing by the gun, torn and bleeding, the little Cockney vanboy who had been faithful unto death.

XVI

Wednesday, May 31, and
Thursday, June 1, 1916

Wednesday, early evening

H.M.S. *Chester*, having gamely taken on the light cruisers of Admiral Bödicker's 2nd Scouting Group, had sustained eighteen direct hits in five minutes, with thirty-five men killed and forty-two wounded. But Admiral Hood and the 3rd Battle Cruiser Squadron were swift in vengeance. By six o'clock H.M.S. *Invincible, Inflexible* and *Indomitable* had crippled the *Wiesbaden*, severely damaged the *Frankfurt* and sent the *Pillau* limping from the scene. Almost at the same time the 2nd Cruiser Squadron, led by Admiral Sir Robert Arbuthnot, arrived to close in on the kill. They had barely opened fire when a new German force appeared out of the mist, including four Dreadnoughts of the 5th Division. With them were battle cruisers of Admiral von Hipper's 1st Scouting Group. It was the cruiser *Derfflinger* which at twenty minutes past six sank Sir Robert Arbuthnot's flagship, H.M.S. *Defence*, with the total loss of all the nine hundred lives aboard.

Before the end of this fierce and highly concentrated action, in which every attack led to an immediate counter-attack, one more calamitous loss was suffered by the British. The 3rd Battle Cruiser Squadron, to avenge the *Defence*, now opened fire on Hipper's cruisers. Hits were registered on his flagship, the *Lützow*, and the *Derfflinger*. Admiral Hood's own flagship H.M.S. *Invincible* was replying to the concentrated fire of five enemy vessels. At 6.33 p.m. she received, as *Lion* had done before her, a direct hit on her "Q" turret. *Lion*, thanks to Major Harvey, had been saved from what now happened to the *Invincible*, the ignition of the charges in the magazine rooms, which exploded in rapid succession. The flagship, another victim of the *Derfflinger*, blew up exactly in half and sank with only six survivors out of a crew of one thousand and thirty-two.

It was upon this scene of disaster, and at a moment when the British losses far exceeded the German, that the Grand Fleet now appeared at full speed and began its majestic deployment. Jellicoe's irritation with the Admiralty's misinformation had somewhat subsided. The information he was receiving from his own ships was not much better, and as late as six o'clock, when he signalled his Vice-Admiral for news of the enemy's battleships, Beatty's reply gave news only of the German cruisers. But from the quarter in which firing was now heard it was plain that the Grand Fleet and Scheer's Battle Fleet were rushing towards each other, and Jellicoe, with the roar of combat all about him and visibility reduced by an impenetrable curtain of coal smoke, had to take one of the vital decisions of the day. He decided to deploy the Grand Fleet to port, towards Jutland Bank. This permitted him to "cross the T", placing his fleet in a single line across the German advance, so as to bring its broadsides to bear on an enemy capable of replying only with its forward turrets.

Admiral Scheer was not aware of Jellicoe's presence until the Grand Fleet opened fire on the German battle cruisers which had done so much damage in the first phase of the action. He found himself faced with twenty-four battleships in a line just over five miles long, while his own twenty-two were strung out along a nine mile line. Not so much in number as in disposition of their force, the British had the advantage, and as salvo after salvo belched from their guns Scheer decided that discretion was the better part of valour. He refused to join battle, ordered his fleet to execute a single point turn to starboard and form line ahead in the opposite direction. By a quarter to seven the High Seas Fleet, disappearing into the mist behind its own tremendous smoke-screen, was steady on a south-westerly course. Jellicoe altered course to place the Grand Fleet between Scheer and his base at Wilhemshaven, about one hundred and fifty miles away.

Admiral Scheer was as much in the dark about the general situation as his adversary. He had received no wireless reports at all and like Jellicoe relied on often contradictory information from his own captains. He had only two ambitions—to stave off a major gunnery duel until darkness fell, and then to escape from the Grand Fleet, through the Skagerrak if he must, back to Jade Bay if he could. Believing Jellicoe's line further south than it actually was, he reversed his course and steered straight back into the arms of the Grand Fleet.

The firing which then began, and lasted till half past seven, proved the value of Jellicoe's insistence on long-range gunnery practice. The Grand Fleet, receiving only two hits itself, and supported by Beatty and the battle cruisers, scored success after success: the *Wiesbaden* sunk, von Hipper's *Lützow* out of action, Scheer's *Friedrich der Grosse* badly damaged, the *König* and the *Grosser Kurfurst* crippled. Scheer in desperation ordered the 1st Scouting Group to a suicidal action, a "death ride" as it was called, to ram the British line. With the flagship and Admiral Hipper unable to lead the attack, it was led by Captain Hartog in the redoubtable *Derfflinger*, which had sunk H.M.S. *Defence* and *Invincible*. The German cruiser now suffered the same agony as she had meted out to others, for as hit after hit pierced her armour there were explosions inside two of her turrets, killing one hundred and forty-five men. But the German system of magazine protection was better than the British, and the catastrophe which had overtaken four British ships was not repeated. Badly holed like her three sister ships, the *Derfflinger* was not sunk; she survived to carry on the death ride of the battle cruisers until Admiral Scheer called it off.

Scheer had made up his mind to escape for the second time. As he retreated to the south-west, only too well aware that he was moving away from his home base but unable to stand up to the British guns, he ordered his destroyers to attack the Grand Fleet with torpedoes.

This was the second crucial decision Jellicoe had to take. To avoid the approaching torpedoes on their 10,000 yard run, he ordered two 2-point turns, with the result that the Grand Fleet was, for the time being, steering south-east. He had thus "turned away" from an enemy he had tactically beaten and reduced to headlong flight, at the very moment when a "turn-towards" might have led to the annihilation of the German Fleet. The total victory, the new Trafalgar, was there almost within Jellicoe's grasp; it was his own, overmastering instinct to save his ships and crews at all costs which allowed it to slip away. He could hear firing going on in the south-west, where there were several engagements between Beatty's force and the German battle cruisers, but he declined to act upon the signal Beatty made at ten minutes to eight, suggesting that the van of the battle fleet should follow his battle cruisers to cut off the whole of the enemy fleet. This, he thought, was insubordinate. Jellicoe was aware of his strategic advantage while the Grand Fleet lay between the Germans and the Jade, and certain, as night began to fall, that the decisive victory was only postponed until the morning light. Dawn would usher in a day already memorable in the Royal Navy, and 1916, too, would have its Glorious First of June.

Wednesday night

When Admiral Jellicoe signalled to the Grand Fleet that he had "no night intentions", David Flett had been on duty for nearly five hours. He knew that this was nothing, that the duty of officers in other ships had been far heavier, and like most of the ship's company of H.M.S. *Hampshire* he began to suffer from the old sense of frustration as the afternoon and evening of May 31 wore on. As the linking ship between the easterly and westerly halves of Jellicoe's cruiser screen, the *Hampshire* had little chance of bringing her relatively small guns into action. About five o'clock, when forming line ahead on their own flagship, H.M.S. *Minotaur*, the cruisers began to see the flashes of the battle cruiser action, and as they raced full speed ahead to the scene they heard more than one tremendous explosion and felt considerable underwater shock. By seven, when the range had closed to 10,000 yards and the Grand Fleet was in the thick of the fighting, the *Hampshire*'s gun-layers were quite unable to see their targets through the dense German smoke screen.

"No night intentions, well, thank God for that!" said the senior searchlights officer. He and David were still at their post, wrapped in duffel coats. The night was growing chilly, and a servant from the Wardroom had brought each of them a mug of cocoa. It took the filthy taste of cordite from their mouths.

"Short and sweet," said David. "The C.-in-C. likes to keep his signals to the point."

"Sometimes a damn sight too short and sweet. He composes them himself, in the good old-fashioned way, and never thinks of including the details. The fleet in action needs more guidance than concise orders to open and cease fire."

"Aye, that's right enough," said David, "but the main trouble today was that every movement had to be signalled through and from the *Iron Duke*. Should the fleet not use the W/T more?"

"I bet you half the W/T was smashed or unserviceable by seven o'clock tonight. J.R.J. hates it anyway, and I hear the First Sea Lord told him to use it as little as possible. That's modern scientific thinking for you, Flett old boy! Back we go to our beloved lamps, there seems to be something doing astern."

"There's a devil of a lot of firing astern," said David, staring into the darkness. His eyes were red and sore with concentrating, and there was a rim of salt on his cracked lips.

Some of the men were resting on the deck, which was covered with cinders from the funnels of the next in line. The stokers, down below, had come out to the alleyways, and covered in sweat and coal-dust were lying propped up against the bulkheads when at the sound of renewed firing Captain Savill himself came out of the charthouse and viewed the situation from the bridge. There was something like a fireworks display five miles astern, where the British destroyer flotillas were following the battleships. There were bursts of German star shell—something quite new to the British—and the white flashing of searchlight beams. There was the exchange of recognition signals, for which the High Seas Fleet used coloured lights, and also the flicker of the white lamps which they used to impersonate the British ships. Something was undoubtedly up astern, but Jellicoe, once again handicapped by misinformation supplied from the Admiralty, concluded that nothing very serious was going on. He lay down about eleven o'clock for three hours' rest, until first light, in his shelter at the back of the flagship's bridge; being roused, during this brief respite, by several more reports from the Admiralty and his commanders. He knew nothing about two of his battleships which had been blown up and sunk; neither did he know that while the Grand Fleet waited for the dawn the fleet under Admiral Scheer's command was on its way home to Jade Bay.

This was the dark hour of the British destroyer flotillas. Some destroyers had covered themselves with glory earlier in the day, like H.M.S. *Shark* and *Acasta* of the 4th Flotilla, which went to the rescue after the attack on *Chester*. The *Shark* had gone down with colours flying, and in the *Shark*'s spirit of tackling a superior enemy the 4th Flotilla now took on a squadron of German battleships.

By ten o'clock the High Seas Fleet was in its night formation, eight miles east-south-east from the British Battle Fleet steering south. Scheer's ships were advancing by Squadrons, with the Scouting Groups screening their port side and the van, and were steering for Horns Riff off the Danish coast, from which the Amrum Channel led to Wilhelmshaven and safety. Seven times between ten o'clock and 2.15 a.m. the British destroyers stood in the way and challenged the retreating enemy. Some solid successes were won: the sinking of the light cruiser *Frauenlob* and the old *Pommern*, "the five-minute ship"—the pre-Dreadnought in which Kommandant Karl Ritter was "eventually" to serve—and the disabling of the *Rostock* and the *Elbing*, later abandoned and sunk by their crews. The British lost the *Tipperary*, whose survivors were later found on a Carley raft singing an appropriate song, and the *Ardent*, only two of whose crew survived after taking on an entire division of German battleships. Of all the destroyer captains engaged in those recklessly brave encounters, very few made any attempt to report to the Commander-in-Chief. Captain Stirling, leader of the 12th Flotilla which sank the *Pommern*, three times tried to get a wireless message through to the *Iron Duke*, indicating that the High Seas Fleet was literally fighting its way home along a south-south-westerly course. None of these messages were received in the flagship.

The gallantry of the British destroyers was not rewarded. Scheer was only one hour's steaming from the Horns Riff lightship, which was flashing the way for his passage back to port, when dawn broke on that not-so-glorious first of June.

Wednesday night and Thursday morning

When Jellicoe's message announcing that the Grand Fleet was going to action was received at the Admiralty, there was tremendous rejoicing. The news had been anticipated for nearly two years, and there could be no doubt of the outcome: in some offices there was already talk of buying champagne to toast the victory. Liz Flett's day's work was officially over, but she was still in the precincts of Room 40 when the great news came, and at once begged Sir Alfred Ewing to let her stay on.

"Now, Miss Flett, since when have you been allowed to work on the night shift?"

"Not since the third week in April," she said with a smile, and Sir Alfred acknowledged that she had a point there. The third week in April was when Liz had worked at night with the team preparing the fake code book for David to take to Amsterdam.

"Everyone will be needed tonight, sir. Do let me stay!" she said.

"You like to be where the excitement is, don't you, Miss Flett?"

"But this is so tremendously exciting—and we've waited for so long!"

"Very well, by all means come back later, I'll be very glad to have your help. But only after you've had a proper meal and a good rest, Miss Flett. Why don't you go home to your rooms and have a nap?"

"I never had a nap in the daytime in my life!"

"Haven't you really? What it is to be young! All right, be off with you now, and come back when you feel like it. I'll tell Mr. Combermere to expect you," he added with a twinkle. What a darling he is, Liz thought as she went off to get her coat and hat. He must have guessed about Adrian and me.

Not that there was anything to guess. A few meals together, a few theatres and concerts, mid-day walks in the Park—that was about all it had amounted to since the night they had to give up dinner at the Trocadero to meet David at Liverpool Street Station. They were the best of friends, of course, but the tenderness, the excitement of the early spring had never ripened. Liz, as she walked along Whitehall, was frowning. She had no intention of going back to Nottingham Terrace to lie down on her bed like an old lady, all alone on this beautiful evening, listening to the whisper of the poplar tree in the back yard.

She had a pot of tea and poached eggs at an A.B.C. It was the sort of place she usually despised, preferring to eat a sandwich out of a paper bag in one of the parks when she couldn't afford to visit one of the solidly good restaurants where it was now permissible for professional women to go alone. The crowd in the teashop reminded her of the typists who wanted her to go about with them when she first came to work at Mr. Neroslavski's London office. They had expected a Scots girl newly arrived in town to be homesick, friendless, humble. Well! she had shown *them* what ambition and hard work could do! But Liz, looking round at the pale office faces and the cheap summer finery (there was hardly a man in the place) was not as satisfied as usual with the image of Lucky Liz Flett, the girl in the know, one of the best cryptographers in the Admiralty.

She finished her meal quickly and walked back to the Strand. There was a Western film showing at one of the new cinemas— just the sort of rubbish her Dad and Davie liked, all cowboys and Indians and guns going off. The alternative was a Mary Pickford movie. Liz bought a ticket and went in. She thought it would be restful to sit still in the dark, but she left again before long, so that a motherly attendant followed her to the foyer and asked if she would like a glass of water.

"Aren't you feeling well, madam? You do look pale!"

"Thank you, but I'm quite all right—"

"It's the 'eat, I expect. Takes it out of you, a warm spell like we've been 'aving."

"It does rather."

"Shame, reely, you missing the end of the film, it's ever so nice and sad. Mary Pickford's sweet, i'n't she?"

"She's very pretty." How to explain to this friendly Londoner

281

that the star with her pretty simpering face and those artfully arranged curls seemed intolerably divorced from real life, the story a sham, and the nice sad ending, obvious from the beginning, having nothing to do with real suffering?

The Fleet is going to action, Jellicoe had signalled. Real suffering was on its way to England as coldly and as surely as Breithaupt had once flung down his bombs over this very Strand. For the first time Liz regretted the special knowledge of which she had been so proud. In all the Strand, most likely she was the only person who knew a battle was raging in the North Sea. How many of the people who drifted by, looking at the darkened shop windows, enjoying the long summer evening prolonged by Daylight Saving, would be heartbroken in a day or two when the casualty lists came in?

She returned to the Admiralty at nine o'clock. In her own room the Commander, the elderly don, and Adrian were at their desks. The room was very quiet. Through the open window came the hum of London. Adrian got up, unsmiling, as Liz came in.

"I'd like to have a word with you, Miss Flett, may I?"

"Of course, Mr. Combermere."

In the corridor he dropped his formal manner, and sat down beside her on a broad windowledge.

"You might have waited for me, Elizabeth. We could have had something to eat together, since we were both planning to come back."

"I didn't know how long you'd be with Blinker."

"He let me go just before half past five, but Alfie said you'd left."

"Have you *had* some food, Adrian?"

"I had a beer and a sandwich at the pub across the street. Look, dear, I told the Commander I would put you in the picture. It's been a pretty rough night so far, I'm sorry to say."

"What's happened?"

"The Germans claim to have sunk four of our ships already, with a heavy loss of life."

"*Four?*"

"*Queen Mary, Indefatigable, Invincible* and *Defence.*"

"My God!"

"You can guess how Captain Hall feels about the *Queen Mary*."

"Yes, but—what about *their* losses, Adrian?"

"Don't know yet. There's very little coming in from our side so far."

"Well, then, we only know half the story!"

"That's the worst of this game we're in—you only see a bit at a time. For the past hour the intercepts have shown the Germans apparently retreating, and moving west. If only those heroes in the War Room would order Harwich Force out to nobble them!"

"What's going *on* in the War Room?"

"God knows. Blinker's trying to find out."

"Well," she said, getting up from the windowsill, "Let's carry on, shall we? Thank you for telling me about the losses, Adrian. You've saved me from going in to see the boss whistling, and making blithe remarks about success."

"He wants us all in the big room anyway."

Sir Alfred had decided that on this night of crisis his cryptographers—the regular night shift and a few dedicated volunteers like Liz—should be together, pooling their knowledge, while on a map the positions of the two fleets were plotted as best they could be from the German intercepts. These were coming in thick and fast as the enemy ships signalled their positions; already Sir Alfred Ewing had his doubts if all the signals were accurate. Ships at sea were often out in their reckoning of other ships' positions, and the smoke of Jutland had obscured more than the targets in the late afternoon. This improvised map, of course, was only for the information of the cryptographers. The real war map of the North Sea was in the War Room, where the Chief of the War Staff, Admiral Oliver, was complaining bitterly that whenever he wanted to look at a chart people kept getting in his way.

These troublesome visitors included the First Lord, Mr. Arthur Balfour, and his assistants, and the First Sea Lord, Admiral Jackson, he who had instructed Jellicoe not to overdo the use of wireless telegraphy at sea. They were in and out of the War Room all afternoon and part of the evening, giving their approval to the orders sent to Jellicoe; but the prime responsibility for these orders lay in the hands of one man: the Director of Operations Division, Captain Henry Jackson.

When Liz Flett joined the cryptographers they were struggling with a particularly difficult intercept. From the first words decyphered it was obviously of great importance, and copies were passed round so that all could work on it simultaneously. It was from Admiral Scheer to the German Airship Detachment, and read "Early morning reconnaissance at Horns Riff is urgently requested." It was passed on to Ops at ten minutes past ten. For some extraordinary reason it was not sent on to Jellicoe.

"Then the Huns are going to try to get back to port by Horns Riff and the Amrum Channel," said the R.N.V.R. Commander in Room 40, looking at the map.

"Plenty of time to catch them yet," said Ewing cheerfully. He had always been a buoyant man; now he drew on his reserve of optimism for the sake of his cryptographers, who were aghast at the changing pattern of the British fortunes as the night wore on. After the request for airship cover they decyphered a new intercept which read that the High Seas Fleet had been ordered home, giving the course but not the route. This indeed was sent to Jellicoe, but without the vital earlier intelligence which showed that the Horns Riff route was the chosen one.

After this signal was despatched from the Admiralty at 10.41 the War Room seemed inclined to rest upon its laurels. The distinguished visitors had gone to dinner long ago, and Admiral Oliver might well have studied his charts in peace. But Oliver was now overtaken by fatigue, and went to take a rest. His temporary deputy was Captain Everett, R.N. naval secretary to the First Lord. He unfortunately was not accustomed to evaluate German operational signals, which put the responsibility more squarely than ever on the shoulders of the Ops Director, Captain Jackson. Of seven intercepts decoded by Room 40 between 11.15 p.m. and 1.25 a.m. on June 1, only one was sent on to the Commander-in-Chief. It had to do with the movements of German submarines. A German signal of the same importance as the earlier request for airship reconnaissance, reaching Ops at

11.15, ordered all the German flotillas to assemble at Horns Riff by 1 a.m. Even then, if this second confirmation of the Horns Riff rendezvous had got to Jellicoe, the Grand Fleet could have cut Scheer off in time from his retreat to port. The message never reached the Admiral, for the good reason that it was never sent.

In their closed little world, behind the locked door of Room 40, the cryptographers of course knew nothing of what was being done, or not done, in the War Room. But they remembered the delays in communicating with Jellicoe at the time of the raid on Lowestoft, and all those who had realised Jackson's blunder in placing the DK sign at Wilhelmshaven earlier in the day were consumed with anxiety to know what the Ops Director might be doing now. Sir Alfred visited Captain Hall's office more than once, and came back looking grim. Nobody dared to ask any questions. Pots of tea were brewed, and teacups containing dregs stood unremoved at everybody's elbow. Liz smoked her way inexpertly through a packet of twenty cigarettes. She felt a dull ache between her shoulder-blades, and her cheeks were burning under the harsh electric light. There was a flurry of work after midnight, when the methodical Germans always changed the cypher key, but it was found with less trouble than usual, in time to decode a signal giving Scheer's position at 1 a.m.

It was Liz's pride that night that every intercept given her to decode was in the Ops Room within twenty minutes, and in fact forty-five minutes was the longest stop on any intercept between its reception in Room 40 and its arrival in Ops. Liz had never worked so fast or well. Her pale blue eyes, so like her father's, were reddened with the strain, almost as if she were a searchlight officer on duty in the North Sea, but she knew she was "beating the room", as she loved to do, though this time there was no enjoyment in the thought. This time, the cyphers represented a possible defeat for Britain—and the lives of men.

They had opened the windows, and the summer dawn whitened the tired faces in Room 40 as the birds began to twitter in St. James's Park. The cryptographers stretched wearily, yawned, listened compulsively for the thud of the shuttle as new intercepts came up from the telegraph room.

285

"I've been telephoning to some of your colleagues," Sir Alfred said at three o'clock. "They're coming along to relieve us on a special shift at four o'clock. Then the morning shift will be coming on as usual, and you can all rest until this afternoon."

"You're going to rest yourself, I hope, Sir Alfred," said the Commander.

"Yes, I am, the Fleet Paymaster is going to take my place."

"We may as well shut up shop anyway," said Adrian with no expression in his voice. "Just have a look at this."

He handed over the most recent intercept. Decoded, it showed Scheer's position to be thirty miles distant from Jellicoe's flagship, and only sixteen from the gateway of his road to safety.

"Yes," said the Head of Room 40, "that does it, of course. Send it on to Ops at once, for what that's worth. Scheer will be safe in the Amrum Channel before Jellicoe sets eyes on this."

Someone said, "Poor Jellicoe!" but that was all. Wearily, hardly speaking, the cryptographers cleared their desks for the relief shift. They threw the scribbled-over paper, the record of so many people's errors, into the waste baskets and left the brimming ashtrays for the cleaners. In the sour smell of stale tobacco and disappointment, the battle fought off Jutland Bank came to an end for Room 40.

A little while later, Liz and Adrian walked up Whitehall. Nelson on his column presided over Trafalgar Square. Big Ben struck four, at sea the beginning of the morning watch.

"Let's get a taxi," Adrian said.

"I do want some fresh air, Adrian."

"Better pick up a taxi while we can." There were few cabs about at that hour of the morning. Adrian hailed one as it came out of the Strand and told the driver to take them to York Gate.

"Sure you don't want to go straight home, dear?"

"I'll die if I have to be shut up inside four walls now!"

Adrian said nothing. The taxi went north through a sleeping London, up Regent Street and Portland Place to Regent's Park. He became aware that Liz was crying. She made no attempt to hide her tears as he paid off the taxi.

He took her arm, and Liz leaned her shoulder against him as they walked towards the park, across the little bridge over the canal. It was still dusky there beneath the trees, as if the night lingered on, and there was nothing to be heard but the cheep of the moorhens which nested under the banks. Adrian stopped and took Liz into his arms.

"Why are you crying, Elizabeth?" he said gently. "Are you worrying about your brother? I think he's safe enough as long as he's in *Hampshire.*"

"As safe as any man at sea was, yesterday."

"You poor girl, you're just exhausted!"

"Who cares about me?" she said indignantly. "It's the *people* —the poor people I saw in the streets last night, and everybody waking up this morning, not knowing that we lost the battle—"

"We don't know yet that we lost it, dear."

"We didn't win it, anyway. And God knows how many have been killed or wounded—"

"But Elizabeth, we've known in our job all along that there would be a battle some time. It isn't just a game we play with letters and figures, with Liz Flett very nearly the best player of us all—"

"I realised that yesterday," she said, and laid her head against his coat, and sobbed. Adrian waited. Presently he raised her head and kissed her.

"You're very pretty, Elizabeth," he said, "but you're beautiful when you weep for the sorrow of the world."

"Adrian—darling—"

"You know," he said, holding her close to him again, "when you came to work in Room 40 I was absolutely fascinated by you. I'd never in my life met any girl like you. I wanted to find out everything about you, what made your mind work, why you were so desperately anxious to succeed, and everything added up to this: I began to fall in love with you."

"Then David came back from Holland," said Liz Flett, "and you stopped loving me."

"I thought you weren't very gentle with him, Elizabeth. He felt it himself, obviously. He didn't go to you when he came back

287

from Amsterdam the second time. And Ewing says he was in a pretty bad way then; he needed help."

"Poor Davie!"

"And . . . I couldn't help thinking . . . that if you could be unfeeling to your own brother, some day you might be pretty rough with me . . . And I'm a chap who needs kindness, Elizabeth. I want peace and friendship and contentment round me . . . God! just what thousands of poor devils are deprived of, every day."

"I know what I said that put you off," said Liz. "At the station that night. 'God help the man that's chained to our Davie'—wasn't that it?"

"I thought it was a cruel story, dear. But I'm not Scots, you see."

"Did it make you think 'God help the man that's chained to our Elizabeth'?"

"I think the man who married Elizabeth would be the happiest man in the world—if he were sure she loved him too."

"And if *she* were sure?"

"But is she?" Adrian's thin intelligent face was alive with feeling. "Elizabeth darling, you've got to be dead sure! You know I'm a humdrum sort of chap, and you're an adventurer, just like your brother! You're the brilliant First, and I'm the good safe Second; I don't suppose I'll ever have the thundering sort of success in life you care about. But I've seen your tender heart now, my darling; this ghastly night has brought us close again. Say you love me, Elizabeth! Say you'll let me try to make you happy!"

She gave him her lips, and after that long embrace Liz said in delight:

"Happy? But of course we'll both be happy! What I can't get over is how *lucky* I always am!"

Thursday afternoon

About one o'clock on that same day, June 1, Frau Blum, whose husband was an inspector at the Imperial Dockyard, hurried down the stair of an apartment building in Wilhelmshaven and knocked at the door of the porter's lodge.

Frau Schmidt looked out, suspicious as always, but her face brightened when she saw Frau Blum.

"Have you heard the good news, then?" she said excitedly. "Does the Herr Inspector think it's true?"

"Oh, it's true beyond a doubt, Frau Schmidt. A great victory in the Skagerrak, the fleet is entering the Jade Canal now."

"That's what my man heard, he's gone into town to see the fun. *Gott strafe England!*" said Frau Blum enthusiastically.

"Have you any idea where Frau Ritter's gone?"

"I only know she went out half an hour ago."

"If she went to the shops I could try to catch up with her. I don't think she should hear it from anybody else—"

"Hear what, Frau Blum?"

"My husband just telephoned from the Dockyard. Commander Ritter's ship was sunk in the small hours of this morning—"

"The *Pommern*? No! They said none of our ships were sunk."

"I'm afraid there must have been *some* losses . . . Let's see if Frau Ritter is on her way back from the shops. The shopkeepers can't know about the *Pommern* yet."

The fat portress and the plump Jewish lady crossed the courtyard, where the lime tree shook its scented blossoms over the cobbles, and looked up and down the quiet street.

"No sign of her. Oh dear! She may be anywhere!"

"She doesn't usually go far afield. Not since the children took to shouting '*Engländerin!*' whenever they saw her coming."

"Frau Schmidt, I have a very high regard for the Frau Konteradmiral . . ."

"A good quiet householder," said the portress grudgingly.

". . . But don't you think, just lately, she has been—quite peculiar?"

"Ever since the Herr Kommandant came home on leave, if you ask *me*."

"Does he write to her?"

"Not a single letter has come through the lodge, I can assure you."

"Still, it's only six weeks since he was here. That's when she told me he was posted to the *Pommern*." Frau Blum sighed, and

289

gave up the idea of a long walk in the heat. "We can only hope he's one of the survivors."

. . . Muriel Ritter, meanwhile, was walking aimlessly into the town. It was one of her confused days, when she had woken up believing herself to be back in Dresden, the pretty English governess whom Hans Ritter loved, and she had gone about the apartment talking aloud to him all morning. Now her head was clear again, but enough was left of the governess feeling to remind her of the need for exercise and a proper afternoon walk. She put on a lace scarf and carried a parasol to mark the formality of the occasion. The children had been very noisy lately, and it was a pleasure to find the wide leafy streets deserted. There was a great deal of noise down by the harbour, however, and she went to see what was happening, feeling confused again, and planning to call at Hans's office, ask grandly for Admiral Ritter and get him to escort her home.

The High Seas Fleet came through the Jade Canal and proceeded to its anchorage in Jade Bay. Ever since the ships were safely through the Amrum Channel the news had gone ahead of them, and Wilhelmshaven had turned out to the last man to cheer the victors of what was already being called the Battle of the Skagerrak. The ships in harbour were dressed overall. The townspeople gathered armfuls of roses and flung them into the Canal in the path of the advancing Battle Fleet. Admiral Scheer, leading the procession in the *Friedrich der Grosse*, allowed the ships next in line to overhaul the flagship at the entrance to the bay, and stood at the salute as each ship's company cheered him while they passed.

On the conning-bridge of the *Friedrich der Grosse* there was a celebration. A telegram from the All-Highest had been received by Scheer and was reverently passed round. The imperial syntax, never very sound, was choked with emotion: Kaiser Wilhelm II intended to visit the fleet and congratulate his victorious admirals in person. The flag officers, pressing round the Commander-in-Chief, assured him for the hundredth time that he had destroyed the myth of British naval supremacy. The spell of Trafalgar was broken after a hundred years. From now on, by sea as by land, the watchword would be *Deutschland über alles!*

Vice-Admiral Reinhard Scheer was an honest man and a good sailor. His square, firm face, with the clipped moustache and beard, showed little emotion as he listened to the compliments. He knew the whole thing was a fraud. If Jellicoe had lost fourteen units of his fleet, Scheer had lost eleven, and those he had brought into port were so badly damaged that weeks, if not months, must pass before he could take them to sea again. Worse still, the "victory" he claimed was nothing but a full retreat. If he was a victor, it was only because he had refused to fight. Scheer, when the fleet had passed into Jade Bay, did not linger over the champagne.

Long after the celebrations had shifted to the inns and beer gardens of the town, an old woman trailing a lace scarf and a parasol was still wandering by the waterfront, stopping all the men in uniform, and whimpering:

"Why has the *Pommern* not come into harbour? Has nobody seen the *Pommern*? Has nobody seen my son?"

XVII

Friday, June 2, to
Monday, June 5, 1916

While the church bells rang in Wilhelmshaven, and in Berlin the propaganda chiefs handed out news of the "victory" to neutral newspapermen, the British fleet was returning to its bases across the sea from which the enemy had fled. That was the only consolation: the British were still masters of the North Sea; but it was cold comfort on the first day of June, as communication of a sort at last took place between the units of Jellicoe's command. News of the appalling losses spread from ship to ship, and funeral services were held at which the poor bodies, each man wrapped in his own hammock and shotted at the feet, were slid off into the grey waters under the cover of the Union Jack. Out of a fleet of sixty thousand men over six thousand had been killed in action. There were relatively few wounded, and these were taken to hospital ashore as soon as possible. While the Grand Fleet returned to Scapa Flow and Beatty's battle cruisers to Rosyth, some of the badly damaged ships put in to the Humber, the Tyne and Aberdeen. The arrival of these ships and men late on the first, or early on the second day of June, informed the British public that the great sea battle had been fought and incompletely won.

It was not until the afternoon of June 2 that the Grand Fleet passed the Pentland Skerries and steamed through Hoxa Sound into its anchorage at Scapa Flow. The fine weather which had lasted through the battle had broken in the Orkneys, and under cloudy skies and rain the fleet grimly began the routine work of coaling. It was a matter for pride to the Commander-in-Chief that before ten o'clock that night he was able to advise the Admiralty that the fleet was once again ready to put to sea, and at four hours' notice for steam.

Few of the officers and men engaged in this tremendous effort were fit to do anything more than turn in to their bunks and hammocks when that long day was over. The post mortems and the recriminations had to wait; sleep was the first need of the Grand Fleet, back in its shelter behind the hills of Hoy. The next was to get in touch with parents and wives; to hear the home voices by telephone when that was possible, or to send telegrams; commanders gave shore leave generously on Saturday, and one of the heaviest burdens of the war fell upon the communications centre at Long Hope.

David Flett stood in line for nearly an hour in the Long Hope post office before his turn came to use the telephone. Earlier in the day, when written messages were collected aboard the *Hampshire*, he had sent off a telegram to Aberdeen—not, he imagined, that his imperturbable little Dad would be worrying about him, but the pink sheet would be something Mr. Flett could show to Mr. Garden, and swank about in Maggie's Diningroom. The telephone call was the really important thing, and the over-burdened operators, opening circuits to all parts of the United Kingdom, were gratified by the simple request for Hamnavoe 1.

It was Agnes who answered, he could hear her bawling "Ingrid! Ingrid!" and the rush of feet downstairs. Then Ingrid's voice was in his ears, coming from only a few miles away, with nothing but Scapa Flow between them, and he could picture her mouth close to the vulcanite as well as if her lips were parting beneath his own.

"Oh, Davie darling! Are you all right?"

"I'm fine, Ingrid, how are you?"

"We knew last night that the *Hampshire* came back safely. But Davie, did we *win*?"

"Well, the other side ran," said David, "but it was a right dust-up while it lasted. What about Magnus?"

"He was wounded, Davie, but not severely; we had a telegram late yesterday."

"I hear the *Chester* took an awful licking."

"That's what they're saying in Kirkwall. There was an Orkney man aboard and he telephoned after *Chester* reached the Humber."

"Oh, that's where they're at, is it?"

"Magnus is in hospital at Grimsby. That's what he said in the wire: "Slightly wounded, am in Grimsby hospital, don't come, hoping telephone tomorrow." So he can't be very bad, can he, Davie?"

"Not if he can get to the telephone. How's your father taking it?"

"Of course he wanted to rush off to Grimsby. I was thankful Magnus said not to come; and then Daddy has been asked to take part in the funeral tomorrow, so he has to stay."

"Is that the funeral at Lyness?"

"Yes."

"Can you come over with him, Ingrid? I've *got* to see you."

"Yes, we must talk. I can't go on like this, Davie—"

"No, I know. I've got something planned—I'll tell you about it tomorrow."

"Will you get leave?"

"I'll try. Don't be down-hearted, darling! So long just now!"

David opened the door of the telephone booth and let the next man in—an unknown Lieutenant-Commander, who had been glaring at him through the glass during the whole of his conversation with Ingrid. As he went off to Long Hope pier and the *Hampshire*'s cutter, through throngs of seamen and dockyard hands from H.M.S. *Victorious*, he wondered if the time would ever come when they would be alone together. One picnic at Birsay Bay— that was all they had had so far, and yet in the stress of war, death and treachery his feeling for Ingrid Sabiston had ripened into a true passion, however uncertain their future might be. He had heard the note in Ingrid's voice when she said "I can't go on like this"—a note of mingled fear and determination; and he knew quite well that the death of Karl Ritter might become a barrier to their happiness unless he went to work at once on the plan he had hinted at to Ingrid. Back aboard the *Hampshire* he procured writing materials and shut himself up in his cabin at the first opportunity.

He intended to tell Captain Hall about the return and death of Ritter. Before the action at Jutland started he had thought of consulting Captain Savill, but he knew quite well that would mean an almighty row *on the spot*: first, Contraband Control would be brought into it (and for all David knew the *Thorfinn* was still at Kirkwall), the Gloup of Deerness would be searched for the body, and there would be no way of keeping Ingrid out of the thing at all. But he had confidence in Blinker; Blinker Hall knew the whole story (and David had a dismaying vision of himself telling Captain Savill about *Swan Lake*) and would certainly put his own subtle interpretation on how justice should be done. So David wrote, under H.M.S. *Hampshire*'s letterhead:

Sir,
   I have the honour to enclose a German passport and a plan of the Stromness golf links and surrounding country, and to report
1. That these documents were removed from the body of Commander Karl Ritter, I.G.N., deceased, at approximately 2300 hours on Saturday 27 May 1916.
2. That appropriate action was taken with respect to the golf links plan.
3. That Commander Ritter stated before his death that the submarine base in Norwegian waters is sited off or at Namsos.
                    Respectfully,
                    D. Flett,
                    Lieutenant, R.N.V.R.

David made a copy of this letter and put the original, with Ritter's papers, into a manila envelope. He felt, if not light-hearted, at least considerably relieved. Blinker would know how to handle a thing like this without a public hue and cry, and Ingrid's part in the story need never be known outside the four walls of Blinker's office. He went off to the smokingroom, thirsting for a Scotch and soda.

A "Wardroom cag" was naturally in full swing. On June 1, when the sun rose to reveal a North Sea swept bare of the enemy, most of the *Hampshire*'s officers had been too stunned with disappointment to do more than curse; and after eleven o'clock, when Jellicoe gave the order to return to port, all were occupied by the routine duties of getting the cruiser back to Scapa Flow. But now the numbness had worn off. The terrible toll of dead and wounded and the losses of so many ships were almost completely known: in the *Hampshire*, as in every other Wardroom in the fleet that night, frustration and anger found a free expression. David stood near the door with Bill Ramsay and two young Engineer Lieutenants. They were better educated men than David Flett, and much more articulate, but he knew in his bones that what all four of them really felt would remain unspoken. To say in public that they believed the failure to win a complete victory at Jutland had disgraced the Royal Navy, destroyed the legend that was part of British history—this was unthinkable. They criticised the separate shortcomings instead.

Both the Engineer officers complained that the "Plumbers" and the stokehold gangs were never given sufficient credit for their efforts.

"Out of sight and out of mind, that's us," said one, "but we got you there and back, didn't we?"

"Never mind, old bean," said Bill Ramsay, "there's one bit of comfort: it'll be a long time before you have to worry about competition from our dare-devil bird men. Will someone kindly tell me what happened to the *Campania*?"

"She never left the Flow," said David.

"Like hell she didn't!" said one of the Engineers. "She didn't get her sailing signal on Tuesday night—don't ask me why—but she followed the fleet before midnight and was ordered back to base on Wednesday morning early."

"Carrying about ten seaplanes, fully equipped with wireless—"

"That's right."

"For God's sake, *why*?"

"Because J.R.J. thought she was too far behind and would never catch up with the battleships."

"*Campania* couldn't, but the seaplanes could. Didn't he realise that?"

"He's never had much faith in air reconnaissance. Scheer hasn't either. None of the Zepps were up as far as I know."

"And Beatty didn't do much better. He ordered up one Short from *Engadine*; it was only airborne twenty minutes."

"Engine failure as usual, I suppose?"

"God knows."

"I've been wondering why Harwich Force was never heard from," said David. "I thought a fighter like Tyrwhitt would have been in the thick of the fray."

"He made one sortie and got a bottle for it. Didn't get sailing orders from the Admiralty until Scheer was practically at Horns Riff."

"Oh, hell!" said one of the Engineers violently. "What does all that matter? We could have won without an air recce, and surely we never expected Harwich Force to defeat the High Seas Fleet. The devil of it is, we had them cold, on toast, sewed up, and we let them through our fingers because we were mugs enough to think the Huns would go to bed like good boys and wait for us to come along and kill them in the morning. That's the long and short of it, my lads, and we'd better face the facts."

"But what about that bloody turn-away?" said David, allowing his voice to rise to trawler pitch.

The Commander came over to the group of younger men. "Are you chaps planning to write your memoirs?" he said pleasantly. "You'll have the next fifty years to argue about Jutland; I wouldn't get too heated about it tonight."

"We weren't getting heated, sir," said Lieutenant Ramsay. "We were just saying how nice it was that we'd got back in time for the Long Hope sports."

The funeral to be held at Lyness on the island of Hoy was that of the officers and men who had died of wounds after the Grand Fleet returned to Scapa Flow. All ships were to be represented at the service, but there had been no casualties in the *Hampshire*, and there was no rush of volunteers for this sad duty. David Flett easily obtained permission to leave the ship.

The mourning party fell in at Lyness pier and were marched to the little cemetery. It was a raw, misty afternoon, and the only note of colour in the sombre island landscape was provided by the Union Jacks on the row of coffins. The hills of Hoy were shrouded in low-lying cloud through which invisible seagulls circled and screamed as the firing party and the Marine buglers took their places by the open graves. David saw Ingrid immediately: Lyness was not easy of access for civilians, so there were few spectators and still fewer women. She was standing alone, pale in her black dress and hat, not far from where Dr. Sabiston in his black gown waited with the white-surpliced naval chaplain. She looked across the graves at David, not smiling, but with the hint of brightness in her face.

The firing party presented arms as Sir John Jellicoe walked quickly across the springing turf. It was the fourth time David had seen him in as many weeks, and at first sight the Admiral seemed quite unchanged by the ordeal of Jutland. The trim small figure was as erect as ever, the lean face as composed. It was only the eyes, as they travelled along the coffins of his men, which revealed the emotion of the Commander-in-Chief who had been denied the full fruits of their sacrifice. He must be feeling like hell now, thought David Flett.

The service ended. The three volleys were fired over the graves. The Marine buglers sounded the "Last Post". Jellicoe and his flag officers exchanged a few words with the clergymen and went off to the admiral's barge, and the mourning party fell out at the entrance to the cemetery. David was free to wait for Ingrid; he saw her speak to her father, and then hurry to join him. Their meetings were always hurried; he was due back at Lyness pier in twenty minutes.

"Hallo, darling." He was getting more accustomed to that extravagant word now, and Ingrid said "Darling!" too, as she put her hand in his. They walked away through the hamlet of Lyness, so strangely altered by the war, and as they went she told him about Magnus. He had been wounded in both arms, but not severely, the surgeons said he would soon be fit for duty. As "walking wounded" he had been allowed to use the telephone, and had spoken to his family that day.

"He was asking for you, Davie."

"I wish I'd told you to give him my best, when he called."

"Oh, I did! We're so thankful he's no worse off. David, did you know there were thirty-five killed aboard the *Chester*? That nice Lieutenant-Commander who came to tea, remember him? He was killed outright, and the poor boy Magnus told us about that day died of wounds in Grimsby Hospital."

"The boy who saluted Jellicoe."

"Jack Cornwell, yes. He was terribly brave, and stood by his gun quite alone to the end. Magnus says he'll be awarded the V.C."

"Good for him. Well, I didna get a chance to win a medal for you, Ingrid—"

"As if that mattered!"

"But I would like you to take a look at this."

He gave her the copy of his letter to Captain Hall, and stood waiting with the manila envelope in his hand. He saw the colour rise in Ingrid's pale face, from which the childish look had vanished: it was a woman flowering in the forcing house of war who was studying what he had written to the Director of Intelligence.

"I see," she said when she had read it twice. "Thank you for showing it to me."

"Keep it," he said, "it's for you; and will you post this for me tomorrow in Kirkwall? I would have sent it off from here if today hadn't been a Sunday."

"I will, of course. I'm going to the Red Cross in the morning."

"It would be better registered."

"I'll take care of that."

"Then what's the matter, Ingrid?"

"David, do you really think this is the way to do it?"

"It's the best way I can think of. They have their own ways of working in the Intelligence Division; they'll handle this all right."

"You mean the whole thing can be hushed up?"

"That's what we want, isn't it? I can't take the chance of Ritter's body turning up some day—"

"Oh don't!" Ingrid began to shiver. "I keep thinking about it and *thinking* about it! Every time I go into the kitchen I fancy

299

I see him, bleeding on the floor! I can hardly bear to ride the bike since you took away his body in the sidecar—"

"Well," said David reasonably, "would you rather fancy you saw *my* dead body lying on your linoleum? Because he would have had me strangled, if—"

"If I hadn't given you the knife," said Ingrid. "We murdered him."

David took her arm. They had come close to the sea's edge now and were only a little distance from the pier.

"Look out across the water," he told her. "Nothing there but ships, eh? When we came west on Thursday we saw dead Germans by the hundred, all dressed up in their life-saving waistcoats, floating among the wreckage of their ships. And we would have killed hundreds more if we could have but won at them before they turned tail and fled. Do you think it matters a damn to me if I killed one more German—and maybe saved John Jellicoe?"

"You didn't know about Jellicoe until after you killed Ritter," Ingrid said. "Don't you remember the first thing you said when you found us together in the kitchen?"

"What did I say?"

"'You'll not break this one like you broke Elena Petrovna,'" she said defiantly.

"So the wind's in that quarter, is't?" said David. "If we're to start casting up who said what, I heard you call Ritter a murderer, and say you'd do your best to see him hanged."

"You were *thinking* about Elena Petrovna all the time!" Ingrid disregarded his last words. "You weren't thinking about protecting me, or all the harm that man might do: you were thinking about avenging *her!*"

"Listen to me, Ingrid. Don't you know I love you? Don't you know I want to marry you some day?"

"You never said so before."

Still reasonably: "I havena had much chance so far. Will you give me your promise, Ingrid—darling?"

She pulled her hand away from his like an unhappy child. "Oh —not yet—so much has happened to us both so quickly . . . Davie, you'll have to give me time!"

"Time!" he said. "God knows how much time we have left!"
She faced him resolutely, the sea-blue eyes very grave and true.
"Darling, I'm going to tell my father about Ritter."

"Your *father!*"

"I can't go on like this, David. I'm living a lie, in the same
house where it happened, every day of my life. I must tell Daddy
the truth about Hans Kolberg, I must tell him what happened to
Karl Ritter . . ." She hesitated. "How can I ever receive the
Sacrament again, if I don't?"

"All right, Ingrid," he said. "If that's the way you feel about
it! I'll only ask you to do one thing—post that letter to Hall first.
Then wait till my shore leave on Tuesday before you say anything to your Dad. I want to stand beside you when you do."

Next morning the London papers of Saturday reached Scapa
Flow, and spread rage and consternation through the whole of the
Grand Fleet.

The Germans had got in first with their story to the neutral
press, and the British Admiralty had done the rest. A message
from Jellicoe on June 2, giving a few details of the action at
Jutland, had been used as the basis of a communiqué drawn up by
the First Lord, Mr. Balfour, and slightly modified by the First
Sea Lord and Admiral Oliver, whose absence from the War Room
on Wednesday night had contributed to the fiasco of the untrans-
mitted signals. This communiqué, given to the press in time for
the Saturday morning papers, gave the impression that the Fleet
had been totally defeated and that something like a national
disaster had taken place. The comments in almost every newspaper
of importance were written in tragic terms, as if the Navy,
England's pride, had now become the country's shame.

There were grim faces in the fore-cabin of the *Hampshire* when
Captain Savill sent for all his officers later in the morning. Someone said, as they went along the alleyway: "Winston Churchill
should have written that communiqué. He'd have made Jutland
sound like the greatest victory of all time."

"I've just come from the Fleet Flagship," Savill began
abruptly, and indicated the pile of newspapers on a side table.

'You've all been worrying about this, I know. I'd like to tell you, first of all, that the Commander-in-Chief was told about the Admiralty communiqué on Saturday. He protested immediately, and I understand that there is a much better account in today's papers of a battle which, when all is said and done, left us with the mastery of the seas."

There was a slight relaxation of the unsmiling faces round him. Captain Savill went on: "I don't know when we'll have an opportunity of reading the Admiralty's—er—revised version. Gentlemen, I have good news for you! I'm quite aware you all experienced some frustration when we were in action. *Hampshire* had a useful job to do, but one which hardly put us in the fore-front of the battle. Now we've been selected for a very important operation: we're to take the Secretary for War, Lord Kitchener, on an official mission to Russia."

He smiled. "I thought that would surprise you! As a matter of fact, the Commander-in-Chief proposed the *Hampshire* for this mission as long ago as the twenty-seventh of May, but as—certain other matters required attention in the meantime—we didn't receive our final orders until yesterday. Lord Kitchener left London last night; he's on his way across the Firth in the *Oak* at this moment, and is expected for luncheon in the *Iron Duke.*"

"May I ask what our sailing orders are, sir?" said the Commander.

"They won't be issued until half past three. The weather forecast isn't very promising, so there may be a last minute revise, but I expect to sail about five o'clock. For security reasons, no one is to leave the ship before sailing time, and the Master-at-Arms has been so informed. Any questions?"

"Is Lord Kitchener bringing a large staff aboard, sir?" asked the Paymaster.

"He is, Pay; we'll have to review the cabin accommodation. His Military Secretary goes, of course, and five other gentlemen, plus a detective, a shorthand writer and four servants—thirteen in all."

"Unlucky number!" someone murmured in the rear.

"If we're going to keep strict security, sir, may we not know

302

something about Lord Kitchener's mission?" suggested the Commander. "Or is it to be top secret in his own entourage?"

"I don't know very much about it," confessed Captain Savill. "Except that he goes to Russia on the personal invitation of the Czar. Probably he'll be asked for a British loan, or a supply of munitions, or closer co-operation between the Allies; your guess is as good as mine, Commander."

"And our port of destination, sir?"

"Archangel."

The sailing orders were duly transmitted from the *Iron Duke*, and Captain Savill studied them with care. The usual route to the White Sea, which the *Hampshire* had taken many times in the previous winter, was eastabout by South Ronaldshay, and then north-east; but Sunday's bad weather had blown up into a heavy north-east gale, and Jellicoe's judgment was that the *Hampshire* should steer westabout by Hoy, using the shelter given by a lee shore. There was no time to have the western channel swept for mines, for Kitchener was impatient to be off, but the cliff watchers reported the area clear of surface minelayers. No one, of course, was aware of U75's night visit, and what U75 had left behind.

Kitchener came aboard the *Hampshire* at a quarter past four, and David Flett, on the quarterdeck as he was piped aboard, for the first time saw the living face of the Secretary for War. It was very like the chromolithograph, not so much tanned as tawny, with strange, blue, rolling eyes: he almost expected it to say "Your King And Country Need You!" while they all stood stiffly at the salute. Kitchener's entourage looked miserable already, for it was raining heavily, but they all remained on deck until the *Hampshire* slipped her buoy and moved towards Hoxa Sound. Kitchener was on the bridge with Captain Savill. In spite of the latter's mild security precautions, the news of his arrival at Scapa had spread very quickly, and he stood at the salute, apparently enjoying the situation as he was "cheered round the Fleet" by ship's company after ship's company as the *Hampshire* left the Flow. To the disgruntled seamen Kitchener's sudden appearance and dramatic departure to the mysterious land of Russia was just the tonic they needed after Jutland.

Lieutenant Flett was officer of the watch in the second dog watch, beginning at six o'clock. The bell had just been struck when he reached the bridge and reported to the officer he was relieving. Captain Savill had just been sent for, he was told: the wind had backed several degrees and was blowing hard ahead since they rounded the southerly point of Hoy. While the Captain, who had been entertaining the guests below, was on his way to the bridge David began the usual routine: hearing the report of the man he was relieving, checking the ship's course by the standard compass, making sure that the watch on deck, their reliefs and the look-outs were all present and correct. Captain Savill arrived and ordered the speed rung down to 15 knots.

"Report says the destroyers can't keep station, sir," said David.

"Of course they can't; 10 knots is about their limit in a near gale," said Savill. "What infernal luck to run into a nor'nor-westerly! I wish to God we'd been ordered to take the old route after all."

He beckoned to a wireless messenger. "Send this to Flag: 'Weather so bad am returning escort to harbour.'" When this went off by short wave through Long Hope to the *Iron Duke*, the two destroyer escorts were signalled to turn back to Scapa Flow, and H.M.S. *Unity* and *Victor*, giving a farewell hoot on their sirens, were left astern off Rora Head.

Captain Savill had speed rung down to 13½ knots before he left the bridge. "I'll send the Commander up," he said, "I don't like the look of the weather. Don't hesitate to send for me again if necessary, Mr. Flett."

"Aye, aye, sir."

By the time the Commander arrived, looking as if he preferred the bridge to the distinguished company below, David had ordered the hatches battened and shored down. The wind had increased to gale force, and the *Hampshire* was shipping very heavy seas. Although two bells had just been struck for seven o'clock the weeping skies gave the effect of an early nightfall, and the bridge was in a half-darkness in which the faint glow of the binnacle lamp threw into relief the features of the quartermaster at the wheel. They were steaming very close to the shore, and had left the Old Man of Hoy behind them; David could see the cliffs below the Black Craig where Ingrid did her cliff-watching. He hoped she wasn't out on such a night.

He wondered when she would hear that *Hampshire* had gone to sea. Almost immediately, he guessed: Agnes would get the news at the shop, and Ingrid would know it was no common mission that had taken him away from her again when he most wanted to be by her side. He hoped with all his heart that she would say nothing to her father until he got back, and leave it all to Blinker and his men; but he was not quite certain that she would. What was it Blinker Hall had said? "The vagaries of the feminine mind are beyond me!"—well, they were beyond David too; but this was not a vagary: Ingrid's determination to make the truth known at all costs was a moral force, the proof of a strong character, but she was just a bairn too; she needed a man to look after her! She was still jealous of Elena Tamirova, and maybe she was right: it was daft, the way his heart had moved when Savill said Archangel was their destination. Archangel, Elena's birth-place: the name would always make him think of her, just as that seagull, fluttering white-winged on the gale, brought a recollection of a white tutu and a dancer in a swan's-feather crown.

David cursed himself, and went on with his duties. He checked the battens on the fo'c'sle hatch, which had been giving trouble, spoke to the coxswain of the sea boat and the petty officer in charge of the falls. Everything was secure, the gunports and scuttles closed and tight. The midshipman and the corporal of the watch presented their half-hourly report as three bells struck for half past seven. *Hampshire*, in the teeth of the gale, bucked her way up the coast to Marwick Head.

She struck one of U75's mines at twenty minutes to eight o'clock, when Lord Kitchener was holding court below. There was one tremendous explosion, which threw every man to the decks, the funnels crashed down, the aftermast fell pinning men beneath it, and the cry of "Fire!" was heard from below. David ran along the canting deck shouting "Boats away! Boats away!" A wave swept him off his feet against a funnel stay. The larger boats and pinnaces forward of the aftermast could not be freed or even reached. The cutters, as soon as they were slung out on their davits, were smashed by the huge seas. The seamen worked frantically to lower the rafts. Captain Savill was on deck, struggling to help the men, and Kitchener appeared, in khaki service dress, without a greatcoat; the Captain shouted something Kitchener failed to hear. The *Hampshire* was going down, and rapidly; David for the second time in his life heard a captain's terrible cry:

"Abandon ship! Abandon ship!"

He saw the fo'c'sle break off as he tore off his oilskin coat and jumped for the tilting rail. The crew were jumping fast, and David saw the upturned faces swept away. The water was icy cold, he felt numb in a minute, but he swam away from the ship as hard as he could and then turned on his back. He saw the *Hampshire* go down by the head, turn what looked like a somersault, and sink. Then he felt a violent blow on his own head, swallowed water, and went down into the Atlantic surge.

Ingrid Sabiston was at work ironing while Agnes prepared the vegetables for an unusually late supper when she heard the telephone ring and her father answer. He had been in Kirkwall all day for a series of meetings, and had just come home, very wet and cold, in his Session Clerk's machine.

"I wonder if that's a call from Magnus?" Ingrid said. She put the iron on its stand and opened the door to the hall. She heard her father say "What?" . . . "Where? . . ." and then "God help them all!"

"Daddy, what is it?"

"Yes, I'll tell her, certainly," Dr. Sabiston said into the telephone, and hung up, shaking his head sadly.

"It was the cliff patrol people, Ingrid—there's been a tragedy, my dear. A ship down off Marwick Head—they want all the cliff watchers they can muster, to help look for survivors—"

"Oh, Daddy! Of course I'll go at once—Agnes can give you and Olav supper. I'll go up and change—"

"Wait a minute, girl." The minister restrained Ingrid at the foot of the stair. "I honestly don't think you should go out tonight."

"Why, Daddy? Because of the bad weather?"

"No, it's worse than that. My poor dear, they're very much afraid that it's the *Hampshire.*"

"The *Hampshire*?" she said stupidly, "but she's in Scapa Flow."

"You hadn't heard, then?"

Impatiently: "What was there to hear? Neither Agnes nor I have been outside the house since the heavy rain came on."

"She sailed at five o'clock on a special mission, with Lord Kitchener aboard."

She ran headlong upstairs then, paying no attention to her father's call of "Ingrid!" nor to Olav, coming out of his bedroom, staring, with his homework in his hand. She tore off her dress, pulled on her breeches, sweater, boots; ran down for her oilskin jacket and sou'wester. She spoke to her father only once, as he stood helplessly at the study door, with Agnes wringing her hands in the background.

"Off Marwick Head, you said? They're certain?"

"Yes."

"If they ring again tell them I'll be at the post at Birsay."

They heard the roar of the Harley-Davidson. Ingrid had detached the sidecar earlier in the day; she hated the thing now, as she had said to David—*David!* Out there drowning, perhaps dead, never to hold her in his arms again, never to hear her promise, never to make her his wife! She drove faster than she had ever driven before, with the bike sending up waves of rainwater on each side, through Stenness, past Skara Brae, along the road where David himself had driven her one sunny afternoon. And it seemed to Ingrid Sabiston that he was driving still, one with her; that she could see his face, with the dark hair and the serious dark eyes, that his big hands were firm above her own. "I love you, David!" she cried out, as if he could hear her above the howl of the wind and the roar of the motor-bike, and in a waterfall of rain drove into Birsay, where he and she had been happy together.

Ingrid had been so quick, and the night so wild, that there were not many people, beyond those who lived in the hamlet, gathered with the cliff patrol outside the little post office. But already officialdom had taken over; there was talk of a Very Important

307

Person, and of sabotage, and the need to throw a security cordon round the whole area as soon as the Kirkwall police arrived.

"What does security matter when all those men are drowning?" Ingrid cried. "We ought all to be searching along the shore!"

"Now then, missy!" It was an Englishman, a sergeant, who spoke soothingly, "this ain't no place for a young lady. You be off home, and leave it to the military; we don't think there's much chance for them pore devils now."

"Nothing can live in that sea," said a voice, and there was a murmur of agreement.

"I saw two rafts capsize, I tell you!" said another. "Two rafts —hundreds of men aboard—all swept away—"

Ingrid looked helplessly out to sea. The long Atlantic rollers came tumbling in on the Brough of Birsay, and in all the waste of water beyond Marwick Head she could see no ship, no boat, no living thing.

There was a Carley raft afloat, although not visible from Birsay beach. It had drifted south, and was now caught in the pull of the Atlantic tide, not one of its few passengers having as yet the strength to try to reach the shore.

When David Flett came back to consciousness he was lying face downwards in a pool of oil and water, mixed with his own blood. He had swallowed fuel oil while in the water, and vomited it up; he could smell and taste the filth but not see it, for the same oil had clogged his eyes. He tried to raise his hand to rub them clear, and with the first ray of returning sight saw that his left hand too was covered in blood, the wrist bent at an odd angle. Someone was saying "Is there an officer aboard? Is there an officer aboard?" He tried to mumble an answer and could not.

"Who's that over there?" David felt hands on his body, turning him over; the pelting rain fell cold upon his face.

"It's Flett, looks like 'e's done for,"

"What's that he's trying to say?"

"Says 'e's not done for."

"Let's have a look." Someone was taking charge, beginning

to sort things out; someone felt his bleeding head, and David moaned.

"Got a right nasty scalp wound. Here, sir, let me try this—" Something, some sort of pad or cloth was held to the back of his head, where the pain was; this time the pain knocked him unconscious, until words and dreams began to form once more.

Last time . . . last time . . . on the Carley float in the North Sea . . . but he could swim then, had swum till the Dutchmen picked him up, but this was different. This could be death. Ingrid! He had to get back to her, had to look after her! What would she do if the police came, if they found Ritter in the Gloup of Deerness, and himself not there to take the blame? I left her, I left her just like Ritter left Elena, I dragged her into it, like Ritter dragged Elena; Ritter and I are the same person, like Odette and Odile, and the sea will hold us both or carry us in a golden barge to heaven . . . What was it she said that first day I came back, a ballad? "Do not fear, heaven is as near, by water as by land!" Then sight and clearer senses came and he saw that it was dark.

"Where are we?" he forced himself to say.

"We're not doing too badly, sir, we're still in sight of Marwick Head."

"You must steer for the Yimna Yamnas," he told them, and saw them stare and shake their heads. They were all unrecognizable, faces black with oil and mouths gaping, wide with fatigue; some of them had been struck by wreckage, like himself. Black and beaten, a crew of demons, all that was left of six hundred and fifty men, the *Hampshire*'s gallant company. "The Yamnas! The Yamnas!" he repeated—it sounded like the ravings of a drunken man.

He went under again, and far deeper this time, as someone turned his head on one side to let him breathe. The blood, the oil, the vomit, the water, all seemed to have broken over his head now, the flashes of dream were gone into the darkness which had fallen over the world. He was not aware that one of the men had contrived at last to wrench off the nipple of the Holmes light lashed to the raft, so that the carbide was ignited by sea water, or that this pathetic flame was quenched almost immediately by the great waves carrying them back on the rocks of Marwick Head. He was only aware of the pain wrenching his whole body as a freak wave caught the Carley float and threw it, with the sole survivors of the *Hampshire*, into a cleft far up the cliff. But at last, after light-years of suffering, he heard a cry:

"It's the water tug, mates! It's the *Flying Kestrel!*"

"She's seen us! Oh my God, she's seen us!"

"Saved—we're saved!"

It was the only word they knew. There were no cheers, no songs, no shouts; merely a dumb gratitude for the recall to life, the silent endurance of utterly broken men, that lasted while the rescuers came, and raised them one by one with pulleys to the cliff top as the first light which comes before the dawn was appearing in the sky. There were many people there, and many sobbing; David heard one of the *Hampshire*'s men say "Kitchener is dead!" and became aware that a silence had fallen, as if the world had stopped.

Then someone was kneeling on the grass beside him, and the wet gold hair fell over Ingrid's face, looking in an agony of love into his own. Thus he was given strength to raise himself a little, and lay his wounded head on the breast that would be his for ever.